E. & M.A
THE HEEL OF ACHILLES

EDWIN ISAAC RADFORD (1891-1973) and MONA AUGUSTA RADFORD (1894-1990) were married in 1939. Edwin worked as a journalist, holding many editorial roles on Fleet Street in London, while Mona was a popular leading lady in musical-comedy and revues until her retirement from the stage.

The couple turned to crime fiction when they were both in their early fifties. Edwin described their collaborative formula as: "She kills them off, and I find out how she done it." Their primary series detective was Harry Manson who they introduced in 1944.

The Radfords spent their final years living in Worthing on the English South Coast. Dean Street Press have republished three of their classic mysteries: *Murder Jigsaw, Murder Isn't Cricket* and *Who Killed Dick Whittington?*

E. & M.A. RADFORD MYSTERIES
Available from Dean Street Press

E. & M.A. RADFORD

THE HEEL OF ACHILLES

With an introduction by Nigel Moss

DEAN STREET PRESS

Published by Dean Street Press 2020

Copyright © 1950 E. & M.A. Radford

Introduction Copyright © 2020 Nigel Moss

First published in 1950 by Andrew Melrose

Cover by DSP

ISBN 978 1 913054 97 7

www.deanstreetpress.co.uk

To
'ELI', our best
friend.

Requiescat in Pace.

INTRODUCTION

DOCTOR Harry Manson is a neglected figure, unjustly so, amongst Golden Age crime fiction detectives. The creation of husband and wife authors Edwin and Mona Radford, who wrote as E. & M.A. Radford, Manson was their leading series detective featuring in 35 of 38 mystery novels published between 1944 and 1972. He held dual roles as a senior police detective at Scotland Yard and Head of its Crime Forensics Research Laboratory. In 2019 Dean Street Press republished three early novels from the Doctor Manson series—*Murder Jigsaw* (1944), *Murder Isn't Cricket* (1946), and *Who Killed Dick Whittington?* (1947)—titles selected for their strong plots, clever detection and evocative settings. They are examples of Manson at his best, portraying the appealing combination of powerful intellect and reasoning with creative scientific methods of investigation, while never losing awareness and sensitivity concerning the human predicaments encountered.

Having introduced the Radfords to a new readership, Dean Street Press have now released a further three titles, each quite different in approach and style, written during the authors' middle period but retaining the traditions of the Golden Age of Detective Fiction. They include two Manson novels: *The Heel of Achilles* (1950), an inverted murder mystery; and *Death of a Frightened Editor* (1959), a baffling murder by poisoning on a London-to-Brighton train. The third, *Death and the Professor* (1961), is a non-series title featuring an array of impossible crime puzzles and locked room murders solved by the formidable mind of logician Professor Marcus Stubbs.

The Radfords sought to combine in Doctor Manson a leading police detective and scientific investigator in the same mould as R. Austin Freeman's Dr John Thorndyke, whom Edwin Radford keenly admired. T.J. Binyon, in his study of fictional detectives *Murder Will Out* (1989), maintains that the Radfords were protesting against the idea that in Golden Age crime fiction science is always the preserve of the amateur detective, and were seeking to be different. In the preface to the first Manson novel *Inspector Manson's Success* (1944), they announced: "We have had the audacity to present here the Almost Incredible: a detective story in which the scientific deduction by a police officer uncovers the crime and the criminal entirely without the aid of any outside assistance!"

The first two Manson novels, *Inspector Manson's Success* and *Murder Jigsaw* (both 1944), contain introductory prefaces which acquaint the reader with Doctor Manson in some detail. He is a man of many talents and qualifications: aged in his early 50s and a Cambridge MA (both attributes shared by Edwin Radford at the time), Manson is a Doctor of Science, Doctor of Laws, non-practising barrister and author of several standard works on medical jurisprudence (of which he is a Professor) and criminal pathology. Slightly over 6 feet in height, although he does not look it owing to the stoop of his shoulders, habitual in a scholar and scientist. He has interesting features and characteristics: a long face, with a broad and abnormally high forehead; grey eyes wide set, though lying deep in their sockets, which "have a habit of just passing over a person on introduction; but when that person chances to turn in the direction of the Inspector, he is disconcerted to find that the eyes have returned to his face and are seemingly engaged on long and careful scrutiny. There is left the impression that one's face is being photographed on the Inspector's mind." Manson's hands are often the first thing a stranger will notice. "The long delicate fingers are exceedingly restless—twisting and turning on anything which lies handy to them. While he stands, chatting, they are liable to stray to a waistcoat pocket and emerge with a tiny magnifying glass or a micrometer to occupy their energy."

During his long career at Scotland Yard, Manson rises from Chief Detective-Inspector to the rank of Commander. Reporting directly to Sir Edward Allen, the Assistant Commissioner, Manson is ably assisted by his Yard colleagues—Sergeant Merry, a science graduate and Deputy Lab Head, and Superintendent Jones and Detective-Inspector Kenway of the CID. Jones is weighty and ponderous, given to grunts and short staccato sentences, and with a habit of lapsing into American 'tec slang in moments of stress; but a stolid, determined detective and reliable fact searcher with an impressive memory. He often serves as a humorous foil to Manson and the Assistant Commissioner. By contrast, Kenway is volatile and imaginative. Together, Jones and Kenway make a powerful combination and an effective resource for the Doctor. In later books, Inspector Holroyd features as Manson's regular assistant. Holroyd is the lead detective in the non-series title *The Six Men* (1958), a novelisation of the earlier British detective film of the same name released in 1951 and based on an original story idea and scenario developed by the Radfords. Their only other non-series police detective, Superintendent

Carmichael, appeared in just two novels: *Look in at Murder* (1956, with Manson) and *Married to Murder* (1959).

The first eight novels, all Manson series, were published by Andrew Melrose between 1944 to 1950. The early titles were slim volumes produced in accordance with authorised War Economy Standards. Many featured a distinctive motif on the front cover of the dust wrapper—a small white circle showing Manson's head superimposed against that of Sherlock Holmes (in black silhouette), with the title 'a Manson Mystery'. In these early novels, the Radfords made much of their practice of providing readers with all the facts and clues necessary to give them a fair opportunity of solving the mystery puzzles by deduction. They interspersed the investigations with 'Challenges to the Reader', a trope closely associated with leading Golden Age crime authors John Dickson Carr and Ellery Queen. In *Murder Isn't Cricket* they claimed: "We have never 'pulled anything out of the bag' at the last minute—a fact upon which three distinguished reviewers of books have commented and have commended." Favourable critical reviews of their early titles were received from Ralph Straus (*Sunday Times*) and George W. Bishop (*Daily Telegraph*), as well as novelist Elizabeth Bowen. The Radfords were held in sufficiently high regard by Sutherland Scott, in his study of the mystery novel *Blood in their Ink* (1953), to be highlighted alongside such distinguished Golden Age authors as Miles Burton, Richard Hull, Milward Kennedy and Vernon Loder.

After 1950 there was a gap of six years before the Radfords' next book. Mona's mother died in 1953; she had been living with them at the time. Starting in 1956, with a new publisher John Long (like Melrose, another Hutchinson company), the Radfords released two Manson titles in successive years: *Look in at Murder* (1956) and *Death on the Broads* (1957). In 1958 they moved to the publisher Robert Hale, a prominent supplier to the public libraries. They began with *The Six Men* (1958), before returning to Manson with *Death of a Frightened Editor* (1959). Thereafter, Manson was to feature in all but two of their remaining 25 crime novels, all published by Hale; the exceptions being *Married to Murder* (1959) and *Death of a Professor* (1961). Curiously, a revised and abridged version of the third Manson series novel *Crime Pays No Dividends* (1945) was later released under the new title *Death of a Peculiar Rabbit* (1969).

Edwin Isaac Radford (1891-1973) and Mona Augusta Radford (1894-1990) were married in Aldershot in 1939. Born in West Bromwich, Edwin had spent his working life entirely in journalism, latterly in London's Fleet Street where he held various editorial roles, culminating as Arts Editor-in-Chief and Columnist for the *Daily Mirror* in 1937. Mona was the daughter of Irish poet and actor James Clarence Mangan and his actress wife Lily Johnson. Since childhood she had toured with her mother and performed on stage under the name 'Mona Magnet', and later was for many years a popular leading lady appearing in musical-comedies, revues and pantomime (including 'Dick Whittington') until her retirement from the stage. She first met Edwin while performing in Nottingham, where he was working as a local newspaper journalist. Mona also authored numerous short plays and sketches for the stage, in addition to writing verse, particularly for children.

An article in *Books & Bookmen* magazine (1959) recounts how Edwin and Mona, already in their early 50s, became detective fiction writers by accident. During one of Edwin's periodic attacks of lumbago, Mona trudged through snow and slush from their village home to a library for Dr Thorndyke detective stories by R. Austin Freeman, of which he was an avid reader. Unfortunately, Edwin had already read the three books with which she returned! Incensed at his grumbles, Mona retaliated with "Well for heaven's sake, why don't you write one instead of always reading them?"—and placed a writing pad and pencil on his bed. Within a month, Edwin had written six lengthy short stories, and with Mona's help in revising the MS, submitted them to a leading publisher. The recommendation came back that each of the stories had the potential to make an excellent full-length novel. The first short story was duly turned into a novel, which was promptly accepted for publication. Thereafter, their practice was to work together on writing novels—first in longhand, then typed and read through by each of them, and revised as necessary. The plot was usually developed by Mona and added to by Edwin during the writing. According to Edwin, the formula was: "She kills them off, and I find out how she done it." Mona would also act the characters and dialogue as outlined by Edwin for him to observe first-hand and then capture in the text.

As husband-and-wife novelists, the Radfords were in the company of other Golden Age crime writing couples—G.D.H. (Douglas) and Margaret Cole in the UK, and Gwen Bristow and Bruce Manning, John and Emery Bonett, Audrey and Wiliam Roos (Kelley Roos), and Frances and Richard Lockridge in the USA. Their crime novels proved popular on the Continent and were published in translation in the major European languages. However, the US market eluded them and none of the Radford books was ever published in the USA. Aside from crime fiction, the Radfords collaborated on authoring a wide range of other works, most notably *Crowther's Encyclopaedia of Phrases and Origins*, *Encyclopaedia of Superstitions* (a standard work on folklore), and a *Dictionary of Allusions*. Edwin was a Fellow of the Royal Society of Arts, and a member of both the Authors' Club and the Savage Club.

The Radfords proved to be an enduring writing team, working into their 80s. Both were also enthusiastic amateur artists in oils and water colours. They travelled extensively, and invariably spent the winter months writing in the warmer climes of Southern Europe. An article by Edwin in *John Creasey's Mystery Bedside Book* (1960) recounts his involvement in the late 1920s with an English society periodical for the winter set on the French Riviera, where he had socialised with such famous writers as Baroness Orczy, William Le Queux and E. Phillips Oppenheim. He recollects Oppenheim dictating up to three novels at once! The Radfords spent their final years living in Worthing.

The Heel of Achilles

Published in 1950, *The Heel of Achilles* is the eighth of the Doctor Manson detective novels and their last from the publishing house of Andrew Melrose. Thereafter the Radfords were to take a break of six years until their next detective story. Having established a reputation as writers of ingenious whodunits, this book represents their first attempt at the "inverted murder story form", a sub-genre well suited to mysteries featuring scientific detection. With Doctor Manson, Head of Scotland Yard's Crime Forensics Research Laboratory, already pre-eminent in this field, the premise is an intriguing one and the story does not disappoint. The inverted mystery novel reverses those features of the traditional whodunit concerned with working out the identity of the murderer and motive for the crime, usually kept hidden until the denouement when the detective reveals all. Instead, the murderer is known from the start, and their thoughts, plans and actions are shared. The reader knows everything and the detective knows nothing. The suspense comes in following the detective's investigation at close hand, as he works to uncover the factual mistakes that upset the apparently perfect crime.

The storyline of *The Heel of Achilles* falls into two parts. The opening section 'Story of a Murder' outlines the background events and motive behind the murder, together with its planning and execution. The protagonist is Jack Edwins, a likeable and decent young motor mechanic. While on holiday in Paignton, Jack meets and falls in love with a local girl, whom he later marries. By a cruel twist of fate, on the same holiday Jack also makes the acquaintance of James Sprogson, a charming but disreputable character. Their association is a disastrous one. Jack is inveigled by Sprogson into unwittingly assisting in a country house jewellery robbery which goes badly wrong. This ill-fated episode becomes Jack's 'Achilles heel'; a vulnerability he is unable to shake off, despite subsequently becoming an honest, hard-working owner of a garage business, happily married, and with a new identity.

Some years later, fate intervenes again in Jack's life. A chance encounter with Sprogson (also now living under an assumed name, James Canley) leads to a course of increasing blackmail demands about the robbery and to the destruction of Jack's happiness. Jack becomes desperate as he perceives his livelihood and marriage to be threatened to the core and feels compelled to resort to murder as the only way out of his predicament. He conceives an ingenious plan to commit what he believes will be the perfect murder, with no personal traces left behind and made to look like an accident. The murder is carefully planned and rehearsed in meticulous detail. We witness the brutal act of murder and the surrounding events of that night, sharing Jack's thought processes and emotions at each stage—concerns, fear, panic and finally relief when everything is over. The authors succeed in creating the compelling portrait of a murderer with whom the reader sympathises.

The second half of the book 'Cherchez l'Homme' opens with the discovery of Canley's decapitated corpse lying on the tracks of a railway branch line, a few hundred yards from his cottage in Thames Pagnall, the fictitious Surrey village which also featured in the Radfords' earlier novel *Murder Isn't Cricket* (1946). Initially the local police regard Canley's death as an accident or suicide, but the railway company's doctor is unsure and insists on Scotland Yard being called in. Enter Doctor Manson and his colleagues Detective-Inspector Kenway (CID) and Sergeant Merry (Lab Deputy). Manson's careful examination of the body at the trackside is a masterclass in scientific deduction. His portable laboratory, known as 'the Box of Tricks', is put to good use. Manson rounds on the local police for having been blinded by superficial appearances, for having seen but not observed: "It was obvious to me within a few minutes of seeing the body that the man had not been killed by the train . . . From that moment I ceased any investigation into the cause of the man's death and concentrated all my efforts into the circumstances of his death."

Subsequently, we follow step-by-step Manson's painstaking piecing together of how the murder was committed and working out the identification of the perpetrator. The investigation is adroitly handled, a highly elaborate game of cat and mouse, and the story becomes an absorbing page-turner. But it is not a one-sided affair. Other suspects are identified, and each needs to be eliminated by process of deduction. In places the authors soften the tone of the investigation by introducing some gentle humour. The local Chief Constable, Colonel Mainforce, a bluff ex-military type with dialogue to match, joins the investigation (he previously appeared in *Murder Isn't Cricket*). While the novel is firmly rooted in the Golden Age style, there is a more modern feel to the narrative.

There is a steady remorseless and deadly probability about the way in which the investigation, using logic and scientific analysis, works its way inexorably towards Jack. The room in Canley's cottage in which the murder took place, the reconstruction of the act of murder and removal of the dead body to the railway line—all are examined and considered thoroughly by Manson. The authors explain Manson's thought processes and the various deductions he makes, so that the reader can follow each stage. The field is narrowed down and the net tightened. It is a masterly piece of scientific detection, erudite but never dull. The pursuit is gripping and enthralling. To make Manson appear more fallible, the authors catalogue a surprising number of mistakes and wrong assumptions on his part, usually in footnotes to the text. The ending is sombre and emotionally charged; a powerful conclusion to a morality tale which is reminiscent of the novels of Freeman Wills Crofts. The police always get their man, but sometimes at a heavy human cost.

The Heel of Achilles is the Radfords' homage to R. Austin Freeman and his series detective Dr John Thorndyke. Freeman is the acknowledged 'parent' of the scientific detective story and Edwin Radford greatly admired the Dr Thorndyke stories. Both Thorndyke and Manson are first and foremost forensic scientists, who apply their professional skills to the furtherance of detection. They are highly intelligent and knowledgeable men, possessing acute powers of logic, reasoning and judgement. It is no coincidence that the observant railway company doctor who significantly disagrees with the local Police over the cause of Canley's death is one Dr Jervis, the same name as

Dr Thorndyke's junior scientific assistant. Thorndyke is renowned for his portable miniature laboratory, the famous 'green square box' used during site investigations, and similarly Manson has 'the Box of Tricks'. Critical opinion attributes the invention of the inverted mystery story to Freeman, and particularly to his Dr Thorndyke short story collection *The Singing Bone* (1912), which includes the classic inverted tale 'The Case of Oscar Brodski'. Like Manson, Thorndyke notices things which others overlook, and the police and the reader are in awe of his deductive prowess and abilities. One reviewer in 1913 wrote that reading Dr Thorndyke stories was akin to "a course of mental gymnastics conducted under the pleasantest conditions". The author Raymond Chandler also had a high regard for Freeman's stories and applauded their "even suspense".

The experimental form of the inverted mystery story was adopted and developed with success by various leading UK Golden Age authors who sought to be innovative. Some notable examples include Francis Iles (Anthony Berkeley) in *Malice Aforethought* (1931) and *Before the Fact* (1933); Anthony Berkeley in *Trial and Error* (1937), which cleverly manages to combine the inverted form of Iles' writing with the puzzle mystery of the earlier Berkeley detective novels; Richard Hull in *The Murder of my Aunt* (1934) and *Murder Isn't Easy* (1936); Henry Wade in *Heir Presumptive* (1935); Freeman Wills Crofts in *Antidote to Venom* (1938); the novels of Anthony Rolls; and the Roy Vickers short story collections about the Department of Dead Ends. A significant variation developed by Iles in *Before the Fact* was to shift the inverted perspective from murderer to victim. Today, the inverted tale remains an effective and familiar form of crime writing, helped by popular appreciation of the long-running *Columbo* TV drama series which used the inverted murder form as its anchor.

Nigel Moss

Note

ACHILLES was, in Greek mythology, the son of Peleus and Thetis. The story goes that when he was born, Thetis took her son by one heel and dipped him in the Styx—the river of the dead—in order to make him invulnerable to death. The waters of the river washed over every part of his body except the heel in his mother's hand.

Achilles became the mighty hero of the Trojan War, on the Greek side. He slew Hector and other Trojan champions. But he fell before Troy was captured. An arrow, shot according to legend by Paris, pierced the *heel, the vulnerable spot of his body.*

FOREWORD

IN THIS novel—the eighth of the cases of Dr. Manson—we have deviated from the traditional style of the detective novel. The standard mystery follows along the lines of a perpetrated crime, the details of commission and the *particeps criminis* of which are unknown to the reader as well as to the investigator, whether he be famous amateur or professional detective.

The reader follows in the track of the investigator, and sees unravelled the plot of the crime, sometimes without being able to appreciate the points which are regarded by the detective as clues, because they are hidden in the detective's mind in order that he may at the end pull one from the hat to surprise the reader!

Sometimes—as we have always done in the 'Manson' stories—the clues are plainly presented, without artifice, and the reader is challenged to fit them into the jigsaw of the developing case, and name the guilty person. That constitutes the *modus operandi* of the normal detective story.

In *The Heel of Achilles* we have inverted the procedure. The complete details of the crime are presented to the reader in advance; he (or she, for it is a striking fact that the greater readers of detective stories today are women) is, in fact, an eyewitness to the murder and has the advantage over the investigating officers striving to trace the story, and the details, through the normal channels of investigation.

The authors hope that this 'inversion' will arouse as great an interest in the mind of the readers as does the traditional story of detection. They trust, too, that it will serve a useful purpose in revealing the mechanics of detection and how modern criminal investigation works in the police forces today; for there is nothing in the trail through Part Two of this story which can be said to be outside the realm of actual modern police investigation. The scientific and medical arguments given are such as are part and parcel of the C.I.D. in any case of major inquiry.

The case of Mrs. Ruxton (so ably reconstructed by Dr. J. Glaister, of the Department of Forensic Medicine, of the University of Glasgow), the Rouse case, and one or two others of even more recent date are all examples of the harnessing of science to the detection of crime and illustrate the methods and conclusions arrived at in this story.

Finally, the story may act as a warning to those people who may think that they can commit a crime and get away with it. They can't! *We,* who know something of Scotland Yard, and its men and methods, are quite sure of that fact. The detective novel, so long as it is written without fancy thrills and after the style of actual police investigation, is not the menace which so many people would have us believe. It preaches a moral—the detective invariably 'gets his man'!

E. AND M.A. RADFORD

Hampton Court,
  Surrey.

PART ONE
STORY OF A MURDER

CHAPTER I

THE SUN was climbing slowly to its zenith in the arched sky of periwinkle blue as the judge began his slow walk from the church to the assize court.

He walked majestically in scarlet and ermine, but with the inevitable monotony of established habit: thus had he pilgrimaged week in and week out on his round circuit of assizes over a span of years.

His hands, almost transparently white in their fragility—for he was an old man—clutched his robes which a desultory breeze cutting across a junction of roads blew apart, and drew them tightly round him.

His chaplain, who had minutes before asked at the altar of the parish church that Divine guidance might be vouchsafed to the man of Justice, walked behind him; alongside him the sheriff. Police officers rode slowly in front, their horses nosing gently and delicately to the pavement edge the lines of watching people.

In panoplied, leisurely dignity the cavalcade reached the market-place. Press photographers saw here their 'picture'; a news-reel man with Technicolor cameras saw it, too. The ancient market-place had been a mart of commerce since before the Norman landed on our shores, as he said 'for your good, for all your goods'. (A wit, in view of subsequent happenings, commented that he should have added 'and chattels'.)

City councils with a rare understanding had throughout the years preserved the ancient market-place for commerce; the latest council had even beautified it; rickety and haphazard stalls had been replaced with permanent sitings, each with a two-slope roof of pantiles in delicate shades of green, amber and blue. The tiles, struck by the sun's shaft of light, threw off rays of shimmering white. The rays combined with the scarlet of the judge, the silver and blue of the sheriff and the colourful produce piled on the stalls themselves, to add picturesque hue to the dignity of the cavalcade.

If the judge saw anything of this, he gave no indication; he walked with eyes looking straight ahead without a sparkle from out the face set beneath the full-bottomed wig. Only when he moved past the King's

Stone did he turn his glance aside to eye it, grey and chipped behind its guard of iron fencing; for his Lordship was a man learned and loving in the history of the past (which are good English words for the Latin word *antiquarian*), and he knew that Saxon kings had been crowned on that stone after Egbert, King of England, had been gathered to his father, and Westminster Abbey was as yet unthought of.

Because of the stone the City had come by its Royal title and its name of Kingston. Later generations, inspired by the river flowing gently and softly past added to the name the description 'on-Thames'. The King's Justice eyed the King's stone until, like history, it passed out of his sight.

Two men intrigued by the crowd lining the pavements approached, and each paused to eye the scene. They came from varying directions, drawn from their intended course by curiosity. The curiosity of women is a much maligned characteristic; the majority of spectators drawn as though by a magnet to a hole in a road, with a couple of men working within it, were men! However, on this day two men drawn by curiosity approached the procession. Or perhaps, in the light of subsequent events it might be argued that they were drawn by Fate, and not by curiosity.

One of them was James Canley. He lounged indolently against a convenient lamp-post and peered over the heads of those in front of him. He was a man of no more than medium height, with no characteristic to stamp his identity on the mind of an observer unless the observer was one skilled in judging men; then he might well have noticed the hard lines of the face, the shiftiness of the eyes set too closely in the head for honesty of purpose and uprightness. And he would have said that here was a man not to be confided in, not to be allied with any adventure where danger might be said to lurk—a man for the law-abiding to keep clear of.

His prying gaze turned first to recollection, then identification, and finally to bitter sneering regard as he saw the face of the robed figure. Years before he had stood in front of a judge in court and listened to blistering words that had sent him to penal servitude. His hands now clenched in threats of revengeful violence at the remembrance. But he made no move to turn into action the promptings of his rancour. He watched the passing of the judge.

The second man who had come to pry only in curiosity, stayed in sturdy independence, noting the pageantry and appreciating it. There was no remembrance to embitter his enjoyment of the wasted few moments of the morning. A virile-looking figure of muscle, Jack Porter had the appearance of the traditional English artisan; he was, in fact, a competent motor mechanic forging a way towards a satisfying fortune of achievement; he was as honest and industrious as Canley was insufferably idle and dissolute.

Two men in variegated pattern from the loom of Lachesis, waiting for Atropos to cut the threads at her fancy. And the threads were running out, had the men but the gift of knowing it.

Once in the years passed Fate had brought Canley and Porter together in a tangled web of circumstance. The result had been disaster for the one, and prison for the other. Nor had they set foot near, or eyes on, each other from that day.

The judge reached the entrance to the courts and stood for a moment as the trumpeters sounded the fanfare of arrival. The moment was set for pageantry, but not for the drama which followed. Nor did that concourse of people ever come to a realization that drama had been played out before their eyes; drama that was to lead to murder, and to the scaffold. Only two men knew it at the time. Both were to die without telling it. Only the workings of the mind of Superintendent Dr. Manson[1] and the logic of his deductions were to seek out, months later, the pattern of the Three Sisters of Mythology, and follow it in its unwinding.

As the fanfare sounded and the police sat stiffly to attention on their horses, a dog suddenly shot from between the legs of the people at the pavement edge and darted across the road under the legs of the horses. One of the animals, startled, reared and threw its rider. A gasp of alarm

1. Our regular readers may be surprised at finding that Chief Detective-Inspector Dr. Manson has, in this volume, blossomed out into Superintendent Manson.

This is by no desire of us, or of Doctor Manson; it is inevitable in order that the 'Manson Stories' may follow with accuracy the set-up of Scotland Yard. Up to July last year (1949) a yard man detailed to conduct a murder investigation was always a chief detective-inspector. Because he had to meet, and not infrequently, entertain local superintendents, he was allowed an annual emolument of £65.

In July last year, Scotland Yard authorities took the view that the investigating chief detective-inspector should not be placed in the peril of being junior in rank to a superintendent of police in the investigating area. So all chief detective-inspectors were raised to the rank of superintendent. Because a superintendent is not officially an 'investigating officer' but an 'executive officer' he no longer draws the extra £65 a year! But thus, Chief Detective-Inspector Dr. Manson, has, willy-nilly, to be a superintendent.

from the crowd seeing the hooves of the horse over their heads, was followed by a surge backwards. The officer, however, though falling heavily, managed to keep grip of the reins, and quieted his mount with a few words and a pat.

The dog vanished down the street, yelping. It might well have been the spiritual descendant of that hell-hound of Cornelius Agrippa, which whisper said was a spirit incarnate: for its escapade caused James Canley to edge towards the front of the line in the wan hope that he would see that someone had succeeded in getting his own back on the figure of Justice. He glanced up at the court steps and found himself looking into the face of Jack Porter.

His eyes passed from Porter to the judge, and then suddenly returned and again scanned the face of Porter. Puzzled wrinkles lined his brow, and he searched back in his memory for some clue to the air of familiarity which seemed to attach itself to the man opposite him. Suddenly it came. In a flash he saw in his mind's eye a large house in the woods above Paignton, the Devonshire seaside resort built in the manner of the townships on the *Côte d'Azur*, with palm trees lining the front, and the gaily coloured homes set in tiers on the hillside climbing up from the waters of the sea.

He heard again the shrill scream of police whistles, the alarming call of his companion. He recalled the climb out of a window, the dash for safety, followed by police officers, the blow with which he felled one of the men in a vain bid for escape, and the failure. He saw again the grim interior of an assize court and the face of the judge, so like that of the figure now standing on the steps of the assize court in front of him as the fanfare came to its finale.

'Jack Edwins, by God,' he said to himself. 'Jack Edwins, found after all these years.'

He took another sidelong look at the man, who had not as yet seen him. 'Looking pretty prosperous, too,' he added to his identification. 'On my money.'

The fanfare ended. The judge turned and entered the doors of the court. The police rode their horses slowly away, and the crowd broke its ordered line and in its individual members dispersed on the day's lawful occasions.

Jack Porter, his dalliance over, strode quickly down the street in the direction of the market-place. Canley, noting his direction followed a little behind until his quarry reached a less crowded street. He quickened his pace, and reaching Porter's side, placed a hand on his shoulder, swung him round, and. . . .

"Damned if it isn't old Jack Edwins!" he said.

Face to face with his past, which he had accounted for many years as dead, Porter fought desperately for recognition. He stared blankly at his accoster, and then slowly let the stare soften to a smile of pleasant regret.

"I am afraid you must have made a mistake, sir," he said. "My name is Porter."

He moved away, only for Canley to link an arm through one of his, and further to detain him. He guffawed.

"Well, that's as it may be," he announced. "Porter or not Porter, what's in a name anyway? You may be Jack Porter out here, but you're Jack Edwins to a Devonian. Come and have a drink. There are old times we have to talk over."

"I tell you . . ." Porter began again.

Canley interrupted, and with a menace in his voice. "It doesn't matter a damn what you say. Do you think I don't know my old pard, Edwins, even though it's been years since I saw him? Now I know somebody who would. . . ."

"All right." Porter gave up in forlorn surrender. With Canley he turned into the bar parlour of an hotel.

The stage was set for the first act of tragedy.

It was the pre-lunch half hour, and the bar was thickly lined with appetite stimulators.

"Can't talk here." Canley grumbled a protest after a drink. "And there's lots of things we've got to talk about that it won't do for anybody to overhear. Better come along to my place. It's only a bus ride away."

He led the way. Ten minutes saw them alight at the entrance to the village of Thames Pagnall: and a walk of some five minutes landed them outside a small cottage hidden away in a quiet lane. For solitude at the gateway of convenience Canley's home could hardly have been equalled. A railway station was no more than three minutes' walk from the lane, bus routes within five minutes. Yet there was no other dwelling in sight of the house. It is true that another cottage stood some two hundred yards further up the lane, but it was completely hidden from view by a high hedge bordering an orchard. Canley's cottage, again, had a second high hedge between it and the same orchard.

The lane itself was bordered by hedges, and a wide grass verge. It was, in fact, less a lane than a track. Originally it had been marked out, probably by the passage of feet of strollers through the grass. Then someone had dumped over the track a lot of rubble and rubbish so that it now made a track unmetalled and rough. No wheeled traffic would have made any effort to drive a way through it.

"Nice and lonely, eh?" Canley drew the attention of his companion to the surroundings. "That's how I am, Jack. Lonely. I haven't a friend these days. Nobody wants to be friendly with a gaolbird, you know."

He leered into the face of Porter.

"You've never seen the inside of a prison, have you, Jack—? A little stone room with a plank bed, and a window—A window so high up that you can't even look out of it *let alone climb through it*. Wouldn't like that, would you, Jack?"

He leered again, and poured out a couple of whiskies. "So the cops never caught you? You got clean away?"

Porter spoke for the first time. "That wasn't in any way due to you," he said. "You know that I had nothing to do with the business, that I went in all innocence, and yet you gave my name to the police. Hadn't even the honour of a thief, had you Canley?"

Canley ignored the accusation. "When you went out of that window, Jack, you had £1,000 worth of jewellery in your pockets. I put it in, so I know. That's what I'd gone there for. All the time I was in prison I said to myself that Jack Edwins had a nice nest egg for me when I came out, something on which I could start up again. We'd agreed to share it out at a pub, hadn't we?"

"We hadn't, and you know it." Porter denied the allegation. "You know very well that I knew nothing of what you were going to do."

"But the police never recovered the jewellery did they? Oh, no."

"I sold it, and I sent the value of it to the owner years after, when I made good in a business I bought with the £300 I got for it."

Canley sat back in his chair and roared with laughter. "That's a good story, Jack. Three hundred pounds for stuff that was worth more than a thousand. Don't expect me to swallow that, do you?" His voice changed. It grew dangerously quiet with intimidatory and transparent menace.

"Trying to do me out of my five hundred quid, are you? Don't try that game on me, Jack. I served three years in quod for that five hundred, and I'm going to have it. Else—" He let the sentence remain unfinished.

"I tell you that I sent £1,000 to Paignton for the owner of the jewellery. Ask the police there, if you don't believe me."

"Then the more fool you. You'll have to find the money yourself, then—Oh, don't get into a panic. I don't say I want it all at once. But I'll have a fiver now, just to be going on with. I've struck a bad time and a fiver will come in handsome."

"And a fiver is all you're going to get, now or at any other time." Porter turned on his blackmailer. "I had nothing to do with the Paignton business, and you know it." He handed a five-pound note over, and rose to go.

Canley placed it carefully away in an inside pocket of his waist-coat. He escorted his visitor mockingly to the door.

"I'll be seeing you again, Jack," he said. "You've bought a little business, have you?" He laughed loudly.

* * * * *

The five pounds became ten pounds, and twenty pounds. Within a few weeks five hundred pounds had gone from the pockets of Porter into those of Canley.

Each demand had grown in size, until—

At the office of the garage which Porter had built up on the by-pass road at Staines, a letter was handed to its owner by the post-man. It was marked 'private and confidential'. Porter opened it.

> *Dear Jack—I've got to come to you again. I said that with the five hundred the account between us was settled. But I've had a spell of bad luck, and I'm on my uppers again. Bring me a hundred pounds to the cottage on Friday night. And don't fail me. You know what to expect if you do.*

It was at that moment that Jack Porter knew he had to kill James Canley.

CHAPTER II

SOME years before the meeting of Porter and Canley in Kingston two men wended a precarious passage up Shorton Valley Road. The road climbs a strenuous way from the back of the seaside resort of Paignton to Shorton Woods, which stand on what once were, indeed, wooded heights midway between Paignton and its larger and more garish neighbour, Torquay. The woods have now mostly given way to houses; but a country lane wending between trees still exists, and a copse here and there with a house set in its shadows continues to justify the name Shorton Woods.

The two men walked precariously because they were both the worse for drink; to put it bluntly, they were drunk. It was a warm evening, and the climb in the sultry air combined with the beer to bring beads of perspiration to their brows, a circumstance which necessitated frequent applications of handkerchiefs.

James Sprogson was less drunk than his companion. Old William was twice his age to begin with, and he had drunk much more beer, though he didn't know it; Sprogson had played him for a purpose and was still engaged in the play, which was the reason for his accompanying William to the house in which the old man was butler when the family were in residence, and caretaker when they were not. They were not in residence at the moment.

Yew Tree House hove into their sight at long last. It was a large manor house built of grey stone in the manner of the good builders of old, when money was no object, and only comfort regulated the size of the dwelling and the style of it.

The house was set in grounds of about a quarter of an acre and shadowed by some of the few trees still left in Shorton Woods. There were no yew trees, strangely enough; but doubtless yew trees had stood there when the house was built some forty years ago. On one side of the grounds ran a large and high bay hedge in close proximity to the kitchen—which made it handy for the cook to snip a couple of leaves off when she desired a little vanilla flavouring for the custard to the sweet course!

The house and its grounds were fairly secluded; some two hundred yards away a wooden bungalow stood, screened by yet another bay hedge, and sheltering beneath a row of poplars. Its occupants were two women—and a cat. With the exception of this dwelling and a castellated farmhouse (a queer architectural parody) there were no other residences until the summit of the hill was reached; along the high road which skirted the summit, buses ran on their way to Torquay.

Old William paused at the entrance to Yew Tree House, and regarded his companion with the comic solemnity of a drunken man.

"Very goodsh of you to come along old man," he said. "Couldn't—made it on me own. Come in and have a bite to eat?"

Sprogson looked doubtful. "I'd like to, old boy, but—er—what will the family say? Eh?"

"No family." William waved a hand comprehensively, taking in everything. "Gone away—London—for a week."

Sprogson had already acquired that information after considerable and guarded inquiry; but he wanted the butler's confirmation.

"Got a tasty bit of chicken," announced William, invitingly.

"All right. May as well. I'm feeling a bit peckish," agreed Sprogson. They entered together.

Half an hour later Sprogson sat back, comfortably satisfied inwardly. But not so satisfied mentally.

He looked round the room.

"Nice place you've got here." The suggestion was couched in a voice that might have suggested uncharitable envy. "A nice cushy job, too, I'll be bound."

"Not so bad," agreed William. "Not at times. But a lot of 'sponsibility when family's away. See?"

"Responsibility?" Sprogson looked inquiringly.

"Antiques. See. Very old—"

"They would be, if they're antiques," sneered Sprogson.

"And silver," added William. "Come and see it."

He led the way to the butler's pantry. The pantry was a large square room at the side of the house. It was provided with a large table, and a smaller side table, a comfortable armchair and two plain wooden chairs. A window gave a view from the side of the house when it could be looked out of: at the moment it was sheathed with double steel doors or shutters fastened on the inside and secured with a padlock through the horizontal bar which ran from side to side.

Sprogson gazed at it with surprise. He waved a hand in its direction. "Bit hot, isn't it?" he asked.

"Hot?" William looked puzzled.

"Are they afraid somebody will lam the butler over the head or something?" interpreted Sprogson.

"Ah!" William looked mysteriously round the room. "Valuables—kept in here. See?"

He opened a large cupboard and displayed a quantity of silver table-ware. Sprogson examined it with interest, and disappointment.

"Crested," he snorted. "No good to a burglar. He couldn't sell it, and it wouldn't be worth anything melted down. Doesn't seem worth the iron curtain."

"Ah!" said William again, only more mysterious-like than before. "That ain't all. It's the jewels, see."

"Jewels? What, in this room? In cupboards?"

"You'd never guess, would you?" Old William became arch.

"No, I wouldn't. You telling me a fairy story, old boy? Where are they?"

"Ah!" William's monosyllable was becoming monotonous. He leaned against the wall. Sprogson, who was still gazing round the room seeking a possible hiding place for jewellery, turned at the sound of a slight grinding noise, and stared. A section of panelling had parted, disclosing a cavity behind. What Sprogson stared at was a safe in the cavity. It looked out from its hiding-place, a cache of considerable size, and of burnished steel, with an obvious combination lock wheel in the front of it.

"So that's it," said Sprogson. "And you say there are jewels inside it?"

"Full of jewels, old boy."

"Let's have a look at 'em. I've never seen a lot of valuable jewels all in one little nest."

"No. Can't do it." William shook his head. "Can't show 'em. In me custody. See? 'sponsibility."

"Oh, well." Sprogson looked regretful resignation. "Silly of me to ask. I don't suppose you could open the safe, anyway."

William bridled. His custodianship, complete custodianship, was a point of pride with him—a fact of which Sprogson had been made boringly aware during the last three or more evenings. The suggestion that he had not been trusted with the means of opening the safe during his custodianship, annoyed him. He gave vocal vent to the annoyance.

"Ho! Couldn't I?" He protested. He leered still half-drunkenly, in spite of the meal just concluded. "Couldn't I? Got combination. See? In me head," he added, sagely.

"Good story, old man," said Sprogson, and laughed.

The laugh incensed William. He snorted. "I'll show you," he said. He turned to the safe. A few turns of the wheel and he pulled open the doors.

Sprogson peered inside. William had exaggerated when he had announced that the safe was full of jewellery. There was, however, quite a valuable collection. Sprogson valued it at, roughly, several thousands of pounds. He had time for only a hurried look, for William, repenting his bravado, and scared for his charge, slammed the door and swung the wheel again. At the same time he slid the panel back into its place, hiding the safe from view.

Sprogson examined the panel. It showed no mark of a join, and no hint that it was any different from any other panel which lined the walls in light oak.

"Clever," he commented. "Clever. Open it again, William." William obliged. The panel slid open almost silently, and again returned.

"Blessed if you aren't a Maskelyne, old man." Sprogson looked at him admiringly. "How the devil do you do it?"

"Hidden spring," William grinned.

"Let's see if I can do it." Sprogson felt and pushed at likely spots in the embroidery of the panel, but without result. William watched him for some moments, and then giggled.

"You ain't nowhere near the place," he chided.

"Then where the devil is it? Go on. Show me again. Then we'll go and have another drink up at the Hole. They've got your favourite wallop there, haven't they?"

"They have." William moved to the wall again. "It's the little rose," he explained. "Secret spring, see."

He pressed the rose and the panel disappeared. Another pressure and it returned and closed.

"Derned cute," said Sprogson. "Well, come along and have that drink before they close."

It was two hours later that the pair left the ancient smugglers' inn at the top of the hill overlooking the golf course. By that time half a dozen glasses of powerful black wallop had reduced old William almost to helplessness coming on top of the earlier libations.

It is doubtful if he would have left the hostelry even then had not the landlord refused to serve him with more drink.

"No. You're drunk. Out you go, William," he had dictated. "I'll lose me licence if the police find you here like this."

So out the pair went, Sprogson, with a grin, supporting his butler friend. He felt for the keys in the man's pockets and unlocked the front door of Yew Tree House.

"I reckon I'd better get you to bed, William," he suggested. "You're too drunk to get there by yourself."

"No!" emphasized William. "Got—ter—look in safe. Shee if things ish a'rightsh," he explained. "It's me duty, see. Every nightsh, look in safe."

"All right. Come on, then." Sprogson escorted him to the butler's pantry. "Better let me open the safe for you, hadn't you?" he asked.

"No!" William showed alarm. "Word's a secret—never tell—living soul," he protested.

Sprogson shrugged his shoulders.

William lurched to the safe and leaned against it. Sprogson watched him amusedly as he swung the wheel a full turn and began to work the combination. Suddenly he sprang to stiff attention. The old man was muttering under his breath, as though counting or repeating something he had difficulty in remembering in his drunken state. Sprogson, still as a mouse, listened.

"T," and the wheel moved. "R," another turn, "E—E—S," the wheel being gyrated at each letter.

Satisfied, William pulled open the door of the safe and with difficulty of vision decided that the contents were whole and untouched. He swung the door to again, touched the spring which slid the panel into position, and turned to Sprogson.

"Ish a'rightsh," he announced with solemnity of a custodian and the comicality of a stage 'drunk'.

"Good," responded Sprogson, and meant it. "Now come along and I'll get you into bed."

The operation was concluded not without some intractability on the part of William. But he expressed his gratitude at the end.

"You're a good fellow. Dunno your name, but you're a gennelman. Anybody can shee that," he lisped. "Gennelman, that's what you are. Like—meet you—again—have more wallop."

"That's all right, William. Call me Fred. Now, look here. Be at the Hole again tomorrow night at 9.30. If I'm not there at the time, wait for me. I'll be along, but I may be a few minutes late. We'll have another evening out, eh?"

"Tomorrow at 9.30—tomorrow at—" William sought to impress the date on his mind.

"Here. I'll leave you a note on the table to remind you," promised Sprogson, and wrote it on the back of an envelope.

That was the end of a perfect day for William. And for Sprogson, who left the house and walked rapidly down the road into Paignton, and on to the back-street boarding house in which he had a temporary room.

It was eleven o'clock, and as he approached the house a man ahead of him walked up the steps and opened the door. Sprogson called a warning to him as the door was about to close. "Half a minute, Jack!" he shouted.

Jack Edwins turned and recognized Sprogson. He frowned. He had at that very moment been thinking of the man. Not with any feeling of pleasure, or anticipation of seeing him. In point of fact, he had only a quarter of an hour before parted from his sweetheart after a heated argument over Sprogson and his companions. The discord which still jangled in Edwins's recollection, was over the desirability of Sprogson as an acquaintance for himself. The argument had been unsparingly acrimonious on the part of Mary Reed; in fact, it had amounted to an ultimatum threatening to end a love romance which had developed unexpectedly from a chance holiday. It was also their first quarrel.

The holiday belonged to Edwins. With work slack in the London garage where he was a mechanic Edwins decided to take an early break. A spell of fine weather which looked like lasting over a fortnight helped his decision; his employer attracted by the idea of not having to pay a man during the slack weeks had agreed with enthusiasm. Newspaper paragraphs recording hours of sunshine in Devonshire had led to Edwins deciding on Paignton as the location for his break.

Bed and breakfast, and meals where I want them, had been Edwins's idea for the holiday. 'No boarding house meals for me and paying for food I'm not there to have,' he had added to himself. It is, by the way, the argument of twenty-five per cent of the family holiday-makers today at most of the resorts; and is a popular course with landladies, since it relieves them of the task of preparing meals, and of the presence of lodgers throughout the daylight hours, except on wet days.

After a tour of the town Edwins decided on the Café Rouge as his regular lunching place. He liked the red tables with their snowy-white tablecloths, the clean red chairs and the atmosphere of quiet luxury about it. He liked, too, the welcoming smile of the girl who came forward to wait on his table.

Mary Reed took to her customer from the first meal she served him—after she had found a shilling tip underneath the plate, which was an advance of ninepence on the average tip. She looked on him with considerable favour when he appeared at the same table the next day.

Mary was an attractive woman of about twenty-three years of age. Her face was not pretty, as the word is understood of the female sex. She had no glamour; but there was a likeable something in the pleasant smile of her grey eyes, which drew customers back to her table after a first visit. She dressed neatly and becomingly; a woman observer would have remarked that her frocks had been well worn over a long period, for there were neatly done darns, and embellishments of embroidery which told most women of frayed or shiny parts thus disguised by a covering.

Edwins, lonely in the evenings of his holiday, whispered to the girl after his third meal.

"What time do you close here?" he asked. She smiled.

"Six o'clock. We don't serve evening meals. It means double staffs," she explained, "and doesn't make it worth while with the additional expense. At least, that is what the management says."

"Then how about you and I going to the pictures?" Edwins looked anticipatingly pleased.

"I'd love to," replied Mary Reed.

The evening's meeting was repeated. Edwins found that his liking for her grew with each evening's jaunt along the promenade, or at the cinema, with a night-cap of fish and chips in a late café. He also found that his liking for her had an echo in Mary's regard for him. The mutual pleasure of each in the other's company was sufficient to convince Edwins that his future lay not in London. Mary Reed agreed, enthusiastically; she had been living a lonely life since coming to Paignton, and the company of a sound, good-living artisan such as Jack Edwins was something she had for long desired.

The bargain was struck; Edwins set about looking for a job in Paignton. There was no difficulty about that; he was a skilled motor engineer, and they are scarce enough anywhere. He obtained a remunerative job in a garage and service station in the seaside resort. The Café Rouge continued to provide him with his lunch, and Mary's company at the table. The courtship progressed and soon they accounted themselves an engaged couple. Their evenings were spent together walking in the country lanes at the back of Paignton, away from the madding crowd of holiday-makers, and in the number of lovers from time immemorial.

Into this Eden of romance the serpent of Sprogson intruded. After six weeks the couple had become officially engaged. From his wages in the garage Edwins was putting away a percentage towards the purchase of a home; Mary was saving the amount represented by her tips; beyond that she could not go, her wages being no more than a few shillings a week, the customers making the amount up to a living wage with tips, which is the bad custom of the restaurant trade, or was the custom at the time of this story.

Edwins had wanted to borrow the money to enable them to marry and set up house, thus avoiding the double cost of their lodgings; but Mary would have none of it. "I am not going to start married life by getting into debt," she insisted. "There is no security in that. A few weeks' illness, or if you're on short time or lose your job, then we are finished, and it's the same with furniture on hire purchase. I'd sooner have a bed, a table and a couple of chairs paid for, than a home which isn't ours at all, but the property of a furniture company."

So the couple were saving hard.

Within three months they had acquired the sum of fifty pounds, and decided to celebrate. In the Red Cow, a quiet hostelry towards the back of Paignton, Mary drank delicately, a glass of port, and Edwins a whisky and soda. They toasted each other. Before the glasses were empty Sprogson stepped into their lives.

James Sprogson had journeyed to Paignton because it, and the neighbouring Torquay, were holiday resorts, and therefore crowded. Sprogson lived on the takings he could get from other people in any way that was not legal; he could not have made much by legal means, in any case, for he lived on his wits. But it was not until much later that the company and Edwins and Mary knew that. All they knew at this time was that Sprogson was an open-handed man who bought drinks for the house, and seemed to have plenty of money to flash before envious patrons of the Red Cow.

He had on several occasions dined at the Café Rouge, and he recognized Mary as the waitress there. His insistence on buying her a drink with the remainder of the company effected an introduction to Edwins. Mary regarded this as essential to avoid the attentions he seemed anxious to show her.

Sprogson talked racing. It was a subject, he said, on which he had information straight from the horses' mouths and from their jockeys.

"Thinking of getting married, are you?" he said, to Edwins after the introduction. "Then you can do with a bit of the ready. Back Royal George tomorrow—you'll get twenty to one on it now, and it's a dead cert. Listen."

He crossed to the telephone and called up a bookmaker. "That you, Joe?" he asked. "Put me twenty pounds on Royal George at twenties? You will? Right. That's how sure I am, love birds," he announced.

The following morning Edwins ventured two pounds; the result increased their savings by forty pounds. After that he renewed the acquaintance with Sprogson and his cronies.

Mary saw the growing intimacy with concern. Her lover, she noted, was drinking more than was good for him. She remonstrated without much effect. The weekly savings from his salary grew less; Mary protested against the money spent on betting and on drink.

The climax had come on the evening that Sprogson paid his visit to Yew Tree House with Old William. Edwins had failed for the first time to add any money to Mary's tips for the bottom drawer. He had, he said, to pay Sprogson money he owed. Mary, who had sacrificed many luxuries to save her tips for the future, was tearfully protestant at the lapse of her lover. She arraigned Sprogson.

"He's no good, I tell you, Jack. Those ferrety eyes give him away to anyone who can see through them. He gives me the creeps." She shuddered. "Why on earth you want to go round with the man I can't think. He's no good to you, Jack, and will land you in trouble one of these days."

"Oh, for Heaven's sake give it a rest, dear," grumbled Edwins. "He's all right. We only have a few drinks and a game of pool on the nights you're at the cookery classes. Surely there's no harm in that. I need a little fun after I've been in that blasted garage all day."

Mary looked thoughtfully at him. "I thought you liked being in the garage, Jack," she said, and her eyes regarded him anxiously.

"You know I only took the job to be near you. Else I'd have gone back to London after my holiday. Joe's garage isn't my idea of a job. I want my own place and I'll get it before long—with a nice little flat over it where Mrs. Edwins will be getting the supper ready while her loving husband is locking away the day's takings, eh?" Edwins put an arm round Mary's shoulders and drew her close.

Mary pouted. "Well, darling, I can't see that that man is going to help in getting it. I know I can't get out every night, but surely you could find a friend belonging to the place or to your garage; there's several nice men there. Sprogson is too crafty to be buying you drinks and taking you about in that rat-trap car of his for nothing. Darling, I wish you'd listen to me."

Edwins swung her into the shade of the bandstand past which they were strolling. He kissed her full on the lips. "Now, will you stop nagging, Mary," he said.

Mary laughed. "Well, have it your own way, Jack dear. But do be careful."

Edwins took her into his arms again. "Now, darling, I'll relieve you of your anxieties," he said. "Sprogson is leaving for London again this week-end. I'm having a farewell drink with him and the other two pals of his tomorrow night. I don't suppose I'll see him after that."

Mary nestled contentedly against his arm. "Did you mean that about the garage, Jack?" she asked.

"Yes, dear. I meant it. I'd got it all planned out as soon as I met you. I knew you fitted into my scheme of things. Don't worry. This time next year we'll be settled in our own little home. Whatever may happen always remember that's what I'm working for—just you and I, partners in every way."

They kissed in the shadow of the doorway of her lodgings, and Jack Edwins strode away towards his own boarding house.

It was on the steps that he met Sprogson.

CHAPTER III

It was not until nearly ten o'clock on the following night that Edwins turned up at the Red Cow for the final drink with Sprogson. A breakdown order had kept him employed in a rush job at the garage until after nine o'clock, and a hurried wash and change gave him just time to get to the rendezvous before closing time.

Sprogson was arguing hotly with his two cronies. They looked up as Edwins entered. He hung on the outskirts of the company until the argument should be ended; though he tolerated Sprogson for the benefit he gained from his racing tips and his talk, he had no wish to make the further acquaintance of his companions.

From the back Edwins heard snatches of the dispute.

"It isn't our kind of game"—this from Thatcher Stevens. "No, I reckon I'd better be getting home to the missus," was the contribution of Cow Evans.

"I tell you there's money in it. Easy money," said Sprogson.

"Reckon we've got enough for the time being, Sprogson," replied Thatcher. "Take the kid; he can do with some. He wants to get spliced, don't he?"

Sprogson uttered a foul oath. "All right. I'll take him. And to hell with the lot of you."

He turned.

"Time, gentlemen, please," called the landlord.

Sprogson turned away and beckoned Edwins. "Come on, Jack," he said, "we're going to see Old William up at Yew Tree House. He can put me in the way of some money. And you, too. I suppose you can do with a bit of easy money, eh?"

"I reckon I can, and the sooner the better," replied Edwins.

"Come along, then. We'll have to buck up. It's later than I meant it to be."

The two men walked rapidly up the hill to the house. It was now getting dark. The long hill was practically deserted. Few people passed along at that hour. Those who frequented public houses and hotels had not yet started their journey homewards. And the cinemas had not closed for the night.

"You know Old William, don't you, Jack?" asked Sprogson.

"Yes, I've met him several times in the Red Cow when he's been with you," was the reply.

"I was with him last night. We got drunk together. He's full of his secrets when he's had a few," explained Sprogson. "He showed me how to get hold of a few hundreds. I reckon there's as much as I want and a bit over for you. More than you can earn in months at the garage you slave in. A smart chap like you ought to get hold of money easier than oiling yourself up under motor-cars."

"I should have thought if there was easy money going, Old William would have been after it himself," suggested Edwins.

"He hasn't got the nerve, Jack. That's why it's coming to me and you. 'Nothing venture nothing have' is my motto."

They arrived at Yew Tree House as the last of the light was going. Sprogson led the way up the drive, keeping in the shade of the high hedge. At the door he produced a key from a pocket, unlocked the door and motioned Edwins inside. He followed, locking the door again behind him.

The place was in darkness. To Edwins it seemed to exude an air of bleak emptiness, and oppressive desolation. He felt a chill of nervous apprehension: curiously enough his thoughts turned not to his present position in the house, the darkness of which affected him adversely, but to Mary who, except for this farewell night, he would now have been escorting towards her home.

Before he could give vent to his feelings, Sprogson, standing in the hall gave a low whistle. There was no response, and after a moment he moved in the direction of the butler's pantry and tried the knob. It turned in his hand and the door opened.

"Good!" said Sprogson. The two men entered. Sprogson, closing the door behind him, switched on the light.

"Butler's pantry. Old William's domain," he explained to Edwins. He pointed to the iron shutter which covered the window. "See, no light shows out of the room," he pointed out.

Edwins nodded. "Funny do, isn't it?" he asked. "Why couldn't they use a thick curtain?"

Sprogson smiled. "Don't worry your head about things which don't matter," he recommended.

"Anyway, where's your friend? I don't want to stop here too long. Can't we hear about the money and get home?"

Sprogson did not answer. Instead he crossed to the inside wall of the room and pressed on the panelling. A door slid back and in the recess Edwins saw with surprise the outline of a safe.

Sprogson pointed to it with a grin. "There's thousands of pounds' worth of stuff in there, Jack," he said. "I've seen it. Old William showed it to me last night."

"Then I reckon they *want* a good bit of steel on the windows," retorted Edwins. "But I wish your friend would come. It doesn't seem right to be messing about with things in here like this without him."

Sprogson made no reply. He had moved to the front of the safe, and was twiddling with the combination wheel. He was reading from a paper and twiddling the wheel at the same time. After a minute of two of fiddling there was a sudden click, and Sprogson pulled the safe door open.

Seeing the contents of the safe laid bare, there came into Edwin's mind with wounding and nauseating realism the explanation of their presence in the house; the reason for the non-appearance of Old William; the wait after Sprogson had given his low whistle on entering the hall and closing the door behind him. Edwins knew for the first time since he had entered the house that the place was empty of any butler or caretaker, and that Sprogson had come deliberately, knowing that, to burgle the safe.

Edwins backed away from the violated cache and challenged his companion. "William isn't in the place and you knew he wasn't going to be here." He directed his indictment against Sprogson fiercely. "You're robbing the place. I'm not having anything to do with it, Sprogson. I'm getting out."

Sprogson eyed him, grinning. "Don't be a damned fool, Jack," he said. "There's a fortune here for the taking. Nobody but me knows that there's nobody here in the place, and by the time they find the safe rifled we'll be two hundred miles away in London. Besides, there's nothing to show that you and I have been here. Old William doesn't know that he gave me the combination when I got him blind drunk. If he thinks of it later, he won't speak. It's as much as his job is worth. Don't be a damned fool. It's the easiest crib I've ever cracked, and the safest, too. Can't you do with a few hundred quid?"

"Not that way I can't," Edwins spat out the words. "And I'm not going to, either. I'm getting out—now."

"All right," Sprogson hissed venomously. "Get out, you damned fool. I thought I was doing you a good turn. But keep your mouth shut when you *do* get out. If anyone gets on to me I'll know you've been talking, and I'll slit your throat. See?"

Edwins turned to the door. As he did so the note of a police whistle shrilled from outside the house, and near it. Sprogson's hands came away from the safe as if he had received an electric shock. He stared at his companion.

"The cops!" he said.

A grin came over his face. The humour of the situation appealed to him in spite of the danger. "Well, you're in it now, all right, kid," he said. "No good telling the cops you didn't have anything to do with it, when they find you in the place. The side of the house is the best. Run for the trees; they'll never catch us among them."

He moved quickly to the safe again, and his hands came away crammed with jewellery.

"Here," he snapped. He stuffed the jewels into Edwins's jacket pockets. "Get out and run like hell. Don't go near the Red Cow. Get up to The Case is Altered, at Babbacombe, and I'll meet you there tomorrow night. And mind you bring the stud along with you. We'll share half and half. Now we'd better part. We'll stand a better chance that way."

He climbed out of a window at the side of the house, darted to the shade of the hedge and began to run. Edwins watched him reach the end of the hedge and make a dart for the shelter of the trees in a copse. A policeman came running from the direction of the side gate. Another whistle shrilled out, and two other officers converged back and front on the running man.

Edwins realized at that moment the idea in Sprogson's mind in putting the jewellery in his, Edwins's, pockets. If they were caught by the police it would not be Sprogson who had the stolen goods in his possession but himself. Sprogson would not have a single piece of stolen property on him. It would be easy for him to say that he had seen a man break into the house and was waiting for him to come out, follow and identify him. That, he judged, was the reason why he had brought him along at all; he wanted a second man as a safety-first plan.

These thoughts in his mind, Edwins stood quietly behind a window watching the chase. The dalliance served him an unexpected good turn, for when Sprogson and the officers were out of sight, the consciousness came to him that there was a quietness about the place that suggested isolation. He listened for a moment or two but heard no sign of movement outside the house. It occurred to him that the police had used a ruse, and had overshot their mark. The whistle, he worked out, had been to alarm the intruders, cause them to bolt for it, into the hands of the triangular-arranged covey of police. Seeing only one man emerge from the house, they had figured that the 'started' hare was the only one on the job. That meant that the way was clear for him to escape.

Climbing out of another window Edwins kept in the shade of the bushes, where they were thickly planted, until he reached the bottom of the garden. Then, instead of taking the route mapped out by Sprogson and followed by him, he forced a way through the thick hedge into a field behind, in the opposite direction to the town. He followed the hedge, keeping low down in its shelter, and continued likewise across two further fields until he reached the high road at the top of the hill. A bus was approaching; he signalled the driver, and climbing aboard was taken on to Torquay.

For ten minutes he waited at a coach stop, his heart beating wildly at the sight of every policeman who patrolled the busy centre. Once, as an officer crossed the road in his direction he nearly made a run for it; the policeman passed on without a look at him, and he realized that there was no hue and cry out for him.

The arrival of a coach for Newton Abbot relieved him of any immediate anxiety, and put him a further stage on the road to safety. At the Devonshire rail junction, he searched the timetable. There was no train due out until 1 a.m. for London. That meant a wait of two hours.

Edwins, thus far on the road to safety, realized that hanging round the junction at that hour of the night might occasion suspicion, and with the jewellery still in his pockets any quizzing of him by a police officer would have fatally unfortunate results. He accordingly walked sharply out of the town, as would a late reveller walking home after the last bus had run.

Seeing a field that had but recently been cleared of the hay crop, he settled himself comfortably in the screen of a hayrick and thus passed the midnight hour. A cautious approach to the railway station shortly before one o'clock failed to reveal any waiting police or officials of the station. There was no hesitation in giving him a ticket on the part of the booking office clerk, who was too sleepy anyway to take note of any intending passengers. Edwins, ticket in his pocket, waited until the train was about to move out, and then jumped aboard.

At 7.45 a.m. he walked out of Paddington Station and vanished in the maze that is London.

Twenty-four hours later he learned that he was by no means yet out of the Paignton wood; Sprogson, said a newspaper report, had been apprehended after he had attacked and knocked unconscious one of the police officers pursuing him. He was sent for trial on a charge of burglary, and a further one of inflicting grievous bodily harm on a policeman.

The police stated that jewellery worth £1,000 was missing from the safe at Yew Tree House, but no jewellery was found on the prisoner when he was apprehended. Sprogson, they added, said that the jewellery was taken by a companion he had with him, who was named Edwins.

After reading of the betrayal, Jack Edwins died that morning. He became Jack Porter.

At Sprogson's trial a month later, the police stated that none of the jewellery had been recovered. They had so far found no trace of the man whom the prisoner said had been with him, and who got away with the jewellery. They had learned that a man named Edwins had been in the town for some time but had now disappeared. The surface of the safe at Yew Tree House revealed the fingerprints of the butler at Yew Tree House and of Sprogson, who was known to them by another name. They believed that the prisoner might have cached the jewellery during a period when they lost sight of him during the chase from Yew Tree House into Paignton. He had been picked up later at Paignton Railway Station, having been recognized by an officer. He denied that he was the man who had been pursued, but his fingerprints identified him. The judge sentenced him to three years' penal servitude.

* * * * *

In the Café Rouge on the morning after the Yew Tree House burglary, Mary had glanced from time to time at the table where her fiancé had made a habit of sitting for his lunch. Her momentary surprise at the lateness of his non-arrival was later turned to wonderment when, at 2 p.m., he still had not put in an appearance. It was the first occasion on which he had not taken his lunch at the café since that day he had first entered for a meal and met her.

Her feelings gave way to anxiety when Edwins was not at their usual rendezvous at seven o'clock, and although she waited for an hour, he was still missing. Fears that he might have been taken ill, and unable to communicate with her, sent Mary hurrying to his lodgings. There she found, to her alarm, that he had not returned to his bed the night before and had not been seen that day.

The garage in which he worked was closed by this time and no information was available from his workmates as to whether he had been sent away on a job. She felt certain, however, that had that been indeed the case, he would have sent round to tell her.

After a night's tossing, in which sleep was chased away by fears that some tragedy had happened to her lover, Mary, hurrying round to the garage on her way to the café next morning, heard newsboys calling out "Police chase man at Shorton."

She remembered that Jack's disappearance followed the night he was to have spent with Sprogson at the farewell drinking party, and her fears and warning to him returned. Nor were they long in being confirmed. She purchased a paper and turned to the headlined report and Sprogson's statement that he had had a companion named Edwins.

Her faith in her lover, though shaken by the reports, still did not accept the allegations made against him. She remembered her distrust of Sprogson and insisted in her own mind that Jack, if he was concerned in the outrage, had been 'framed' by the companion against whom she had warned him so tearfully but without any effect, the man who was so sure of himself and of his capacity to walk with bad men and keep his virtue, to misquote Kipling.

At the end of the second day her trust was rewarded. On reaching her lodgings after her day's work in the café, she found a letter from him bearing a London postmark. She read it, half aloud:

Darling—You were right about Sprogson. He led me up the garden path. You'll have seen by now the trouble I am in. Dearest, I knew nothing of what he was doing until the police whistles went, and it was too late. I had to run for it when I saw the police after Sprogson. I've got to London safely, but I can't come back to you yet.

Darling, I've done nothing to be ashamed of. You must believe that. And when I've found another job I'll go on saving if I know you aren't disappointed in me, and are not giving me up. You mustn't do that. I couldn't live without your help now, after I've known you.

You've got my share of our savings with yours. Hang on to that, and collect the things from my digs and keep them for me until I can let you know where to send them. God bless you, darling. I love you so much.—Jack.

There passed slowly weeks of anxious days and nights in which Mary's agony of dread and suspense fought with her need for sleep. Only now and then a postcard reached her, unsigned, but with a London postmark; and with these new hope stirred in her heart.

Then, at long last, came blessed relief for Mary that hurt in its unexpectedness. A letter lay on her table awaiting her return from work. She opened it with feelings equally divided, it seemed to her, between dread and hope.

Good news, darling. Come to London on Friday and I will meet you at Paddington. I think we have found what we have waited for.—Jack.

CHAPTER IV

THE TOWNSHIP of Staines, in Surrey, straddles the wide Thames close by those meadows, lush in history as well as in grass, where John made his mark on the *Magna Carta* and thus gave a measure of justice to the people of England.

Some time in the seventh century saintly persons built a church on the banks of the river. A community grew around the church, which was the way of most of the villages of England—first the church and then the congregation; always the church gave birth to the village. In the fields nearby the church more than five hundred years later, when the *Magna Carta* was signed, the place was still no more than a church and a hamlet. Sixty-five years passed with their winters and summers and someone else, whose name had been lost to history, placed reverently on the river-bank hard by the community, a rough slab of stone with, on it, the inscription 'God preserve the City of London.'

Why the sudden invocation, and from what the Almighty was to preserve the city nobody can even now conjecture.

But the Saxon word for stone was 'stane'; from the stane the community came by its name of Staines—'the place of the stone'.

The years passed by again; the old saintly church fell into decay—disappeared. A new church rose in its place, bigger and mightier. There it stands still as St. Mary's Church. The 'place of the stone' grew from its hamlet to a village; from a village to the busy town which is Staines today. Roads took the place of the rude tracks and paths; the newest of these roads is the great by-pass which takes traffic on towards the West Country.

A mile or two out of the town along the by-pass on its Surrey side there stood a small garage. It looked unprosperously out, a square brick building, its ground floor a large concreted 'shop' with room, perhaps, for a dozen cars. Stairs in a corner led to an upper floor of two rooms.

The floor of the garage was dirty and oil-stained; the doors and windows were bare for want of a lick of paint. A run-in from the road on either side was no more than a muddy piece of land rammed to some degree of hardness by the wheels of cars and commercial vehicles. Two petrol pumps stood at the roadside edging the run-in. A couple of cars were jacked up in the garage itself, while a mechanic in overalls tinkered with the innards of one of them.

Jack Porter had walked with Mary Reed from a bus stop two hundred yards or so up the road. He pulled her to a halt outside the building.

"What do you think of that, Mary?" he asked. He waved a hand in the direction of the garage.

"It doesn't look very prosperous, Jack." The answer came spontaneously. "Is this where you are working?"

"No. But's where I may be working, Mary, with you at my side."

"With me?" The girl looked her puzzlement. "Why with me, dear?"

Jack Porter hesitated. This was the moment for which he had been hoping—and yet fearing. The fear sprang from his knowledge of Mary Reed's character; from the honesty which looked out from her eyes; the faith which she had in him, and which misfortune had not dimmed—as yet. There were things that Mary Reed did not know of Jack Porter, and which she had to learn; now, he realized, was the time for the learning.

"Because, Mary," he answered her question slowly, "this may be the beginning of the dream we had—of a garage of which I shall be the boss, the two rooms in which we can be together and build a future."

The words came quietly, and he inflected into his voice hopeful ambition, which, at the moment he was very far from feeling.

"It doesn't look much now, Mary," he agreed, "but that is because it is neglected. A coat of green and cream paint all over—I can do that myself—a concrete run-in—I can do that, too—and the entire place cleaned up and made attractive and there would be a nice little business here, on this busy road. In a couple of years' time we could extend it with a show-case or two for spares, and so on. And it's going for £500 freehold. It's a snip. Can you see it?"

Mary Reed nodded, interestedly. "Yes, Jack, dear, I can visualize what can be done, and what it would look like. But £500 is a lot of money. We have exactly £100 saved up, haven't we?"

The crisis had arrived; the moment Jack Porter had dreaded since the minute that Mary Reed had stepped off the Devonshire train at Paddington, and had run forward and kissed her lover for the first time since the night on which Sprogson had all but led him into the hands of the police, and the gates of a prison.

"What is the good news, Jack?" she had asked after the greeting, and when they were seated side by side in a train hurrying its way to the Surrey Thames-side.

"I will tell you at the right time," he had replied. He knew that his procrastination was the coward's device to gain time foolish though it was, since the *dénouement* must of necessity come eventually. Through his worried brain was drumming the realization that there was much more than a cliché, a tag, in the bewailment of Hamlet:

Conscience doth make cowards of us all.

Now there had arrived the time when the truth had to be told to Mary. On it, he knew, rested her future—and his.

"I have £450, Mary," he replied quietly to her comment, without looking at her; his eyes rested on the garage which stood in front of him, with his hopes.

His words startled Mary into an ejaculation. "Good Heavens!" she said. "Where on earth have you managed to get that, Jack?" she asked.

"Well, I've lived pretty plainly in a cheap lodging-house, Mary, and I've saved £150 out of my wages, and a bit of spare time work I put in on my own. It's been a sacrifice, but I've done it—for you."

"And the other £300, Jack. You could not have saved that in the time." A sudden suspicion came into her mind. "You've borrowed it. Don't let us start on borrowed money. I'd rather wait than have the anxiety of knowing that we may at any time have a demand for repayment after we've started out."

"I knew you'd feel like that, Mary." Jack Porter turned and faced the girl. "But chances like this on a busy road and so cheap, do not occur every day. In fact, only once in a lifetime. However, I haven't borrowed the money, at least, not in the way you're thinking. We'll have to pay it back, but there is no time named for when we have to pay it."

Mary looked puzzlement from her grey, steadfast open eyes that looked into those of her lover. "Then how *have* you got it, Jack?" she asked.

"From the jewellery, Mary. The jewellery that Sprogson pushed in my pocket when he ran for it. I was the one whom he thought would be caught with the goods on me. But I was the one who got away. I sold the jewellery in London."

"You kept the jewellery, Jack!"

The grey eyes looked lustreless into those of Jack Porter, and Mary's voice lost its timbre of contentment. It came to him with a cadence of drabness. Mary's world, it seemed to her, had come to an end. The meeting with her lover to which she had looked forward throughout the journey from Devon had lost its joy, now.

"You kept the jewellery, Jack," she said again, and horror looked out of her gaze.

"I had to, Mary. What else could I do?"

"You could have sent it back, Jack. You didn't willingly steal it. You could have posted it back to Yew Tree House."

"It wasn't as easy as that, Mary. I had handled it. It had my finger-prints all over it. The wrappings would have had my prints, too. And don't forget that the police were still looking for the other man—for Jack Edwins. They would have been told by Yew Tree House if the jewels had been returned. They would have got my prints from it. If they ever connected me with Jack Edwins I was done, innocent though I was of wishing to steal. I had to get rid of it."

"But you sold it, Jack. Wasn't that dangerous?"

"Not to me. I was living in a pretty low quarter in the East End, Mary. I soon found where there was a 'fence' who would take it and ask no questions. The police said it was worth a £1,000. All I got was £300, and I only got that much because the jewellery was convenient for getting rid of, and because I stuck out for that much. So I have £450 and there is the £100 you have. That leaves us £50 over to carry on with."

He saw the refusal in his woman's eyes. "It's our chance, Mary—the chance to make a living together," he pleaded.

"No! Not on stolen money, Jack. I would rather die than that," she said. "We could never be happy on stolen money. I'd—I'd be afraid all my life. I'd never have an easy conscience."

Jack Porter turned his back on the garage. He took Mary by an arm. "Let's walk back into Staines," he said.

Mary walked slowly beside him. Once she half-turned and looked back at the garage receding from her—and from him; and the pain in her heart at the lost hopes was reflected in her demeanour, in the listlessness of her walking, the sad solitude of her silence.

For five minutes they walked without a word. It was Jack who broke into the painful reflections of both of them.

"I was not asking you to live on stolen money, Mary," he said gently. "I was planning to use the money until we were settled and then return it. That was what I meant by saying that I had not borrowed it in the way of which you were thinking."

"Return it, Jack? How?"

Jack glanced sharply at her face. He sought for a sign of relenting; the glance showed him nothing.

"Well, Mary, I've seen the figures of the garage, and I know what I can do with it. I can double the earnings in a few months, because I know my job and the chap who's there now doesn't. I work it out that we would be able to put by five pounds a week, every week, as a first charge on our takings. Bank it in a separate account. That is £260 a year. In just over four years at the outside it will reach £1,000, which is the value the police place on the jewellery. Then we can send the money to Yew Tree House, and I am quits. And we will have a good business, a home—and each other. That was the plan I had thought of. Nobody loses anything; and we gain everything."

They had reached Staines and their hotel before Mary replied to the suggestion. "Let me sleep on it tonight, Jack, and I will tell you tomorrow morning what I decide," she said.

Jack nodded. "All right, Mary," he agreed. "But—"

"Yes, darling?"

"If it means a shadow, or something between us, I'd rather wipe the whole thing out. I couldn't stand that."

Mary eyed him gravely and levelly. "If I say yes, Jack," she said, "there will be no shadow between us. I shall be a partner in it, won't I?" On that they parted, a feeling of restraint between them; a shadow which kept their eyes averted from each other's.

She had her decision ready at the breakfast table next morning. Long hours of argument with herself and her conscience during the silent watches had fought a losing fight with her love. Jack kissed her as she entered the room and waited, anxiously. Mary caught him eyeing her face anxiously. She smiled when she could no longer tease him.

"I am saying yes, Jack," she announced. "But—" she held up a hand—"there is one condition. That is, that the five pounds a week must be put into a separate account and never touched. It must be put in every week, even if it means that we may not have enough for more than one meal a day after it has been subtracted. I don't know whether I am doing right, but—"

She said no more.

Three weeks later the name Jack Porter appeared over the garage on the by-pass. The rooms over the workshop had been furnished, and there Mary kept her housewifely duties while her man repaired cars as they came in, sold petrol, and in between times cleared up and painted the garage in cheerful tones of green and cream. The name 'The Green Service Station' proclaimed itself to passing motorists.

The bargain with justice was religiously kept. Every Monday morning five pounds was paid into the 'A' account of Jack Porter. In the later months when trade had a summer fillip more than the five pounds stipulated sum was invested; in a little under three years the owners of Yew Tree House, Paignton, opened a registered packet and found to their astonishment a thousand one-pound notes, and on top of them a typed letter on plain paper which read:

"Restoration by the second, burglar of three years ago."

It caused complications with the insurance society. But the memory of Paignton was wiped out from the mind of Jack Porter and the mind of Mary.

The three years had seen the Green Service Station expand. There were now two garages and an extensive clientele who came for monthly overhauls of their vehicles under Porter's Service Scheme. Reasonable charges, and work that was never scamped had established for the garage a reputation.

A bank balance was growing even after expenditure on new machinery and on improvements. The work was arduous, for the paying out of the £1,000 which would otherwise have gone into the business was a circumstance which obviously had called for rigid economy. The result had been that Jack Porter worked on repairs from early morning until late at night, when he otherwise could have employed a garage hand, or mechanic. Nor could the labour-saving machinery on the market for shortening the time spent on, say, decarbonizing, be afforded; the decarbing had to be done by hand.

Nevertheless, Jack Porter, seeing his business grow, and the future bright with Mary, sang cheerfully at his work and with the thousand pounds repaid looked with ambitious gaze to a rosy future of prosperity; the Promised Land of his early ambition drew near.

Until that day when, pausing to watch the procession of the Judge in Kingston, he had come face to face with Sprogson—and found that the past can never be buried.

So does Chance play its cynical part in the life of a man and a woman. Thus do the Three Fates around the loom and the web of Life disport themselves in wanton and malignant pleasure.

CHAPTER V

JACK Porter had been four years in his garage on the Staines By-pass when Sprogson made his first appearance in the village of Thames Pagnall.

Of the sentence of three years' penal servitude he had served two years and six months, good conduct having earned him the full remission of two months for each year of sentence. Where and how he had spent his period of ticket-of-leave only the police to whom he had to report, and himself, knew; when he made his way to the Thames-side village, he was free of all regulation to visit the police. He was also free of the name of Sprogson.

His coming was spectacular. As the last of the race crowds left Hurst Park behind them and entrained at the terminus station for London, Sprogson stepped into the Miller's Arms.

"A whisky, landlord—large one, and soda." His voice boomed over the room. The hum of chatter ceased momentarily as the crowded bar turned to look at the intruder. Sprogson eyed back the stares.

The Arms was an historic hostelry with a sedate company of regulars, all resident in the place. It was so far at the back of the village that few strangers found it out. Its clientele had little truck with the race crowds, particularly those members of them who appeared in check suits, a flower garden in the buttonhole, and a loud and hearty good-fellow voice. Sprogson sensed the hostility.

"And a big cigar, landlord, too, and a drink for yourself," he invited.

Mine host hesitated. The customer did not appear of the class for which the Miller's Arms desired to cater. He had, however, no grounds for refusing to serve him—not that grounds are necessary; a publican is not bound to serve anyone entering his house. That he is so compelled is a popular fallacy. He can refuse a man a drink for any or no reason, even for the fact that he does not like the colour of his eyes.

Quietly the landlord ('Ted' to his regulars) poured out the drink, produced the desired cigar, and then poured out a drink for himself. "Good health!" said Sprogson. "And to you," rejoined Ted.

"Had a good day at the races, I take it, sir?" he added, with a desire to appear social.

"Not bad," Sprogson winked. "Won just over fifty quid. Generally do win. But you have to know something to do that."

"Something outside the form book, I take it?" suggested the landlord.

Sprogson grinned, and winked again. "That's so," he admitted. "If you want to make a bit of money, back Philo tomorrow. He hasn't a chance, they say." He winked a third time. "I'm putting a pony on it." He finished his drink. "I'll look in tomorrow, and we'll celebrate. By the way—keep that to yourself. Don't want to spoil the price."

Sprogson made his second appearance in Thames Pagnall and in the Miller's Arms the following night. The fact that the landlord had risked a pound on Philo at Hurst Park and had netted eighteen pounds induced from him a somewhat more cordial greeting to his customer. Ted worked out that if Sprogson had had twenty-five pounds on the horse, he must have won at least £360, even at starting price, and he would probably have got odds, for the betting forecast had given the probable price as twenty to one.

"Did you do it?" asked Sprogson after he had ordered a whisky and soda and another cigar. The landlord nodded. "Thanks, yes. I had a nice little win." He broadcast the news to those of his customers in the immediate vicinity; and Sprogson celebrated his and the landlord's winnings by buying a large round of drinks.

A company inclined to regard with favour a man with such knowledgeable insight into racing as to tip as a certainty a twenty to one outsider, eagerly sought anything good that might be going at Brighton next day. Sprogson shook his head. "I never bet or advise my friends," he said, "except on reliable information from the inside. There's nothing certain at Brighton, but I've good friends in the game and there may be something at Birmingham at the week-end. I'll be there, and if my friends give me the O.K., then I'll wire the landlord here, and he can pass the news on, for you to get on to it."

From that day Sprogson was regarded as an authority on racing. He gave from time to time a number of quiet tips which produced handsome dividends. But not as Sprogson. It was later in the evening of this second visit to the Miller's Arms, during a chat with the landlord, that he revealed the identity by which the village was to know him.

"I'd like to settle in this place," he explained. "I haven't had a place for some time, and this seems very handy for racecourses, with Sandown, Hurst Park; and Kempton Park on the doorstep and Ally Pally only half an hour or so away. I suppose there isn't a furnished place going, is there? Somewhere quiet?"

The landlord thought diligently. "Well, as a matter of fact, Mr.—?" He looked inquiringly.

"Canley is the name, landlord. James Canley."

"Well, Mr. Canley, as it chances, there *is* a small cottage. The owners are friends of mine and have gone abroad for a year or so. They would be prepared to let the place furnished for that time. It's a bit isolated. If that doesn't matter, I think you could do a deal."

Canley chuckled to himself. "If it's isolated, then it's all the more desirable. I like a bit of peace and quietness at night," he said. "Where can I find the agents?"

Canley saw the agents the following day. He guffawed at the request for references. "The best reference I know is six months' rent in advance," he rejoined, and paid it over in notes. He went into occupation of the cottage the following week, with Mrs. Skelton, an honest but formidable female, as his daily help and cook.

Despite his occasional racing tips and the profit from them, Canley was not a popular figure in the village. Nor in the Miller's Arms, which he frequented most nights. He was dogmatic in his views, rude in his arguments, and apt to dominate all conversation, with little regard to the niceties of debate.

Again, he was too familiar with the womenfolk of the regulars. There were a number of disputes over his conduct towards women, and on one occasion at least a bout of fisticuffs, in which he retired for several days with a black eye, and a warning of more to come unless he left a certain lady to herself.

This did not, however, prevent a succession of affairs with a number of young women in the village and the neighbourhood. One of these was concerned with Margaret Harker, a girl of eighteen years.

The affair had been developing side by side with another with a woman of more experience and *sang froid*, and Canley's ingenuity in keeping the pair apart had been the topic of amused, and somewhat anxious, conversation in the Miller's Arms. The affair with Margaret Harker was pretty general talk in the village; the only person, seemingly, who knew nothing of it was William Harker. He learned of it through overhearing a conversation over the partition in the canteen of the concrete company for which he worked.

William Harker was a well-built man of considerable physique, who had been a concrete mixer some fourteen years. He held strong religious opinions, and was a local preacher of some reputation. Curiously enough, this did not affect his pleasure in the cinema or a drink when he felt like it. There were some of the chapel congregations who looked on these practices with a jaundiced eye. William's reply when the point of view was put to him, was to refer to the making of wine at the marriage feast at Cana in Galilee; it was an argument to which the Band of Hope brigade found no answer. William usually celebrated his victory with another pint!

It was over one of these pints that William learned of the acquaintance, and certain facts in connection with it, of his daughter and Canley. He confronted his daughter's accuser and called him by a number of names which would not have passed the elders of the chapel. Then he laid the man low with a heavy blow.

The man, rising, was about to get clear of the place, when he was halted and told, somewhat belatedly, to prove his words. He made answer that, since everyone in the canteen knew it, he wouldn't mind. Harker listened to the tale. He looked round at his mates, and in their avoidance of his eyes, he saw confirmation.

Harker did not go back to the yard; he left the canteen and walked briskly away. A few minutes later he entered the back door of the council house which he occupied. He entered quietly, slipped through the passage from the back door, turned the key in the lock of the front door and put it in his pocket. His wife, coming from the living-room bumped into him as he returned to the kitchen.

"Good heavens, Will, you didn't 'arf give me a start," she protested. "I didn't hear you come in. Early, ain't you?" She looked at the clock. "What's happened? Everything all right at the works?" she added, anxiously.

Harker removed his boots, white with dust from the concrete powder. "Oh, yes. Everything's all right, mate," he replied. He washed his hands at the sink, and glanced at the table. One cup and saucer, he saw, had been used. "Margaret *had* her tea?" he asked.

"Yes, she's upstairs getting washed." Harker asked no further questions, but listened for the sound he expected. Every nerve in his body was strained and hard, and a dull flush crept up his neck as he heard the stealthy step on the stairway, the hurried rush to the front door—a tug at the handle, and the muffled 'damn' as Margaret discovered the door locked, and the key missing.

Mrs. Harker looked up at the word. "What's the matter, Margaret?" she asked.

No answer came from Margaret as she stood, white-faced, in the doorway of the kitchen. She guessed that something had been heard by her father, and since there was no way out of the house now except through the kitchen, she knew that her only chance of leaving the house was by brazening the position out. Her father stood between the sink and the back door, wiping his hands slowly and with elaborate care.

"Well," said Margaret. "I must be going now. Shan't be long."

William Harker looked at her bright pink blouse and checked box coat. His gaze passed to her high-heeled platform shoes and silk stockings. It moved again to the brightly painted lips of his daughter, and his eyes blazed.

"And where are you going, may I ask?" He almost spat the words out.

"Oh, just out," she smiled weakly.

"I said *where*. Now I'll have the truth, Miss."

"I'm going for a walk."

"Liar."

"Will!" gasped his wife. "Please!"

"Liar!" said William again. Margaret braced herself.

"I won't be spoken to like that, by you or nobody else," she said.

"Liar!" said William again.

Mrs. Harker stood up from the table. "Will, that's no way to be talking," she protested. "Whatever's come over you?"

William pointed to the girl. "Ask her where she's going," he said. "Ask her—that dirty little slut of a daughter of yours. Ask her why she's dressed up like a trollop. Ask her what she does when she leaves this house."

There was silence, and William returned to the attack. "You don't ask her because you don't want to know. Because you're afraid to know. Well, I'm not. I *do* know. So does everybody else round here. Every tattling woman for a mile round talks about her, and the foul-est-mouthed men in the place have a name for her. It's time you opened your eyes, mate, to what sort of girl your daughter is. Now ask her." He pushed his wife towards Margaret. The girl saw her chance.

"I'm not going to stop here to be insulted by you, Dad," she said. "I'm no longer a child, I'm eighteen and it's time you realized it. I'm going out." She flung herself towards the door. Harker grabbed her by the shoulders, shook her, and as he released her, suddenly, she over-balanced and fell, catching a cheek on a corner of the table. Mrs. Harker ran towards her. "Will! Will, have you gone mad?" she called.

"If I have," burst out Harker, "it's she that has driven me mad. Even now she wants to brazen out like the jezebel that she is. She won't tell you where she goes. Well, I will. She's going with a man I wouldn't trust my dog with, in his house, too." He looked at the girl now whimpering in a corner of the room. "You're no longer a child, eh? You're eighteen. Well, do you know the difference between right and wrong, 'cause if you don't somebody's going to teach you." He made a step towards the girl.

"Don't you hit her, Will. If she's done anything wrong, we'll put it right."

"Nothing can put it right," said Harker. "But I won't hit her. Now listen to me, my girl. I swear before God that if I get my hands on the rat who's dragging you down, I'll kill him like I'd kill any other rat. Even if I swing for it."

Margaret, looking at him, shrank back and ran upstairs, slamming her bedroom door behind her. Harker watched her go, trembling with the passion into which he had thrown himself. His wife sat at the table crying quietly into her hands, and wondering how the quiet God-fearing man who was her husband could be changed into the demon that he had shown himself during the last few minutes.

A few minutes passed, only the dripping of a tap and the weeping woman were the sounds heard. Then, putting a hand across his moist brow, Harker sat at the table and tears rolled down his heavy, red cheeks—tears of sorrow and humiliation. All his world had tumbled about him. He who had urged men to mend their ways, had shown them the error of their old ways, he now had a daughter at whom those same men pointed a finger of scorn. He, who had taught see no evil and think no evil was now steeped in the Slough of Despond, with murder in his heart. A great happiness died in those moments and despair was born.

He rose to his feet, placed a hand on his wife's shoulders and walked out of the house.

Many minutes passed before Mrs. Harker crossed to the staircase, and listened for any sound from her girl's room. As she was considering what she could say to Margaret, the latch of the kitchen door clicked. She turned expecting to see her husband; instead the form was that of Harry Johns, a friend of them both. He smiled.

"Will in?" he asked.

"No, Harry. He's just gone out."

"Oh, well, I'll call again. Maybe I'll catch him at the allotment."

"Harry?" Mrs. Harker choked slightly. "You've been our friend for nigh thirty years. You know Will better than any other man knows him. What's happened to Will?"

"Oh, nothing, Elsie. He was upset at the works this afternoon, that's all."

"Harry, don't hide anything. It's about Margaret, I know. How shall I know what to do if nobody tells me anything."

"Yes, Elsie." Johns was a little diffident. "There was something about Margaret that Will overheard. They said that there he was putting on airs, and being a chapel-goer and a preacher and his daughter going into men's cottages at night. He heard the man's name and threatened to kill him. Enough to make a man want to do it, of course. I came along to see him as soon as I could, because Will's a good man. Where is he now?"

"I'm frightened, Harry. Frightened," cried Mrs. Harker. "He went out just now—"

"All right, Elsie. Don't you worry. I'll go and look for him. He can't be far away. If we don't come back for some time, don't be thinking things. I'll calm him down." He patted the back of the woman's hand resting on his coat, and left the house.

It was the following morning that Canley was found dead on the railway.

CHAPTER VI

JACK Porter opened the letter from Canley in the seclusion of the office of his garage. He read through the words until he knew them by heart.

> *"Bring me a hundred pounds to the cottage on Friday night. And don't fail me. You know what to expect if you do."*

It was at that moment he decided to kill James Canley.

It was not altogether a new idea; he had considered it before on several occasions, in fact each time that he had received from Canley requests for a loan, which he knew would never be repaid. On such occasions he had toyed with the idea of ridding himself, and the world, of the man; but the self-suggestion was more in the nature of a mental protest at the demands than as a serious suggestion possible of achievement. It seemed to afford him some degree of satisfaction to think of the secret enmity towards Canley, the strength of which Canley did not recognize.

Porter had borne in mind the words of Canley at their first meeting after the market-place encounter. The man had said that he had done three years' penal servitude, and had looked to his £500 share of the jewellery to start him in life when he came out. He realized a certain amount of justice, if somewhat perverted justice, in the expectation. The fact that the share would have been only £150, half the amount realized from the 'fence' for the jewellery, seemed not to occur to Canley.

But that he was entitled to have half the value placed on them, Porter conceded. Thus, while he protested to Canley at each of the demands, saying that he had already paid back the value to the owners of the jewels, he acknowledged the debt, up to the £500 asked for by his blackmailer.

With the last of the amount paid over a week or two before, Porter breathed a sigh of relief. He was now clear of the mythical debt which Canley had claimed. That was what the man had asked for, and now he had received it. The debt was passed and done with.

And only just in time. There had been for Porter increasing difficulty in hiding from Mary the fact that money was going out from the garage account in considerable sums for which no corresponding advantage in the business could be seen.

Mary had been from the first his adviser on developments and extensions of the garage business. It was she who had worked out the possibilities of new ventures, and the cost plus the time needed to get back the money. She had decided that a hoist to ease the task of greasing, and to enable greasing by pressure to be carried out, would be an advantage to the garage. In addition it would greatly reduce the labour on certain types of underneath repairs. She had recommended, and the recommendation had been adopted, the putting aside of a small sum each week towards the cost of the hoist, together with the cost of installation. This was the money, the only money, with which Porter had been able to satisfy the demands of Canley.

Mary, who knew to a shilling what should be in the account, had been urging that the hoist should now be obtained. At his wit's end to find a way out of the impasse, Jack had invented an excuse that hoists were not available at the moment, but that the makers would let him have the first one that they could release after the completion of earlier orders.

Unfortunately, a few days before the arrival of Canley's letter, Mary had read an advertisement of hoists for immediate delivery, and had suggested that now was the time to acquire the one wanted.

By scraping together every penny he could get his hands upon, Jack had acquired a little over £100, which would be sufficient for him to take delivery, whatever else was owing to be paid off at a later date.

The demand for £100 from Canley put paid to that idea. The thought of murder that he had toyed with as a mental escape from Canley, now became essential. He decided to kill Canley as a way out of his continual blackmail—and to save the £100 which was the only chance of keeping from Mary the story of the presence of Canley to trouble them for the rest of his life.

The decision made, he found that his earlier mental planning had given him a good background for the perpetration in reality. It had been his habit during his visits to the cottage with money, to note the lay of the land, and subsequently to spend many pleasant hours in working out on paper how simple it could be to get away with Canley's murder.

It sort of cheered up Porter between the spells of paying out to think that he was plotting to end it all. Building castles in the air, so to speak. Now that he had decided that the castle should have a more permanent anchorage—on the ground—he proceeded to examine the position more closely, and to co-relate all the knowledge of the man which he had gained by introspective thinking. The more he looked into the idea the more sure he became that the murder of Canley could be done easily and safely.

The fact that Canley lived in the small and secluded cottage on the outskirts of the village, and that he lived alone was an advantage. Porter took the view that the absence of a woman or a man in the cottage was less meanness than, probably, necessity. There had been a number of burglaries in the district, in which he, Porter, thought he recognized the hand of Canley, or rather of Sprogson. With his cottage lonely and empty at night, there was nobody to say what time he came in at night, or if he left again after he had once returned, or even whether he had been out at all.

Porter's visits to the cottage and seeming willingness to make the 'loans' to Canley had led to a feeling of friendliness between them, or so it had seemed to Canley. In consequence, Porter had learned much of the mode of living of his intended victim. He knew, for instance, that the day woman left in the ordinary way about 7.30 p.m. after she had prepared the evening meal for her employer, and that she did not appear again at the cottage until the following morning when she came to make breakfast.

Still another advantage was that the cottage was one of the only two in the lane, and was, in fact, some distance away from the other. In between were high hedges which shielded any vision of one from the other. The lane itself was not so much a thoroughfare as a track between fields. It seemed to have been started by people walking along the grass. When this became a habit, someone apparently dumped rubble in the centre so that there was a definite track, rough and unmetalled. Grass grew on either side of the track. It was one of those country lanes that hikers like to find, because it is lovely and rural!

Some 200 yards below Canley's house the path passed under a bridge which carried the railway line to Thames Pagnall station, and thence on to the terminus. It was this fact that had interested Porter during his journeyings to Canley's cottage and in his metaphorical murder planning, for he saw possibilities in the railway. He was not such a fool as to think that he could *obviously* murder Canley and get away with it. He had too much fear of the law. If Canley had to die, then it would have to appear to be accidental death. It was in that connection that Porter saw possibilities in the railway line.

One of the reasons for the path which passed Canley's cottage was that it was a short cut from the outskirts of the village on the west side to the station, and also for the neighbouring village which joined Thames Pagnall. Also, it was a short cut from that part of the village to the main street and the popular 'local'.

It happened this way: immediately past the railway arch and on the left of it a narrow path led from the lane up to the railway lines. It was not a prepared path, but a kind of trodden path made through the grass of the embankment by people who had used it for a short cut; they had, as it were, established a kind of right of way, if you understand what is meant by that. If one wanted to get to the station one walked up this path until the gravelled bank was struck, which led along the side of the metals to the platform some hundred yards away.

If a person were making a short cut to the village, then at the top of the path he stepped over the two sets of train lines, walked a few yards in the direction of the station, and then descended a similar path on the other side of the railway embankment, which was, of course, on the other side of the bridge. This performance put the pedestrian within five minutes' walk of the shopping centre of the village and of the shops and 'local', whereas if the road was followed round it meant a walk of over a quarter of an hour.

The spot was pretty lonely on a winter's night. The people of Thames Pagnall did not go in for a great deal of night life; a concert by the children of the school sometimes, a whist drive in the church hall, the annual performance of the Choral Society was about the extent of the night haunts, except for the once a year dinner of the cricket club.

Again, only one or two of the villagers ever used the path after dusk, and they were mostly home-goers taking the short cut from the station. Nobody tried the short cut to the village after dark; it meant stepping over two live rails in darkness, for the line was pretty well shadowed by trees which grew along the bottom of the embankment on which the railway was laid.

When he had decided that his only safeguard was to remove Canley, Jack Porter turned over these facts in his head; they were pretty familiar to him already, for he had noted them on his comings and goings from the cottage on the occasions which in the past few months he had visited Canley. With an idea of linking the railway with the murder he set himself to testing an idea that came into his mind.

Making an excuse to Mary that he had to visit a customer who was occupied in his London office during the daytime hours, he took a bus to Thames Pagnall. At the stop at the back of the village, he left the bus and proceeded on foot to the lane. Noting the surroundings in the darkness as best he could, he walked past Canley's cottage, which was in darkness. Thence he proceeded along the lane, climbed the path to the railway lines, stepped over both the live rails and stood at the top of the path on the other side. He did not descend, however, but walked along the side of the metals to the up-line platform of the station. There he spent some time in the waiting-room studying the timetable which was displayed on a large board.

This showed that the last train down to the terminus passed through the station at 11.35 p.m. It stayed at the terminus until the following morning. There was no train up until 6.30 a.m., so that there would be six hours in which to make an alibi, and render himself perfectly safe, because if his plans went right, Canley's body would not be found until the first morning train.

Two nights later, Porter, his plans worked out, made the journey again, timing its progress with his watch, and checking off the programme which he was proposing to carry out. Again he passed no person in the lane, or on the path over the railway. The only light to be seen on this second night was in the cottage of Canley.

Creeping quietly to the window, he peered through a crack in the curtains. Canley, he saw, was in the living-room with a woman—a large red-haired woman with whom the man had been consorting at race meetings. Porter had seen them together on various occasions; he had ruminated that there on the woman's back was going the money he had earned so hardly, and of which he was being bled by Canley.

He made a change in his walk on this second night. Instead of making for the station and leaving by the runway down to the road and a bus stop, as on the previous occasion, he turned in the opposite direction after crossing the live rails, and, still on the permanent way, walked in the direction of the junction station a mile or so along.

The time was shortly after 11.30 p.m. and within a minute or two the noise of an approaching train and the singing of the metals told him that the last train down to the terminus was approaching. A glance at his luminous-dialled watch told him that it was on time.

As it turned the bend and accelerated on the run to the station, Porter lay down flat on his stomach at the edge of the embankment. If he put into operation the plan he had in mind, it would have been dangerous for the driver of the train to remember having on any night seen a man walking along the permanent way. Such a recollection might well, he argued, arouse suspicion, and examination of the line could lead to the discovery of footprints—a source of identification that might lead to his undoing.

The train passed on, and Porter, secure in the knowledge that it would be impossible for the driver to have seen him, rose to his feet and continued his walk along the permanent way for half a mile or so, until he reached another bridge which, in this case, crossed over a main road. There he clambered down the embankment and climbed over a fence on to the road. The junction was a matter of half a mile or so, away. Ten minutes later he walked on to the junction railway platform and took a train back to Staines. There were no more than a dozen people in the train, and he occupied a compartment to himself.

It was a long way round to reach home again, and the journey from Thames Pagnall could have been shortened by taking a bus from the village. Porter had considered this as a possible means of transport back to Staines, but had discarded it as being not so safe as the train journey. If his safety was to be assured, then it was vital that there was no possibility of his being recognized as having been in the vicinity on the night of the murder—for he had now decided on the murder and the means of it. He figured that to make the return journey by bus would mean that the conductor would have about half an hour to take a good look at him, and be able to recognize him as a passenger from Thames Pagnall if he were required to do so. Not that Porter thought there was any danger of that, since the death of Canley was to have the appearance of pure accident; but it was best to leave no loophole to chance.

At each stage of the journey, Porter took note of the times in order that there should be no snag when it was put into serious operation. The journey on this second night was, in fact, corresponding to the dress rehearsal of a play on the stage, in which the final form and timing of the presentation are settled once and for all.

But with one difference: whereas the stage presentation has its dress rehearsal only when the play is actually in being and settled, the rehearsal of Jack Porter was in the nature of a test of whether, indeed, the performance should be given at all; whether his suggested plans should be proceeded with or whether they should be abandoned and the money paid out to Canley.

More than the blackmail was at stake; if anything went wrong, then Porter knew his life would probably be forfeit.

For the next two days he studied carefully the stages of the journey he had made and the stages which at the moment existed only in his imagination, and which had to be translated into deeds. Between the times of his entering and leaving Canley's cottage there had to be done things on which his neck depended; he sat down carefully and cautiously to plan them and decide whether they could be accomplished.

Gradually The Plan was born in his mind. He turned it over step by step, remodelling and altering proposals here and there until, at last, he chuckled to himself that he had a cast-iron plot of murder that nothing could detect as being other than an accident.

He planned to put it into execution on the following Friday night—the night on which the note from Canley ordered him to take the hundred pounds, the first sum over the £500 at which he had placed his responsibility to Sprogson and the proceeds of his unwilling burglary.

CHAPTER VII

FRIDAY passed through its hours very little differently from any other day for Jack Porter. He handled a number of repair orders on half a dozen cars, interspersed with the filling of petrol tanks and the supply of the various odds and ends associated with a garage and service station. Dinner was taken with Mary as usual and so was tea. At nine o'clock he closed the garage for the night—his customary hour.

He had intimated to Mary that he would be attending to a business job after the closing of the garage and would probably not return until somewhere about midnight; the consequence was that she had prepared a meal for nine o'clock instead of the usual snack which they took just before retiring to bed. At nine-thirty o'clock Jack kissed her *adieu* and set out on his errand.

He found himself remarkably unconcerned and well at ease. The fact astonished him. He had thought that he would inevitably be under some nervous strain at the thought of the murder for which he was setting out, that he would feel some anxiety at the perpetration of the deed. Instead, he had within him a feeling of peacefulness and satisfaction at the knowledge that within a very few hours his life would be free from the menace of Canley. Any thought of failure, or of discovery, was missing from his mentality; his plan, he was quite sure, was beyond fault, and outside the bounds of failure.

The first part was put into operation immediately he had waved a farewell to Mary from the roadway. He drove his garage car in the opposite direction to Thames Pagnall. Two hundred yards down the road he turned into the yard of the Bricklayers' Arms. In the bar were several men he knew by sight, and who knew him and his garage. For one of these he purchased a drink, at the same time ordering a brandy for himself.

Over the drinks he led the conversation round to business, bemoaning the fact that he had to go at this time of night, after a hard day's work, to a car job near Guildford some twenty miles away. That, he thought, would ensure that in the event of any inquiries—which was not at all likely so far as he could see—would give him an alibi in the opposite direction to Canley.

With the commiserations of his acquaintances in his ears he left the 'Arms' and drove away in the direction of Guildford. Within a few minutes, however, he turned into a side road and doubled back on his tracks. Parking his car in a market car park where it would attract no attention, since cars were often left there until the small hours, he walked to Staines station and took a train to the junction. From there he put into operation the time-table of his two nights' rehearsal, *but in reverse*. That is to say, he walked along the main road until he reached the bridge down the side of which he had climbed to regain the road on the rehearsal night on leaving the permanent way. He climbed the bank and reached the track. From there, keeping to the edge of the ballast, he walked in the direction of Thames Pagnall station.

Once, as on the night of his test, he lay down by the side of the embankment as a train came along, lest he should be seen by the driver or the guard. The train passed, and, rising, he continued his walk. Within twenty minutes he had reached the path across the short cut leading to the lane in which stood the cottage of Canley. There he crossed the two lines of metals and descended into the lane. But not by the path. It was part of his plan that no footsteps should be found there, at least not any that could be identified to him; he descended carefully down the grass of the embankment a few yards further along.

Once in the lane he walked in the direction of the cottage, keeping in the long grass verge that edged the track. Such marks as he made would be obliterated, for the grass would recover during the night and spring upright again by the morning, thus hiding any evidence of traversing. The verge ran up to the gate of the cottage, and there Porter put into operation the second part of The Plan. From the gate to the door of the cottage there ran a flagged path, made of concrete slabs such as those used for pavements for the ordinary footwalks of a city street. Porter had noted them on his many visits to Canley, and recognized that they represented the danger that on a night such as this traces of visitors to the cottage might be left on their tell-tale surface.

That was the first thing that Porter had prepared against.

Before he left the grass verge of the lane he took off his boots, and in his stockinged feet crept quietly up the path to the door of the cottage. One of the points of his plan was that there should be no bootmarks left on the path; at least no bootmarks other than those of Canley himself.

Arrived at the door, he peered through a crick in the curtains at the corner of the window. It was essential to ascertain that Canley was alone. If the woman whom he had seen before with Canley was present, then the plot would have to be put off to another night. The inspection, however, showed Canley sitting in an armchair and nobody with him. Satisfied, Porter put on and laced his shoes and the operation completed, he knocked at the cottage door.

It opened within a few seconds. Canley stood outlined in the aperture.

"Who's there?" he asked. He peered into the darkness and recognized his visitor. "Ah! Come in, Jack," he invited.

Anyone seeing or hearing the greeting would have imagined from the bluff heartiness of it that the two were bosom friends.

Porter made no response, but entered the cottage, closing the door behind him. Canley led the way to the sitting-room, and pulled forward a chair for his guest, placing it opposite that in which he had been sitting.

Porter looked round the room. There was not, so far as he could see any trace of another occupant or visitor. Nevertheless, it was vital that he should be sure that he and his intended victim were really alone in the cottage. The woman might be upstairs, waiting for the expected visitor to come and go again before she made her reappearance. Such a circumstance, Porter realized, would spell disaster to his plans. He decided on a ruse that would allow him unsuspectingly to search the house. He held up his overcoat to his host.

"I think I'd like a wash and brash-up, Canley," he explained. "I've been working late, and haven't had time to change. And I'll hang this coat in the hall while I'm about it."

"All right, Jack," Canley agreed without any enthusiasm or otherwise. Porter nodded and went into the kitchen, where he made a pretence of washing. He mounted the stairs to Canley's bedroom, whistling the while as he used a hairbrush and comb. This operation over, he moved stealthily to the doors of the other two rooms. They were empty. It was plain, however, that the woman *had* been in the cottage, for there were a number of articles of feminine wear lying scattered about. Porter concluded that Canley had got rid of her on some excuse to leave him free to wait his (Porter's) arrival.

Canley was sitting in his chair when Porter re-entered the sitting-room. He greeted his guest jovially.

"Thought you'd gone to bed, Jack." He chuckled at his joke. "I reckon that after your journey on a night like this you can do with a spot of something, eh? It's a damned nasty night, I guess, though I haven't had to go out in it."

He fetched a bottle of whisky from the sideboard and placed it on the table with a couple of glasses and a carafe of water. Then he poured out two fingers of the whisky. He raised his glass. "Good health," he said.

Porter stifled a chuckle. He reflected that his host little knew how his health would soon not matter to him at all, or how soon it would be before he need not trouble about his health. "And to you," was all he said, and downed the drink in a gulp.

He wanted that whisky. Now that the time was approaching for the deed on which he had decided, Porter felt a sinking feeling within him. There was but a short time to go before what would be for him the crossing of the Rubicon, an act from which there could be no recall. He began to wonder whether he had really covered every point of danger. It is much easier to kill a man when you are, say, eight miles from him, than it is when he is sitting at your elbow.

Porter welcomed that drink in order to keep his nerve going and quieten the fears that now began to crowd in on him. As a matter of fact, he had come prepared with a flask in his hip-pocket for just such a drugging; but it pleased him to let Canley give the drink that was to fortify his murderer.

"I think I'll have another whisky, Canley," he said. He pulled a couple of cigars from a pocket, and handed one over. "Have a cigar?"

Canley took it, and bit off the end. Porter struck a match, and the two smokes were lighted from it. The match-end Porter placed in the ashtray on the table. One of those cigars was a 'prop' in the plan to end Canley's existence. So was the match-end. Porter reflected that his plan so far had gone according to time-table.

A few minutes passed in blowing the smoke from the cigars before Canley introduced the reason for the visit. "How's business, Jack?" he asked.

Porter laughed silently. He realized the kind of business to which Canley was referring; he played with his desire with a pretence that the query was concerned with just everyday business.

"Oh, it isn't too bad," he replied. "I've a good bit of work in hand and things are looking up. I think they'll be even better next week." He chuckled as he spoke. Canley looked up. It was a pity, thought Porter, that he could not share in the joke. He did, however, show some interest in the observation; doubtless he saw a vista of more money from the business finding its way into his pockets.

"I wish they were looking up for me, Jack," he answered, and shook his head sadly. "I don't want to be sponging on you for money. You've been very good to me. But I've got this house to carry on and I can't get money. Went for a job again today. They asked for references. I ask you, can I give a reference? a gaol-bird?" He shook his head mournfully.

"Damned hypocrite," said Porter under his breath. In Canley's bedroom he had seen a race-card for that day at Sandown, which was a course only twenty minutes' walk from the cottage. That, Porter soliloquized was the job Canley had been after.

Canley was now exhibiting signs of impatience. Porter was talking rapidly and easily about the weather, racing, the government and any topic that came into his head; his host answered in monosyllables, and fidgeted in his chair. At last he broke into the small talk with a peremptory demand.

"Have you brought the money?" he asked.

"No, I haven't," Porter replied.

Canley stared, in surprise.

"Oh! And why not?" he demanded.

Porter blew a whiff of his cigar smoke towards him. The time for the deed was now coming close. His heart was beating a little more quickly, but he showed no outward concern. Indeed, he managed to bring up a little smile of unconcern as he answered the question.

"Because I'm not paying any more blackmail," he said. "That's why." He worked himself into a simulated temper. "I can't afford it for one thing, and for another I'm not going to, even if I could afford it. You've had all I can spare, and now I've finished. That's why I came here to tell you." He banged his hand down on the table in emphasis.

Had Canley had the sense to see the red light, and to realize that his money-making was ended, he would have been alive next day. But he hadn't the intelligence to know that he must stop blackmail some time.

He jumped out of his chair. He cursed and shouted. "I've done three years for you," he said, "and now you're doing well out of a good business, and won't help me." He swore again, and came towards Porter menacingly. Porter took up a boxing stance, and he backed away, but went on cursing. Porter kept silent and waited.

That seemed to quieten Canley. He seemed to realize that violence was not going to pay him. He stopped and sat down in his chair again. Then he began speaking, all quietly and nastily.

"So," he said. "You won't play any more, eh? All right. The police will have a letter tomorrow. It will tell them that Jack Porter, who has a flourishing little garage business on the Staines By-pass is Jack Edwins, wanted for burglary and assault on the police at Paignton."

He waited. Porter made no reply but sat calmly—at least to outside appearance—smoking his cigar.

"You'll get a taste of what I had—clink. See. We were partners once, and—"

He paused. Porter, watching, saw that he had suddenly thought of something.

"Well, fancy me never thinking of that before." Canley grinned. "Staring me in the face, too. Partners. We were partners once before and we can be partners again. A partnership in that little garage of yours is just the very thing. I could keep an eye on things, and then I wouldn't be taking your money, would I? I'd be earning my own money. Damn it, it's the very thing. What do you say to that, Jack?" He leered.

Porter saw red. If he had had any scruples about killing Canley, they vanished at that moment at that foul scheme. Canley in *his* garage, the place he had built up with the sweat of his brow, and with toil, for the woman he loved and who even now was waiting for him. The man in front of him read his thoughts.

"Call it a deal, Jack. Or will you pay the hundred pounds?" he asked.

The alternative finally made up Porter's mind.

"All right," he said, "you win. I've brought the money. I just wanted to see how far in vileness you'd go. Now I know. I'll know what to do in future."

"Never mind the future," retorted Canley. "Hand over the money."

"It's in my overcoat pocket," said Porter, and got up to go into the kitchen. He had the money on him, but the weapon which was to end Canley's life was in the overcoat. Porter had chosen a big flat garage jack-spanner, a heavy and formidable weapon. In the hall he took it from his overcoat and slipped it into his right-hand trouser pocket, lifting the flap of the waistcoat over the top of it to keep it in position. Then, taking out the packet of notes he went back into the sitting-room with them in his hands.

"There you are," he said. "You'd better count them to see none is missing. I'll stand by the side of you while you do it—just to see you don't make any mistakes."

Canley snatched the wad, and zipped the notes through his fingers, as one does a pack of cards. Then he began to count.

Porter stood there, talking in as natural a voice as he could muster. As Canley came near the end of the notes, Porter took out the spanner. He need not have troubled to talk; Canley's only concern was the counting of the money. At last the counting was finished. Canley bent his head slightly sideways to see into his inside pocket, as he tucked the hundred pounds away.

That was Porter's opportunity. At that moment he struck.

If his plans were to go off without a hitch, it was necessary that there should be no sign of attack on Canley's body. That would be fatal. Provided the blow was struck at the exact spot Porter had worked out, nothing would be visible of the blow when the body was finally disposed of.

That spot was where the neck joined the spine. And it was there that Porter's spanner fell, with all his strength behind it.

Canley sagged in his chair, lurched forwards, and then fell out of it, face downwards on the carpet. He had not spoken a word, or made a sound. Porter hit him twice again on the same spot.

Then he turned him over. The heart was not beating.

Canley was dead.

CHAPTER VIII

JACK Porter stood staring down at the figure of Canley. In his hand he still held the jack-spanner with which he had ended the man's life. He looked at it, in his right hand, and from it to the body and back again. The fire shot out bursts of flame, throwing the two men in relief against the background of the room, lighting the macabre scene with shafts of yellow, which died as the flames went down, only to be revived once more when the new gas jets in the coals again roared the flames into being.

Canley lay on his back, flat, except that one leg was resting over the other; it had been dragged into that position when Porter had pulled him over. The eyes of the man stared glazingly up to those of his watching murderer. His face was unchanged from that which had greeted Porter in life; the sneering leer with which he had taunted Porter into producing the £100 was fixed as though it had been carved there by a sculptor. Death had come upon him with a suddenness and unexpectedness that left no opportunity to reveal itself. Nor had the ruddiness of colour yet faded from the face; the pallor of death had still to come. Indeed, so disturbingly natural an appearance did the body present that Porter, looking down on it, wondered whether his persecutor could really yet be spoken of in the past tense.

He bent down and felt again the heart. There seemed to be no beating. Still unsatisfied he let his gaze wander round the room, searching for something. Crossing the floor he lifted down from a wall an oblong mirror measuring some two feet by eighteen inches. Polishing it with his handkerchief Porter held it, cumberously, close to the mouth of Canley, letting it remain there for a quarter of a minute. He looked anxiously at the surface; it showed no sign of vaporization. With a sigh of relief he replaced the mirror on the wall; there remained no doubt in his mind that Canley was dead, and that he, Porter, was free.

Free—but for the moment only; only the first stage in his freedom had so far been reached. Up to now the murder of Canley had gone according to plan; there remained the second and final stage. To make him completely safe Canley must appear to have died from an accident. That was what Porter had planned with such care. On his subsequent movements, he realized, rested safety and final and absolute security.

During his deliberations on the means of ridding himself of Canley he had debated whether the best plan was to steal away from the cottage as quietly and unnoticed as he had arrived. Was that, he had asked himself, the best course. He could very easily obliterate all traces of his personal presence, and thus leave the cottage without fear of discovery. He had never been seen in the presence of Canley, except on that one occasion in the market-place of Kingston, and never at all in Thames Pagnall. He had not visited the cottage in daylight; on such occasions as he had come down with the blackmail money it had been always under cover of darkness.

Only once had he passed a living person in the lane leading to Canley's cottage, and that person had been too drunk to recognize him, or even probably to remember that he had seen anyone there. So there could be no connection between the dead man and himself. Porter had considered these points before elaborating his plan. The result of his split-mind discussions was that such a course of action constituted a position which might well become dangerous.

Canley would be found dead by the charwoman when she arrived next morning. That meant, inevitably, that a doctor would be called in: a consequence as fatal as the blow which had stretched Canley in the position in which he now lay. The doctor would diagnose immediately that death was not due to natural causes. His examination would lead to the discovery of the injury to the top of the spine. It would be equally obvious that such an injury could be due only to a blow. A blow on that part of the body was impossible by self-infliction; some extraneous cause was the only possible explanation. Accidentally received? There was nothing in the room that could by any stretch of imagination have caused an accident of that description.

The result of the doctor's report would be that the police must instigate inquiries. Therein lay the danger as Porter had seen it. He had accordingly dismissed the plan to leave the dead man in the cottage and vanish as silently as he had come. Canley, he had decided, must die from an accident. The decision made, Porter had set himself down to plan such an accident. Stage by stage he had plotted, revised and remodelled his ideas until, finally, there had emerged a plan that was fool-proof, and perfect.

The time had now arrived to put that plan into operation. To ensure success it was necessary to work to a time-table. Porter's planning in this direction had called for the death of Canley at 10.30 p.m., allowing for a few minutes either way. In point of fact, the fatal blow had been struck almost to the minute. Porter glanced at the clock; there now remained exactly three quarters of an hour for him satisfactorily to dispose of the body.

The body itself was his first concern. On certain conditions in it rested success or failure of his plan. For that reason Porter had devoted a great deal of attention to the conduct of bodies—the biological conduct, that is. An omnivorous reader of detective stories—it was, as a matter of fact, his mental digestion of thrillers that had first led him to think of murdering Canley—he modelled his plan on the mistakes made by lawbreakers in the novels he had read. One of the first clues in a murder case, he knew, was concerned with the time of death. Alibis had (in fiction as well as in real life) been ruined on numerous occasions by proof of the time of death.

A human body, Porter had learned, cooled off at a certain rate. He had gone into a reference library and looked the matter up in a medical book. The outside of the body cooled first, and the rate of cooling depended on the temperature surrounding it. The longer the outside could be kept warm, the longer would be the cooling of the interior be delayed.

To ensure the success of his plan of Canley's 'accidental' death, it was essential that the man's blood should be uncongealed and still able to run freely at 11.35 p.m. In other words, a doctor must be able to certify that death had taken place round about that hour. It was now about a quarter to eleven o'clock, which meant that the time of death had not only to be disguised for an hour from the actual time, but the blood in the body had by some means to be prevented from cooling to any extent. Porter had directed his plotting energies to this end, and he was convinced that he had learned sufficient to be able to accomplish the task with success.

A bright fire was still burning in the grate in the room. On it he heaped the remaining coals in the scuttle standing by the hearthside. This completed, he dragged the body of Canley towards the fireplace until it was stretched out on its back in the full blaze of the roaring fire. Lest there should be any cooling effect of a draught from under the doors Porter rolled up a rug and wedged it under the full length of the side of the body farthest from the fire. Inspecting the completed operation, he nodded his satisfaction, and turned his efforts to the next stage of the 'accident'—the table.

On it were standing drinking tumblers, a bottle half-full of whisky, a carafe of water and an ashtray. The latter contained a certain amount of ash from the cigars which he and Canley had smoked, or rather, partly smoked, during their talking. The unsmoked half of Canley's cigar lay on the floor where it had been shot from his mouth when he had been struck the fatal blow. Porter picked it up and dropped it into the heart of the coals now blazing furiously up the chimney, and stirred it into total destruction with the poker. One of the cigar stumps was planned to play a leading part in the story of the 'accident' to Canley— the simple story of a single smoker in that room who had left it to meet death. Two cigars would tell a story of *two* men, which would be fatally destructive to the plan.

With Canley's cigar now destroyed Porter looked round for that which he himself had been smoking. It was not in the ashtray, nor was it on the table. His eyes searched the floor where it might conceivably have fallen when he struck Canley. There was no sign of it.

Porter panicked. For three long minutes which seemed to him almost an eternity he searched in every place in which he could conceivably have stood since he lit the cigar. At the end he was without any clue to its whereabouts.

Beads of perspiration stood out on his brow, and he was trembling violently. Fantastically, the thought passed through his anxious mind that he should thus be so greatly disturbed by the loss of a cigar whereas he had felt no emotion whatever when he had first looked down at the body of the man he had murdered. He unconsciously analysed the reason. In the missing roll of tobacco he saw a menace to his plan which had up to now, he thought, worked with the preciseness of a clock movement. If this simple part of his plotting had gone wrong, then other points, not so simple, might also go astray. His safety would be imperilled.

Porter steeled his nerves, and stood striving for calmness in which to recall all his actions up to the moment when he had struck Canley down; thinking introspectively, he realized, might lead him to the missing cigar.

It was at this moment that searching round the room he caught sight of the reflection of himself in the mirror on the wall with which he had tested the breathing of Canley. He was shocked into utter and complete surprise. Then a laugh, which was almost a sob of relief, came from his throat.

The cigar was in his mouth!

With a hand trembling in nervous exhaustion he took it thankfully from his lips and placed it carefully on the mantelpiece.

Porter sat down heavily in a chair and passed a hand over his wet brow. The incident had left him still trembling like a leaf. So stupid an action on his part, as the cigar showed him to be capable of, made him fear for the safeguards he had planned. The cigar was a safeguard that had very nearly gone wrong. Was there another safeguard in danger? Despite the fact that minutes were passing and that he had a time-table to work to if his method of disposing of Canley was to be carried out, Porter sat down and reviewed, as far as his brain would allow, all that he had so far done.

Forcing himself to take things quietly and unhurriedly he went over the points of his plan—they were imprinted on his memory—and compared them with the murder and the aftermath so far achieved. After groping cogitation he convinced himself that the cigar incident was a solitary incident; apart from that he had left nothing undone, and that he was safe so far as he had gone in the matter of the disposal of Canley. The reviewing had taken him several minutes and he was now behind with his timing. He had to hurry faster than he really wanted, and almost too fast to be consonant with the meticulous care that safety demanded.

The destruction of Canley's cigar had been intended, of course, to leave in existence only one of the two cigars smoked, in order that it should be quite clear that Canley, and none other than Canley had been in the cottage that night—in fact, that Canley had been alone and without visitors. This led him now to what he regarded as one of the two most important of his operations—the removal, completely, of any evidence of his presence in that cottage.

The disposal of Canley's body in the way he had in mind meant that an inquest would have to be held on the man. An inquest meant police investigation into the death. The presence of two people in the cottage would be bound to be discovered, and if the second person did not come forward to give an explanation to the police, then suspicion against him was certain to be aroused. At the moment there was undoubtedly evidence of two people in the two glasses from which he and Canley had drunk. One of the glasses had implanted on it the fingermarks of Canley, and the other bore the fingermarks of himself (Porter). In fact, both might have imprinted the fingers of Porter on their surface, for he was not sure that he had not handled the glass of Canley, when he had poured out that last drink.

For such a possibility Porter had come prepared. From a jacket pocket he took out a large piece of mutton-cloth—the soft woven material which most motorists use for polishing their cars. Lifting the two glasses from the table one at a time he rubbed them vigorously all over with the cloth, afterwards thoroughly polishing them. Inspection obtained by holding the glasses up against the light showed them to be completely clear of any fingermarks or even stains of any kind. One of the tumblers Porter replaced on the table; the other he carried to the sideboard, where he stood it on a shelf.

Next article to be treated was the bottle of whisky. Porter exercised the greatest care in polishing the entire expanse of glass. Finally, the carafe of water was similarly cleared of all impressions.

The next phase of the plot was one to which Porter in his planning had given much thought. Though it was, of course, essential that there should be no traces of his (Porter's) fingerprints about the place, necessity demanded that there should be prints of the fingers of Canley. A bottle of whisky, a glass and a carafe of water all on the table without the impress of a hand upon them would hardly coincide with the supposed story of Canley drinking to himself in the room, and walking out, probably half-drunk, to his death, in a manner which was so obviously accidental.

Even a common or garden detective of the lowest constabulary rank would examine the drinking necessities for fingerprints—it was now a formal precaution in the Force, as Porter realized. And such an officer would take a decidedly jarring interest in the absence of any. Nobody could drink, naturally, from a glass without leaving the imprint of a finger on the glass. That was where the cleverness of Porter and his plot was to be demonstrated.

The tumbler which he had placed on the table after its polishing he now lifted, holding it by the base with the mutton-cloth as protection. Crossing to the body lying in front of the roaring fire he knelt down, and keeping his face averted from that of the dead man, lifted the right hand.

The flesh was warm and natural to the touch despite its lifelessness. The action of the arm was still flexible, which surprised the man holding it. Porter manipulated the limp hand into a certain position, inspected it in relation to the tumbler which he was holding in his left hand, and shook his head in a negative decision. He released the hand which dropped at once to the side of the corpse. Slightly changing his position by the side of Canley, Porter once again raised the hand. Once more he flexed the wrist and opened the fingers. This time a nod of satisfaction escaped him. Gently, he lowered the glass into the dead man's hand, and then with his right hand pressed the thumb and fingers of the hand of Canley round the surface of the glass. The operation required considerable dexterity to ensure that the prints gave the appearance not of a fellow fumbling for the glass, but of a firm picking up by a holder who wanted a drink, and knew that he wanted it.

Rising, Porter held up the glass to the light and inspected the impressions made by the dead hand. They appeared to him to be quite natural and in the position which the hand of a man picking up the glass to consume its contents would naturally assume. With a chuckle of appreciation of his dexterity Porter stood the glass on the sideboard. Then, with the same careful and sinister caution, he repeated the operation with the bottle of whisky and the carafe of water. In the case of the former, he imprinted the dead man's fingers about half the way down the bottle surface. To ensure accuracy he had himself gone over the action of picking up the bottle and noting where his hand had taken natural hold of it. He had then to re-polish the glass surface before pressing the hand of Canley similarly round it. The carafe of water he caused to be seized by the dead man by the long neck of the vessel. In each case he had been meticulously careful to hold the article through two thicknesses of the mutton-cloth.

The result was that he now possessed three articles—the tumbler, the whisky bottle and the water carafe—all bearing the marks of having been used by Canley—and by nobody else. Thus he had, simply and emphatically, realized his safety plan of leaving behind the story of a man who had poured himself out a tot of whisky, drank it, smoked half-way through a cigar and had then, still alone, left the house, never to enter it again.

Porter surveyed the scene with mental and physical satisfaction. So far so excellent! But still more work remained to be done in the way of fingerprints. There was also the table to arrange to present an emphatic confirmation of the picture drawn by the prints impressed on the drinking vessels. He turned his next efforts to the table.

Taking it in sections he proceeded to polish with the mutton-cloth every square inch of the surface. As each section was completed he peered along it at table level to make sure that there remained no vestige of marks. The detailed nature of his planning was evidenced by the fact that he polished equally thoroughly the edges of the table, and even the *underside* of the edges.

Similarly, he treated the two chairs on which Canley and he had sat. Here again he was sufficiently cautious to wipe with the cloth the underside of the chair which he had used; he recalled having read in a detective story of a man whose presence was proved by an inspector from prints made on the undersides of a chair which he had drawn towards him while still sitting in it. Porter had tried the experiment himself, and found that the natural way of so moving a chair was to grasp the edges of the seat, partly lift oneself and then jerk the chair forward. He remembered that he had several times moved the chair backwards and forwards while with Canley. He accordingly wiped the underside of the seat thoroughly.

This operation completed, he sat in Canley's armchair letting his hands rest on the upholstered surface of the arms. It tickled him thus to leave marks—secure in the knowledge that no such marks or prints could be identified or taken from the rough tapestry! From his vantage point he let his eyes wander round the room, dwelling slowly and thoroughly on each article of furniture, and deliberating with himself whether he had at any time touched it since he entered the cottage. Not until he had surveyed everything at least twice, and had finally wiped the poker with which he remembered he had stirred the ashes of the burnt cigar, did he feel satisfied with his work.

The time had now arrived in accordance with his prepared time-table, for him to leave for any investigation which might be undertaken a picture of the last hours of the life of Canley—a picture that would be easy to read, and he was sure, impossible to be misunderstood by any police officer.

Holding the whisky bottle by the rim with the mutton-cloth, and taking care not to smudge the prints of Canley, he poured a little whisky from it into the tumbler, also bearing the prints of Canley's fingers. This he swished round inside the glass. The inference to be drawn from a subsequent investigation was that the glass had been filled and drunk from. Placing the tumbler on the table, Porter proceeded to carry from the sideboard to the table the carafe of water and the whisky bottle, arranging them in a casual manner just behind the tumbler, as they would be to a person wanting them near his hand for the purpose of drinking a nightcap.

Then came something which had not originally been in his plan. It came spontaneously, a sudden idea that raised a smile on Porter's face despite the corpse that lay, still and warm in front of him; a regular ornament for the *mise en scène*. Lifting the tumbler once more with the mutton-cloth he moistened the base with whisky and rested it on the table top. He proceeded to lift and rest it again several times, making the resting places overlapping each other. Every time a ring of moisture was left on the polished surface.

Simple but ingenious. The rings would dry but still leave their marks on the table. They would tell now emphatically the story of Canley in the house. Four or five drinks of whisky which he must have taken. If it led to the belief that Canley was pretty well under the weather, so to speak, when he went out of the cottage on that night, then it would be of incalculable help to the plan. Porter regarded it with great satisfaction, and with no little pride at the thought of it.

He proceeded further to set the final scene. The chair which he had used during his talk to Canley and which he had polished free of all prints, he placed against the wall at the side of the room, whence Canley had pulled it forward on his arrival. Canley's chair he placed by the side of the table, in front of the drinking requirements, but pushed slightly sideways as a chair would be if a drinker rose from it to go out of the room.

Stepping back he surveyed the setting. It looked to him quite natural; he saw nothing that could be said to be out of place.

He nodded his head contentedly. He was quite satisfied now that he had eliminated all traces of Jack Porter from the room.

It now remained to make perfectly certain that the room was equally clear of all traces of Jack *Edwins*. Wrapping his fingers in the utilitarian mutton-cloth he pulled the papers and wallet from Canley's pocket and looked through them. There were bills, a demand from a bookmaker for the settlement of an account within seven days—apparently, said Porter to himself, that was the reason for the request for the £100 to be brought tonight. The remainder of the contents of the pocket were a cheque book and a few letters. Porter pushed them back into the pocket and crossed to a desk standing in front of the window. In its recesses and drawers were more letters, a bank statement of account, photographs, racing form books and bookmakers' accounts. There was also an accounts book which seemed to refer to Canley's income and payments out.

Nothing in them, so far as Porter could see linked him with Canley. Not that he had expected to find anything, but he had to make sure. The least suspicion pointing in his direction, or in the direction of Jack Edwins, might prove disastrous.

Upstairs in the bedrooms the same security seemed assured. The drawers in the dressing-table and in the tallboy contained only the usual things to be found in such places. There was nothing in the pockets of other suits of Canley which were hanging in the wardrobe.

Mutton-cloth in hand to take hold of any article requiring investigation, Porter wandered through the remainder of the house, searching for danger. The kitchen showed nothing within of peril for himself, the other room in the house, with a door opposite the room in which was Canley, had no furniture in it. He had been in no other place.

The time had now come for the final stage in the death of James Canley. Glancing at the clock Porter saw that it showed 11.10 p.m. He had twenty-five minutes left. He walked back into the hall and lifted his overcoat from the hallstand. It was then he realized that it was possible that in hanging up the coat his fingers might possibly have come into contact with the wood of the stand. That must be made negative. He polished the stand with the mutton-cloth. Then carrying his overcoat over one arm, he lifted down the overcoat of Canley and went alertly and determinedly back into the room.

In just under twenty minutes' time the last train of the night on its way to the terminus station down the line would be passing over the bridge within sight of the cottage.

That train was to end Canley's life for the second—and last—time!

CHAPTER IX

JACK Porter had now reached the last stage of his plan. Though the other stages had been of great importance, this final preparation represented the crowning point, the high spot of the murder. So far he had eliminated all evidence of himself, or of his other self, Jack Edwins, from the house and from the actual contact with Canley. But that was not sufficient; he had now in the final move to eliminate any other person of any kind, or any suspicions of another person in the company of Canley, or any suspicion, however slight, of foul play in connection with the death. He flattered himself that nobody could have evolved a simpler, yet completely watertight way of achieving those two ends than the way he had worked out.

It had been decided upon only after long and logical consideration of the position from every angle. The outcome of it was that Canley's body would be found on the railway line next morning. The cause of death would be obvious to everybody; the victim, crossing the lines by a short cut, had been caught by the train in the darkness, knocked down and killed. It would be given in evidence that people were in the habit of using the short cut despite the warning of the railway company. Should the question of how he came not to see the train and thus be knocked down arise, that would probably be answered by the evidence shown in the living-room of the cottage. It would disclose that the man had been indulging in alcohol, was evidently half-drunk and had failed in his fuddled state to notice the train, or alternatively had seen the train but not realizing how close it was, or misjudging the speed, had tried to cross ahead of it, and had been trapped.

Reviewing his activities during the past three-quarters of an hour Porter convinced himself that all had gone well. The worst was now over. What had to follow was—Porter thought round for a suitable word—was tricky but not really dangerous. He saw very little difficulty about it, so long as he kept his head should certain unforeseen circumstances arise, and provided that he did not fall down on any detail of his planning. Since he had gone over this part of the plan not once, but a hundred times until he knew them as well as a moneylender knows his interest tables, there was little danger of his failing to do that.

With a cheerful but subdued chuckle at the thought that the long night was at last nearing its end, Porter began these final preparations. Canley himself was to renew an active role in them.

Porter's first actions, however, were peculiar. He sat down in Canley's armchair, unlaced his shoes and kicked them off. He started a little at seeing a bare toe protruding through one of his socks, grinned, and examined his toenail. A psychologist, doubtless, would find some explanation for the incongruity of the incident; but Porter himself could not, for after a moment he stared at the toe in amazement. 'What the hell does it matter?' he asked himself, 'What's come over me?'

Shrugging his shoulders, he walked over to the body of Canley, and knelt down. Unfastening the laces of the corpse's shoes, he drew them off the feet and, rising, carried them to the door of the room. There, he switched off the light, walked the length of the little hall and opened the front door. He was still carrying the shoes.

For the space of a couple of minutes he stood, shoeless, on the concrete path underneath the shade of the porch, his head on one side, listening.

The night was pitch dark, and damp with the November mist. Porter strained hard to distinguish the many sounds that came to his ears, sounds that in the daytime would have passed unnoticed, but in the darkness seemed so loud as to have been amplified through a microphone. The rustling of leaves in the surrounding trees, stirred by the slight wind mingled in the ears of the listening man with the monotonous drip-drip of water from the overflow pipe at the side of the house.

An owl hooted in the darkness a few feet away from him. Porter's heart missed a beat. He was not a countryman, and the hoot sounded to him like a hail from a wayfarer who could see him outlined against the doorway of the cottage. Not until the hoot was repeated did he recognize it.

Once, he drew back into the darkness of the hall as he heard what he thought was the cry of a baby from the lane. He deluded his ears into identifying actual footsteps along the lane, and cursed the ill-luck that had brought parents and a child in the neighbourhood of the cottage on this of all nights, and at this particular time when minutes were precious to him. The cry came again, and he then recognized it as the mating wail of a predatory cat.

At last, satisfied that the lane was deserted he stepped clear of the porch, and in his stockinged feet walked down to the gate and through it into the road. But not along the flagged path! Instead, his progress lay along the grass edging to the path and the grass verge of the lane itself. Standing on the latter, he put on his feet the shoes of the dead man, lacing them comfortably. For a few seconds he stood thus in the soaking wet grass, shuffling the shoes into the turf until they were sodden and muddy. Then he stepped from the verge on to the lane, *backwards* so that he faced the cottage. Pushing open the gate he walked slowly and heavily up the flagged path to the doorway, and entered the cottage.

Behind him were the footsteps of Canley.

Now there could be seen the reason for Porter's stockinged feet approach to the cottage when he had come to call on Canley.

The only person to enter the cottage along that path since the rain ceased, was Canley. There were no footprints of anyone else to show. Only the identifiable footsteps of the tenant.

That was the corroborative evidence of the loneliness of Canley in the cottage that night, which Porter had planned, and which the removal of fingerprints from the articles in the cottage room accentuated.

Back inside the cottage, he closed the hall door, and returned to the living-room. The fire was now burning lower but still threw long flickers of yellow light over the darkened room. Porter standing in the doorway and feeling for the light switch felt a sense of the eerie as he watched the light of the flickers pass over the still figure, lying like a silent sentinel asleep on duty. He switched on the lights. A glance at the clock threw the feeling of eeriness from him.

A final glance round the room convinced him that he had missed nothing of the plans he had prepared. Everything looked perfectly natural; the chair by the table, the bottle, glass and water carafe were all cosy. Perhaps, he said to himself, there was one thing that could improve the scene; the ashtray which he and Canley had used for cigar ash was on the sideboard; it would look better and more natural on the table with the other things. Porter placed it there. Then, walking to the mantelpiece, he took from the shelf the half-smoked cigar which had given him so great a fright, and pushed it in one of the pockets of his waistcoat. It was to be a link in a chain of accident.

The only blot on the story of the room now was the body of Canley. To complete the night's narrative, it had to be transported to the railway line between 100 and 200 yards down the lane. This, Porter had regarded from the first moment of his planning as the only real risk he ran in the murder. There was the danger that, contrary to the general run of custom, someone might be walking along that lane at that hour of the night. True, on no occasion had he seen a soul, save for one drunk; and it was unlikely that anyone would use it since it led only up to the railway line. But there was always the danger that it could be used. A courting couple, for instance, might choose the spot because of its darkness and remoteness. An encounter by anyone with a person carrying a bundle of any kind on his back would be likely to arouse very considerable suspicion when, next morning, a body was found at a spot a few yards away from the line.

Such an encounter could, of course, be avoided, Porter realized, by his pushing himself against the blackness of the hedge until any such wayfarer or wayfarers had passed on their way. That was supposing always that he had sufficient warning of approach to be able to hide himself. But such a proceeding he wanted to avoid if possible; it was necessary for the success of his plot that there should be a definite impression in the lane of walking footsteps from the cottage to the railway. This was one of his most definite safeguards. To deviate from the centre of the lane to the grass verge and into the hedge and then back again to the road might be a proceeding on the part of the footsteps sufficiently curious to court inquiry.

This was the risk which Porter realized he had to run in the final stages of his planning; but it was one which had to be taken, so there was no sense in hesitating about it. The fact that the night was a nasty one for anyone to be out and that it would be well after eleven o'clock when he traversed the lane probably reduced the risk to a small one.

The first requirement was to prepare Canley for his walk. Porter pulled away the rug which he had wedged under the body to keep away any cooling draughts, and spread it out again behind the body. On it he spread Canley's overcoat which he had brought into the room with his own coat. He rolled Canley over on the coat and began gently to ease the man's arms into the sleeves.

The operation gave him many anxious moments. He had thought that it would be a comparatively easy matter to get Canley into the coat; instead it proved a stumbling-block. The heat of the fire beating on him from a foot or two away, combined with his own exertions and the nervous strain of handling the dead man sent him into a bath of perspiration. His clothes stuck to his body.

Glances at the clock did not help him in his task; it was taking considerably longer than he had bargained for. However, there was really ample time when at last he succeeded in getting the man's arms into the sleeves, and was able finally to button the coat round the body. Provided there were no more delays, the time-table would still stand. His next task was to carry Canley from the room into the hall and prop him up in the chair standing at the side of the hallstand.

Canley's shoes he now fetched from the flower bed just outside the front door, where he had left them to ensure that they remained thoroughly damp from the wet soil. Slinging his own shoes round his neck, he returned to the sitting-room, and put Canley's shoes on his own feet. Another glance round the sitting-room assured him that nothing had been left behind, and that there remained nothing undone that he had planned to do. He switched off the light. Only the fire flickering over the room remained alive in the place.

The darkness of the interior of the house complete, he opened the front door. Then, with much grunting and heaving he hoisted and pulled the body of Canley on his shoulders, pick-a-back fashion and, thus laden, stepped out of the cottage on to the flagged path. Steadying himself against the porch, he took out the mutton-cloth from his overcoat pocket and grasping the knob of the door pulled it to. With the same caution he turned the key in the lock, afterwards dropping it into a pocket of Canley's overcoat.

For a moment or two Porter stood in the shade of the porch, listening intently. No sound alien to the night was to be heard. Satisfied that there was nobody about he walked as quietly as he could down the path, through the cottage gate and into the lane.

The last walk of Canley had started.

Down the centre of the lane Porter progressed with his burden. He walked slowly, treading heavily and squarely to make certain that every impression of his shoes, or rather Canley's shoes, was left sufficiently deeply and clearly in the wet softness of the lane to form a recognizable print. This was the groundwork—if the pun may be used—of the scheme which he had so patiently evolved and carried out for the disposal, finally, of his blackmailer.

Canley was no great weight, and Porter was strong. The more so since he was buoyed up with the prospect of a future free from the menace of Canley's demands upon his purse, and upon his happiness with Mary. He was, however, bathed in perspiration, not from the burden of Canley, nor from the exertion of the walk—it was a cold night, anyway. The perspiration was that which is generated from fear. He had known that this walk with the dead man would be the hardest of the night's tasks for him. Now that he was in the middle of it, and with no chance of turning back without imperilling his entire plotting, fear ruled his heart; his future, indeed, maybe his very life, rested on the success of this walk, and its outcome. Every sound of the night brought a feeling of terror to him; a stone flying from beneath his feet as his tread caught it on an edge, tip-cat fashion, sent his heart into his mouth. The shock caused him to stumble, and almost drop Canley, a circumstance which would have been fatal to his evening's work. In time, however, he recovered, and after a pause resumed his walking.

Once, he thought he heard voices close to. The pounding of his heart and the throbbing of the artery in his neck seemed to him to be striking hammer blows loud enough to have been heard by the owners of the voices. He stood stock still, unable for the moment to move even a hand to ease the weight of Canley from one side to the other. Had a passer-by hove into sight Porter could not have moved away, even to save his life.

Nobody, however, did approach, and the beating in Porter's ears died down. He realized that the voices must have been carried from people on the road on the far side of the railway line, probably from a couple of people calling good night near the bus stop. He continued with his walk. Within a couple of minutes he had reached the railway bridge and passed underneath it. In front of him a path ran up the side of the embankment leading to the railway lines.

He had now reached much harder going, and was slightly out of breath, for the ascent to the embankment top was rather steep even without the addition of a burden such as Porter was carrying. Then it was important for him not to slip on the wet surface of the slope. Porter, before approving the details of his plan had studied the effect of weight on footsteps. Such was the care with which he had gone into details for the killing of Canley. If a slip mark was heavily scored in the path it might be assumed, he had realized, that the man who had slipped was carrying a weight of some kind, and a heavy one at that. No trace of a weight would be found beside Canley when his body was found, and that would be a suspicious circumstance.

In any case if he did slip on the ascent it would be impossible for him to recover and Canley would probably be sent flying from his shoulders to the bottom of the path. Nothing would ever be able to remove tell-tale signs of that happening. So Porter trod carefully and slowly, tensing his legs and making sure that each foot was safely holding before he went ahead with the next step.

At last, he reached the top in safety, and breathed a sigh of relief. He let Canley slip down on the grass at the side of the metals. He had been nearly four minutes climbing the short slope. If his breath was coming heavily, his heart was beating lightly, and he hummed jubilantly to himself. He was safe! He paused and again strained his ears for any sound of passers-by. There were none. It did not matter now if there were, so long as they remained on the roadway, or in the lane. They could see neither him nor Canley from there. It was a thousand to one chance against anyone coming up the bank for the short cut now, for the last train of the night was due to pass within a few minutes' time, and most of the villagers knew it, and would avoid the line until it had passed. By that time Canley would be dead—dead, that is, from the accident which he, Porter, was going to stage for the benefit of himself. The stage was, therefore, clear to arrange those final obsequies of the man.

These he now proceeded to carry out. He lifted the body of Canley and placed it in the permanent way, between the two sets of metals, and just past the spot where people taking the short cut stepped over the metals. Then, lifting it by the shoulders he laid the neck over a rail of the down track, so that Canley was lying clear of the lines except for his head.

Stepping back he peered through the darkness at the position of the form. It looked perfectly natural for what it was supposed to show after the passing of the train. Porter nodded in satisfaction.

From the waistcoat pocket where he had placed it, he now extracted the cigar which he had half-smoked. Walking half a dozen paces up the line, he turned and flicked it with a sharp action towards and over Canley's body. It was as he threw, that the first sounds of the approaching train sounded. The time-table which he had compiled had worked out perfectly, despite the one or two delays which had caused him some anxiety at the time.

Taking Canley's shoes off his feet, Porter placed them on the feet of the corpse, and laced them up. His own shoes were still hanging by their laces round his neck. *The plan was now completed.*

In less than three minutes' time the last train of the night would come along that line, racing as it always did up the slight rise to the station before the driver began to brake.

Canley's severed head, the cigar knocked from his mouth by the impact and lying between the lines, his footsteps from the cottage along the lane, together with the mise en scène *inside the cottage would tell their own story, and plainly, to the police when they came to investigate.*

The noise of the train was now growing louder and the rails were vibrating. Within a moment or two the engine would be rounding the bed. Porter, still in his stockinged feet, began walking towards the up-line embankment. He was bending almost two-double in case his figure should be silhouetted against the sky to a pedestrian on the road below. And he was whistling softly.

Suddenly he stopped dead, as though shot. His heart came into his mouth again, for the third time that evening. Fool that he was, he said to himself, he had again nearly given himself away, and rendered useless all the thought, care and work which he had put in at the cottage.

Canley's shoes! He had handled those shoes half a dozen times. His fingerprints were all over them. If any suspicions chanced to be aroused and the police began to look for clues they might well find suspicion in shoes marked with the fingers of someone other than the wearer.

He ran back, still bending low, to the body, and taking from a pocket the piece of mutton-cloth which had done such useful service in polishing that night, rubbed with it every part of the shoes, going over them three or four times.

The train had now just turned the bend; in the darkness Porter could see the reflecting glow of the window lights on the bordering trees. He again crossed the metals to the up-line and walked rapidly on the grass verge towards the junction. As the train approached he lay flat down in the wet grass, completely hidden from view, even if the driver had had sufficient light to see him.

The train rumbled past; Porter remained supine for a full minute after its passing in case anyone should be looking out of a window, the guard for instance, and should see a figure outlined.

He saw the train stop at the station, and resume its journey to the terminus. Then, as the tail lights grew smaller and smaller, and finally disappeared round a curve, he rose, elated, and with a song in his heart continued along the ballast way, following the course that he had pursued on the night of the final rehearsal of his plot.

He had walked for a quarter of an hour when he reached a bridge near the junction—the lights of the junction platforms were, in fact, in view. A road lay beneath him. Carefully he descended the embankment and stepped out on the highway. Not till then did he put on his shoes. Shod at last he walked smartly to the junction, and walked on to the down platform. He did not buy a ticket; by that omission there could be nobody to identify him as having been at the station at that hour. A wait of only ten minutes was necessary before the last train of the night for Staines drew in. Porter stood by the side of an empty compartment until the guard signalled the train away. Then he slipped into the compartment. Again, as he had planned, there would be nobody with him to give any evidence of identification if, somehow, suspicion was directed towards him.

At Staines he walked to the market car park. His car was there, and with two others. He drove back to the garage, locked up and went upstairs to the bedroom.

Mary was asleep. She stirred slightly, but did not awake. He bent over her and brushed her brow with his lips. "Mary—" he whispered, under his breath. In the darkness he undressed and crept into bed beside her.

He was *safe*!

PART TWO
CHERCHEZ L'HOMME

CHAPTER X

ON THE tick of 6.30 the first train of the day drew out of the Surrey terminal station on its torpidly slow journey to London. It negotiated the long curve into Thames Pagnall at a slumbering ten miles an hour.

The handful of passengers huddled together for warmth in a party-compartment designed by a considerate railway for convivial gatherings of executives up to a number of twelve, looked sleepy-eyed out of the windows at the dawning light.

"Old Charlie on it agen today?" The question was thrown at large by an artisan holding his bag of tools across his knees.

"Reckon so, mate." Pained resignation found an echo in the faces of the other passengers.

"Frightened of speed, Charlie is," he added. "Ain't never known him do more than twenty miles a'nour at his best."

There were nods. "'Fraid train will run away with him, he is. That's what I reckon."

Silence followed as the company gloomily contemplated the fell possibilities of the train running past itself. The sight of the gently moving countryside dispelled any fear. The morose-looking man in a corner broke the silence.

"It's all along o' his bicycle," he said.

The gathering looked up in concerted interest.

"Whose bicycle?"

"Old Charlie's. He learned suddenly to ride a bike. Fifty he was at the time. He was going down a hill and the bike ran away with him. Lost his nerve, Charlie did. Forgot he'd got a brake." He ceased talking and gazed out of the window, ruminatingly.

"What happened?" asked the girl.

"Bike threw Charlie over a hedge into a pond. Never rode it again. Hadn't the nerve." He paused. "Nearly drownded him, it did."

"And he thinks the train will run away with him some time?" The stranger among them spoke for the first time.

"Could be," said the morose man. "Happened ten years ago," he added, inconsequentially.

"No ruddy fear of that." The artisan waxed sarcastic. "Not at the speed Charlie drives the engine."

The train pulled up at Thames Pagnall platform. "All stations to Waterloo," chanted a porter. "Close the doors, please."

"As if we'd leave the ruddy doors open on a morning like this." The morose man pulled his overcoat closer.

"Your language!" The girl tittered as the train got under way again on its trek.

Two minutes passed. The sudden silence in the carriage was broken by a loud screeching of brakes. The train came to a standstill.

"Gawd's truth. He's at it again," said the artisan. "Every time Charlie's driving this 'ere train, he stops here. What's 'e do it for?" he demanded passionately. "Young Masters don't do it. Charlie damn near always does, and I misses me bus and has to wait ten minutes for the next. What the hell for?"

"The signal's against him, I expect." The girl looked resignation.

"Can't be." The artisan emphasized the fact with a forefinger. "We're on the local line. There's no other train for ten minutes except the fast from Esher that stops at Surbiton. That's on the fast up-line. There's nought on the local line except us."

"Perhaps we're before our time," said a fellow traveller. The suggestion of the stranger was brushed aside. "Old Charlie ain't never been before his time in his life," insisted the artisan.

"Don't need no other train for signal to be agen us." The morose man glowered. "Signalman works signals. Mebbe it's about this time he's making a cup o' tea. So he don't pop the signal down till he's made it. See?" he added, darkly.

Three minutes passed in immobility. A mood of depression descended upon the company. The artisan saw in mental vision his bus passing into the limbo of forgotten things. The stranger looked at his watch. "I'll miss my connection at Surbiton," he announced. He became plaintive. "And the one at London," he added, after a pause for mathematical checking.

After four minutes an air of restlessness rustled through the company. The girl voiced alarm. "Perhaps the train's broken down," she suggested.

"No," said the artisan. He elucidated. "Compressor's working. Listen." The staccato stabbing of the air being drawn into the brakes sounded somewhere ahead.

"Must be signals then." The girl was definite.

The morose man let down a window and poked a head out. The green of the signal winked down at him in the semi-darkness. "Signal's all right," he announced. He dropped his gaze to the line, and bellowed.

"Cor suffering Mike," he said. "He's sitting down between the rails."

"What!" A second head screwed through the window. The artisan peered out in the lightening dawn. He recognized the black-and-white-striped box beside the driver and relayed the news. "He's telephoning," he explained.

"Oh, dear. Perhaps we're being broadcast," the girl's spirits returned. "I shall tell my friends—"

A shout from the next carriage sent up startled heads. "Crumbs, old Charlie's done it this time. He's knocked a bloke down."

There was a rush of heads through the windows on the other side of the train. In the faint daylight the figure of a man was visible lying beside the lines.

Death spoke eloquently from the body. It lay stretched out straight, as comfortably as though the man had lain himself down to sleep. The girl took one look and retreated hurriedly into the carriage, a handkerchief to her mouth. Everybody looked the other way.

"There are so many ways to let out life," quoted the stranger. "Massinger," he explained. It conveyed nothing to the company.

Meanwhile, Charlie at the telephone was talking to the signal box at the terminus. "Bill, there's a body on the line," he announced. "Knocked down by train. Not my train." He put forward the defence hurriedly.

The signalman chuckled. "No, I reckon it wouldn't be, Charlie. You ain't fast enough to knock a fly down. Dammit, you're five minutes late now and Surbiton's asking where the hell you are. Where's the body?"

"Just past the bridge at Thames Pagnall."

Bill started in alarm. "Cor lumme, Charlie, ain't you any further than that?" he demanded. "You'll have the slow Guildford running into you."

Charlie squeaked a protest. "I had to make sure it were a body, hadn't I? Then I had to get to this 'ere phone box. It ain't got no head. Cut off by train." The explanation seemed superfluous.

"Then it must have been the last down train last night. You get away, quick, Charlie. I'll have to put the down train on your line. Hop it."

Charlie replaced the receiver, closed the box and climbed back on to the driving cabin. The train whistled and set off for the third time. The passengers, now warmed by the excitement, settled down to discuss the shortness of life in general, and the sudden and dramatic terminations they had in their various walks of life witnessed.

In the signal box the operator waited until Charlie had passed the distant signal, then set it at danger. He pulled over the points of the down line on to the up-track and signalled Surbiton the warning. Then he hurried to the station-master's office.

A telephone call to the police station came through just as the inspector was on the point of departure. Mackenzie was a tall, burly man in plain clothes, whose features some freak of heredity had assembled into a perpetual expression of ferocity, so that to be in his company was like consorting with a man on the point of committing violent assault. He listened to the tale of the dead trespasser on the company's premises.

"I'll be along," he announced. "With the police surgeon and a sergeant. You'd better send some of the staff down to see nobody goes near the body. And tell 'em not to go near it, themselves."

"I'd like the railway doctor to be there, Inspector, before anything is moved," announced the station-master. He was old in the service of the company, and a cautious man.

"All right. You get him to the station, and I'll pick you up—say in a quarter of an hour."

The inspector was as good as his word. He led a procession of five along the ballast way to where a couple of plate-layers were already waiting. One of them was sitting with his head between his knees; he had been violently sick.

Mackenzie looked down at the corpse. "Anybody we know, Bunny?" he asked of the sergeant.

"Don't know yet, sir." The fact was not altogether surprising.

"Where's his head?" demanded the inspector.

A plate-layer nodded in the direction of the grass at the edge of the ballast way. "It took a toss over there," he announced. He was the plate-layer who had not been vomiting, having twice within thirty years been engaged in the process of prodigious and lawful shedding of men's blood in two wars.

The sergeant took a quick peek at the face peering up at him from between blades of long grass. He thought of the Japanese executions he had seen along the Burma road. The Japs buried their victims up to the neck in the earth, and then lopped off their heads.

"It's a fellow named Canley, sir," he announced. "Lives—lived," he corrected himself—"in a cottage in the lane there. He indicated with a wave of a hand the rural lane below the railway line.

"Anything to do with you, Mr. Station-master?" asked the inspector.

"Really, sir." The braided official pardonably mistook heredity for malignity in the policeman's face. "If that's meant to be serious—"

The inspector stared at his indignation. "Don't be damned silly," he chided. "I mean is he an employee of the railway?"

"No."

"Then he was trespassing?"

"Yes."

"Everybody trespassed," said the plate-layer. He pointed to a well-defined track across the lines. A width of a foot was trodden hard like a rabbit run across a field. There was a certain petulancy in his voice at the idea that a train had the right to knock down only one trespasser out of so many.

"People use it as a short cut to the other side of the village," the station-master explained. "They aren't supposed to."

The inspector turned to the body. "Well, we know who he was and what he was doing here. You two medical gents better have a look at the corpse while the sergeant and I browse round the scene of the accident."

The first discovery was made a few yards in the direction of the station. The inspector picked up a butt-end of a cigar. Although he searched carefully all round, that was the only discovery of any article that might not be expected to be on the spot in the ordinary way of things.

He parked it in a pocket of his waistcoat as Sergeant Bunny called him across to the edge of the embankment, and pointed to a line of footprints, the toes pointing in the direction of the ballast way.

"Better make sure they're his, Bunny." The sergeant crossed to the body and returned with one of the shoes. He looked at the sole and compared it with the marks of the prints. The impressions were about a quarter of an inch deep; the sergeant fitted the shoe into one of them. "It matches, sir," he reported. "I reckon he came up this path from the lane like they all do when they're making the short cut."

Inspector Mackenzie was looking at the prints and wrinkling his brows. "They're overprinting others in one or two instances, Bunny," he pointed out. "And there are none overprinting Canley's." Something he had read in the criminological library of his city police station as a constable, came into long-delayed use. "What time did it stop raining last night? Anybody know?" The constable nodded vigorously. "Yes, sir, half past ten pronto."

"Sure of that?"

"Quite. I was just finishing my beat, and it had rained all through my duty time."

"Then that settles the time they were made. In my humble opinion, the man walked up the bank after 10.30." He smirked smug satisfaction at the inquiry in the sergeant's eyes. "Matter of observation, Bunny," he announced, grandiloquently. "If rain had fallen after footprints were made, then the prints would have filled with water, and the marks of the patch on the sole would have been smoothed out by the water. Then, the edges of the impressions are sharp. Water would have taken the edge off them when the rain beat on the ground. Ever read Gross's *Criminal Investigation*, Bunny?"

"No, sir."

"You should. Every police officer ought to study it. I did. Well, I think it's pretty clear now. Let's see what the doctors say about the death."

The police surgeon looked up at their approach. Dr. Gaunt's duties rarely went beyond certifying that an obstreperous man was drunk, or had had such drink as made him unfit to be in charge of a motor vehicle. He was a cheery soul, with a round face, the projecting part of which bore unmistakable signs that whatever he might think of women and song, he was in attune with the wine part of the triplet. On the other hand, the railway doctor was a worried, ascetic-looking and elongated man. He seemed to be meditating the scene with some secret inhibitions.

"You'll be wanting to know the time of death, Inspector?" suggested Dr. Gaunt. The inspector indicated acceptance. "Well, we agree that it was some time between 10 p.m. and midnight. Can't put it any nearer than that."

The inspector glanced for confirmation at Dr. Jervis. The railway doctor nodded.

Inspector Mackenzie detailed the discoveries of his sergeant and himself, including the evidence of the footprints.

"Then that settles it." Dr. Gaunt looked his satisfaction. He also looked at his watch; he was thinking of breakfast. "The fellow crossed by the short cut, got on the lines, and was knocked down by the train, fell across the line and was beheaded. I'd better be getting away now."

"I dispute that."

"What!" the ejaculation came from Dr. Gaunt. He glared at his professional colleague.

"I said I dispute that he was taking the short cut and was knocked down by the train. I don't accept responsibility so far as the railway is concerned until the circumstances have been investigated."

"You—you—" Dr. Gaunt, the vision of his breakfast receding into some dim future, became incoherent.

"I should have thought the facts were plain enough, Doctor," said the inspector. "I realize that it may be a question of damages from the railway company for the death of the man, but—" He paused for thought. "What grounds have you for doubting the means of death?"

"Perhaps he thinks the man cut off his own dashed head."

Dr. Jervis ignored the police surgeon's outburst. "I think there are several grounds on which it could be argued that the facts are not quite as simple as they look," he insisted. "I shall report what I think to the Company at Waterloo, and I shall ask for Scotland Yard to be called in."

"This is Surrey, not London, Doctor." Inspector Mackenzie's face acquired a ferocity additional to his hereditary one. "It is *my* area."

"It is also the railway company's property, Inspector, with its own police, and headquarters in London. I shall demand that the Yard be called in. In the meantime, I must ask that the body shall not be moved until a new examination has been made by a pathologist." He turned to the station-master. "And I think you had better have a thorough examination made of the train which is supposed to have knocked the man down."

Sergeant Bunny scratched his head. The inspector looked from one to the other of the two medical men. "And what am I supposed to do?" he asked in high dudgeon.

"I should say that it would be best to take the greatest care that none of the footprints are disturbed, and that somebody is left here to see that there is no disturbance of what may be vital facts."

The inspector decided. "You take charge here, Bunny," he said, "until you receive further instructions." He turned on his heel and began his walk back to the station. Dr. Gaunt followed him. The railway doctor crossed to the side of the station-master. After a few words, he, too, left the lines.

Sergeant Bunny, after due consideration, expressed his opinion to the police constable. "It's a rum do, Perkins," he said.

The constable, who was born a yokel and after twenty years in the force remained one, gave careful and apparently painful thought to the problem.

"Ah!" he said.

CHAPTER XI

THE telephone bell shrilled out in the hall of a flat in Whitehall Place, which runs alongside the War Office. A manservant in the dull black of 'service' answered it, placed the receiver gently on the table, knocked at a door and entered the breakfast room.

"Scotland Yard, sir," he proclaimed sombrely; it might have been a Lord Bishop at the other end, judged from the solemnity of his voice.

Dr. Harry Manson rose, dropped his napkin on the table and crossed to the hall. He picked up the receiver.

"Manson here," he announced.

The voice of Superintendent Jones reverberated through the purlieus of Whitehall Place.

The superintendent was a big man; and his voice was in proportion. But it differed from his personality. The super was slow and lumbering in gait and thought; his voice spoke in *staccato* jerks—they resembled as much as anything a machine-gun firing rounds of explosive bullets in bursts.

Crime reporters who gathered in the Press Bureau of the Yard added that he spoke in shorthand; they meant that the super left out of his conversation the little words between the essential ones, thereby saving much time and energy.

Newcomers to the Force were wont to wonder how Jones ever became a detective at all, and by what miracle he, having insinuated himself into that occupation, had climbed to the rank of superintendent. No make-up man on earth or in Hollywood—which is not of the earth earthy—could have disguised Jones, not even to a person stricken with blindness. He could not have approached within a hundred yards of a suspect without being recognized.

But Old Fat Man—his nickname in the Yard—had two remarkable aids to detection. Firstly, he had a large and innocent-looking face—'baby-face' is the description usually given to it—which looked out on the wicked world with such lack of guile, and surveyed malefactors with such trusting innocence in their protestations and explanations of this and that endeavour or dispute, that they were persuaded to pull the long bow until it broke and left them defenceless. His second attribute was a painstaking genius for delving into a mass of verbiage and coming to the surface with all the essential facts.

His lack of imagination was a joke in the force. But nobody had ever known him to miss a fact. He might not reveal it at the time, because he had not the imagination to realize that it *was* a fact. But sooner or later, when that particular fact was essential to an investigation, Superintendent Jones would conjure it from the pigeon-hole of his memory with the same dexterity that an illusionist produces a rabbit out of a hat.

The fat man told over the telephone to Doctor Manson the story of the headless man.

That was the instruction of the Assistant Commissioner (Crime) of Scotland Yard. All corpses were taken to Dr. Manson. He was a doctor, not of medicine, but of science; he was also the head of the Yard's laboratory of crime, and the Force's scientific investigator and adviser. He had, in fact, founded the laboratory, equipped and established it as the greatest scientific criminal investigation institution in the world.

At first the doctor was called in only when actual violence had been used on a body. Until the day when lack of appreciation of a piece of scientific evidence had pretty nearly resulted in a murderer getting away without a hanging.

The Assistant Commissioner had promptly ruled that all cases of death reported to the Yard, whether they appeared to be due to natural causes, or whether violence was actually suspected should be handed over to the scientific and logical mind of Dr. Manson to investigate and express an opinion.

The doctor listened to the story of Canley to the end. He became plaintive.

"That's all very interesting, Old Fat Man," he said. "But why unload the man on to me? Thames Pagnall is in the Surrey country, isn't it? Let them set loose *their* police dogs to worry it."

"Can't!" The super chuckled gleefully. "There's a row—Everybody—Surrey—Force happy—gent wandered line—" he staccatoed, "walked—train—half-sozzled—"

"What! The train?" asked the startled scientist.

"No—man." The super never saw a joke until long afterwards.

Mitheration still held the doctor. He invited enlightenment. "Well, what do you want me to do, Old Fat Man—certify that the chap *was* drunk? If everyone's happy, why make my breakfast miserable."

The super burst out again. "Railway doctor—won't have bloomin' train—says—s'matter—compensation—see? Line not fenced—ought to—relatives—bring action—damages."

"Have they said so?" Manson was beginning to see the trend of the conversation.

"No—doctor says—might."

"I see, Old Fat Man. And because the railway headquarters are in London, they've come to us. Is that it?"

"S'right, Doctor. Insisted on Yard being called in—Corpse—all—yours."

"All right, Jones. Get hold of Merry and tell him to get things ready. I'll come round and pick him up. I'd better have Kenway, too. Let them know at Thames Pagnall."

"Right you are, Doctor." A sudden crackle of laughter roared over the wire. Manson recoiled as though swept by blast. "What the deuce is the matter now?" he demanded.

"Joke, Doctor." Another roar followed.

"Joke?" Doctor Manson deprecated uneasily. "I don't see any joke in the corpse. It was no joke for him."

"Not man—train, Doctor—sozzled." Manson groaned. The thing was getting beyond him. "It sounds as though *you* are," he began— Enlightenment suddenly dawned. "Oh, I see. You don't mean to say that you've assimilated *that* joke *already*, Old Fat Man." He chuckled with delight. "It must be a record for you."

"Not that one, Doctor. Ho! Ho!" Another frenzied burst swept over the scientist. "Train *must* have been sozzled after all. All trains—well oiled!"

The line went dead. Manson hung up with a chuckle.

Inspector Mackenzie greeted the London party on the permanent way with neither enthusiasm nor disappointment. It was, he soliloquized, all one to him whether the Surrey police or Scotland Yard delved into the proclivities of the corpse on the railway. The effect would be the same as far as he was concerned; he would have to 'carry the can' of routine inquiries and searches.

Mackenzie was, in fact, a little bored with the whole thing. He saw no reason to doubt that the man had been knocked down by the train on a dark night such as the previous night had been. Lots of people crossed the line there and the only marvel was that nobody had been killed there before.

What the celebrated Doctor Manson could deduce other than that from the evidence which he, Mackenzie, had collected he was unable to conjecture. But he was prepared to learn from the big noise. He advanced to the five arrivals.

"Dr. Manson?" he inquired. His eyes passed from one to another of the company; Inspector Kenway grinned as they stayed on his face. The scientist acknowledged himself.

"I am Inspector Mackenzie, sir," was the reply. He made the necessary introductions.

The scientist glanced round. "I take it that this is the spot where the body was found?"

"It is that," replied the inspector. He stepped towards the bank, invitingly. "The man came—" Doctor Manson waved the sentence into silence.

"Just a moment, Inspector," he urged. "Let me have a look round before you talk." He walked a few paces up the line. "I like to start with a clear mind," he flung back.

A watery sun had appeared low in the sky. It caught the mirror of gleaming steel of the rails and ricocheted on the faces of the little crowd waiting near the body of Canley. From the centre of the down-track Doctor Manson gazed along the line. The station was apparent a few hundred yards ahead; Manson measured the distance with his eye. About the same distance in the opposite direction the lines disappeared round a curve.

"He'd have heard it, Harry," said Merry who had followed him.

The doctor turned, startled. "Psychic, Jim?" he asked the deputy scientist.

"No. Just following your line of reasoning." Merry slinked in the riposte slyly. "Your thoughts were easy to translate. You were obviously looking for anything that might have obstructed the sight of the train from anyone crossing the line. All there is is the curve round which the train would not be visible until it entered the straight. You measured the distance mentally, and frowned, and I then said that the man even if he could not see the approaching train would have heard it at that distance. It's elementary, my dear Watson."

"You're right, of course." Manson nodded. "So long as the speed of the train was not excessive he should have had warning enough. We'll have to get that from the driver."

The two men returned to the waiting group which opened out for them. The doctor let his eyes stray over the immediate vicinity. A dark rusty-coloured stain showed up on a section of the rail and on the white flints in the ballast way.

"Blood?" Manson looked at Inspector Mackenzie.

"Yes, sir. The man was decapitated."

Manson nodded, and walked a few yards up the line. He was looking intently along each side of the ballast and between the rails.

"Is the driver of the train here?" he asked. A man in railway uniform stepped forward.

"I was driving." He spoke pugnaciously.

"What speed would you have been travelling past here last night?"

"Just under twenty miles, sir. That was the usual speed."

The doctor brooded over the point. He walked again up the line and made a more meticulous examination. He made no comment on his journey on his return, but produced a circular object from a pocket and pressed a button on it.

A shining tongue of polished steel tape shot past the constable standing nearby. He jumped an inch in the air. Manson, mildly surprised, looked at him. "A tape measure." He explained the obvious.

With Sergeant Merry writing down figures in a notebook the scientist measured the area of the bloodstains. They extended eighteen inches one way and about two feet the other way. The extent seemed to worry him, for his brow furrowed, and crinkles appeared in the corners of his eyes, the stormy petrels of his detection. He said nothing, however; but crossed to the edge of the embankment and looked down into the lane below. A single trail of footsteps showed plainly on the path. They were pointing towards the railway line, and were plainly marked.

It was for this that Mackenzie had been waiting. He patted himself on the back. "They were made by the dead man, sir, walking up to the line. I compared them with his shoe measurements, and you'll notice a patch on the sole of one of the shoes is reproduced. I also fitted a shoe into one of the prints—" he indicated a smudged outline—"and it fitted perfectly." He exuded self-satisfaction.

Doctor Manson nodded. "Most commendable," he said, absently, and crossed to the other side of the line. The path was clear of prints. He returned to the group.

"The body now," he said.

The mortal remains of James Canley lay in the ballast way. He had been lifted by the two plate-layers after the doctors had concluded their examination before the quarrel between them which had led to the call to Scotland Yard. A tarpaulin had been placed over them. This the plate-layers now removed, and displayed to the gaze of the Yard men the grim spectacle underneath.

Canley had been left as he had been found, even to his overcoat, still buttoned round him. The head, however, had been wrapped in a separate covering.

"Just as he was found," Mackenzie announced. Doctor Manson looked up quickly.

"Do you mean that literally, Inspector?" he asked. "That he was lying as he is now—on his back?"

"Yes, sir. I took particular notice of that. The body itself was flat in the space between the lines of metals."

"That's right, Mister." A voice came from the group. Doctor Manson sought the owner. He looked inquiringly at the Surrey police chief.

"One of the men who moved him, sir. The other's here, too. He's got to be moved again when you have finished with him." The inspector shuddered slightly.

The plate-layer stepped in front of the group. "Flat on his back he was, Mr. Policeman." Manson eyed the body.

"And straight out, just as he is now?" he asked.

"Yes."

The doctor turned away and started on an examination of the body. He began with the shoes, paying particular attention to the soles. Merry brought up a suitcase, placed it on the ground and opened the lid. Inspector Mackenzie peeped into its interior.

"This is where the doctor starts the ball rolling," Inspector Kenway whispered in his ear. The Surrey man sought enlightenment.

"That's what we call the Box of Tricks," explained Kenway. "We used to laugh at it when the doctor first brought it round." He left no doubt in the mind of Mackenzie that there was no matter for jesting now.

The Box of Tricks was the name given to a portable laboratory which Dr. Manson carried with him on his investigations. It was a laboratory in miniature, all the contents, even a microscope, being equal to the full-sized instruments, except in size. Ridicule, which greeted its appearance in the earlier investigations of Doctor Manson, was quickly silenced after the success attending scientific examinations on the actual scene of the crime.

From the box Merry lifted a packet of small white envelopes of the kind usually used by seedsmen for the packaging of their wares. He laid them with his fountain pen on top of the case. Manson continued with his examination of the shoes; he had taken from a pocket a small lens through which he was scrutinizing closely the welts. The operation seemed to tickle Inspector Mackenzie's sense of humour.

"Wonder he didn't bring a telescope," he whispered to his constable. "Shouldn't have thought he wanted a magnifying glass to see them. They're big enough, aren't they?"

The doctor smiled; he was blessed with acute hearing. But he made no reply. With a pair of tweezers taken from the box of tricks he plucked a tiny length of thread from a crick between the upper and lower sole of the right foot.

Merry and he examined it together, heads bent closely over it. The pair then moved to the shoe of the other foot, which they inspected without a glass this time.

After Manson had drawn attention to some aspect of the inspection, Merry slipped the thread into one of the seed envelopes. He sealed it, and wrote on the outside a description of the article, and the circumstances of its finding. The doctor looked up at Mackenzie.

"I would like these shoes handled carefully and kept, Inspector," he said.

"Very good, sir." Mackenzie hesitated, and then added: "I should say, sir, that we have compared the soil on the soles of the shoes with the soil of the path, and it seems to correspond, if that is what you are thinking of."

"It was in my mind," Manson admitted. "Together with another point of interest."

"That being?" The inspector put the query with some anxiety at the thought that he might have missed something of importance.

Doctor Manson did not reply. He was feeling the overcoat on the body of Canley. He looked up and caught the glance of the inspector.

"Not very wet," he remarked. "Just damp. Do I gather that it was not a wet night here last night? I recall that it rained fairly heavily in London."

"Not exactly wet, sir, if you mean was it raining." Mackenzie pondered a moment. "There was no rain after about half past ten o'clock, but there was a nasty November mist. That would account for the dampness of the coat. The body must have been here since 11.35."

"Quite so." The doctor gave the coat a comprehensive glance. "It seems, by the way, to be undamaged."

The inspector agreed. "I work out," he explained, "that the train hit him and threw him clear of the lines, except for his head and neck, which fell across the nearside rail. The trunk was clear of the metals when we found him. That would account for the coat not being torn."

"But—" The doctor clipped off his sentence with a wave of a hand. It seemed a gesture of resignation. He eyed the inspector morosely. "I see," he said. "That is your observation and deduction."

The driver of the train had been manifesting considerable nervous objections to this exposition on the part of the inspector. He hopped from one foot to the other, and shook his head in violent objection. Dr. Manson now turned towards him.

"I gather you are not altogether at one with the police officer," he insinuated. "What I cannot understand is how you did not see the man walking or standing, even though it was a dark night. It seems to me looking towards the station from here that you have a certain amount of skyline which would give you a reflection from the lights of the station. Is that not so?"

"That's what I'm getting at, sir." A grimace lent expression to the driver's assent. "I always keep a good look-out after I pass over the bridge, because I have to watch for the station signal and my distance for braking."

"And you saw no sign of the man?"

"No, sir."

"Did you feel a bump at all?"

"Not a thing, sir."

The doctor eyed him reflectively.

"Suppose the man had been standing in the shade cast by the trees at the edge of the bank, and as you were nearly level with him, ran in front of the train. Would you, do you think, have seen him?"

The man looked doubtful. "It's a bit hard to say, sir. It would be only a matter of a few yards. If I was looking up for the station signal, I might have missed him, especially if he was bending. But—" The doctor eyed him keenly.

"Yes?" he invited. "But what?"

"Well, sir, I've been driving a good few years, and mostly of nights. We get a kind of sixth sense, especially in the dark. I think that I might not have *seen* him to recognize that it was a person, but I think I would have *sensed* a movement in front or at the side of me with that sixth sense. It's happened like that before with a dog, sir."

Doctor Manson nodded his satisfaction. "That, driver," he said, "is just what I was trying to get from you without putting the direct question. And you can recall no such feeling on that night?"

The man shook his head.

"I regard the point as of some importance." The doctor addressed the company at large. "But," he added, "it helps only in an indirect way at the moment. There is no doubt, of course, that the man was decapitated by a train—"

He broke off suddenly. The significance of the phrasing he had automatically used struck him with some force. He turned to Mackenzie.

"Has the train of this particular driver been examined. Inspector?" he asked. He put the question sharply.

"Yes, sir. We made sure of that. There are bloodstains on the wheels of the second bogie of the leading coach." He put in an addendum. "That is the coach containing the driving cabin."

"Ah! Then that disposes of that point," said the doctor. "And blood, of course, on the undercarriage," he added, with conviction.

"No, sir."

Doctor Manson had bent over Canley again. But at the inspector's remark, he jerked suddenly upright. He stared at the Surrey officer. "Say that again, Inspector," he invited. Mackenzie obliged.

"There was blood on the bogie wheels, sir, but none on the undercarriage." He was stubbornly convincing. "But you can see for yourself if you doubt it. We have had the coach run into the goods shed, and the station-master has sent out one of the reserve driving coaches in its place."

"I am not doubting your facts at all, Inspector. The circumstances seem a little odd, that is all," said Doctor Manson.

The inspector shifted uneasily. It appeared to him that the scientist was *sorrowing* over him. If he was, he showed no further sign of it. He was, in fact, busy with the tweezers picking particles of what appeared to be sodden fluff from the back of the dead man's overcoat. They had been brought to light when the doctor and Merry had turned the body, having finished their examination of the front. The pair bent over the particles in a close scrutiny.

"Possibly from a scarf, or something like that, Doctor," suggested Merry. "They would cling to this rough-surfaced material."

"I should have thought they were more fibrous than woollen, Merry. That would not fit any kind of scarf of my acquaintance. Still, we'll know better after we have had them under the microscope. Into an envelope with them."

The doctor turned again to the coat. "Here are a few more, Merry," he called out. He indicated them to the deputy scientist. "They form an interesting corollary to our discussion, I think. Note their position."

"Meaning, I take it, that the man would hardly wear a scarf round his seat." Merry chuckled. The chuckle was too much for Inspector Mackenzie, who was feeling the effect of having not had his breakfast. He went off in a gentle explosion.

"Do bits of fluff matter, sir?" he demanded. "The man was plainly run over by a train. You have said so yourself. What he was wearing it seems to me makes no difference to the fact that he *was* run over. Nor does it carry us any further as to how he came to be run over."

"It may make a deal of difference." Doctor Manson corrected him sharply. "Everything that is not natural about a body matters in a case like this, Inspector. This man is found dead on the railway. It is presumed that he was knocked down and killed by a train on a section of the line which is not guarded to prevent unauthorized people gaining access to it. A great deal may depend on the condition of the man—where he had spent the night before he, presumably, climbed up to the line. I know nothing more indicative of a man's surroundings as attachments to, or markings on, the outside of the garments which he is wearing."

Some glint of illumination penetrated into the mind of Mackenzie. "You mean that he may have been drunk and wandered on the line?" he asked. The doctor shook his head impatiently.

"I have no evidence that he was drunk," he said. "But such a state, now that you mention it, might conceivably account for his failing to notice the train, which otherwise he should have seen or heard quite easily."

"Perhaps he had lain down to sleep it off." The local constable made his first contribution to the discussion.

"Don't be a fool, Perkins." Inspector Mackenzie turned on the man. "Why should he walk out of his house, where he could sleep comfortably off the effect of drink, just to drop off on the railway."

Merry grinned. "Trouble in the family," he said. "What next, Doctor?"

"The head, I think." He unwrapped the grisly relic, and looked down at it. Kenway dug Sergeant Bunny in the ribs. "Alas, poor Yorick," he quoted. "I knew him, Horatio." He had played Hamlet in the Metropolitan Police Dramatic Society's production.

"You knew him, Inspector?" ejaculated the sergeant, whose knowledge was nearer bacon than Shakespeare. Kenway let it pass.

Doctor Manson, after a cursory examination of the features of the dead man, and the facial markings, forced open the mouth and examined the interior. "There seems to be no fracture of the teeth, Merry," he pointed out. "And they are quite firm in the gums, you notice. That would seem to be of importance." He probed further into the mouth with a pair of forceps, which came out with between them a minute brown fragment that had clung to the gums. The doctor examined it through his lens.

"Seems to be a particle of tobacco leaf, probably from a cigar," he said. "What do you make of it?"

"I should think that is quite likely." Inspector Mackenzie interrupted. "We found a stub of cigar some five yards down the line. It seems to have been knocked out of his mouth by the blow from the train." He produced the exhibit. Manson took it.

"Practically dry."

"Which makes it dropped after the rain last night—that would mean after 10.30 p.m." Mackenzie emphasized it pointedly.

The doctor looked up in marked surprise at the deduction. He smiled and nodded. Merry slipped the stub into another of the seed envelopes and labelled it. Into a third he placed a few of the hairs from the dead man's head, which the doctor had snipped off with a pair of surgical scissors.

Manson straightened up, and stretched himself. "Well, I think that is all we can do with the body," he said. "Except—" He gazed at the corpse, and at the head, as if searching for something. The inspector watched him.

"Was there something?" he asked.

The scientist made no reply. Instead he walked to the edge of the embankment and let his eyes wander over the grass and down the slope, walking a few yards in each direction. He returned still in a state of dissatisfaction. The inspector reiterated his query.

"Yes, inspector, there *is* something." His eyebrows went up, questingly. *"What has happened to the man's hat?"* he asked.

"His hat? We haven't seen a hat."

"Well, it can't be far off. Perhaps, while you tell me your story, some of these men will make a search for it. Possibly the wind from the passing of the train whirled it away."

He watched the sergeant and constable separate and begin the search.

"Now, Inspector, who and what was this man?" he asked.

CHAPTER XII

INSPECTOR Mackenzie dived a hand into one of his pockets and produced his notebook. With a moistened thumb he flipped over the pages until he arrived at the *collectanea* appertaining to the present tragedy.

The process was regarded by Doctor Manson with a frown. He had little enthusiasm for notebook recitals. While it was well, in fact, advisable, for facts to be put into writing as an aid to future memory and for filing, it should be, he held, within the mental compass of an inspector of police to relate the salient points of any investigation without having recourse to his notes. He waited with patient tolerance, however, until Mackenzie, having digested anew the data, began his story.

"His name is James Canley," said the inspector. "He is about fifty years of age, and he lives—lived" (he hastily corrected the slip) "in a cottage down the lane there." A wave of the hand incorporated about 300 yards of the area below the railway embankment.

"What was he?" asked Manson.

"I don't know. So far as we are aware he was of independent means. But we have had no reason up to now to inquire into his circumstances. I've never known him to be in any employment. But he used to do a good bit of race-going."

"Any relations?"

"Not to our knowledge. He lived alone in the cottage with a woman coming in daily to clean for him. She also prepared his breakfast and an evening meal. She—"

"Just a moment, Inspector," interrupted the doctor. "The cottage, I take it, has not been interfered with?"

"No." A touch of acidity crept into the monosyllable, a frigidity that announced a state of dudgeon that so elementary a precaution should have thought to have been neglected. "The woman," he added, "has been told not to touch anything in the place, and there is a constable there to see that she doesn't—and nobody else, either. She is waiting in case you wish to question her."

"Most commendable, Inspector." Manson re-established amicable relations. "You were saying," he added, "that this man Canley was apparently independent. He had no business, then, on this railway line?"

"He had no right, officially," replied Mackenzie. "But"—he waggled an admonitory finger—"unofficially he sort of had."

Doctor Manson looked bewilderment. "Sort of had?" he said. "What do you mean by that, Inspector? He was not apparently employed by the company. Therefore he had no right to be on the lines. Do you mean that he had some sort of honorary connection with the company? Either a man has a right to be somewhere or he has no right. There cannot be any 'sort of had' a right about it."

The inspector goggled, and looked inquiringly at the station-master. That official met his eyes with a blankness that conveyed plainly the message that he was not talking out of his turn. Mackenzie took the bull by the horns. "Well, sir, he had a sort of a right of way, if you get my meaning."

"I don't, Inspector."

"Well, sir, the villagers have for years and years been crossing the lines here. They look upon it as a right of way by custom. And the company has always winked at it."

"I protest at that statement." The station-master flared up at the insinuation. He had a vision of the ogre of damages for neglect looming. "There are notices posted," he insisted, "at the extreme ends of the station platforms warning that passengers must not cross the lines except by the subway." He added as an afterthought, "Penalty five pounds."

"But these people were not passengers," said Doctor Manson, peeved. "And anyway they couldn't see the notices from here unless they used binoculars."

"They knew it, all right," the station-master insisted.

"The fact remains," the inspector swept into his interrupted stride again. "The fact remains that for years people have been crossing the lines at this spot. And as for the company not winking at it, drivers during the daytime sound their whistles as they reach the end of the curve there to warn anybody who may be on the permanent way."

Doctor Manson glanced down at the track. "And they have to cross two live rails," he pointed out. "Why do they do it?" he asked plaintively.

"As a short cut, Doctor." Mackenzie delved into geography. "The railway embankment cuts this village into halves."

Doctor Manson's eyes twinkled. "It looks a lot more modern this side, Inspector," he suggested. "Possibly a nearer approximation to the truth is that this part of the village which I see possesses no shops, was built on the wrong side of the railway. Eh?"

The niceties of the argument had no place in Mackenzie's retrospect. "It still cuts the village in two, sir," he insisted. "And it's a good walk from this side to the village centre, shops and the popular 'local'. I live at the back, so I know. Somebody years ago saw that if they climbed the embankment from this lane, crossed the lines, and went down the embankment on the other side, they strike the main road and are in the main street of the village in about five minutes. The cut became popular, and now, as you see, there is a regular path worn by feet up and down the embankment on each side."

"I see." The doctor digested the information. "And you assume that this man Canley, while making this short cut was caught by the train and killed?" A note of combativeness crept into the scientist's voice.

"That is how I look at it, sir. Take the facts as we have them—"

"How long has Canley lived here?"

"I am not sure," began Mackenzie. The sergeant chipped in. "Just over eighteen months, sir."

"Then he would know the times of the trains, I suppose?"

The inspector acknowledged the probability that he did.

"Sufficiently well not to cross the lines when one was due at the spot?" The scientist allowed time for the implication to sink into the inspector's mind, and then switched with disconcerting suddenness to another line of inquiry. "What kind of night life have you in this village, Inspector?"

Mackenzie goggled. He appeared stupefied at the suggestion. "Night life? You mean—"

"Gilded palaces, riotous clubs, drinking dens, Inspector. 'All the fun of the fair.' What do the denizens do with their time?"

"There's nothing like that here, sir. It's a very quiet sort of place."

"Not a picture house?"

"Not nearer than the junction or the terminus, sir."

"No Buffalo bean-feasts, or such-like?"

"There's the cricket club annual dinner, which has a bit of entertainment. And there's a dance at a local hotel on Saturday nights."

"Was there a cricket club dinner or a dance last night?"

"No."

"Was there any festival of any kind last night?"

Mackenzie shook his head. He was beginning to have doubts of the scientist's ability seriously to investigate the riddle confronting him.

"Not even a whist drive?" The doctor was plaintively insistent.

"Nothing at all. I walked through the village myself round about ten-thirty o'clock, and there were no more than a dozen people about. Those were on their way home after closing time."

"That is what I should have expected in a village of this description," announced Doctor Manson. "Now, Inspector, may I invite you to consider these facts in conjunction with the theory of the manner of Canley's death, and try to reconcile the two."

Mackenzie applied himself laboriously to the elucidation of this problem, and then, finding the effort too much, abruptly abandoned it. "I don't see what you are getting at, sir," he confessed.

"No?" The doctor looked surprised. "Not in the time of death?" he asked.

The inspector shook his head. "It must have been the eleven thirty-five train, sir. That is certain. The body would have been noticed by the driver of a train either on the up or down line if an earlier train had caused the death."

"Doubtless. That is not the point I am trying to convince myself of, Inspector. Granting the time of death was eleven thirty-five, and the cause of death the last train, do you not find something peculiar in the circumstances of the man being on this line?"

"Everybody used the line, sir."

Doctor Manson made a gesture of despair. "So you have told me before," he said, testily. "What for?"

The inspector looked stupefied. The Scotland Yard expert, it seemed to him was either lacking in memory or was singularly hard of hearing. "What for?" he echoed. "I have told you—to get to the other side of the village."

"To go somewhere, in fact?"

"That is so, sir."

"Where do you suppose Canley was going at eleven thirty-five o'clock at night, Inspector? Where *could* he have been going?"

"I don't know, sir."

"No, and neither do I. That is what I meant. It is the time of death that has intrigued me from the start. Dash it all, Mackenzie, look at the circumstances. Here is a man in a village which is sound asleep at eleven o'clock. He is drinking comfortably in his own home apparently, from what you tell me, alone. He leaves that home shortly before midnight, and takes the short cut into the village—the short cut over a dangerous route in the dark, mind you. Where was he going? There wasn't a place open. There wasn't any kind of entertainment in the place."

"Might have been going for a walk before bed, sir," suggested the inspector. "I take a walk myself often."

"On a foul night like it was last night, Inspector? When he was comfortable at home with a drink, and so on?" Doctor Manson waited for any comment; none was forthcoming.

"All right," he said. "We will suppose that like you, he occasionally took a late before-bed walk. He has a mile or so of road on this side of the line, nice country roads from what I remember of them. He could indulge in a nice walk round the houses. But, instead, he takes a dangerous route down a lane, up a railway embankment and across lines which have two separate live rails to touch, either of which could mean death. And there he allows himself to be run down by a train. Why, Inspector? Do you take your nightly stroll over the railway lines? You live on this side, don't you?"

"Had the footsteps been mounting the path on the other side of the rails there would have been a certain degree of probability. He might have been coming back from some carousal and on the way home. As his cottage is within 200 yards of this spot he might well have taken the short cut."

"That is precisely my point, sir." The interruption emanated from the railway doctor. It came emphatically. "I maintain," he asserted, "that this man was trespassing on the company's premises for some unlawful purpose—"

"What unlawful purpose?" demanded Mackenzie.

"Something, I should say, in connection with this train," replied the doctor. "Otherwise there is no doubt that he would both have seen and heard the train. He could not have been knocked down by mischance."

"You can add to that that I should have seen him—almost certain," put in the driver.

Inspector Mackenzie looked from one to the other. The investigation, he thought, was going haywire. Doctor Manson broke the strain.

"I cannot go with you about the something unlawful." He addressed the railway doctor. "But I will go so far with you as to state that there are, to my mind, strong indications discounting the accidental knocking down."

A satisfied sigh escaped the station-master. His face took on cheerfulness of relief. Inspector Mackenzie, on the other hand, darkened. He confronted the scientist.

"Indications?" he snorted. "Such as? The man's head is cut off. If he was not knocked down how did he come to be killed?" A thought struck him. "Are you suggesting that he cut his own head off?"

"Suicide," said the railway doctor, "was one of the unlawful purposes I had in mind." He sought confirmation from the scientist.

Doctor Manson shook his head. "I rule out suicide by lying on the rails," he said.

There was an uneasy silence at his words. It was broken by the inspector suddenly banging excitedly on his notebook and becoming slightly distraught.

"If he wasn't knocked down by the train and he didn't commit suicide, then what the hell *did* happen?" he demanded.

He looked quickly round at the spot where the body was lying, as if expecting to find that Canley had, in the meantime, behind his back, resurrected himself and taken to flight. Reassured, he felt more strengthened.

"He's dead—in two parts. He's on the railway lines." The inspector became passionate. "The engine wheels have blood on them. Is this a debating society? For the love of Mike tell me, what *did* kill him?"

"I don't know," said Doctor Manson. He was apologetic. "By the way I ought to have asked before, what time do you medical gentlemen say he died?"

Both doctors began to speak, and stopped in confusion. The police surgeon was the first to recover. "From the temperature of the body when I saw it, and from the minimum temperature of the night hours," he said, "I put the time of death as between ten-thirty and midnight. If I were pressed to give a more definite time, I should say eleven-thirty or thereabouts. I admit"—he became self-excusing—"that I am influenced there by the fact that the last train on this line was at eleven thirty-five last night."

The railway company's doctor confirmed. "I agree with my professional colleague," he snorted. "It is about the only point on which I *am* in concert with him," he added.

Doctor Manson's eyes wrinkled over the Bone of Contention. He straightened himself up. "Well, that seems as far as we can go here," he announced. "Suppose we follow the man's tracks, Mackenzie, which you say lead to his cottage. Your men can then get the body to the mortuary for Dr. Gaunt. I think a casual examination of the body surface will be sufficient for the doctor to telephone me certain information." He had a quiet word aside with the police surgeon.

The railway doctor pushed forward towards them. "I should like to be present at the *post mortem*, in the circumstances," he requested.

"I shall be glad to accommodate you," said the police surgeon. The two went off, happily, side by side.

The plate-layers prepared to carry the body of Canley to an ambulance waiting in the main road on the other side of the embankment. Doctor Manson halted them.

"We will keep the man's shoes here," he said. Inspector Kenway unlaced and removed them.

The *cortège* crossed the lines.

CHAPTER XIII

STANDING at the top of the embankment Inspector Mackenzie pointed out to Doctor Manson, Inspector Kenway, and Merry, the double row of footprints pointing towards them.

"There, Doctor, is the story, as I see it," he abrogated, "and plainly outlined. Canley's cottage is some 200 yards down the lane there. You can't see it because of the tall hedges on either side of the lane."

"Now, he seems to have walked from his cottage down the centre of the lane." He paused as Manson was about to speak. "I'm stating a fact now," he hurried on. "I'll show you the proof presently when we go down the lane. Er—where was I?"

"You were walking along the centre of the lane with the late Mr. Canley," prompted the doctor, gravely.

"Oh, yes. Then he climbed up here, which is the normal way of reaching the cut. Whatever may have happened on the line"—the inspector showed plainly that he regarded the circumstances to be as plain as the handwriting on the wall of Belshazzar's palace—"these facts are, I think you will agree, obvious."

"The obvious is not altogether reliable, Inspector," said the doctor, chidingly. *"Quodcumque ostendis mihi sic incredulus odi."* He quoted Horace. "You may have seen the performance of sawing through a woman on the stage."

He was kneeling down alongside one pair of the prints inspecting them closely through a lens. The result seemed to afford him matter for concern, for he moved farther down the slope subjecting the remainder of the prints to a similarly close scrutiny.

Finally, after a brief conference with Merry, the latter climbed slowly up the bank, collected the shoes of Canley and returned, whereupon the doctor compared the soles with the prints, again through his lens. Finally, he measured the depth of the impressions with micro-callipers, Merry noting the figures on a note-pad.

Mackenzie was shifting from foot to foot in exasperation—like a greyhound straining at the leash, thought Kenway, watching him. Presently he slipped his collar.

"We have already examined the prints, Doctor Manson," he burst out. "I have had some experience of prints, and there is no doubt that these were made by the dead man."

Doctor Manson glanced up. "There is no doubt at all in my mind," he said mildly, "that these prints were made by the dead man's shoes." The inspector, mollified, relapsed into silence. It was not until considerably later that he appreciated the distinction drawn by the scientist's phrasing.

"I was wondering, Inspector, if there was anything else you could tell me from the prints?"

"Yes. They were made after ten-thirty last night," said Mackenzie, triumphantly. He emphasized his theory that rain would have washed out the details of the impressions shown in the steps. Manson nodded appreciation of the point.

"I give you marks for that," he said. "But the fact does not help us a great deal further. We are already pretty certain of the time of the tragedy. The condition of the overcoat, you know," he added. "I mean, do you see anything in the prints likely to give us any material help in solving the riddle of how he came to be on the railway line?"

The inspector, after a mental recapitulation of his examination, intimated that he saw no further facts of importance in them.

"Now, I find them extraordinarily interesting," said the doctor. He oozed satisfaction. "I'll give you a clue. You must have noticed that the outside of the heels of Canley's shoes are considerably worn down. The natural assumption is that the man took long strides and came down with his feet splayed a little. Most men who stride do so."

The inspector took up the point. "You mean that the distance between the sets of prints is shorter than one would expect for the length of Canley's legs, sir? I had thought of that, but the man, you remember, was mounting a slope."

"Well," said the doctor, who, after a momentary anticipation as the inspector began to speak, was now beginning to look unhappy. "I agree with that, so far as it goes. But what else?"

"M'm!" said the inspector. He felt that something more was expected of him, and gazed into nothingness.

"Possibly," suggested the scientist, "a still closer scrutiny of the prints may lead you to a further conclusion." He proffered his lens. Mackenzie bent down and stared hard through it, without adding anything further to his store of knowledge—and said so.

"Never mind." The doctor sounded regretful. "Perhaps it will occur to you in the lane where there are, I think you told me, a number of other prints. In the meantime it may be advisable to preserve the more plainly marked of these impressions. The weather may deteriorate and we should lose some valuable evidence."

Merry had forestalled the intention. He had opened the Box of Tricks and taken from it a collapsible bowl, a water-bottle and a packet of Plaster of Paris. He proceeded to mix the water and plaster in the bowl to the consistency of thick paste. The doctor himself, exploring the box, extracted an insecticide spray and from it blew a layer of dust into the first two of the prints. The inspector eyed the process with curiosity.

"Shellac," Manson explained. "Just a safeguard to prevent the paste when it is poured in, obliterating the more delicate points of the impressions. It is not absolutely necessary, but in this case I think it advisable."

He took from Merry the bowl of plaster and with the spoon ladled the mixture into the prints until the outline of the impress was covered. Then, while it was setting a little more stiffly, he broke a few twigs from a bush on the embankment and arranged them cross and longwise over the plaster afterwards pouring more plaster on to the thickness of the print.

"The twigs?" He answered the unspoken question of Mackenzie. "To strengthen the cast and bind it more firmly."

Within a minute or so the casts were sufficiently hard to be lifted. Doctor Manson examined them closely.

"Excellent," he pronounced, and wrapping them in separate rolls of tissue paper, placed them carefully in the Box of Tricks.

"Now, Inspector," he said, "while Merry and Inspector Kenway here take one or two more casts here and elsewhere, we might walk to Canley's cottage, making one or two observations in the lane, if necessary."

Inspector Mackenzie led the way, keeping carefully to the grass verge and pointing out the trail of footsteps as they walked. He dilated on them.

"You see, Doctor Manson," he said, "they are quite steady. That is why I do not think the man was drunk. There is no sign at all of staggering."

The doctor protested. "I have never suggested that he *was* drunk," he said, plaintively. "The suggestion came from you in the form of a question. Nor, on the other hand, have I denied it. It seems. . . . Ah! here is an excellent print."

He had stopped beside a circle of clayey earth and was looking down at a perfect imprint of a shoe sharply outlined in soil that was still damp. Once again he examined the exhibit with cryptic concentration, and then turned his gaze speculatively on the inspector.

"I should say, Mackenzie, that you at a rough guess are the same weight and height as Canley?"

"As near as makes no matter, I should think, sir."

"Then would you go a few steps up the lane and then walk back, taking care to step in this soft spot alongside the mark already there. Proceed as you would if you were walking casually along to the short cut."

On the print resulting from this operation the doctor expended more of the meticulous care with which he had hitherto examined all the other footprints.

"Illuminating," he said. His voice exuded satisfaction. "Most illuminating. Much as I expected, but pleasantly confirming."

"Of what, Doctor?" Mackenzie inspected the two prints without finding anything to cheer about.

"Not even in the heels, Mackenzie?" Manson chaffed him. "No? Well, let us get on."

A few more steps brought them to the end of the tall hedge which had hitherto lined the side of the lane, and Canley's cottage came into view. It was a two-storey structure built with brownish-yellowish bricks in the square-box shape customary with rural cottages. Doctor Manson put its age at probably thirty years, since the roof was of rough tiles. They had probably been a shade of dark brown but were now green with moss and weather-stain, except where rain had poured down round the sides of the chimney-stack keeping a clear passage as does a centre stream of water in a weed-choked river.

The cottage stood some twenty yards back from the road. Its garden was bounded on the two sides by tall hedges, these being linked up by a privet. The inspector, pushing open the gate, drew attention to the path. Along it, here and there, a number of footprints stood muddily, but not obtrusively muddily, against the light cement of the stones.

"Coming and going, sir," he said. Manson thought the explanation a trifle redundant. "And undoubtedly the same shoes as those in the lane." He pointed to the marks of the patch.

"Yes," said Manson, promptly. "Quite definitely, yes."

This disconcerting and unexpected agreement with one of his suggestions encouraged Mackenzie to draw his bow at another venture. "I think they make things a little clearer, Doctor?" he said.

"They certainly do, Mackenzie." Manson beamed. "I would go even further and look upon them as a definite pointer to the manner of Canley's demise. But what evidence do you find in them yourself?"

The inspector mentally marshalled his facts and having filed them in due order, unloaded them in a rota. "There are two or three omissions, sir, which have a bearing on the evidence of the path," he began. "One of them concerns this lane. Yesterday was a day of rain-showers. The lane is overhung by tall trees, as you can see. The result is that it is nearly always damp, even in summer-time.

"Now, the daily woman arrived at eight o'clock. She made breakfast. Canley left the house, according to her, at ten o'clock, and he was back again at eleven. He went out once more some time later. I don't know when, but he was in again at five in the afternoon."

"There is a note on a pad by the telephone with a number written on it. I telephoned the number and the person there said that he telephoned Canley at five, or a few minutes later, was to be called back and gave his phone number which Canley wrote down and repeated back to him. That places the time. Then at eight o'clock in the evening the woman arrived again to prepare the evening meal. Canley was not in the house then, nor had he come in when she left at nine o'clock. Is that clear, sir?"

"Splendidly clear, Inspector."

"Now, all these comings and goings, in view of the state of the lane, would have left their marks on the path, except for one thing—the rain. There is none of them. Rain has washed them all clear. We are left with the sole prints of Canley himself." The inspector became slightly dramatic.

"It ceased raining at ten-thirty o'clock. We know that Canley returned to the house at some time, because the meal prepared by the woman has been eaten. Therefore, these marks were made after the rain had ceased—after ten-thirty o'clock. They are Canley's prints, coming and going, *and there are no others.* He was, therefore, alone in the house."

"M'm!" said the doctor. The comment was strictly noncommittal. "And the order of the making of the prints? Have you any ideas on that?"

Mackenzie became fretfully petulant. "Well, sir, he couldn't very well have come out if he had not gone in, could he?" It seemed a reasonable assumption. His eyes wandered casually over the prints, and then brightened suddenly. "But, as a matter of fact, you will see that in one or two instances the outward prints are imposed partly on those pointing inwards which seems to settle it."

"Then that's that," said Doctor Manson. The inspector stole a glance at him; there was something in the intonation that sent a wave of misgiving over him.

Doctor Manson was walking up the path towards the cottage. He stretched out his hand to the knob and was a little jolted to find it slip through his fingers and the door turn slowly open, apparently of its own volition. "Open Sesame," he muttered.

Mackenzie laughed, the first sign of light-heartedness he had shown since the inquiry began. "It will be the constable, I expect," he explained, and peered into the dark interior of the hall. The constable did, in fact, materialize from the shadows and switched on a light. It disclosed the hall as a small oblong-shaped lobby, with doors each side facing each other, and one at the top end.

"That is the kitchen, Doctor," said the inspector, and led the way into it. He pointed to the dinner things still in the sink, and unwashed. "The remains of Canley's meal. I told the woman to leave them there as they were."

"She did not put them there, then?"

"No. Canley himself always carried the dirty dishes into the kitchen and dumped them in the sink ready for her in the morning. So we know it was Canley who ate the meal."

"Did he eat in here?"

"No. In the sitting-room. That is the door on the left of the hall as we came in. He carried the dishes from there. Then he seems to have returned to the sitting-room, settled down to drinks and a smoke and then, for some reason we don't know, turned out again and walked to the railway line. Do you not think so?"

"Er—what, Inspector?" The doctor spoke absently. He was looking at the hall stand. "Is that day woman here now?" he asked.

"That I am." The voice floated down from above them. It was followed by an angular belligerent figure in a dingy dress which swept the ground. The woman's forbidding aspect was emphasized by a boned collar. She wore with it an air so militant as to look positively destructive.

"That I am," she repeated, "and I want to know how long I'm supposed to stay. Skelton's the name, Hannah Skelton, a respectable married woman, with five children what are waiting for me, and a husband to cook a meal for. I've got me work to do as well and can't hang about here for—" She paused to draw breath, and Doctor Manson intervened before she succeeded.

"Tell me, Mrs. Skelton," he asked, "did the late Mr. Canley wear a hat?"

"A hat!" she snorted. "'Course he wore a hat. Who do you suppose wore 'em if he didn't?" She jerked her head in the direction of the hall stand.

"Then I wonder," mused the doctor, quietly, "why he didn't wear one last night?"

Mrs. Skelton stared at him and turned again to the stand. Two hats hung there. Sudden surprise illuminated her face. "Now, that's funny," she said. "They're there. What was he a'thinking of to go out without his hat. And a night like last night. He might'a caught his death o' cold."

"As it happened, he caught it in another way, madam," Manson reminded her, grimly humorous. "He hadn't bought a new one, I suppose?"

"Not him, Mister. He wasn't the sort to go buying new hats when he had two of 'em here."

"A careful man, eh? All right, Mrs. Skelton. You hurry off home and cook your husband's dinner now. But come back here for half an hour or so in the afternoon."

The woman's going was followed by the arrival of Inspector Kenway, reporting progress. "Merry is just taking a last cast of a print in the lane. He thinks it's interesting, Doctor," he explained. "He'll be along in a few minutes. Oh, and the men report that there is no sign of a hat anywhere. Your sergeant's here, too, Inspector, and the constable is still on guard on the line. I think that's all. You made any progress, Doctor?"

"A little, Kenway, I—"

The telephone rang. Kenway, standing beside it, lifted the receiver and listened. "For you, Doctor," he said. Manson took it. A few smothered words came over the wire to the ears of the other three.

"And no other injuries of any kind?" inquired the doctor. "Many thanks. It's what I expected you *not* to find." He chuckled, at the laugh that came over the instrument at the *bon mot*, and hung up.

"That," he announced, "was your police surgeon, Mackenzie. He found one or two abrasions on the hands and arms, but no other injuries other than the severed head."

"Isn't that enough, Doctor?" Kenway giggled. Inspector Mackenzie seemed stupefied.

"No. It is *not* enough, Kenway."

Mackenzie found his voice. "His head was cut off," he said. "That would kill *any* man. Why worry about any other wounds? We've got a mountain; no need to make one out of molehills."

Doctor Manson stared at him in astonishment. He had not judged the inspector capable of a literary simile. Mackenzie met his stare with an abashed and faintly furtive look, as might have done a Roman leader venturing to question the prognostications of an Augur on the Capitoline Hill. He licked dry lips.

"There again, Inspector, you are accepting as definite what appears to be the obvious," said Doctor Manson. "The very thing against which I warned you just now. I do not think you are doing yourself justice. Suppose that Canley had been knocked down by the train"— he propounded a theory—"and had not fallen with his head over the rail, and had not been killed. Would you have expected him to have risen and walked away, leaving the train trundling on at twenty miles an hour?"

"Not quite, Doctor," answered the inspector.

"Why not?"

"Well, he'd have had a bit of a shock and he would certainly have had a few black and blue—" He stopped.

"Bruises, Mackenzie?" Doctor Manson interposed. "Is that what you were about to say? If so, by all means complete the sentence. You are right, you know. And because I saw no sign of violence other than the decapitation, I asked Doctor Gaunt to let me know at once whether there were any bodily injuries or bruising."

The inspector grinned a little sheepishly. "I should have seen that, of course," he admitted. "Can't think how I missed it."

"Because, as I have told you, you were misled by the obvious," retorted Manson. "The man was on a short cut on the line with his head cut off. *Ergo*, he was knocked down by a train. Never accept the obvious, Inspector. Always test an alternative. If the obvious is correct, you have not lost anything; if it isn't, you've gained something."

"Doctor Manson?" The voice came from the sergeant who had been following the lecture with interest. The company turned towards him. "You told Dr. Gaunt over the telephone that you had expected him *not* to find any injuries," he said. "Do you mean by that that you knew all the time that the man had not been knocked down by the train?"

Mackenzie transferred his gaze from his sergeant to the doctor. He waited anxiously for the answer. Something of the Yard's respect for Doctor Manson was beginning to penetrate into Mackenzie's understanding.

"I was sure of it," said the doctor. He met Mackenzie's gaze. "And you must admit, inspector, that I tried to make you see it when I referred to the undamaged state of Canley's overcoat. If you were struck by a train travelling at that speed and hurled to the ground, which in this case is composed of rough and sharp flints, would you expect that nice blue overcoat of yours to escape without a rent, a tear or an abrasion of any kind on the nap? You see, man, you were blinded in your judgment by superficial appearances."

Mackenzie slowly digested this essay on observation and deduction from observation. He was a cumbersome thinker, and it took some time. Presently, however, his jaw dropped, and a look of consternation spread over his face.

"Then how did the man come to be decapitated, Doctor, if he was not knocked down by the train?"

"Suicide!" burst out the sergeant. "That's it. He committed suicide. Just laid down and put his head over the rail."

"The doctor has said that he ruled out suicide," pointed out Inspector Kenway.

The sergeant looked flummoxed, but not defeated. "Perhaps the further inspection has changed his mind," he said.

Mackenzie looked at the doctor. "Is that it, sir?" he asked.

For the first time since the investigation began, the doctor allowed himself a smile.

"Not unless he was able to double his own death, Inspector," he answered. *"Not unless a dead man can get up, smoke a cigar, walk a hundred yards or so, and climb up a bank."*

CHAPTER XIV

"A DEAD man!"

The exclamation came in a wail from Inspector Mackenzie. Like David mourning for Jonathan, or Saul for Absalom. "Do you say, then, that the train did not kill Canley at all?"

In so sinister a possibility Mackenzie saw his whole morning's work of laborious tracing of the tradings of Canley from his house, along the lane and up to the railway track, gone for nothing, together with his worked-out theory of the tragedy.

Doctor Manson shrugged his shoulders. He had not from the first gained any great opinion of the capabilities of Mackenzie. But he was prepared to put down the overlooking of what, to his mind, were vital facts to that officer's small experience of homicide.

There was not, he realized, a great deal of practice in such crimes in places like Thames Pagnall and the surrounding area; and when a case of homicide developed, the local people usually called in Scotland Yard. Without actual experience of homicide, and the requisite knowledge of medical jurisprudence gained by such practice, excuses could be made for omissions by local officers, whatever their rank.

It was true, the scientist knew, that a certain amount of elementary background can be acquired by reading and study; but the difference between an academical knowledge and the ability to see in actual surroundings and circumstances the points that can be adduced from books, is a very different matter. In any case, he thought it unlikely that there would be such textbooks as Gross's *Criminal Investigation* or Smith's *Forensic Medicine* in the police station of Thames Pagnall, of at the junction for that matter.

But he had hoped that the peculiarities in the case upon which he had patiently dwelt, and the hints conveyed in his examination of the body and the ground, particularly in the case of the footprints, which the inspector himself had made side by side with those of Canley in the lane, would have awakened some suspicion in the inspector's mind. It was obvious, however, that he had seen nothing of the implications of any of these things; his surprise at the possibility of the man being dead before the train decapitated him proved that. Meanwhile, he was waiting for an answer to his question. Doctor Manson supplied it. He replied quietly, without apparent interest in his conclusions. He stated it not as a suggestion, nor as a possible conclusion, but pertinently as an established fact. "It was obvious to me within a few minutes of seeing the body that the man had not been killed by the train," he said.

Mackenzie gazed at him in bewilderment. He knew of the doctor as what the Force called a book-learning detective, and book-learning did not always conform with the facts required by detection, any more than theory always works out in fact. Inspector Mackenzie wondered whether he might suggest something of the kind and put it to his distinguished colleague that he might be wrong. He decided to get round the point in another way.

"But Doctor Manson," he said. "Look at the facts. The man is on the line and he is dead. He has in fact lost his head, which is lying by the side of the rails. Moreover, his blood is spilt between the rails, and a cigar which he was undoubtedly smoking is a few yards farther down the line. You say he was not killed by the train. Why, Doctor Manson? Why?"

"May I ask you a few questions?" replied the scientist, surprisingly. Mackenzie nodded.

"Then, they are concerned with three points of investigation, Mackenzie. When I arrived at the scene you pointed out to me an area of bloodstains. Had you measured those bloodstains. Inspector?"

"No, Doctor?"

"Why not?"

Mackenzie looked his astonishment. "Why not?" he echoed. "Why should I, sir. There was the man, and there were the blood-stains. It obviously came from the body, minus the head."

"I see." Doctor Manson spoke a little peevishly. "Well, we'll leave that for the moment, and pass on to question number two. When you exposed the body to me, do you remember what you said?"

Mackenzie thought hard for a moment or two. "I can't say that I recall anything particular, sir," he answered. "All I can think of is that I assured you that the body was exactly as we had found it."

"That is what I meant, Inspector."

Mackenzie scratched his head. "Well, so it was, sir," he insisted. "The plate-layer if you remember confirmed that."

"I know he did, Mackenzie. Now the third question. When I inquired of you if the train had been examined, what did you reply?"

"That it had, sir. And that there was blood on the wheels of the second bogie of the leading coach."

Doctor Manson nodded confirmatory agreement. "After that I made a remark. It was more of a thought spoken aloud, but you answered it. Do you recall that, by any chance?"

Mackenzie peered back into the recesses of his mind, contorting his face into a painful physical effort of thought. He shook his head. "I can't place anything particular, Doctor," he answered.

"Well Mackenzie, I said 'and blood, of course, on the under-carriage. You answered. . . .'"

"No." The inspector supplied the answer. "There isn't any blood on the undercarriage, either," he confirmed.

"Quite so." Doctor Manson nodded. "Now, your answers to those three questions told me that the man had not been killed by the train. From that moment I ceased any investigation into the cause of the man's death, and concentrated all my efforts into the *circumstances* of his death. That is the answer to your question to me why within a few minutes of seeing the body I knew that Canley had not been killed by the train." He ceased speaking and eyed the inspector interestedly.

There was silence for a moment or two. Then: "You don't see the significance of them even now, Inspector?" asked Manson. Mackenzie shook his head.

"Then we'll take the consequences arising from your answers one at a time," said Manson. "Tell me what cases of violent death you have been associated with?"

"A few drownings in the Mole, sir. And a couple of stabbings when I was in Guildford as a constable."

"Any collisions with vehicles, shall we say?"

"Yes, sir. A woman knocked down and killed by a motorcar a few months ago."

"How was she found—I mean her condition?"

"In the middle of the road."

Doctor Manson made a gesture of impatience. "Crumpled up, I suppose?"

"Oh, yes, sir. All in a heap, so to speak."

"Quite so. That is the usual way, of course. Sent sprawling in a heap. Yet you want to tell me that this man, hit by a very substantial train, was left lying peacefully on his back as if he had gone to sleep in a natural way, Inspector, without, as we have already agreed, having his overcoat scratched or torn. Of course, a man might have fallen like that but it is a thousand to one against it. That is why I asked if you meant it literally when you said the body was exactly as found. You see that, now?"

Inspector Mackenzie nodded glumly.

"Good. Now we'll take the question of the area of the bloodstains which you did not measure. You did not record the area because you assumed that as the man had been decapitated by the train there were bound to be bloodstains, and hey presto, there they were. Can you remember the area covered by the stains on the track?"

"Eighteen inches one way and a couple of feet the other," said Kenway before Mackenzie could recall the figures. "Merry wrote them down," he added.

"Yes. Eighteen by twenty-four." Manson repeated the words slowly and with emphasis. "It worried me." He looked up sharply. "Does it worry you, now, Inspector?" he demanded.

"Doctor?" Kenway suddenly interrupted the questioning. Doctor Manson turned towards him. "Yes, Kenway?" he asked.

"Re the lying flat on his back. Would that not be a natural way for a man to lie if he were committing suicide?"

"It would, Kenway. Either that way or on his stomach, if he feared to see the train overtaking him."

"Then might not suicide be the solution? I remember that you ruled out suicide, so you told the railway doctor."

"I did for a few moments consider suicide as a possibility, Kenway," replied Manson, "but Inspector Mackenzie's statement about the undercarriage of the train disposed of that. That brings us back to the area of bloodstains."

"My statement?" Mackenzie looked up, startled. "How was that, sir?"

"You haven't answered the question that I asked you," retorted Manson. "I wanted to know whether the area of the bloodstains worried you at all now?"

"N-no," said Mackenzie, and appeared a little doubtful about it. He felt that if they worried the scientist, there was apparently something which should make him, too, concerned.

"Um! Have you ever seen a man beheaded? Guillotined, shall I say?"

"No, sir. I have not." Mackenzie shuddered at the thought.

"And I suppose you have not any knowledge of the action of the heart on the arteries, or the blood in them?"

The inspector, who had risen naturally in seniority from a street beat, disclaimed any knowledge of anatomy.

"Then let me illustrate the point with a few simple facts about the heart, Inspector. The heart is the most efficient motor in the world. It goes on and on every second of the day and night without any of the frequent breakdowns of the mechanical motor. Its daily performance is equivalent to the energy required to lift a load of 40,000 lb. one yard, or an elevator containing three persons a height of 100 yards. Every twenty-four hours it despatches into the circulatory system of the body 20,000 pints of blood, pumping it through the arteries. And the power of the pumping I have already given you as being able to lift three persons in an elevator 100 yards into the air during the course of a day."

The inspector fought valiantly against the boredom creeping over him. Doctor Manson continued. "Supposing you have a pump, Mackenzie, pumping up water, and you suddenly severed the pipe at any point along the system. What would happen?" Mackenzie grasped the simile. So did the sergeant. "It would gush out." The answer came from them simultaneously.

"Quite!" Doctor Manson looked pleased by the realization. "And so it is with a decapitated person. I have seen a man guillotined. So soon as the head is severed, the blood spouts from the neck artery in a gush, projecting the stream some three or four feet, probably more. Now you see why the blood area of eighteen inches by two feet worried me. I realized that the little area shown on the railway track was incompatible with the amount, which should have been left by the beheading. But there was one point in my mind which could still leave little blood there and not yet negative the idea of suicide."

"And that, sir?" asked Mackenzie.

"That the stream of blood might have gushed *upwards* and distributed its force on the undercarriage of the train . . ."

"I get it, Doctor," said Kenway. "And when Inspector Mackenzie said there was no blood on the undercarriage . . ."

"Then I knew, Kenway, that the man was dead when the train ran over him."

Mackenzie digested this explanation with considerable misgiving. It appeared to put him in an even worse position. Kenway came to his assistance.

"I suppose, Doctor, he *could* have died on the line while going over the short cut?" he asked. "And have fallen the way he was found? A man in a sudden heart attack, or in a fit, generally drops flat."

"Nothing *in the attitude of Canley's body*, when found, discredits the possibility." Manson emphasized the qualifying words.

"Then that's it," whooped Mackenzie, and rubbed his hands.

"Only he didn't die on the line," added Manson, devastatingly.

Mackenzie bowed under this new blow. The sergeant rubbed a hand over his unshaven chin and whispered to Kenway.

"Bunny wishes to ask, Doctor," Kenway interpreted, "how come about not dying on the line?"

"A pertinent question, Kenway, and one raising interesting possibilities. But too long to explain at the moment. Let us get the man on the line first."

"He didn't die on the line . . . he was on the line . . . and the train ran over his body." Inspector Mackenzie declaimed like a schoolboy reciting blank verse. He thought it over. "That can only mean that he was *taken* there, Doctor." He put the statement as a query.

"Well, Inspector," challenged the Doctor. "And what is wrong with that?"

"The person, or persons, who took him there had to arrive at and leave the spot," Kenway said ruminatingly. He made it sound like an algebraical equation.

"And there is no trace whatever of a second person," said Mackenzie, triumphantly. "Only Canley's footsteps going and not coming from." He placed the doctor in the position of having his back to the wall.

Manson stared at them and then began to laugh—silently at first, and then loudly. *"Cucullus non facit monachum,"* he said. "The cowl does not make a monk. In other words, do not look at the coat but at what lies under the coat. I gather you did not study logic, Mackenzie?"

"They didn't teach logic at the Board School, sir," the detective said, reproachfully.

"No! They don't even teach it in the present elementary schools, Inspector. How they expect children to think correctly, I don't know. But there, that has nothing to do with us and this problem. However, a little lesson in logic ought to be beneficial here. You have said that there is no trace of anyone having been on the scene other than Canley who was found dead?" Mackenzie nodded.

"And you have now agreed with me, following the description of what happens when a living man is decapitated, that Canley was not alive when the train severed his head?"

Another nod, after some hesitation.

"You will agree with me that a dead man cannot walk up an embankment and on to a line and throw away a cigar of his own volition?"

Once again Mackenzie nodded his head. He looked like a rabbit being mesmerized by a watching serpent.

"I have said that Canley did not die on the line, and that a natural outcome of that is that he was taken there."

Mackenzie waited.

"Then what do you mean by saying that there is no trace of anyone other than Canley having been on the scene? The very circumstances which we have discovered *proves* that someone else was on the line with Canley. If someone was there, then there is evidence somewhere that they *were* there. What you mean, Mackenzie, is that there is no *obvious* evidence of their presence. It has to be searched for.

"There was a case some years ago which might illustrate the point. The landlady of a boarding house, unable to make a woman guest in a room answer her knocks, sought the help of a man living in the house. He secured a ladder and with the help of a stranger called on from the street, he climbed the ladder to the window of the room, which was on the second floor. He broke a pane of glass in the window, unfastened the catch, pushed up the window and climbed in. Within a minute he was out of the room again on the ladder shouting 'murder', and calling for the man below to fetch the police. When questioned later, he said that he had left the room exactly as he found it.

"The police found the woman dead on the floor with a bullet in her head. Now the room door was locked, with the key still in the lock. And it was bolted from the inside. The window as we have seen was fastened from the inside. There was no way of getting into the room from the outside. A revolver was in the right hand of the dead woman. If ever there was an obvious suicide, this was it. Yet, there was one little mistake on the part of a murderer that gave it away—the revolver was held in such a manner that the woman could not have fired it herself." Doctor Manson paused for comment.

"There is nobody in the room except the woman, and it was bolted from the inside?" Inspector Mackenzie wrinkled his brows. "Then how was the woman killed, Doctor?"

"By the man who entered by the door, committed the deed, left by the door which he afterwards locked by turning the key with a pair of pliers, Mackenzie."

"But the shot bolt, sir?" The question came from Sergeant Bunny.

"That, Sergeant, gave the murderer away. There was one person who could logically have shot that bolt, and one person only. It was as logical as the day follows night. It is a nice little problem for you to solve."

The three men reviewed the circumstances; they wrestled keenly for the key to the riddle; and failed.

"Who was it, Doctor?" asked Kenway. Manson smiled, broadly.

"You, Kenway, ought to have seen it," he chided. "The only person who could have shot the bolt, and was therefore the murderer, was the helpful man who climbed up to the window with the landlady and the stranger watching, broke the pane, released the window catch, climbed in, reappeared and called for the police to be fetched. During the seconds he was in the room *he stepped across to the door and shot the bolt*, thus rendering the room inaccessible, seemingly, from the outside.

"He, you see, overstepped himself in his anxiety to show that nobody could have got to the woman."

He became grimmer. "There is a similar carelessness in the case of Canley," he added.

"Do you mean that you have found evidence that there was someone with Canley on the line?" demanded Inspector Mackenzie.

"My view, Inspector, is that there is ample evidence."

The inspector groaned. "You mean it's a case of murder?" Depression centred over and around him. The last thing he wanted on his hands was a murder investigation.

"Not so far." The doctor spoke comfortingly, and in reflective tones. "Canley *might* have died naturally. I can conceive certain circumstances in which he could have come by a natural death in the presence of a companion who did not want to face questioning."

"Conspiracy in an unlawful act?" queried Kenway.

"It could be, but not necessarily, Kenway. Canley and his companion could have been in some place, and with company or material with which it would have been inconvenient for them both to have been found. To avert such a discovery the companion, it is possible, staged the supposed accident. I am not putting that forward as a definite view," he warned. "It is merely a reasonable supposition until further investigation supports or destroys it."

The conversation at this stage was halted by a loud clanging in the roadway, followed by a screeching, and ending with a wail like that of a frightened banshee or a doomed soul in torment. Doctor Manson jerked into involuntary tautness.

"What in God's name is that?" he gasped.

"Sounds like Ypres." Inspector Mackenzie giggled.

"Like Ypres! It sounds like the entire battlefield of France in action at one and the same time. What, may I ask, is Ypres?"

"My Chief Constable's car," said Mackenzie. He volunteered an explanation. "That's the name he calls it."

He walked to the door and looked out. "Yes, that's him in person," he announced. "Here he comes—the old warhorse."

CHAPTER XV

COLONEL Mainforce, Chief Constable, ex-Guards officer, stood six feet two inches in his socks, and was broad in proportion. A military moustache bristled white and fiercely above shoulders that were as straight and pretty nearly as powerful as they had been in the war that was to end all wars, and didn't. He was never tired of telling the story of how he had on one occasion seized two Germans who came at him one in each hand, held them off their feet and cracked their heads together until their skulls were fractured.

Doctor Manson and he had met on a number of occasions, both official and privately. The doctor standing at the back of the hall now watched him emerge from the innards of Ypres. Kenway watched, too, and grinned. "I know now," he said, "how a chicken gets out of an egg." The simile was particularly apt. The Colonel's head first appeared through the crack that was the open door. A breadth of shoulder followed then, at the expense of a variety of contortions, a leg appeared, followed by more body, and another leg, until at last the height of the Colonel stretched out to its full and the breadth spread comfortably.

The Colonel advanced heavily up the path and stood at the door peering into the shadows of the hall. He half-glimpsed the figure of his inspector. He bellowed:

"Ah! There you are, Mackenzie. What the hell is all this fuss and bother over a railway accident? Wasting a whole morning." He entered the cottage as he was speaking and spotted a second person. He peered again—uttered a sharp exclamation.

"God bless my soul! Is that you, Manson?" he asked. "What the thunder are you doing here?"

The awful thought struck him.

"Hey!" he roared. "You aren't bringing one of your blasted corpses here, are you?" He glared malignantly. "The last time you were here some damn' nit-wit saw a magpie flying round the place, and he and you landed us with a murder.[2] You aren't on the same lay again, are you?" He became entreating. "For the Love of Mike don't say you are."

Doctor Manson smiled delightedly. "I am, I fear, an Augury of Desolation, Mainforce. I bring bad tidings."

"You've brought another bloody body, I know it," he wailed. "What's it all about?" He pointed an accusing finger at his inspector.

"The doctor says the fellow wasn't killed by the train," announced Mackenzie. "He thinks somebody put him there after he was dead."

"He does? Then he's dead sure right," replied the Colonel, and did not see his pun. "What the hell for," he added, as an afterthought.

Manson, relegated to the role of third person, listened enchantedly to the duologue. The inspector detailed to his chief the extent of the information gleaned from the inspection of the line, the path and the lane.

"Blood on the track did you say, Mackenzie?" he boomed. "Ah, then that makes it all right. Wounds made on dead bodies don't bleed. Been a soldier too long not to know that."

"No more they do. But if the blood is still liquid in the arteries, it will leak," said a voice from behind him. The Chief Constable swung round, to come face to face with Merry, the Yard's deputy scientist, who had come unheard up the path, and now stood in the doorway.

"Hell's bells!" roared the Chief Constable. "Here's the *other* one of the pair. Now it's a certainty. There's trouble . . . there's bloody murder. And how do you keep the blood liquid?" He reverted to the broken-off discussion.

"There are several ways," piped up Manson. "If the body is freshly dead, as it were, the blood will still run."

"And you think this man—what's his blasted name, Mackenzie?"

"Canley, Colonel."

"Then you think this man Canley—Lord, what a name!—was but newly dead, Doctor?"

"I didn't say that, Colonel," Manson corrected. "I don't know when he died."

"Well, anyway, he seems to have walked from here to the line, so he probably died there."

The doctor put a word in. "Oh, no, he didn't," he said.

"Didn't die on the line?" queried the Colonel.

2. *Murder isn't Cricket* by E & M.A. Radford.

"No. Didn't walk from here to the line." Manson paused for a fraction of time. "Come to that, I don't suppose he died on the line, either," he added.

"What!"

Men on the barrack square had jumped when the Colonel spoke with that inflexion of voice. His moustache was standing as stiffly as soldiers on parade. The hairs always bristled like the quills of a porcupine with the wind up when he was annoyed. They were that way now. He swung round from the doctor to his inspector.

"I thought you wrote in your interim report to me, Mackenzie, that you could trace the path of this man—er—Canley, isn't it?—from the garden path down the lane and up the embankment of the railway line. Dammit, man, didn't you check the prints up with his shoes?"

"I did that, Colonel. The shoes match the prints, and the prints match the shoes." Mackenzie, on safe ground there, passed the can to Doctor Manson. He expected at last to get somewhere in the investigation. The problem of the prints was one which he felt was on his side. The Colonel, still bristling, but not so ferociously, retreated on Manson.

"What the devil is going on here? What's the matter with my fellow, Manson?" he asked.

The doctor hauled the shoes of Canley from the Box of Tricks, and dangled them under the eyes of the Chief Constable. "Here they are, Mainforce, the identical shoes. I guarantee no deception, eh?" He looked at the inspector.

Mackenzie nodded sourly.

"Now I say that Canley did not walk in them from this cottage to the railway line. Everybody says he did. Very well, you come along to the line, Mainforce, and I'll prove to you that he didn't."

"Now we're going to get somewhere," said Kenway.

"And about time, too," said Sergeant Bunny, who had a secret fear that the Chief Constable, who had also been his commanding officer, was before long going to notice an eighth of an inch of bristle on his chin.

The company trekked down the lane—"on *safari*," said Merry, brightly. Twenty yards down it, Doctor Manson called a halt. They had reached the spot where Inspector Mackenzie had set his footprint against that of the Canley impress. The doctor pointed the fact out, and suggested a comparison.

The Chief Constable and Mackenzie regarded the exhibit, with mild interest on the part of the latter. He was a little anxious to reach the embankment. With a sniff of disappointment, the doctor started his convoy off again. He halted them for the second time at the bottom of the path leading up to the metals. The Colonel eyed the footsteps. "These them?" he asked, with a soldierly disregard for the elements of grammar.

"Those are they," Manson agreed. "I do not think we shall need them again, for we have casts of the more important specimens. So perhaps the inspector will help prove my case by climbing up the path, placing his feet alongside the prints already there."

"In his steps, or what would Mackenzie do!" Merry quoted disgracefully blasphemous.

"Off you go, Mackenzie," ordered the Chief Constable.

"We'll follow up the grass slope," said Manson.

Safely at the top the Chief Constable, Merry, Kenway and the sergeant gazed at the evidence of the walking.

"Additional evidence," said the doctor "is the fact that the path is a little less moist and squashy than it was last night, so soon after the cessation of the rain." He placed Canley's boots on the bank a foot apart and gazed at them approvingly.

Colonel Mainforce gazed at the boots and from them to Mackenzie and the prints just made, and back again.

"Damned if I can see anything in it, Manson," he protested. Mackenzie was looking round bewildered as a faun in search of a mother which had suddenly vanished *après midi*.

"Oh, yes, you can," retorted Manson. "You don't know you're looking at it." He chuckled. Merry caught his Chief's eye. He received an almost imperceptible nod and turned to the Chief Constable. "Mackenzie wants us to believe, Colonel," he said, "that Canley walked in those boots from the cottage and up this path in the same way that he has just walked. Well—look at Mackenzie's boots."

The eyes of the company sank from the inspector's face to his feet. Mackenzie coloured in embarrassment. He felt like a mannequin, and an untidy one at that; his boots were slimed to the thickness of the sole with clayey mud gathered from the lane and the path.

And then, not only Colonel Mainforce, but Mackenzie himself saw the scientist's point.

The boots of Canley were devoid of mud of any kind. They were dull and smeary, but not muddy.

"By gad! Of course," blurted the Chief Constable. "Must be losing me powers of observation." He paused. "But I still don't get it, Manson." He produced a cigarette and flipped his lighter. "You agree that the boots fit the prints—Blast the damn thing"—he was still flipping the unflaming lighter. Doctor Manson struck a match. "Thanks," said the Colonel, and drew a series of puffs.

"I still don't get it," he repeated. "You agree that the boots fit the prints. . . ."

"The patch on the sole is marked plainly enough," Mackenzie said in a highly pitched voice.

"I have never denied it," protested Manson. "In fact, I reaffirm that the tracks were made by these shoes. Now, what does *that* tell you?" He challenged with his voice as well as his words.

Inspector Mackenzie projected his mind into the realms of thought over the problem, but found the effort too much and gave it up. The argument he decided, was going haywire again.

"Do you mean," asked the Chief Constable, who had also engaged himself on the riddle, "do you mean that Canley's *shoes had been wiped clean of mud?*"

Doctor Manson clapped his hands in acclamation. "That, Colonel," he said, "is just what I *do* mean. The smeary marks are certainly such as would be made by the wiping. You will note," he added, "that it is the upper part of the shoes that have been wiped."

"Then that," said Mackenzie, in tones of deep depression, "answers the other thing of which you were so sure."

"That would be?" queried the scientist.

"That there was another person on the line at the same time. There'd be no reason for Canley to wipe his own shoes, would there?"

"Why not?" asked Manson, interestedly.

"Well, I don't suppose he was intending to camp out on the railway all night." The inspector in a sudden flare of deduction became sardonic. "To get off the track, he had either to cross the rails and go down the bank on the other side, or retrace his steps along the path by which he had climbed up, and return home. Either way the shoes would get muddy again. So why wipe them?"

"Excellent logic, Mackenzie. Now. . . ."

A head appeared with startling suddenness above the top of the embankment. It popped up right under the nose of the Chief Constable gazing, at that moment, into space. He started, slipped and recovered himself with the utmost difficulty from sliding down the bank. He gazed at the apparition, which climbed up with its body and revealed itself as the police surgeon. And he bellowed.

"Damn it all, Gaunt! What the Hades do you mean by popping out of nowhere like that?" he demanded. "Nearly shot my heart through me damn teeth."

Doctor Gaunt chortled. "Thought I was the ghost of Canley come back, I reckon," he retorted. "The dead *do* come back, you know. Sorry, Colonel." He apologized. "I'd finished the *post mortem* and went round to the cottage. The constable there said you had all come here, so I followed. Just climbed up the bank naturally. What do you want me to do? Whistle as a warning, or something?"

He blew through his teeth the opening bars of the 'Dead March' in *Saul*, but ceased abruptly on seeing a hue purpling the Chief Constable's face.

"To business," he said. "Very interesting corpse, Doctor Manson." He beamed on the company. "Very elusive one too. Enjoyed the exploration." He sounded as though he were proposing a vote of thanks to the late Mr. Canley. "You'll want all the gory details."

"Let's hear them, Gaunt," said Manson, pouring soothing oil on the troubled waters.

"First, the cause of death," said the surgeon.

"Yes?" asked Manson.

"Don't know." Gaunt blew out the words. "No idea," he added.

"What!" The Chief Constable stared. "And him with his head cut off?" he roared.

"Didn't kill him, Colonel. He was dead before that. Blood wasn't pumped out of him."

"What do you mean by that?" asked Mackenzie. "He'd die at once, wouldn't he, when his head was cut off."

"Aye, he'd die all right. But heart wouldn't necessarily stop dead—would make a couple of beats and gush blood through the neck artery. It didn't—that's all." He imparted finality to the words.

"What else?" demanded the Chief Constable.

"Nothing, Colonel. Fellow quite healthy, no sign of disease. Had had some whisky just before he died."

"Whisky wasn't doped, I suppose?" asked Mackenzie.

"No. Thought of that, Mac. No poison either, and no sleeping draught. Nothing. That's all the innards," he concluded.

"Marks?" suggested Doctor Manson.

"Few abrasions. Four, I think—no, three," he corrected, looking through his papers. "Made after death, as you suspected"—he nodded at Doctor Manson. "They didn't bleed, sure certain signs," he explained for the benefit of the remainder of the company.

Mackenzie scratched his head. He was still fighting hard for natural death. "Suppose, Doctor Gaunt, the man was on the line, hadn't heard the train and suddenly found it almost on top of him. Would the shock give him heart failure?"

"Aye, it could hae done that tae ony man, if he were a nervous chap."

"Ah!" said Mackenzie, *crescendo*.

"Only it didn't in this case," chortled Gaunt. "It was a good effort, Mac, but it didn't work."

"Why not?" challenged the inspector.

"Heart was natural," Dr. Gaunt explained. "No rupture, no dilation. Would have been if that had happened."

Doctor Manson gazed at him, thoughtfully. "What about the neck?" he asked. "Any injury there—apart from losing his head, of course."

Doctor Gaunt exploded into hysterical Homeric laughter. "Losing his head," he stammered. "Oh, Ho! . . . that's a good one. He lost his head and got it in the neck. Ho! Ho!" He coughed. "But there, nothing to jest about," he said, repentantly. "Ahem! Serious business."

He answered the scientist's question.

"There was a lot of bruising on the neck. Expected it, of course. Bound to be bruising. The neck would be hit and pushed along the lines a bit before the wheels crunched over it."

"And that is the only injury you can find?" asked Manson.

"That's all, Doctor. I had a good look round, of course."

Manson nodded approving acquiescence.

"Then that," he said, "is probably why he had his head cut off."

Gaunt stared. He passed a hand through his sparse locks, rubbing them in puzzlement. "I dinna get that, Doctor!" he said.

Mackenzie grunted. He also stared. "Why he had his head cut off?" he echoed. He made it sound as if the late Mr. Canley had with malice aforethought committed a kind of hara-kiri to set them a problem.

Doctor Manson eyed them both placidly and in mild surprise. "But, of course," he said, judiciously. "There is no alternative."

"I still dinna see it," protested the surgeon.

"Come, come, Gaunt." The doctor was amicably expostulatory. "The organs are healthy and the man did not die any sort of natural death?"

"Aye, mon. I hae said so."

"There is no heart failure. Yet he is dead?"

The surgeon nodded.

"His head was cut off. But that did not kill him. He was dead before that?"

"There's no doubt about that at all, Doctor," agreed the surgeon.

"And there are no marks on the body that could have led to an injury to cause death?" Gaunt nodded again, grimly.

"No *visible* injury." Doctor Manson emphasized the words. He registered disappointment at the inquiring look still on the face of the police surgeon. "Then, since the man is not alive, Gaunt," he went on, "it must follow, *ipso facto*, that the injury has been hidden. Then logically, the only place where there could be any hidden injury, unable to be traced medically, must be on the neck. In other words, the body *had* to be decapitated in order to hide it."

"Mon, ye hae it," said Gaunt. He slapped his hand in delight on the shoulders of Mackenzie. The inspector yowled, in startled pain.

"God bless me soul, Manson," said the Chief Constable. "You mean that someone cut his ruddy throat?"

"No, I don't," retorted the scientist. But he made the assertion half-heartedly, and the wrinkles of doubt appeared in the corners of his eyes. He looked across at the police surgeon. Gaunt shook a negative head.

"The doctor's right, ye ken," he announced.

"How do you know?" demanded the Chief Constable. "You say yourself—or at least Manson does, that the injury has been hidden by the decapitation."

"Ye're no doctor, Chief Constable," retorted Gaunt. "The man's head would hae tae have been cut off with a saw if that were the case. A knife would hae made a *clean* cut in the throat or the neck. I'd hae seen it. I didna. That's all. There was no clean cut, only crushed and torn tissues."

"In any case, if his throat had been cut he would have bled to death before he reached the railway," put in Manson, unhelpfully. "And if it had been cut up here, the blood would have run in streams, and would certainly have run down. The blood on the line came from the decapitation," he added, making confusion more confounded.

The Chief Constable waved his hands in the air. He looked as though he was going off into hysterics. "Cor sufferin' crows," he bellowed. "Where are we getting now? He wasn't killed by the train. He was dead before the decapitation. Nobody cut his throat. And the blood from the body was caused by the beheading. Will somebody tell me something that makes sense." Manson smiled grimly. He was, he felt, beginning to see his way out of the maze. The doctor, he felt, could settle the matter once and for all if he could be led up to the point without he, Manson, putting a leading question.

"When I examined the body first," he explained to the company, "I realized that the decapitation was a staged one. But the reason for staging was not so obvious. Was it to hide violence of some kind. It seemed likely. But what violence? If death were due to poison being administered in some way by another person in the case, that person must have realized that the poison would be found, for every schoolboy knows, these days, that inquests are held in cases of sudden death, and a *post mortem* examination is made on all inquest victims. Such a *post mortem* would have disposed at once of any question of accidental death. It has puzzled me. But now, I think I see the reason for the staging of the decapitation?"

"That being?" asked the Chief Constable.

The doctor begged the question. Instead, he turned to the police surgeon. "Suppose, Gaunt," he said, "that someone wanted to kill Canley without showing trace of injury. Bearing in mind the subsequent decapitation, and that the throat could not be cut because of the loss of blood which would not be left to show the decapitation, where would be the one place, the only place, fatally *to hit him*?"

"Top of the spine, Doctor, I should say," said Gaunt. "The fatal spot—" He broke off and stared. The line of reasoning of the scientist had become suddenly clear to him.

"By gad, sir, that could do it," he said; and showed the excitement of a schoolboy at an unexpected discovery. "It would serve three purposes; conserve the blood for the beheading, the train wheels would obliterate the marks of the blow, or at least by their bruising would not allow an earlier bruise or bruises to be identifiable, and there would be the semblance of accident." He looked at the scientist in admiration. "What the devil made you think of that?" he solicited.

"A cigar stub," said Doctor Manson, cryptically.

"Eh, what?" demanded the Chief Constable. "Cigar stub? It's the first I've heard about that. Why does everybody keep things from me?" He became plaintive. Doctor Manson grinned.

"Now, now, Mainforce," he chided. "There's nothing whatever in it that could have helped you had you known about it," he said. "When I saw the body on the line I decided straight away that he had not been knocked down by the train. I've told you why, already. Nor that he had committed suicide. Later on I was certain that he had been placed there after death by someone else. But the fact confronted me that he might have been placed there after a natural death by someone who was with him at the time of death and did not want to be mixed up with an inquest, or in the business at all—"

"Well, we know all that, Doctor. What about the cigar end?" The Chief Constable was becoming impatient.

"Coming to that now, Mainforce. Don't rush me. I must explain in continuity. It was Mackenzie who told me that he had picked up a cigar stub some few yards down the line. He explained that it had apparently been knocked out of Canley's mouth when he was hit by the train—"

"I see," interrupted the inspector. "As he was dead, and had not been knocked down by the train, the cigar stub must have been planted for us to find?"

The scientist nodded acceptance of the hypothesis.

"Hold hard," said the Chief Constable. "How the devil do either of you know that the cigar belonged to Canley. Might have been thrown out of a carriage window by a passenger."

"There was cigar leaf in Canley's mouth, Mainforce," put in Manson. "Only a small piece, but quite big enough."

"Huh!" said the Chief Constable. "Answer for damn near everything."

Doctor Manson switched the conversation from its wanderings back to the question of the blow. "Could the bruising you found on the neck, Gaunt, have been caused by such a blow at the top of the spine. The blow would have to be sufficiently strong to cause death, you know?"

"Could be." The surgeon fumbled for his spectacles. "I wouldn't like to swear that it *was* caused that way, but there is nothing incompatible with the suggestion."

He stampeded suddenly. "Hoicks!" he whooped. "The only chap I ever knew to get it in the neck twice."

The Chief Constable glared. Gaunt subsided, abashed. A hand dived into a waistcoat pocket and emerged flourishing a watch. "Well, I'd better be getting off." He thrust the *post mortem* report into Doctor Manson's hands, and disappeared below the embankment.

For a moment or two all were silent. Colonel Mainforce mopped his forehead with a huge yellow handkerchief. "That a serious suggestion?" he asked the doctor.

"Quite serious, Colonel. I have little doubt that that is what happened."

"Means murder, I suppose." The Chief Constable sighed. Then he exploded in annoyance. "Murder Hoodoo, that's what you are, damn you, Manson. You and Merry. We are all set for a nice comfortable railway accident that would have stopped damn fools walking over the railway line in future. A nice accident with no trouble. And you run us in for another murder investigation. And Scotland Yard in it. All coming out of the rates. Fifteen and six in the pound they are now—"

Manson and Merry laughed together. The Chief Constable grinned sheepishly.

"You'd better come back, and have a spot of lunch with me," he said. "We can talk things over."

"Accepted!" said the doctor. "I'm a bit peckish. You spoilt my breakfast."

"Me?" The Chief Constable feigned indignation.

"Well, your dashed body did." He paused. "Just a moment," he said. He peeped into the lounge outside the door of which a police constable was on guard. "Keep this room just as it is until I have a chance to go over it, Inspector," he asked.

"In view of our later discoveries the room may be very important. It may hold the secret of Canley's death. Meanwhile, perhaps you will have a few inquiries made into the life of Canley in this village. It will be better if I have some idea of the personal character of the man and his associates."

He followed after the Chief Constable and the others. They piled into the car, and with a series of violent explosions started on the way to lunch.

CHAPTER XVI

THE Chief Constable's car clanged its way through Thames Pagnall, turned into the Portsmouth By-pass and followed the tip of its bonnet at a steady twelve miles an hour in the direction of Guildford, pursued by agonized glances from pedestrians.

Doctor Manson, himself a driver of considerable practice and expertness watched, fascinated, the 'play' in the steering wheel; the Chief Constable had to make nearly a complete turn of the wheel in order to deviate his course clear of a car standing at the side of the road.

"Have you a vehicle inspection department attached to your police force, Mainforce?" he asked.

The Colonel took one hand off the wheel and the car made straight for the pavement. Doctor Manson glimpsed the sins of his past life and sought absolution in time. The Colonel pulled his way clear before he answered the question. The fires of Hell retreated from the scientist's vision.

"We have, Manson, yes," said the Colonel. "And a very efficient one it is, too."

Doctor Manson chuckled. "I take it they do not operate with traction engines," he suggested.

"Traction engines?" echoed the Colonel. "No. We are only concerned under the Act with internal combustion engines. Steam traffic comes under the Ministry of Transport. Why?"

He turned, to see the doctor with his hands over his ears. He laughed. "Ah, I see," he said. "You mean old Ypres." He shook a concerned head. "I'm afraid she's nearly at her end," he said. "But she's an old favourite, you know. I drove her at Ypres, which is why she's got that name. Did good work. Thought, once, of recommending her for a medal or a badge or something. Like Old Bill, the London bus. I don't think Ypres did her much good. That and police work afterwards. Things keep falling out of the engine," he explained.

"It's a ruddy miracle the whole contraption doesn't fall in a heap," said Merry, in an atrocious pun on the name Ypres.

Past Sandown racecourse, Ypres steered an erratic course, and climbed up the busy main street at Esher, thronged with cars and shoppers. At the top, nearly opposite the ancient Bear Hotel, the Colonel, missing a van by inches, turned right—and emerged into so peaceful an oasis that Doctor Manson gasped in surprise.

Gone were the cars, the racket of noise, the throngs; instead, a verdant village green spread itself in virgin loveliness amidst a solitude surrounded by low, rambling cottages of a hundred or more years old, white-washed walls and red roofs, the tiles of which bore the green hallmark of genuine old age.

An ancient church looked greyly and benevolently over the old homes. A few slowly wending pedestrians pursued a leisurely course, in keeping with the quietude, on their lawful comings and goings. Fifty yards away the cars sped on their way noisily and the crowds bustled.

"What a haven," said Manson. The car drew up with a jerk and clatter. The Chief Constable squirmed out, in indication that their journey had ended. He looked his pleasure at the Doctor's surprise.

"Haven?" he echoed. "Nicest little spot in Surrey. Wouldn't believe it could exist, would you?"

"I wouldn't," said Merry.

"Mind you, it's been well known in its time. Beats me why Gray went all the way to Stoke Poges to write his dashed *Elegy*; he was always wandering round this churchyard. And it's a thunderin' sight better churchyard than the one he moaned over at Stoke Poges."

"He didn't," said Merry.

"Eh? Didn't what?" asked the Chief Constable.

"Didn't moan over Stoke Poges."

"Eh?" said the Colonel again.

"What Merry means, Mainforce," Doctor Manson explained, "is that it is extremely improbable that Stoke Poges was really the churchyard of the *Elegy*."

"Gray never said it was," put in Merry. "He never said which was his churchyard. A lot of guessers and wishful thinkers put it at Stoke Poges."

"Why?" demanded the Chief Constable.

"So far as I can see because his ma and sister lived there, and because he died in the place and was buried in the yard."

"Damnitall," objected the Chief Constable, "he describes the place, doesn't he?"

"Sure!" agreed Merry. "He says he heard the curfew tolling the knell of parting day. The only curfew round the place was at Windsor Castle. He must have had damn good hearing to have heard that at Stoke Poges, five miles away."

"H'm," said the Chief Constable, badly shaken, "sounds reasonable."

"That isn't all." Doctor Manson chuckled. "He also remarked on the rude forefathers of the hamlet and the ivy-mantled tower of the church. Ever seen Stoke Poges, Colonel?"

"Not to notice it, Manson. Been through it in the car, of course."

"There you are, you see. Going in for hearsay evidence, and you a policeman. Tch! Tch! There has never been ivy on the tower of Stoke Poges church, and it was always a well-known village with a rural council and never a hamlet."

"God bless me soul," said the Chief Constable. "Then where was his blasted churchyard?"

"Probably Upton, which was a real hamlet near Slough, and is now part of Slough. It still has its ivy-mantled tower, and the curfew could have been heard from Windsor Castle, because it's dashed near next door to the place. And Gray would have gone through Upton to reach Stoke Poges."

"God bless me soul," said the Chief Constable, again. "You mean to say that Stoke Poges pinched the blessed poem?"

"That," said Doctor Manson, "is what literary people and archaeologists believe."

"It was a bit of their old Bucks," supplemented Merry. The pun was received by the Chief Constable in silence. He was cogitating over the sad business of Stoke Poges and seemed, eventually, to arrive at a decision. "He'd have done better to have kept to Esher, which he knew," he said at last, decisively.

He pointed to a house in the middle distance. "See that place? Jane Porter's. She wrote all her novels there. And old John O'Keiffe lived round here, too—chappie who wrote *I am a Friar of Orders Grey*. George Meredith lived round the corner."

"Dear, dear, dear! The decline and fall of Esher," said Doctor Manson. "Now the place houses a Chief Constable."

"Decline and fall!" echoed the Colonel. "Funny you should mention that." He looked quite startled. "Old Gibbon was here—at school. But there, let's go and have that lunch. We've got to solve this Canley business, you know."

He entered the green front gate of a low double-bow window cottage that had in its heyday been the village chandler's. It was one of a number of such houses, each with its roses and creepers clinging lovingly to the old stone work, and each facing the old village green, soft and verdant with age and untouched by the hurrying feet of the busy traffic on the Portsmouth road just round the corner.

The Chief Constable inserted his latchkey into the keyhole, and then pulled up with a jerk.

"Good Lord," he said.

"Now, what's the matter?" asked Doctor Manson. The Colonel grinned. "Just remembered that I ought to have told Mrs. Crouch that you'd be coming to lunch," he said.

With a determination he did not feel, he opened the door, entered the tiny hall, and ushered his guests into the two rooms knocked into one that had made the delightful lounge-cum-living room. It was essentially a man's room, furnished with a mixture of antiquity and club-room comforts. He placed a drink in front of each of his guests, and then, squaring his shoulders, made for the kitchen.

He halted at the door as Mrs. Crouch smilingly looked up from the oven.

"Lunch won't be long, sir," she said. "I'm just dishing up."

"Ah, yes. Very nice," said the Colonel. He raised his voice to a challenging loudness. "I'm very sorry to say, Mrs. Crouch, that I've brought a couple of friends to lunch."

The woman rose slowly to her feet—and beyond. To the Chief Constable she seemed to grow and grow like the Genie out of the bottle. Her eyes flashed red and her hands dropped stiff beside her. Her bosom bulged forward like that of a pouter pigeon.

For one ghastly moment, the Chief Constable thought he would be unable to restrain his laughter as the thought flashed through his mind, 'no falsies there; solid roast-beef woman.'

"Well!" said Mrs. Crouch; and there was no further danger of laughter; he seemed to feel that he was going to be heavily chastised. Hastily, he rallied his forces, and pursued his intended advance. He closed the kitchen door behind him and whispered in a voice like a saw, "Mrs. Crouch, m'dear, the guests—very unexpected. Big noises from Scotland Yard. Everything depends on you. You've never let me down yet. I told the Commissioner, 'wonderful woman is Mrs. C. Would do anything for the Forces.' So now, Mrs. Crouch, eh? Lunch for three? Yes?"

"Well, I *must* say, sir," ejaculated the cook. "This is the limit. You're always doing this, sir." She wagged a finger. "And too late to get anything. It's enough to break a woman's heart, that it is. We've only enough in the place for two. And the Commissioner here. You don't deserve no consideration from me, you don't, the way you treat me. I'm no snack bar just to peck at when you have a mind."

"Now, now, Mrs. C.," soothed the Chief Constable. "Don't get upset. I realize that I've been very stupid, but it's your own fault, being always ready to dash to my rescue. I rely on you too much, I'm afraid. Forget it. I'll just take them over the The Bear and give you no trouble."

"The Bear," gasped Mrs. Crouch. "Indeed you'll do no such thing. Whatever would the Commissioner think if you couldn't give him lunch after asking him. I'll do my best. Goodness knows, no woman can do more. But remember, sir—" she hissed the words—"I don't like it. Now—get out! I'll be ten minutes."

The Chief Constable returned to entertain his guests with local anecdotes, in a slightly nervous voice and apprehensive furtiveness. He heaved a sigh of relief on observing that Mrs. Crouch, entering with the soup, was adorned in the blue-flowered overall reserved only for Christmas and very special occasions. All was going well, he mused; Mrs. C. was 'going to town on the lunch', an expression she had borrowed from the American vocabulary *via* the local cinema.

He was right. A quite excellent curry of the reinforced stew with trimmings of rice that had already been prepared for his evening meal, was followed by a superb sweet omelet *à la Crouch*, and gruyère cheese and biscuits. Cona coffee ended the meal.

She flushed with pleasure at the commendation of the guests at the excellence of the meal. The Chief Constable smiled, as wheeling out the loaded trolley of empty dishes into the hall, she whispered in his ear, "Well, I'm sure I hope you're satisfied, sir. Now, please take a week's notice." She disappeared triumphantly.

Manson sipped the coffee with relish. "Your housekeeper, Mainforce," he said, "is a jewel."

"Yes, quite priceless, I agree," responded the Chief Constable. "But, alas, she is no more. She's given me a week's notice—for the twentieth time." He laughed. "Unfortunately, I always forget to tell her when I have invited guests. I am afraid that one day she'll really get annoyed and I'll lose her. That will put the kibosh on my establishment. However, while I have Scotland Yard at my back I feel safe. She reads detective stories enthusiastically. Oh, by the way, she thinks you are the Commissioner."

"What!" said the startled Manson. "You don't mean to say you've—"

"Don't for the love of Heaven let me down, old chap."

The company dissolved in loud laughter.

Mainforce joined in, but then became suddenly serious. "Now, we'd better talk business, Doctor," he insisted. "My inspector seems to have missed everything it was possible to miss. Sound man in his way. Very trustworthy, you know, but no thinker."

"Don't suppose he has had much practise round here, Mainforce," suggested Manson. "Nevertheless, he ought to have known about the blood."

The Chief Constable looked at him thoughtfully. "I've been thinking, Manson, you might be wrong about Canley not walking to the railway line," he said.

"In what way?" The doctor looked with inquiry and lively interest at his host.

"Well, his shoes. They were mudless, I agree, and doubtless they had been wiped. But couldn't Canley have had a reason for wiping them? If he did, it rather disposes of a second person on the line, doesn't it? I agree it doesn't sound a likely thing to do. On the other hand, it is possible, I suppose?"

"Yes, there is no reason why he should not have wiped them, if he so wanted," replied Doctor Manson. "Folks do queer things sometimes—"

"Ah!" said the Chief Constable, not without a touch of satisfaction. "Then—" Doctor Manson interrupted. He looked quizzingly at his host. "But tell me, Mainforce," he asked. "If he did wipe his shoes, with what did he perform the operation?"

"With what?" The Chief Constable echoed in surprise. "Why with a piece of rag, I suppose. What *would* he wipe them with?" he asked.

"Precisely. And what happened to the piece of rag? When did it vanish into thin air. Because there was none found on him, you know. Nor was there any on the line."

The Chief Constable retired, disconsolately. "Ah, of course," he said. "I ought to have known better. Only it seemed to be a little lacking in your usual clear proof."

"It is not only the fact that the shoes had been wiped that makes me certain that Canley did not walk to the line." The doctor amplified his prognostication. "There is more conclusive evidence."

"What? I haven't heard of that." The Colonel thought introspectively. "What is it?"

"I'll show you that when we get back to the cottage," Manson promised.

The Chief Constable looked at his watch. "Perhaps we'd better get a move on," he said. Rising, he led the way to Ypres. With another variety of clatters they waggled a way back to Thames Pagnall.

A cackle of conversation at the cottage led them to the back room of the house, the kitchen. Inspector Kenway, Mackenzie and Sergeant Bunny were lolling at a table which bore the remains of bread and cheese, the property of the late Mr. Canley. Three empty bottles illustrated the liquid with which the comestibles had been washed down.

At the entrance of the Chief Constable's party, the officers rose, fortified, to render whatever help the Chief might decide. He did, in fact, indicate the immediate problem.

"Before we start on anything else, Doctor," he said, nodding at Manson, "what is the other part of the proof you possess that Canley did not walk from this cottage to the railway?"

"He says," turning to the others of the company, "that the wiping of the shoes is only part of his evidence. Just an elementary fact."

"The proof, Colonel," declared Manson, "lies in the footprints. But I think that the casts which Merry and Kenway made will be sufficient for me to demonstrate the point without us journeying back to the embankment. By the way"—he turned to Inspector Mackenzie—"you can now open the railway line and the path, if you like. I have no further interest in the evidence there."

The Chief Constable guffawed. "I reckon there'll be precious few people using it as a short cut for the time being," he said. "And a damned good thing, too. Now what about those footprints. Manson?" he asked.

Merry had opened the Box of Tricks and from it had extracted the casts of the prints which he and Kenway had taken from the impressions on the path and in the lane. He placed them, soles up, on the kitchen table. Doctor Manson quizzed them carefully for a moment or two.

"Yes," he said. "The evidence is sufficiently plain. There you are, gentlemen."

He replaced the casts on the table, and stood beside them the shoes of Canley, also with the soles up.

"The evidence that Canley did not walk. See if you can find it. Mackenzie already knows part of the solution. You may want a lens," he added. "I did, but then I was examining the actual prints on the path. The evidence here is easier, and, I think, more plainly apparent. But there's my lens." He placed it beside the exhibits.

The officers bent over the table, and surveyed the present but hidden evidence. Merry, more experienced in following Doctor Manson's line of thinking, spent the first few moments comparing the markings of the soles of the shoes with those on the casts. The casts were faithful productions of the markings, which were detailed finely.

After a couple of minutes or so, Merry withdrew from the contest. Inspector Mackenzie quizzed him with his eyes, and received a nod. He returned to the casts and eyed them with enthusiasm, but with little hope, Inspector Kenway did the same. Merry whispered a few words into the ears of his chief, and the scientist nodded. "But you should have seen it earlier, Jim," he said reprovingly.

"What is it, Manson?" The Chief Constable had exhausted his patience.

The doctor moved to the table. "Let me deal, firstly, with the print that Mackenzie knows," he suggested. "And which Kenway knows, too," he added.

"Shoes, you know, can tell many things of the habits of their wearer. Now, these shoes are plainly marked with the walking habit of Canley.

The outside edges of the heels are considerably worn—which is the stamp of the walker who takes long strides, or strides a little longer than the length of his legs justify. The natural result of that is that he comes down on the ground heavily on the outside of the heels, instead of square over the heels as does the normal walker. That is the reason that the heels of Canley's shoes are worn down, thusly."

The doctor demonstrated the amount of the wear by placing the blade of one of Canley's table knives across the heel of one of the boots; it showed a space of a quarter of an inch between the knife and the worn outside edge of the sole.

"That plain?" he asked; after a chorus of "yes," he replaced the shoe on the table and took up the corresponding cast.

"Very well. Now, had Canley walked from this cottage down the lane and up the path to the railway, he would, you will agree, have walked in his natural way—with his feet coming down on the outside of the heels. The result should be, of course, a deep well-defined impression of the outer edge of the heel, and a much less defined and lightly pressed mark of the inside section of the same heel.

"But on the contrary"—the scientist pushed the cast under the eyes of his hearers—"there is here practically no impression at all of the outside of the heels; instead the *inside* of the heel is cut deep and straight."

He demonstrated the fact in all the casts that had been taken by the Inspector and Merry.

"In addition, you have the fact, pretty obvious, that the length of stride as shown by the distance between the prints, is not the normal stride of a man of the height of Canley—let alone that of a man of Canley's height who takes long strides."

"Oh, Lord," groaned the Chief Constable. "Elementary."

"Observation," corrected Manson. "As a matter of fact, it was the shortness of the stride that led me to examine the prints more closely. I had concluded from the shoes that Canley *strode*, and was surprised to find that he had *walked*."

Mackenzie presented the appearance of bewilderment. "Then, Doctor Manson, if Canley did not walk to the railway, how comes it that his shoes made the prints?" he asked. He looked suddenly doubtful.

"Do you mean that the footprints have been . . ." he searched round for the appropriate word, but could think only of—"forged?"

"I should say that forged fits the circumstances, yes," the scientist agreed.

"But," propounded Mackenzie, "a chap would have to walk himself to make the forgeries. He'd have to impress the shoes down in the places and he'd leave his own footprints."

The Chief Constable jumped in with both feet.

"Do you mean, Manson, that someone else was wearing Canley's shoes and walked in them to make the prints appear to be Canley's?" he asked.

Manson applauded. "It has been a long, long trail, but you've reached the end of the winding at last," he said. "That is precisely what I think did happen."

"And where would Canley have been at the time?" asked Mackenzie.

Doctor Manson looked at him long and thoughtfully. "You may remember, Mackenzie," he said at last, "that you were asked to walk up the inclined path to the railway, taking care to place your feet alongside the tracks made by Canley?" The inspector nodded.

"Afterwards, you may recall that I measured the depths of the footsteps you made with a micro-calliper. Similarly you will remember my examination of the print which you made in the soft spot in the lane by the side of Canley's print. What did I say to you then?" he demanded.

Inspector Mackenzie thought back. "I think," he rejoined, "that you inferred that I was about the same height and weight as Canley."

"Excellent, Inspector. You did not, however, notice at your subsequent inspection of the print, any difference between your prints and those of the man who I had told you, and you had agreed, was about your own weight?" The doctor put the statement interrogatively.

"No," agreed Mackenzie, absently. He was thinking back as fast as he could.

"Now, I was intrigued by a peculiarity which seemed to me to tell a remarkable tale. The micro-callipers showed me that the measurement of Canley's supposed footprint was five-sixteenths of an inch deeper than the impression made by you. And your stride was longer than that shown in the lane as the stride of the supposed Canley."

"Being a man with a very suspicious mind, I asked myself what conceivable circumstance could make a man walk with a stride shorter than was his wont, and at the same time make a deeper impression than he normally should make according to his weight. The only reason I could see was *that he was much heavier than usual.*"

"I get it, Doctor." Inspector Kenway broke in on the explanation. "You mean that he was carrying a heavy weight."

*"He was carrying Canley. That's what you are telling us, isn't it?" demanded the Chief Constable.

Doctor Manson spread his hands expressively. "That, Colonel, is the one thing which would explain Canley's shoe-prints showing a tread that was entirely foreign to him, a stride that was not his usual stride, and at the same time explain his apparent walk to the railway line, his death before the train passed over him, and the complete absence of obvious traces of a second person who must have been there."

"And I know no other circumstances," he added, *"that can satisfactorily answer all these curiosities."*

The company digested these facts in silence. They were arguing mentally and individually, that this meant that the supposed accident was definitely a case of murder.

Inspector Kenway ventured the opinion aloud.

"I would not dogmatize that at this stage, Kenway," retorted the scientist. "I think, however, that I shall probably arrive at that conclusion. This cottage should provide us with more data—at least, I hope it will."

"At the moment," declared the Chief Constable, "we have a dead man carried from this house, down the lane, and up a path to the railway lines, and placed over a rail by someone who wore his shoes to give the idea that the dead man was alive, and had walked to his death. In other words, we have a certain chain of circumstances which show a planned and well-thought-out plot to disguise a person's death. That seems quite a lot to be going on with."

His voice had the intonation of a man who sees calamity bearing down upon him; and no way of avoiding it.

CHAPTER XVII

INSPECTOR Mackenzie unlocked and threw open the door of the lounge and made way for Doctor Manson and the Chief Constable to enter. The scientist stood just inside the door and let his eyes take in the general lay-out.

It presented the appearance of a comfortably, but not luxuriously furnished room left undisturbed after the exit of its occupant. By the table stood a chair pushed slightly back in order to allow the occupant to rise. A bottle of whisky half full of spirit stood on the table, together with a single glass and a carafe of water. Near these was an ashtray with, dropped into it, a match end and a quantity of ash. The fire had burnt out.

Across the floor in front of the fender was a patterned rug. A strip of carpet ran diagonally from the fireplace to the door, but the remainder of the floor space was plain polished wood. An armchair stood by the fireplace.

"Looks a placid, contented household, Manson," suggested the Chief Constable. "There is no sign of a struggle or evidence of violence."

"None at all, I agree, Mainforce. This room has not been touched, has it, Mackenzie—either by you or the woman?" he asked the local inspector.

"Nothing at all has been touched, Doctor. We had no reason to touch anything until the railway doctor insisted on the Yard being called in, and after that I thought it best that the place should be left undisturbed."

Doctor Manson nodded a brief acknowledgement and crossed to the fireplace. He lifted from the hearth a formidable iron poker and inspected its heavy knob, first with his unaided eyesight, and afterwards through a lens. The knob dismissed from any complicity in violence, he moved his examination to the length of the weapon. Neither did this afford him any satisfaction, however, and he replaced it.

"Wiped, probably," suggested Merry.

"No," rejoined Manson. "I do not think so. It is well marked with fingers,[3] but I see no sign of any foreign body, such as would have been noticed after violence, and it seems to have been used for no other purpose than that for which the makers intended it."

He called to the men at the door. "Do not tread anywhere near the table," he warned. "Keep where you are for the time being."

His next move was to study the patterned rug in front of the fireplace. After a scrutiny he whispered to Merry, who went into the hall and returned with the Box of Tricks. From it he took an envelope, slit the seal and extracted one of the fluffy fragments which had been collected from the overcoat of Canley on the railway lines.

With a pair of tweezers Doctor Manson pulled a fragment of fibre from the rug and compared it with the fragment from the envelope. He made no comment, but tweaked a number of other pieces of varied

3. Doctor Manson was wrong. The reader knows that Porter wiped the knob after he had realized that he had used the poker to stir up the ashes of the cigar which he had put on the fire.

colours from the rug, and stowed them in another envelope, afterwards resealing the original envelope.

He made only one comment. "It is a point to remember that the coat fragments came from the back of Canley," he said. "That appears to be of some significance."

"Significant of what?" asked the Chief Constable.

Doctor Manson smiled. "I don't know," he answered, naively.

From the fire the doctor's attention was directed to the general lay-out of the room. His eyes roved over the area comprising the table. A spot of greyish-white on the floor caught his eye. It lay in a direct line with the end of the table, and beyond it.

"What is that?" he asked, pointing a finger at it.

Merry approached the spot circumferentially and looked down.

"Cigar ash," he announced. He ringed the ash round with a red chinagraph pencil.

"Dropped from his cigar?" suggested Mackenzie. "We knew he had smoked one."

"Or half-smoked it," added Kenway.

Doctor Manson walked along the side of the room and approached the table and chair from behind. He stood beside the chair, regarding the little pile of ash thoughtfully. His eyes strayed to the table and marked the ashtray with its burden. Then, with a steel tape, he measured the distance of the fallen ash from the chair—it showed three feet four and a half inches.

The distance seemed to cause him some perplexity, for furrows appeared on the broad forehead and there were wrinkles in the corners of his eyes. After a sustained contemplation, he examined through a lens the seat of the chair. The scrutiny seemed to satisfy him, for he looked up at the company and beckoned to Inspector Kenway, who was smoking a cigarette.

"Approach from behind, Kenway, and sit in this chair," he said. "Don't handle it, and don't sit back. There are no marks on the seat of any value, but I have not examined the sides and back. Smoke that cigarette until it has a nice long ash and then stand up, and as you do so, flick off the ash."

The inspector puffed vigorously. Doctor Manson noted the length of the ash and warned the inspector. "Flick the ash fairly strongly away from you in the direction of the cigar ash on the floor, remembering that the ash of a cigar is heavier to dislodge than that of a cigarette," Doctor Manson advised.

The ash fell a foot or so from the chair.

"Try it again, Kenway, and flick as hard as you can," the scientist begged. There followed a wait until the cigarette had burned more ash. The inspector flicked it away again, harder. The further effort scaled just over two feet four inches.

"You could not reach the circle of ash we have ringed round?" asked the doctor.

"I should say it is impossible," replied Kenway.

The Chief Constable, who had watched the proceedings with a measure of fascination, now sought enlightenment. "I don't see what you are after, Manson," he said. "But I gather it doesn't work."

Manson smiled. "It is not quite so bad as that, Mainforce," he replied. "I know now how a certain thing did *not* happen. That is a matter of considerable importance. Having now eliminated the impossible, we are a stage nearer to the possible." He again measured the distance with his eyes, and chewed the cud of his deductions.

Merry was following the lines of his thought. He whispered a few words to his chief. The doctor nodded. "It might be so, Merry," he said. "We'll try it as best we can. But, first, we had better take care of the ash."

With a piece of litmus paper as a scoop, the ash, ringed round with the red pencil mark, was lifted and deposited in another of the scientist's seed envelopes, the outside of which was labelled as usual with the description and position of the contents.

Doctor Manson took from a waistcoat pocket the cigar found on the railway lines. He wrapped a little gummed paper round the end of it and handed it to Inspector Kenway. That officer looked more than a little surprised at the sight of it. It seemed to be an accusation of some sort. Doctor Manson explained its presence. "You are supposed, Kenway," he said, "to be leaning forward slightly and smoking this. Do not be surprised at anything that may happen."

As the inspector put the cigar, with a gingerliness approaching repugnance, between his lips, Doctor Manson moved behind him. Without warning, he pushed the smoker violently on the top of the shoulders. The cigar shot from his victim's mouth, *and dropped within an inch or two of the marked circle.*

"What the devil . . ." began Kenway, and he swung round in the chair.

"Sorry," said Manson. But he did not look it. On the contrary, he appeared to be well-pleased with the result of his assault. "All in the interests of justice, you know. I should say that you have enacted the role of Canley, as he played it in this room last night. Only you have survived the ordeal—he did not."

"God bless me soul." The drift of the experiment had dawned upon the Chief Constable. "You mean that Canley was killed in that chair?"

"I think it highly probable, Colonel. The ash on the floor had a characteristic which interested me greatly, and which seemed to negative the more likely explanation that the smoker stood up, moved towards the fireplace and flicked off the ash, so that it fell to the floor—"

"Seemed a perfectly natural explanation, Manson," the Chief Constable frowned.

"What made you doubt its likelihood?" asked Kenway.

"The fact that, when you drop ash like that, it falls to the floor lightly. Now, this ash has *marked* the polished floor. There is a distinct sign of contact when examined through the lens. You can still see it, though the ash has been removed from the floor."

The Chief Constable came forward and bent over the pencil ring. "I see what you mean," he admitted. "The ash is, shall I say, *impinged*, on the floor."

"Perhaps he dropped his cigar," hazarded Kenway.

"I had considered that." Doctor Manson nodded approval of the suggestion. "But there seems to have been a little more force, and an *obliqueness* of the mark which, I think, discounts the suggestion. The room shows no sign of disturbance. From that fact we are entitled to assume that there was no quarrel. Accordingly, Canley must have been knocked out unsuspectingly."

"And, of course, you have already deduced that he was knocked out by a blow at the bottom of the neck which the decapitation by the train was to hide." Inspector Kenway spoke slowly, and with emphasis.

"Exactly, Kenway. Hence my testing the theory that a sudden blow from behind on the unsuspecting man would jerk the cigar from his lips with considerable force—enough to send it flying just over three feet and make it land obliquely. As you have seen, the experiment in which you shared, lends colour to the view. I cannot, of course, say that that is what actually occurred, but it is feasible."

"Then that would explain the other man upon whom you have been harking all the time," said the Colonel.

"Shall we say the other *person*, Mainforce?" This was too much for Inspector Mackenzie. He rose in open rebellion at the theory.

"How did he get here at all?" he demanded. "Where did he come from?"

There was in him that routine mind which insisted that crime should be solved by police work, not book learning. He now enlarged on his question. "There are no signs of entry in the lane or along the garden path, and we've been all over the garden at the back, and there are still no signs of any approach."

"That is of secondary importance, Mackenzie, compared with the evidence we already have on the line and in this room." Doctor Manson spoke chidingly. "I should draw your attention to the fact that the entire length of the lane has a grass verge, and that a man may walk in that long grass at night-time and leave no sign, since by the early morning the trampled grass of a single footstep would spring back to its upright position, and show no indication of ever having been disturbed. That would be particularly so if the person walked, for instance, in stock-inged feet which would not bruise the grass—a trick which the Red Indians learned in America generations ago."

Inspector Mackenzie gave it up. But he shook a doubting head.

Colonel Mainforce at this stage felt that the time had come to take an active part in the proceedings. He was, he remembered, the Chief Constable, and this was *his* murder.

The fact that Yard officers were present made no difference to him. It was Surrey's murder trail, not Scotland Yard's. He proceeded there-fore, to summarize the investigation as it so far stood. A preparatory cough warned the company to listen to his conclusions; and the Colonel began them:

"I am convinced by the evidence of my eyes, and senses, that this man Canley was not knocked down and killed by the train," he said. "I am convinced that he was killed, and his body deposited on the line, in the belief that the decapitation would hide the evidence of violence on his person." He looked round at the company. Sergeant Bunny nearly sprang to attention. He had heard the Chief use that tone when giving orders on the barrack square.

"I am also convinced that there were two people concerned in the same affair in this room," the Chief Constable proceeded, "and that it was here that Canley met his death. Canley, therefore, was one of the persons. The question we now have to answer is—who was the other?" He turned a waiting gaze on Doctor Manson.

The scientist smiled, and shook his head. "I am no magi-cian, Colonel." The Chief Constable appeared unconvinced by the denial. "And I am no spiritualist medium. I think it probable that there *were* two persons in this room, but there is, as yet, no positive proof of that."

The Chief Constable registered frustration. His moustache bristled out like the quills of a porcupine. "Well, the point is—can we prove it, and how?" he demanded.

"I don't know," confessed Doctor Manson. "This room knows whether there were or were not two people here, and it knows the identity of them both, if there *were* two. Walls have eyes and ears, you know—"

"Then let's pull 'em out and sight 'em," said the Chief Constable. "How do we start?"

"Possibly with the floor," Doctor Manson retorted. "After we have covered that, or uncovered it, we can all come into the room without any danger of destroying evidence. Perhaps you will switch on all the lights, and Merry and I will go over the surface. Once we have cleared that, you can tramp about to your heart's content."

The two men began a methodical exploration, starting with the floor in the vicinity of the furniture. Once or twice Doctor Manson brought his lens into use, but apparently derived nothing of importance.

"Plenty of marks, but nothing at all likely to be helpful," he said.

It was Merry, who, from behind the chair standing at the side of the table, first sounded the tocsin. On hands and knees he had been crawling over the floor.

"He ought to have brought his rompers," whispered Inspector Mackenzie to his sergeant. "What the devil does he suppose he is looking for?" As he ceased speaking, Merry stopped his crawling and examined something which the officers could not see. He called to the scientist. "What do you make of these, Doctor?" he asked.

Doctor Manson crossed the room and bent over two indentures in the polished floor. They were slightly under half an inch long, and were scored in parallel lines. He frowned at the sight of them. "They look to me like scratches from nails, Jim," he said.

After a further scrutiny, he measured them. "I make them one thirty-second of an inch in diameter, and one two-hundredth of an inch deep—one slightly less," he announced. "They are one and a half inches apart, and dead parallel in their entire length. Now, what does that suggest?"

"That, since they are dead parallel all the way, the nails are fixed in some object," hazarded Merry.

"A boot?" suggested the Chief Constable.

Merry turned up Canley's shoes. They were hand-sewn, and the heels contained only the usual rim nails. None was projecting, and none missing.

"Well, they weren't made by *these* shoes," he announced. "It would have been a remarkable coincidence had two nails been sticking up in one shoe, as these must have been, without some very good reason. And heel nails are never so wide apart as these."

"Unless—" Doctor Manson began, and stopped. He searched the floor in the vicinity of the scratches, and then went wider, in circles. "There are no other signs of abrasions," he said. "Can anyone conjure up anything out of that?"

"Rubber-soled shoes any good?" suggested Merry.

The doctor sought enlightenment.

"I mean, rubber bottoms, not just rubber circular heels," explained the deputy scientist. "The heels have generally a couple of nails through the centre of the heels. It might be—"

"I'm wearing that kind, sir." The police constable broke into the dialogue. He had been listening with eager interest from the door. He held up a foot to prove his interruption. The scientist nodded, and the constable unlaced his boot and passed it across to Merry, who bent over it with Doctor Manson.

"There are two nails in the heel," decided Manson, and produced a micrometer rule. "They measure an inch and three-quarters apart." He compared the size of the boot with those of Canley. "About two sizes larger," he announced. "That should bring the distance about right."

"You mean?" The Chief Constable waited the answer.

"If the heels of the boots were well worn it is possible that the nails would be liable to score parallel grooves *in certain circumstances*."

"As for example?" asked Inspector Kenway.

"If a sudden violent pressure was exerted on the worn rubber so that the back of the heel was braced to give power, it would depress the rubber and leave the nails exposed. If the foot was then drawn backwards—that, by the way, is plainly evidenced from the scoring as having happened—then scratches like these would possibly be made, whereas in ordinary pressure, such as from walking, the rubber, though worn down to the level of the nails, would be sufficiently resilient to prevent markings."

"Such as—leverage—for—a—blow?" asked the Chief Constable. He spoke deliberately, with pauses between each word.

"It could be, Mainforce, but again I remind you that we are theorizing without any substantial evidence upon which to base a theory."

"Every muckle helps," burst out Mackenzie, suddenly stricken with enthusiasm—and Scottish.

"Well, you can all come inside now," said Doctor Manson. He beckoned to the Yard inspector. "Kenway, take that chair and go over it for prints. You'll find another insufflator in the Box of Tricks. Use the one marked 'charcoal powder'. And bring me the one marked 'Hydrag c. Creta'—that is the grey powder."

Kenway busied himself with the chair. Merry and Manson paid attention to the table. Seated on a chair brought forward from the wall, with the Chief Constable in another, the doctor looked over the bottle and the glass. He produced a handkerchief, and with it between his fingers, lifted up the glass by the extreme tip of the rim. He sniffed at the interior, which was smeared, and which still contained a few drops of liquid in the bottom.

"Whisky," he pronounced.

"Elementary," said the Chief Constable. "Doctor Gaunt's *post mortem* showed that Canley had had a drink of whisky shortly before his death."

Doctor Manson grunted, held the vehicle up to the light and peered at it closely. Then, placing it back on the table, he puffed over it from the insufflator a little of the grey powder. On the surface of the glass, there appeared, as though by magic, the marks of fingers.

"A right hand," said Merry.

The scientist puffed powder on the other side of the cylindrical surface of the tumbler. Another print appeared—that of a thumb.

"Canley's, of course." The Chief Constable deducted. "He'd be the drinker."

Doctor Manson started in annoyance. "That reminds me," he said. "A very grave oversight, Mainforce. Could anyone else drive that car of yours? Could Mackenzie do it, for instance?"

The Chief Constable scratched his head. "Dashed if I know whether he could," he said.

"I've driven it before," volunteered Mackenzie. He caught sight of his Chief Constable's facial expression, and wished he had kept his tongue between his teeth.

"The devil you have," roared the Colonel. "Now, when would that be? I've—"

"Never mind when it was, Colonel." Doctor Manson grinned. "Mackenzie ought to have a medal for it. Let him drive again. I want some finger impressions of Canley's fingers, and he's in the mortuary—and I want them quickly. Off you go, Mackenzie."

He handed the officer from the Box of Tricks a fingerprint roller, paper and pad for taking the impressions.

"When the devil did he drive Ypres?" the Colonel asked himself, aloud, as his eyes watched the exit of the inspector. "That probably accounts for its condition."

"It doesn't," said Manson, with a wink at Merry. "The only thing to account for the condition of Ypres is its age, so give up worrying." As he spoke, the scientist was puffing more of the grey powder, this time on the surface of the bottle of whisky. Again prints appeared, about half-way up the sides of the bottle. They encircled the circumference, the fingers being on one half of the circumference and a large thumb on the other.

Doctor Manson now began to show signs of keener interest. He pushed the bottle and glass to one side, and concentrated his attention on the surface of the table around the positions in which the vessels had been resting. Some three or four rings showed up plainly on the polished surface. Colonel Mainforce leaned forward.

"Careless blighter, Doctor. Putting wet glasses down on a table like that," he said. "Had a fellow like it in the Mess once. Outsider—plenty of paper mats. But would he use them? Would he, blazes. This chap Canley is the same."

The doctor ignored the lamentable lack of culture in the defunct Mr. Canley. He engaged instead in some intent consideration of the glass and the marks left by it on the table. He looked from one to the other, and back again.

"Deucedly interesting," he announced.

"What is?" asked the Chief Constable.

"All this, Mainforce." He drew the attention of Merry to the set-up. The deputy scientist regarded the rings, and the tumbler with the fingerprints showing up against the colourless composition of the glass. He caught the eyes of his chief, but said nothing.

A clatter came from the distance. "Here's Ypres," announced the Chief Constable. "I'd know the sound of her engine in a thousand."

"So would I," Manson laughed. "Even above the roar of battle," he added.

The car came to silence, and the front door of the cottage opened. Doctor Manson took from Inspector Mackenzie the cards on which had been rolled the fingerprints of the dead Canley. Together he and Merry compared them with the prints showing up on the tumbler and the bottle.

"Well?" demanded the Chief Constable.

"Oh, they're Canley's all right," replied Manson. "Not a doubt about it."

"And nobody else's on the glass or the bottle," pointed out Mackenzie. "Doesn't that show that he was here alone. And that he was drinking before he went out?"

Doctor Manson looked round the room. His eyes brightened at the appearance of another couple of tumblers, standing together on a sideboard, and accompanied with a carafe of water. Taking each in turn with the handkerchief, he held them up to the light, and then placed them on the table. Merry intervened in the proposed use of the insufflator.

"Just a minute, Doctor," he said, and moved a foot farther round, from which angle he eyed the tumblers keenly.

Doctor Manson, joining him, followed the direction of his deputy's eyes. Rays of the electric light striking through the glass gave the tumblers a slight, and decidedly unusual, iridescence.

"A bit odd?" suggested Merry.

"Very," Manson agreed. He laid one of the glasses aside and puffed the grey powder over the other. It fell evenly, and when gently blown to remove surplus powder from any prints that might show, all of it went off. There were no fingerprints.

With a grunt, he packed the second of the glasses into a wrapping of tissue paper, and placed it in the Box of Tricks.

Similar examination of the carafe of water gave results no different from the tumbler.

"It gets odder and odder," declared the scientist. An undercurrent of satisfaction crept into his voice.

"This is definitely the queerest room it has ever been my fortune to examine," he concluded.

CHAPTER XVIII

"ODDER and odder." The Chief Constable echoed the words. "What is there odd about it, Manson?"

"Just a moment, Colonel," begged the scientist. "Let us see if the woman can throw any light on the matter." Inspector Mackenzie bellowed her name from the door.

Mrs. Skelton loomed in the doorway and came forward, slowly. She was a tall, angular woman of forbidding mien, sharp-featured, with a pointed prominent nose, and an air which radiated dolefulness and criticism at one and the same time. Her tight, thin lips pressed to whiteness as she looked round the assembly in the dining-room. There was a pause the while she weighed them up in her own way. Then:

"You wanted me?" The query came arrogantly.

Doctor Manson countered with a charming smile. "Yes, Mrs. Skelton," he said. "We were wondering if you could help us to find out what sort of a person Mr. Canley was. His habits, and so on."

"Ho!" She drew herself up to her full, lean height. "If its habits you want, them as I did see was pretty bad, if I may say—"

"You may, woman," put in the Chief Constable.

"Mind yer, it wasn't much of 'im as I did see. I 'as me livin' to h'earn, so I does me duty and nothing more. If I was to poke me nose into the 'abits of them I works for, I'd be h'out of work 'arf the time. I thinks I knows me place as well as the next one, and I can't afford to be fussy, especially where there's good pickings to be had, which ain't easy these days."

Manson, trying to sort out information from this jumbled mass, seized on the last sentence. "Pickings, Mrs. Skelton," he said quietly. "What would they be?"

"Oh! Bits and pieces, odds and ends." She suddenly tumbled to the implication of the question. "Come by honest, o' course," she added. "Though I wouldn't like to make it me business as to where *he* got 'em. But what's a body to do, sir, these days?" She began to whine. "Big family like I've got, odd bits is useful."

"I've no doubt they are." Doctor Manson tried again. "What bits?" he asked.

"Well, a bit o' butter and cheese and mebbe a rasher or two, or the end of the joint. Plenty 'e 'ad just goin' ter waste, and I will say as very generous e' were whatever else 'e was, and whatever I thought of 'im."

"And what *did* you think of him, Mrs. Skelton?"

"I wouldn't soil me lips with the things I could say about that man." Doctor Manson, looking at her, groaned. He saw the light of fanaticism in her eyes. "Wait till the Day of Judgment, when the secrets of all hearts is opened," she declaimed.

"Can't wait that long," said the Chief Constable, unwisely. "We're in a hurry."

"Ye know not when your time will come," roared Mrs. Skelton. "Prepare to meet thy God." She turned back to Doctor Manson. "On that day such as 'im will be sorry for the lives they've led, the sin and lying and wicked dealings. Everlasting damnation and the fires of brimstone, that's what will happen to him."

The woman stormed with evangelistic fervour. Beads of perspiration stood on her forehead, and her hands twisted round and round the towel which she was carrying when she entered the room. 'A shade too righteous,' thought Manson. 'She's probably a little anxious about those bits and pieces.' Aloud he said, "Well, Mrs. Skelton, none of us is perfect. We should always remember the words of Bishop Bradford, you know."

Mrs. Skelton thought doggedly for a moment. Curiosity overcame her natural reluctance to admit ignorance of the sayings of a Lord Bishop.

"What words?" she importuned.

"There, but for the grace of God goes John Bradford," quoted the doctor. "Now, tell me, Mrs. Skelton, with what do you polish the tumblers?" He pointed to the array on the table.

The woman held up the towel in her hands. "With this 'ere," she said. "Why? What's the matter with 'em?"

"Nothing at all, Mrs. Skelton, I assure you." He took the towel and examined it closely. "You would not, I suppose, use paraffin on them at all?"

"On the glasses?" Mrs. Skelton threw Christian forbearance to the winds at this reflection on her housekeeping. "On the glasses! I'd like you to know as I bin in service on and off since I was fourteen and I knows me job if h'anybody do. I never heard such a thing in all me born life. 'Ow long do yer think I'd a done for a gentleman if I'd washed his glasses in paraffin? You're a'casting a slur on me h'ability as a housekeeper, that's what you're a doin' of. I could 'ave the law on yer for that. Libellous, that's what it is. Libellous—"

"Slanderous," said the Chief Constable, who was a stickler for legal accuracy.

"Wot?"

"I said slander, not libel. Madam. Libel has to be written."

Mrs. Skelton considered this unexpected set-back in silence for a moment. "Are you a'telling of me as I can't have the law on yer for taking me character away?" she demanded.

"No, Madam. I merely said that you couldn't sue us for libel, but you could sue us for alleged slander—"

Doctor Manson chuckled. "Let's get back to Mr. Canley," he said. "You can go to law afterwards." He turned towards the angry woman. "Now, Mrs. Skelton, nobody wants to insult or libel—slander—you," he said. "We're just men, you know, and know nothing of these kitchen affairs. I am sure you are a most praiseworthy housekeeper. I can see that by the state this house is in." Mrs. Skelton deflated.

"Well, I'm sure—"

Manson dropped in hurriedly, lest another tirade began. "We were wondering, you see, if any paraffin could have come in contact with these glasses at all?"

Mrs. Skelton sniffed. "H'impossible," she said. "I never uses paraffin on cloths as has to be used for wiping up things. You don't never keep paraffin in the kitchen 'cos the smell per . . ."

"Permeates?" queried Doctor Manson, smilingly.

"Permeates the place," agreed Mrs. Skelton, "so it couldn't have been in contact with the glasses."

The woman finished with a direct hit. "Anyway, there ain't never bin any paraffin in the 'ouse," she announced. "All the fires is gas and coke fires. There ain't no need to use paraffin, since they 'ad the gas and electricity brought in the 'ouse, and a nice mess they made, too, a'getting of it in, a'taking up of all the floors—"

"Yes, yes, I'm sure you had a terrible job coping with it," hurriedly agreed Manson. "But to return to these glasses. I suppose you wash them after they have been used by Mr. Canley, and carry them from the kitchen back to this room?"

"Well, really! I must say you don't know much about housekeeping. Of course I washes 'em in the sink in the kitchen. There ain't no other sink. Then I polishes 'em and brings 'em back here." A flush came into her acid face. "Are you suggestin' as I've taken any glass?" she demanded.

"Of course we are not, Mrs. Skelton," Doctor Manson assured her.

"And after you have washed and polished them, what do you do with them?"

"Puts 'em on the sideboard alongside o' the bottle."

The words came with venom. Mrs. Skelton's attitude towards the bottle demonstrated her unswerving belief that any man addicted to the use of a bottle containing strong drink of any kind was doomed to the fires of Hell, without the solace even of cool and plain water.

"I see," said Doctor Manson. "And I take it that you would have followed the usual practice with these glasses yesterday?"

"That's right." She gave the impression that her habits were like unto the laws of the Medes and Persians, which alter not. "Did Mr. Canley have any visitors here at all?"

The woman's mouth set in a hard, thin line, and her eyes narrowed in fury.

"Aye. His succubus," she announced.

The Chief Constable startled like a shying horse. "His what?" he gasped.

"Succubus, I said." Mrs. Skelton showed her distaste at having to repeat the lewd word.

"And what might be her name, Mrs. Skelton?" asked Manson. "Succubus is what a church dignitary might call a Scarlet Woman," he explained to the Chief Constable.

"Mrs. Andover is what she calls herself," announced Mrs. Skelton. She drew a deep breath. "He suffered the woman Jezebel," she intoned. "And I gave her the space to repent of her fornication and she repented not. Behold I will cast her into bed, and them that commit adultery with her into great tribulation. Revelations," explained Mrs. Skelton, passionately. "Mind you, I had naught to do with her. Me 'ands never touched her belongings. There's some of 'em scattered upstairs now. And there they will remain. I ain't dipped me 'ands in sin."

"If them upstairs is sin, would I be a sinner," whispered Kenway to Merry. "There's the cutest dressing-gown and pair of black undies I've ever set eyes upon."

"I am quite sure you have not, Mrs. Skelton," comforted Doctor Manson. "Not even the sin of uncharitableness," he added sarcastically. "Was Mrs. Andover a regular visitor?"

"Aye. She comed here a lot."

"You don't know whether she was here yesterday, I suppose?"

"I don't now. But I can soon find out." She turned and left the room. The men heard the stairs creaking under her tread. She returned in a minute or two in a state of burning satisfaction.

"Aye, her must ha' been here," she announced.

"Why are you so sure?" demanded the doctor.

"Because there's some new black—black—"

"Panties is the word," chuckled Kenway.

Mrs. Skelton turned baleful eyes upon him. "Ye son of Belial," she hurled. "Ye—"

"It's all right, Mrs. Skelton." Doctor Manson poured oil on the troubled waters. "He's a respectable married man, and his wife wears them, I expect. You mean that the black—er—thing-a-me-bobs were not there yesterday before you left?"

"That's right, Mister."

"Well, thank you very much, Mrs. Skelton, for your assistance. You have been a great help to us. Now you can go home if you wish. We shall not want you again."

"Vengeance is mine, I will repay," thundered Mrs. Skelton.

"He didn't," said Doctor Manson. The woman looked puzzled.

"Didn't what?" she asked.

"God didn't revenge on Canley. It was somebody human, you know."

The woman glared around her, turned and swept out of the room, banging the door with such vehemence that the glasses rattled on the table.

"God bless me, what a woman!" The Chief Constable saw the back of her with relief. "I bet she still wears red flannel up to her neck and down to her knees. By the way, Manson, what is the point of the glasses. Getting faddy about polishing?"

"Very faddy, Mainforce." He drew attention to the glasses on the table. "Mrs. Skelton washed and polished these glasses yesterday. She carried them from the kitchen into this room, and placed them on the sideboard. Well and good. Then Canley, at some stage during the night, lifted one and brought it to the table. He also carried the bottle of whisky over. He poured himself out a drink. Follow me?"

"I wish I was following Canley; I could do with a whisky and soda," said the Chief Constable.

"Right! Canley had a drink. He had, as a matter of fact, three or four drinks, because you see here the marks made by the glass each time he placed it on the table after imbibing some of the contents, and probably replenishing the glass from the bottle.[4] *Now look at his glass.*"

4. The reader knows that Doctor Manson was wrong in this deduction.

The Chief Constable peered at the circumference of the vehicle. He noted the fingerprints left by the powder puffed on it, and turned a puzzled look at the scientist.

Inspector Kenway broke into the duologue. "There aren't sufficient prints," he suggested.

"Oh!" The Chief Constable became excited.

"Canley must have lifted the glass several times." Doctor Manson illustrated the point. "Once to carry it from the sideboard, and presumably three times to raise it to his lips and partake of the contents. That is proved by the marks on the table. *But there is only one set of prints on the glass*, and they are not in any way superimposed."

"Furs and whiskers," said the Chief Constable. "What about the bottle? That has only one set of prints."

"Only Canley touched the bottle," Mackenzie reminded his Chief, dampingly.

The Chief Constable exploded. "Damn and blast it, Mackenzie, I know that. The bottle's more than half empty. What's missing wouldn't go in a tumbler. So the bottle must have been handled several times. There's one print only, and old flannel says she has never polished the bottle."

"Says she!" Sergeant Bunny said hastily. "You know what these professed teetotallers are like. They tipple on the quiet. I've got a sister-in-law who runs down the drink. She's generally got a bottle of beer in the scullery."

"And you reckon this Skelton woman might be the same?" asked the Chief Constable. He looked round at the company. "She'd be cute enough to wipe her fingermarks off the glass, of course."

Inspector Mackenzie came to life again. "Then that would leave the one fingermark when Canley poured out a drink last night."

"Would it?" Doctor Manson smiled. It looked a wan smile. "You've overlooked the only point that's worth anything."

"He's at it again!" The Chief Constable looked very blank. "Mystery on mystery."

"There's no mystery at all. It's staring you in the face, if you'll look for it. See if you can find an empty bottle with a cork in it, Sergeant, and we'll make the Chief Constable show us the answer."

"Much better find a full one," advised the Colonel. "And get the cork out," he added. There was a chorus of approving gurgles. Sergeant Bunny laughed and left the room.

"Only found a gin bottle, sir," he announced on his return, and held it out. Doctor Manson took it.

"It doesn't matter what kind of a bottle, Sergeant. Now, Mainforce, you imagine this bottle is half full of gin."

"Is there any need to keep harping on drinks, Manson? On a cold day like this?"

"And you want a drink," went on the Doctor unperturbed at the interruption. He placed the bottle on the sideboard. "Go to it," he said, "and pour out your imaginary tot."

The Chief Constable walked to the sideboard, and picked up the bottle. His fingers had reached the cork when the doctor interrupted. "Stay like that," he called.

The Colonel stayed. He looked like a photo-finish picture print of a drinking bout.

"There, gentlemen, is the answer to the one point that really matters," Doctor Manson advised. "Now, do you see what it is?"

A few moments of silent reflection was shattered by the Chief Constable himself.

"How the hell much longer," he demanded, "am I to stand like a bloody waxwork exhibit?"

"It is a matter of everyday observation, coupled with its application to this particular case," the doctor continued, without answering the Colonel's question. "Recall the markings on the bottle of whisky—the only marks. And consider." He looked significantly at the hands of the Chief Constable.

Colonel Mainforce suddenly eased his position, and placed the bottle he was holding on the table.

"You win," he announced. "You generally do."

Doctor Manson eyed him interestedly. "Tell it first," he invited.

"I was holding the bottle with my *left* hand to take out the cork with my right hand fingers," he said. "And so would everyone else. And there's only one hand marked on that bottle—the right hand."

"How about a left-handed man?" Kenway asked.

"That would be different," said Manson. "But Canley was right-handed."

He forestalled the inevitable question as Mackenzie opened his mouth to ask it. "Look at the table lay-out—with the ashtray on the right of the glass, and the chair to the left of the glass. Only a right-handed man would sit down that way."[5]

"However, we did not really want the example of the bottle to prove that there is something fishy about the whole business," Doctor Manson continued. "Take the other glass and the carafe of water. Both, we know, were carried from the kitchen by Mrs. Skelton and placed on the sideboard. *But they have no fingerprints of any description on them.*"

"In other words—" began the Chief Constable.

"They have been deliberately polished," suggested Merry, "to remove any fingerprints which were left by someone who was in the place last night, someone who was obviously drinking with Canley."

"Fingerprints which had been left, or *might have been left.*" The doctor augmented Merry's explanation.

"In other words," began the Chief Constable, "someone with guilty knowledge has removed traces of his presence, eh?"

"That, Mainforce," agreed the scientist, "is the conclusion to which we are inevitably driven. And in doing so he has, like most people, left traces of his presence."

"Ha! The plot thickens." Colonel Mainforce demonstrated his satisfaction. "We now seem to be getting somewhere." He rubbed his hands. "Who'd think of polishing glasses, and such-like?" He answered his own question. "A woman. Just the thing she'd do. Now we know of one woman who was in this place last night. Canley's suc . . . suc . . . his mistress. Know this woman, Mackenzie?"

"Mrs. Andover?" The inspector nodded. "Lives—lodges," he corrected—"in a house near the Green, behind us. Been going round with Canley for some time. Races, and so on."

"What kind of woman is she?" asked Manson.

"Strapping woman, all curves. Red-headed," Mackenzie described her.

"Hey, what's that?" The Chief Constable looked up. "Would she be strapping enough to carry a lump of meat like Canley?"

Inspector Mackenzie took a moment or two to consider the question. "I reckon, sir, she's pretty strong," he decided.

"What about it, Doctor?"

5. Again Doctor Manson's reasoning, though on the right lines, was faulty. For it was Porter, not Canley who had arranged the table.

"I don't know." Doctor Manson looked doubtful. "There is not usually that strength in a woman, but it is a possibility we cannot rule out. I think Kenway will have to see her."

"Don't get the point, Doctor," protested the Chief Constable. "These big women are as strong as some men. Look at Black Maria."

"What! the police van?" asked Mackenzie. "She isn't as big as all that." The Colonel snorted disgust.

"Not the van," he bellowed. "The woman the police van was named after. Boston negress—Boston in America. Kept a boarding house for sailors. When lodgers got out of hand, she'd carry 'em bodily out of the house, and drop 'em in the street. Seeing policeman being attacked one day by a drunken sailor, she went to his aid, picked up the sailor and carried him to the lock-up. Did it several times. Got so well known that police in the district when a chappie was causing them a lot of trouble used to send the SOS 'Send for Black Maria'. When they got vans to carry struggling blokes to the lock-up, they called the vans Black Marias. See?"

"Very interesting and instructive, Colonel," commented Doctor Manson. "Well, Kenway will see what he can learn from this woman of Canley's—and about her. Now, I think we are pretty well finished here, except for the writing desk, and this table. If Canley has a dressing-case about the place, perhaps Mackenzie would put all the contents of the desk into it, and I will go through them at my leisure in Town. Meanwhile—"

He turned his attention to the table, starting with the area on which had been standing the glasses and bottle. Thorough examination, however, disclosed no sign of blemish. Grey powder didn't help, either.

"You see, Mainforce, that again all fingerprints appear to have been wiped clear over the entire area," he pointed out.

Only once did he show any real interest during the examination; that was when, going over the edges of the table he produced his tweezers and loosened a thin curling thread of some sort which had caught on a splinter. This he placed in one of his seed envelopes.

When he announced that he was finished, he had a last word for the local inspector.

"I should still keep the place locked up, Mainforce," he advised. "I may want to confirm something after I've gone through, in my laboratory, the things I've taken away."

As he and Merry walked towards the door, a foot clicked against some object on the floor. Merry picked up the object—a small piece of hard soil, curved slightly in its length.

"A mixture of clay and chalk, apparently," said Manson, and looked more closely at it. "Appears to have dried and fallen out of a heel instep. Put it into an envelope and we'll have a closer look at it later."

"Oh, by the way, sir, we've found that hat about which you were worried," Mackenzie announced. He flashed it into sight like a conjuror producing a hat out of a rabbit for a change.

Doctor Manson took it. The hat, a brown trilby, looked a trifle the worse for wear. The doctor eyed it dubiously.

"Just the kind of hat he'd have picked for a night like last night," Mackenzie suggested.

Doctor Manson nodded, but still dubiously. "And where," he asked, "did you find it?"

"Round the side of the house, near the kitchen window, sir. There are marks of footsteps on the flower bed, but it's loose, soft soil, and there are no definable footsteps."

The scientist walked round the house and inspected the spot. He nodded agreement at the impossibility of making anything tangible of the trampling. He wrapped the hat in a piece of newspaper and packed it into the Box of Tricks.

The Chief Constable walked with the two scientists back to the railway station yard and saw them off for London in Doctor Manson's big black car.

"Anything more we can do?" he asked.

"Only the woman at the moment. Colonel," the scientist replied, "and anything we can find of Canley's movements last night. He had not returned, you remember, when Mrs. Skelton (whom God preserve) had laid his evening meal and left the house for the night. Thanks for the lunch."

The car purred away.

* * * * *

An hour or two later, a car drew into the runway of a garage on the Staines By-pass—a neat, freshly painted garage with green and white facings. The driver crawled out of his seat, stretched his long legs and looked round.

"Hi, there!" he called.

From the interior Jack Porter emerged. He was dressed in a pair of brown dungarees and was wiping his hands on a chunk of mutton-cloth as he approached his customer.

"Petrol—four gallons, please. And you had better put in a pint of oil, too."

"Very good, sir. Nice to see a bit of sun in November, isn't it?"

The man giggled. "All right for them that can see it," he agreed. "Know one chap who doesn't care. He can't see it."

"Who's that, sir?"

"Chappie found dead at Thames Pagnall. On the railway."

"Oh, him! Yes, of course. I saw it in the early evening papers. Knocked down by a train, wasn't he?"

"You're behind the times," announced the customer. "That's the cause of the excitement down there. They all thought that he was knocked down by the train and had his head cut off. Only he wasn't."

Porter's heart stopped a beat. His hand slipped and petrol from the pipe sprayed over the road.

"Hi! Look out, man," warned the motorist.

"Sorry, sir. I'll put a bit more in over the mark. What were you saying about the dead man?"

"Oh, only that he wasn't killed by the train. He was dead when the train ran over him. Rare to-do about how he came to be dead on the track."

"I haven't seen anything about that."

"Don't suppose you have. It isn't public property. Copper friend told me when I stopped at the local. He's been on the business. Seems somebody went over the local police and got the Yard in. They sent down a big noise, and he was scouting round until an hour ago. He said that the chap was put on the lines in order to make people think that his death was an accident."

"How the dickens can he tell that?"

"Don't ask me, laddie. Can't say. Fellow doesn't know himself, according to my copper friend. But he reckons he'll know by tomorrow. That's what I call damned clever."

"Sure," replied Porter absently, as he counted out change for a pound note. "Perhaps the chap deserved to be killed. You never know."

"I know a few I'd cheerfully kill if I couldn't be found out. Good morning."

The customer put his car into gear and drove off.

Jack Porter walked slowly back into his garage. His heart was beating painfully and his legs were trembling so violently that he could scarcely stand. He sat down on a bench to recover himself.

How had the police tumbled to the fact that Canley had not been killed by the train? It seemed incredible. He went back in memory over all he had done during the night, carefully checking off each item.

The marks of Canley's shoes down the lane and up to the line would surely have told the police that he had walked there. And there were not any other prints. Yet they had said that he did not walk to the railway.

But there, what did it matter anyway? The more he thought over the thing, the more cheerful he became. His heart settled down into its usual rate of beating. Suppose they *had* found that Canley was dead when the train went over him, he, Porter, had no cause to worry. There was no trace of him left in the cottage. He was quite certain about that. There was no loop-hole that could send the police in his direction.

Porter looked through his garage doors, and saw another car pull in. He rose and, whistling cheerfully, went forward to service it.

At that precise moment, Doctor Manson began preparing the benches in the laboratory in Scotland Yard for the beginning of the search into the identity of the person whom he knew had killed James Canley.

CHAPTER XIX

LEFT to himself—and Inspector Mackenzie—Kenway debated on the best method of beginning his inquiries into Mrs. Andover. He took the problem to his colleague's local knowledge.

"Now, Mac," he said, "you know this place. Where would be the best place to start searching round?"

Mackenzie, whose way of dealing with the village malefactors was the archaic method of fixing them with the eyes of the Law and thus terrorizing them, as he thought, into subservience, tended in the direction of direct approach. "Seeing as he and she were—"

"On terms of intimacy is what you are searching for, I think," put in Kenway, helpfully.

"—as everybody around here knows," went on Mackenzie.

"It looks strange to me that she hasn't been round to see what's happened to him. All the village knows by now that he's dead. I'd have reckoned that she would have turned up at the cottage. Especially as she's got a lot of things lying about the place. Look's suspicious to me."

"Not if it's true that murderers always return to the scene of their crime," said Kenway.

"Don't believe in that rubbish," denounced the Scotsman, whose superstitious beliefs were only those attested by the Book of Common Prayer and the Bishops. "They keeps as far from the scene of the crime as they can. I know where the woman lives. We could go and give her the works."

"And give her the chance to know all that we know—so that she can set about preparing a nice alibi among her friends! I'd sooner get to know about her and her movements to be able to question her, knowing that we have a good check on her answers—which she won't know we've got. I take it she used to have a drink now and again. Which pub did she particularly fancy?"

"The Miller's Arms, over there on the Green." Mackenzie waved a hand in the direction of the end of the lane.

"Then we will drop in and have a beer. What's the landlord's name, by the way?"

"North. Ted North. Who does your doctor man think did it?" he added, inconsequently.

"The doctor? No idea, Mac. He never says anything about a case until he's sure of what he's saying."

"Don't see what he can do about the case in London, anyway."

"No?" Kenway looked amused. "Now, I reckon that with the things he's taken away with him the doctor will learn more about this case in an hour with his microscope and bottles than we'll get round here in a day."

"Do you mean the things he put in envelopes?"

"I do, Mac, yes."

"Well, I reckon he can't do as well as someone on the spot. Stands to sense. There's the pub," he announced.

The Miller's Arms stood squarely a little back from the road, and in front of a stretch of common land, on which bracken was mixed with blackberry and hawthorn bushes. Whence it derived its name was a never-ending source of conjecture to the clientele, and even to the landlord, for there was nothing in the archives of Thames Pagnall to suggest that there had ever been a mill in the vicinity; in fact, the only mill which did exist in the area was in a neighbouring village, some two miles away, on the banks of the River Mole, or still farther away at Esher; the mill at the latter place still stands.

But, fact or fiction, the Thames Pagnall hostelry bore the title The Miller's Arms, together with a picture of a jolly miller, which looked unlike any miller who ever ground corn!

At first glance the place appeared to be particularly modern, with its red bricks, nicely pointed, and attractively green and cream paint. It was not until the doors were swung open and one passed to the interior that its antiquity was revealed.

A long, low room, carpeted, welcomed the thirsty entrant, with long rough oak beams, blackened with age. (A test of the antiquity of oak beams is usually that they are not of the sawn variety, but merely roughly fashioned with an axe or adze.) A large open fireplace in the side of which half a dozen men could sit, and from the chimney of which hung still the old-fashioned spit, gave confirmation of its age.

Along one of the beams down the centre of the room hung from nails, copper beer-measures, ranging in size from a gill to half a gallon. An air of pleasant quietude and conviviality permeated the atmosphere. Inspector Kenway eyed the bar with appreciation.

"Old place this, isn't it?" he asked.

"More than 500 years," answered the landlord, who had entered unheard from behind them. He greeted Mackenzie. "It has a rare reputation round these parts, has this pub," he added.

"And what would that be, landlord?" asked Kenway.

"You'll hardly believe it"—the landlord chuckled—"but its the only pub hereabouts that Dick Turpin didn't spend a night in. We've got the identical bed upstairs in which he didn't sleep."

He joined in the laughter which greeted the announcement.

"That is probably the reason why Mackenzie here, and the police come," volunteered Kenway. "Patronizing a law-abiding house, as it were. What do we drink here, Mackenzie?"

"Wallop," announced Mackenzie, promptly. "Speciality of the house."

"Then, two pints of wallop it shall be. And perhaps you'll join us, Mr. North?"

"Pleased."

The landlord pulled the beer. "Good health," he pledged; and the three men drank deeply.

"Visiting here?" The landlord looked inquiringly at Kenway.

"Detective-Inspector Kenway, of Scotland Yard." Mackenzie made the introduction. "Mr. North—Councillor here as well as landlord." He paused. "We're in a spot of bother here, Ted," he announced.

"Ah! Canley, I reckon. Accident, wasn't it?"

The swing doors opened, and a couple of men entered. Kenway looked at the landlord. "Can we go somewhere where we can talk, Mr. North?" he asked. "You may be able to give us some assistance."

"Come into my snuggery." The landlord poked his head through the bar hatch. "Tend the bar, Mary, for a bit, will you?" he called out; and then led the way into a small room off the bar, and closed the door. "Only one or two personal friends of mine allowed in here," he explained. "We shall not be disturbed at this time of the day. Now, what can I do?"

"Tell us anything you can about Canley," said Kenway. "I can tell you, in confidence, that he wasn't killed by the train; he was dead before the train touched him. We are seeking some reason why he should have been on the line at that time of night, and something about his habits and acquaintances."

The landlord rubbed a hand over his chin, ruefully.

"There's not much I can tell you," he said. "He was a good customer here—I suppose he spent three or four pounds a week, but we don't know much about him, really. I gathered he was a south country chap."

"Do any work?"

"No. Not so far as I know. It was understood that he had private means of some kind. He did a bit of racing."

"Win anything?"

"He said so. And one or two tips he gave in the bar here have come up. I should think that Dan Hubbard could tell you more of him in that connection. He's our local bookie."

"Any particular friends—or enemies?"

"Not that I know of." The landlord drew puzzled brows together. "It is a peculiar fact that, although he was greeted here affably, nobody really cottoned to him. They'd have his drinks, and buy him a drink, but not like friends. It's hard to explain, but—"

"You mean he had not lived long enough in the place to have ceased being a stranger?" suggested Kenway. The inspector had been born in a country village, and knew the feeling against what are called 'outsiders'.

"No. As a matter of fact, it wasn't like that at all, Inspector. That kind of feeling has died out here. We are so close to London, you know, and most of our people actually work in London and live here. No. It seemed to be some quality in him which did not attract folks."

"Well, supposing that went for men. What about ladies—Mrs. Andover, for instance?"

The landlord laughed. "That was one of the little jokes we had among ourselves, and didn't tell Canley. Everybody except Canley knew all about it. She's rather notorious round here. Canley had the idea that he was the only, and great, lover of the lady. He wasn't. But nobody dare tell him so."

"What kind of woman is she?"

"Actually she's quite good company. And a good-looker. She'd got a little money of her own—left her, I reckon, by some man in the past. I'm told that it is enough for her to live upon. The trouble with her is that she seems to be a 'beauximaniac'."

"Beauximaniac?" Kenway laughed and looked quizzical inquiry. "That's a new one on me," he said.

"Beauximania—one who has a mania for beaux. I invented the word for her," elucidated the landlord. "She can't keep away from men. The obsession made her a bit of a nuisance. I had to stop her coming in here unless she had an escort. I asked Mackenzie's advice about that. Mind you, she had a genius for keeping each of her various men unaware that they were receiving her intimate favours. They knew, of course, that the other men took her into a pub and bought her drinks, but they didn't know the afterwards—in the dead of night. I reckon, though, that Canley had found out. And in the row that followed, I had to turn them both out of here."

"Row?" The inspector started slightly. "When would that be, landlord?"

"Last night, as a matter of fact."

"What!" Kenway became alert. "Do you mean to say that they were rowing in here last night? What time would that have been?"

The landlord thought back. "Now, let me see, who was in here? Bill Adams, Julian Evans, Andrew Melville—he never comes in before nine o'clock, and he'd been in about twenty minutes—it would be about nine-thirty, I suppose. My lady came in with Ted Appleton. He was one of the men Canley did not know about. They ordered drinks. They were drinking snugly and happily and then suddenly Canley himself came in and spotted them."

The landlord chuckled at the recollection. "Ted drank up his port and hopped it. Canley went over to her, and sat down, and then the row started. I asked them to leave, and watched them start off together down the road. You know, I have an idea that Canley had hoodwinked her, because my lady was always very careful not to bring somebody else into a pub if her particular fancy man was likely to be in the same place. And she knew that Canley was mostly in here."

"He did not threaten any violence, I suppose?" asked Kenway.

"Who? Canley?" Mr. North laughed. "No fear! The lady has a whale of a temper and if it had come to any violence, I reckon it would have been Canley who would have been at the wrong end of it."

"Aye, Mrs. Andover could hold him with one hand and spank him with the other," said Mackenzie in confirmation.

"In which direction did they go when they left? You said that you watched them down the street."

"All I can say is that they went in the direction of the crossroads. They have four different choices from there."

Inspector Kenway got to his feet. "Well, we'll be moving on, Mackenzie," he announced. "Thank you very much for your help, Mr. North. I will remember to point out to my friends the inn which Turpin never visited." They laughed together. Outside, they walked along in the direction of the main street.

"Where next, Inspector?" queried Mackenzie.

Kenway wrinkled his brows in thought. "Perhaps before we see Mrs. Andover we ought to check up on that time," he said at last. "Where can we find Ted Appleton?"

"In the grocery shop across the Green in front of us," said Mackenzie. "It's a prosperous business and Ted is what they call 'warm' in money." He looked across as the ting-tong of the doorbell announced the opening of the shop door. "And here," he announced, "here, by a dispensation of providence is Ted himself coming towards us. We can get him alone in the open air." He waited, and halted the grocer.

"Can we have a word with you, Ted?" he asked.

"Sure thing, Inspector."

Kenway introduced himself. "We are trying to trace the wanderings of James Canley last night, before he died, Mr. Appleton. Now, we gather that you saw him in the Miller's Arms during the time you were there with a lady. Is that so?"

"I did, Inspector, yes. But not to speak to." He smiled sheepishly. "As a matter of fact, when he came in I skedaddled. I was with Mrs. Andover, and she was Canley's pigeon—"

"So I've heard, Ted," said Inspector Mackenzie. "I'm surprised at you being with her, seeing as how Canley was about the place."

"Wouldn't have been if I'd known he was around, although I knew her before he ever came here," retorted Appleton. "As it happened, she said that Canley had gone to Esher or somewhere, so I. . . er . . . dallied an hour or two with her. At least, that was to have been the idea," he corrected. "We went into the Miller's Arms for a drink, to start the evening off right, and lo and behold, before we could swallow it, in comes Canley and starts over to me. I wasn't going to have any argument with Canley, so I lit out."

"What time would that be?" asked Kenway.

"I can tell you to within a couple of minutes—twenty-five past nine."

"You saw no more of Canley, I suppose?"

"Not a sign. I went home, and there I stayed."

"Mr. Appleton lives by himself, over his shop," explained Mackenzie.

"No message of goodwill, or otherwise, from Canley, I suppose?" asked Kenway.

Appleton shook his head, waved a hand and resumed his journeyings.

"Well, that's that," said Kenway. "We didn't learn much there we didn't already know, but we've confirmed the time with that given by the landlord. We've got Mrs. Andover with Appleton up to practically half past nine. At that time he handed her over, unwillingly, I suppose, to Canley. After half past nine, Appleton saw them going towards the cross-roads. So it seems to be pretty clear that it was somewhere between a quarter to ten and half past ten that Canley was killed."

"Half past ten, Inspector. Why half past ten exactly?" Mackenzie looked puzzled.

"Because, Mac, after he had been killed and was, I suppose, still in the cottage, the murderer had to make all arrangements in the cottage to show that Canley was alone all night. At least, that is what he thought he was doing. They'd take a pretty time, you know, and then he had to carry Canley to the railway and arrange the accident. I reckon all that would take him the best part of an hour to carry out, so that the last train down was to be the presumed death of Canley, I guess the man was killed about ten-thirty. Inductive reasoning, Mac. We're great on inductive reasoning in the Yard."

Mackenzie grunted. "If I talked like that, old Ypres would call it guess work, and tick me off," he mourned.

"There's a difference between guess work, and assumption based on facts," said Kenway, reprovingly. "In this case we've got a person so keen on removing all traces of having been in the cottage, that we can find out through his over-carefulness exactly what he did. Knowing what he did, Mac, we do not guess, but estimate the time he took to do it. From that estimate we arrive at an approximate time of death. But, anyway, this is getting us nowhere. Having now been left with Canley in the company of Mrs. Andover at the cross-roads, we had better, I think, tackle Mrs. Andover, and see what she did with him. That ought to take us a little nearer the fatal time of half past ten. Where does she live?"

"Only a stone's throw from Ted Appleton," chortled Mackenzie. He led the way to a house just round the corner from the grocer's shop, and rang a bell. "She has a couple of rooms and a bathroom here—a kind of self-contained flat," he explained in a whisper. "Here she is."

Mackenzie had stated that Mrs. Andover could hold Canley in one hand and spank him with the other; and Kenway, when he found himself face to face with the lady, realized that he had not exaggerated.

Mrs. Andover was what is known as a strapping woman. Not in the sense that she was gross or over-sized; she was beautifully proportioned and shaped, with broad shoulders and hips that had the look of strength about them. Her breasts were set high, and stood out from her body, firmly. She stood tall and stately, a perfect animal.

She was, too, a good-looking woman, who earlier in life had undoubtedly been handsome. A hardness in the lines round her mouth, and too much rouge in the cheeks signalled to some extent the beginning of the fading of the fortune of face and figure, but she was still a woman at whom men would look twice. Junoesque, was the description that ran through the mind of Kenway, as he studied her. She greeted the two men surprisingly.

"Do come in. Inspector Mackenzie, and bring your friend," she invited sweetly. "I am sure this will be a most delightful visit—for Mrs. Julian."

"Mrs. Julian?" queried Kenway. 'Where does Mrs. Julian come in, and who the devil is she?' he asked himself under his breath.

Mrs. Andover laughed trillingly. "She's looking from behind her curtain in the window across the street," she explained. "She'll probably write to the Chief Constable or *The Times* about it. Just fancy, a police inspector and another man . . . stopped half an hour, my dear, and in broad daylight."

"Another *inspector*, Mrs. Andover," said Kenway smilingly. "That makes two of them."

He followed Mackenzie into the house. Mrs. Andover placed them in a couple of armchairs, and arranged cushions behind for their shoulders. She lolled herself on a settee, sinking slinkily into its depths.

"Now, let's hear it," she invited. "I suppose it's about Canley?"

"It is, Mrs. Andover, yes." Kenway took over the questioning. He spoke curtly; he felt revolted at the casualness of her mention of the man who had been her lover, and who had died tragically. "You know, of course, what has happened?" he asked.

"I know that he was found dead on the railway, yes."

"We are trying to find out what he was up to on the lines at that hour of the night," explained the inspector.

"Then I am afraid I cannot help you very much." Mrs. Andover made the statement with definiteness. "In point of fact, I would like to know myself what he was up to last night. He seems to have been intent on playing me for a sucker." She gazed in self-appreciation at an ample display of shapely leg.

"Shall we start from nine o'clock, Mrs. Andover?" Kenway developed a business-like air. "Or perhaps a little later than nine o'clock. You left the Miller's Arms with him after a somewhat heated argument, and started out in the direction of the crossroads. Where did you branch from there?"

"I branched into this room, Inspector. Where Canley went I do not know. I told him to go to the devil. He seems to have taken me literally at 11.35 p.m., but where he went in the interim, I have not the least idea."

Kenway had been jerked to surprise at the woman's statement. He watched her face as he asked, quietly, and with a disarming smile: "At eleven-thirty-five? Why do you pick on that time, Mrs. Andover?"

If he expected her to show embarrassment, or confusion, he was disappointed.

"I should hardly think his body could have been missed if it had been lying on the lines before the last train of the night passed," she replied. "But anyway, I am told by my landlady's small child that the 11.35 pm. train knocked him down."

"I see." It was after a moment's reflection that Kenway played his real opening gambit.

"But, Mrs. Andover, you were in Canley's cottage last night, were you not?" The question came in quiet conversational tones.

The woman sat up in surprise, and stared at her visitors. "I told you that I came straight home," she said. Kenway produced his cigarette-case and proffered it. He lighted Mrs. Andover's weed, and with exaggerated care, selected and puffed at one himself. "Why prevaricate with us, Mrs. Andover," he said. "I know that you were in the cottage last night."

"Indeed!" she became sarcastic. "And how, may I ask, do you know that—or suppose you know it?"

"That is simple, madam. You left a—shall we say, an *ensemble* there."

Mrs. Andover laughed. "That, my dear Inspector, is nothing to go by. I was in the cottage most nights and I frequently left—er—*ensembles* there. The ones to which you refer may have been there a week or more."

"Not unless they possess the attributes of a chameleon, Mrs. Andover." Kenway spoke sharply and caustically.

"I don't get that, Inspector."

Kenway explained the attributes of the colour scheme of the *chamaeleon vulgaris*. "If the *ensemble* in question had been left there the previous night, Mrs. Andover, they must have mysteriously changed colour within twenty-four hours because they were not black the previous day."

"I understand. The Gospel thumper has been snooping around again, I suppose? All right. It is true that I was there last night. I expected to spend the night there—at least until the small hours. But at eight-thirty Canley pushed me off, and came out with me. He said that he had some business to attend to, and did not know when he would be back—but certainly not before midnight.

"We parted at the main-road junction. I walked back towards here, and ran into Ted Appleton, told him I was at a loose end because Canley had gone to Esher for the night, and we went into the Miller's Arms for a drink. Then Canley appeared. Ted hopped it"—she grinned broadly—"and Canley and I had a bit of an argument. North said it would be better if we went out until we had decided the matter. Which we did—as I have already told you."

Kenway digested the statement in silence. He was seeking to find a flaw in the timing, but could not do so. It all corresponded with the figures given by Mr. Appleton himself and by the landlord. Appleton's statement did not matter; he might have some reason to shield the woman, but there could be no such argument in the case of the landlord; and his times coincided with those given by the woman. There was one point, however, that might pay for a little probing, the inspector decided. He tried it.

"You said just now, Mrs. Andover, that you yourself would like to know what Mr. Canley was up to last night, and you mentioned something about playing you for a sucker. Do I take it that that referred to his sudden appearance in the Miller's Arms after he had told you that he was going to Esher, or wherever it was he was going?"

"That was in my mind, yes."

"You think he was trying to catch you out?"

"I thought it rather looked that way, which is why we had the argument."

"Did he know that you knew Mr. Appleton?"

"Certainly. He knew that we were acquainted. We have all three shared a round of drinks together before now."

"But did he know you knew him in the phrase which Mr. Appleton used—to dally with you for an hour or so?"

"As to that, Inspector, I do not know—nor do I particularly care. No man orders me about."

"You are quite sure, Mrs. Andover, that you were not in the cottage after eight-thirty?"

"Quite sure."

"What time did you reach the cottage?"

"I cannot say for certain. But I should think it would be about five minutes to eight."

"What did you do with the dinner things?"

The woman stared in surprise. "The dinner things?" she echoed.

"What on earth have I to do with his meals? In fact, I did not see any dinner things. Canley was sitting in the armchair by the fire when I arrived, reading a racing paper."

"Nothing on the table at all?"

"Not to make me notice anything."

"No whisky for instance?"

"None. We had nothing to drink. We had other distractions."

"And after you left Canley you came here?"

"That is so, Inspector."

"And stayed here all night?"

Mrs. Andover nodded.

Kenway reached for his hat and coat. So did Mackenzie. Mrs. Andover accompanied them to the door. She looked across the road and saw the quiver of the curtains in the window of the house opposite. She laughed, placed a hand on the shoulders of Inspector Mackenzie, and waved at the figure behind the curtains.

Kenway looked across at the recipient of the favour, but saw nobody. Mrs. Andover smiled. "Only the lady behind the curtains, Inspector," she said. "I like to acknowledge her kindly interest."

The two men walked away. "Well? What do you make of it?" Inspector Mackenzie quizzed.

"Blest if I know what to make of her story, Mac. I think I'll pop back to the Yard, and see what the doctor can see in it. Meanwhile, you might have a go at some of the other lights o' love of the lady, and see if they know anything. We should, I feel, try for a confirmation that Mrs. Andover was, as she says, in her rooms from just turned nine-thirty onwards. We have only her word for it. Can you get into conversation with the prying Mrs. Julian without Mrs. Andover knowing? She seems to maintain surveillance over the comings and goings from Mrs. Andover's."

"I think there is a back entrance through the garden," decided Mackenzie.

"Then go to it, my lad."

CHAPTER XX

IT WAS not only to Doctor Manson that Inspector Kenway told the story of Mrs. Andover. His arrival at the Yard coincided with a call by the Assistant Commissioner for information on the inquiry.

In the horseshoe-shaped room of the Assistant Commissioner (C for Crime) which overlooks the Embankment from the police palace of Scotland Yard, Sir Edward Allen heard the doctor's story; and then the result of Kenway's inquiries. He looked across at the scientist.

"What does it count up to, Harry?" he asked.

"I would not like to say, Edward," was the thoughtful reply. "I have not seen the woman, Kenway has. He thinks, apparently, that she is of the Amazon stamp who could, in a frenzy, perhaps, pick up Canley and convey him to the line. I have my doubts—not that she *could* do it, but that she *would* do it. I do not think that a woman would have the idea of staging so elaborate an accident. A woman's brain runs in a different groove to that of a man." He thought for a few moments.

"But there is one circumstance that makes me hesitate before dismissing her from the plot."

"That being—?"

"The polishing of the glasses and the bottle. Now that is the *one* thing a woman would think of. Mrs. Andover is a woman, and I gather an intelligent one. There is sufficient in that to make me say that she is worth a little more investigation. Mackenzie, I gather, is probing a little deeper into her various lovers, and I think Kenway here might give him the benefit of his riper experience in such cases."

Kenway nodded. "There is one suggestion I want to make in reply to what the doctor has said," he begged. "That is to inquire what the doctor thinks of a theory that there might be two people concerned in the business?"

Doctor Manson sat up. "In what way?" he asked.

"Well, supposing that it is not a woman's job to carry Canley to the line, which is what we know happened, and it is more like a woman to polish everything up—might not she have done the polishing and her partner the carrying?"

"I have nothing against the idea, Kenway," approved Manson. "What put the idea into your mind?" he added.

"Something that Mrs. Andover said. She thought that she was being played for a sucker by Canley. What she meant was that he told her he was going to be away for the night, left the cottage with her, and locked it up. He walked with her to the cross-roads, and there they parted. Now, at that junction the buses to and from Esher stop. She thought he was going to Esher, so she steps off with Appleton, who was pretty familiar with her before she took up with Canley."

"You mean," Sir Edward looked interested, "that there had been something going on between the woman and Appleton, and that Canley had got wise to it?"

"That, roughly, is the idea, Sir Edward. According to Appleton she was pretty clever at keeping her men apart. As I see it, Canley's shooing her out of the cottage where she had expected to stay for the greater part of the night, his leaving her at the bus stop of the Esher buses saying that he didn't know when he would be back, but not before midnight, seems to suggest that he had learned something of what was going on behind his back, and expected her to be on with a new love so soon as his back was turned."

"And the plan came off," mused Doctor Manson. "It's an idea, Kenway."

"But hardly an excuse for murder, would you think?" Sir Edward challenged the inspector.

"If it was a plan would the couple be content to leave it at that, Sir Edward?" retorted Kenway. "I don't say that it is a ground for murder. But figure it out this way: Suppose the man and woman, irate at being duped by Canley, get together and decide to have it out with him. They go to his cottage, and in the row Canley gets accidentally rubbed out.

Appleton is pretty cute. He could think out the accident theory. He's lived in the place all his life, and knows the short cut pretty well, in fact he's one of the men who has always said that some time somebody is going to get killed on that line, and then something would be done about the crossing. That covers up the doctor's objection to the woman as having taken Canley to the line, and at the same time supports his idea that it is a woman's mind which would think of the polishing.

"As to details," went on Kenway. "Mrs. Andover lives alone in her rooms. Appleton lives alone in the rooms over his shop. Both of them say that they did not go out of their places that night. There is nobody to corroborate either of them."

Sir Edward looked at his inspector. Gratified appreciation showed in his face. "Dash it, Kenway," he said. "I didn't think you had it in you. It's a piece of good logical working out. What do you say to it, Doctor?"

"A very creditable piece of work, I agree, Edward," responded Manson. "But I think there would have been some evidence of some kind of struggle if such an affray had occurred; and I doubt whether a scared woman—and she would have been scared—could have so completely removed all traces, so as to leave not one suggestion for us to discover.

"At the same time I am concerned over one point that Kenway made—his only real arguable fact—and that is the complete absence of proof that either of the people, Appleton or the woman, can produce any corroboration that they did not, in fact, leave their homes after the incident in the Miller's Arms. That is a very important point indeed, and I think it all the more important that Kenway should return to Thames Pagnall and pursue investigations into it. Off you go, Kenway," he invited. "See if you can find any recent association between the woman and Appleton."

Sir Edward waited until the door had closed behind the inspector before he resumed his conference with his scientific investigator, at the point at which it had arrived before the entrance of Kenway.

"I take it, then, that it is murder, Harry?" he asked.

"Oh, yes. There is no doubt about it being homicide, Edward. And I think it was planned, too."

The Assistant Commissioner twirled his monocle on its cord. "Which would mean that you don't accept Kenway's suggestion of a joint visit and a row?"

"I keep an open mind on that—in certain aspects, Edward. As Kenway postulated it will not bear examination—logical examination, that is." He waited a comment.

Sir Edward turned the point over in his mind. "You know, I should have thought it might be possible," he said at length. "They might naturally be expected to go round and ask Canley what was the game. Tempers might flare up in such circumstances—and there you are."

"Granted, Edward. Tempers all het up, and a devil of a row going on. One of the pair sees red. What does he do? He picks up the weapon nearest to his hand, bats Canley one—and Canley goes west. That I can understand."

He paused a moment. "But what I cannot understand in such circumstances, is the actual blow which killed Canley—*in the only place where the injury could subsequently be hidden by decapitation.*"

Sir Edward deliberated the argument. "You don't think it is likely that seeing where the blow fell, Appleton could suddenly think of the train and the neck?"

"Candidly, I don't." Manson drummed his fingers on the arm of his chair, a habit of his when he was worried in his deliberations. "There's another point against it, too, Edward."

"That is?"

"The weapon. There was nothing in the room except the hefty poker that could have killed Canley by a blow. The poker had not been used for such an attack. Would the pair going to Canley to have a row, but without malicious intent to do violence, have carried some weapon with them?"

"H'm! I see the point. But what do you mean, then, by saying that you keep an open mind on Kenway's suggestions, Harry?"

"I qualified the verdict by saying 'certain aspects', you remember. Kenway, being a little impetuous, has not the logically balanced mind to search round all the aspects before stating a case. The two could have been associated in the murder in one way, and Kenway has the ground-work for that, too, in his suggestion that something might have been happening between Mrs. Andover and Appleton before that night.

"It is possible that they may have plotted to get rid of Canley, in which case they could have gone to the cottage with a plan already prepared. Thus, the woman could have kept the attention of Canley fixed on herself while Appleton struck the fatal blow on the spot where it had to be obliterated by the train. That is the reason I told Kenway to trace any possible recent association between the two, and to check, if possible, their presence in their respective homes."

Sir Edward grunted defeat. "Dashed if I know how you think out these snags, Harry," he said. "Without seeming to think at all—Come in," he called, in response to a knock at the door. Inspector Kenway made a reappearance.

"Sorry, Sir Edward, to intrude, but it is rather important," he proclaimed. He turned to the doctor.

"Mackenzie has just been on the telephone. He says that Mrs. Julian—the Paul Pry, you know—is prepared to swear that Mrs. Andover was not in her rooms last night between nine-thirty and midnight. She says that there were no lights, and the blinds were not drawn. When she popped off to bed at midnight, she gave another peep, and the windows were unchanged. Mackenzie wants to know what we want him to do?"

"Nothing." Doctor Manson spoke sharply. "We do not want him bellowing all over the place. Tell him to lie low until you get there, Kenway, and you be off as quickly as you can—in a Squad car."

"It looks as though there is something in the idea, Edward," he commented, as Kenway left the room. "I'd go down myself except that there are one or two matters I must see to in the laboratory."

CHAPTER XXI

MRS. Andover looked from her door in surprise at the renewed appearance of her afternoon visitors. She was dressed for going out, but met the request of the officers for a little further chat by leading the way into her sitting-room.

"What is it now?" she asked, and in less pleasant cadence of voice than she had used on the earlier visit. Kenway appointed himself spokesman.

"There is a little doubt in our minds as to the actual interpretation we each place on what you told us this afternoon," he explained. "Perhaps you would clear it up."

"I thought I made it quite clear. But what is it?"

"You said that when you parted from Canley you came home—that is, to this room, and remained there. Is that correct?"

"Quite correct, Inspector."

"You did not meet Mr. Appleton again? He did not, for instance, come here, and you did not go to him?"

"Certainly not, I had no idea where Mr. Appleton went when he left the Miller's Arms."

The reply gave to Kenway the opening gambit for which he had been angling—the introduction to Mr. Appleton's sudden disappearance from the Miller's Arms. He had thought it strange that the man should have left so unceremoniously at the entrance of Canley. There seemed no harm in his buying Mrs. Andover a drink in a public house— and certainly not any reason for bolting out of the place. Unless—He decided to make his point.

"You told us this afternoon, Mrs. Andover, that you thought that you were being played for a sucker in that Canley had told you he was going away on business, only to walk into the Miller's Arms and find you with Mr. Appleton. Can you tell us why he should play such a trick on you?"

Mrs. Andover hesitated. "No," she said, slowly. "I cannot."

"Would there have been any rivalry between Mr. Appleton and Mr. Canley, for instance? Suppose that Canley had some suspicion that he *would* find you with Mr. Appleton. That would make him lay such a trap, would it not?"

"I don't know what Canley thought, and I don't care, either," retorted Mrs. Andover.

"Come now, Madam," said Kenway, brutally. "Canley was spending money on you. You were his mistress, were you not? You had known Appleton long before you met Canley. Was Appleton also finding you in money?"

Mrs. Andover stood up. Her face coloured. Even the mass of red hair seemed to grow into a more glittering red. She walked, or rather stalked, to the door of the room, and wrenched it violently open.

"Get out," she ordered, *"Get out!" She was quivering with passion.

The two inspectors rose. "Very well, Mrs. Andover. We will go," announced Kenway. "But we shall return. There were no lights in this room or in your bedroom, both with uncurtained windows from eight o'clock last night until after midnight. That can be proved."

The woman stared at him in silence. Then she closed the door and returned to her seat. "All right," she said. "I did not come back here. I went elsewhere."

"With Appleton?"

"No. I did not see Appleton. That is exactly as I have told you. I went to someone else."

"Whom?" demanded Kenway.

"The name I have no intention of giving. He had no connection with Canley, and never has had. He does not even know the name of Canley. And he is not in this village at all."

Beyond that statement Mrs. Andover would not budge, and after a few minutes of unsuccessful efforts to get from her the name of this new man, the officers left.

The search into the probable movements of Mr. Appleton proved even less satisfactory. There was no available assistance from a Paul Pry; the best that could be obtained was from the local constable.

The two men sought him out at his home. At the sight of them he jumped to his feet, and tried hastily and vainly to get into his tunic. Kenway grinned.

"Don't worry, Andrews," he said. "I am sure your inspector doesn't mind you being in your shirt sleeves in your own home, and I don't. Sit down and make yourself comfortable." He turned to Mackenzie. "You know the local ropes, Mac," he said. "See what you can find."

Mackenzie eyed his constable. "This is very confidential, Andrews, and mustn't be mentioned, not even to that wife of yours." The constable nodded.

"Did you see anything of Mr. Appleton in the village last night, after nine-thirty?"

"No, Inspector. Never saw him at all."

"He's on your beat, isn't he?"

"Yes. I tried his shop door, as is my bounden duty, sir. The shop was locked up."

"What time would that have been?" asked Kenway.

"The first time at ten o'clock, after I had traipsed round the places on the village green, sir."

"Any lights in the place. I understand that Mr. Appleton lives above his shop."

The constable shook his head. "No, sir, there were no lights at all in the place."

"You said something about the first time you passed his place, Constable. Do I take it that you were in the vicinity later than that?"

"Yes, sir. I returned that way at twelve forty-five, in the early morning, and tried the door again."

"Any lights that time?"

"No lights at all."

"Did you by any chance see Mrs. Andover last night?"

"Oh, yes, sir. Just after midnight. She was turning the corner near her lodgings."

"Rather late for her to be out, wasn't it?"

The constable smiled slightly. "For a woman, yes sir," he said. "But I often sees Mrs. Andover about after midnight. She generally comes home about that time."

"Home from where, constable?"

"I don't know, sir, of my own knowledge. But if there's anything in rumour, then it's generally from Mr. Canley's cottage—or used to be," he added, remembering that Canley was no more.

"You didn't see whether she came from that direction last night, I suppose?"

"No, sir. I just caught a glimpse of her turning the corner. I did not see from which way she came."

The two inspectors talked the constable's evidence over as they walked back into the main street of the village. Mackenzie was looking a little anxious at the interest shown in Appleton.

"I've known Ted this thirty years," he explained, "and I shouldn't like anything to happen to him. He's a good fellow. But its a bit queer about him saying he was at home, and yet there were no lights in the place either time."

"Well, Mac, I should say that you can forget the absence of lights at half past twelve. He'd probably be in bed by that time. But the ten o'clock darkness is a different kettle of fish. He wouldn't be sitting at home at that time on a cold night with no lights. Perhaps we'd better make a few more inquiries."

Inquiries, however, failed to find anyone who had seen the grocer about the streets, and the landlords of the various inns in the vicinity were quite definite in their statements that he had not been among their clientele at all on that evening.

"That's a funny thing in itself," commented Mackenzie, "for Ted is a sociable kind of a chap and generally spends an hour or two of every evening in the locals."

"Perhaps the experience in the Miller's Arms had put him off for the night," suggested Kenway. "In any case, it does not seem really to matter, because they close at ten-thirty o'clock."

"Perhaps we can get something out of himself," suggested Mackenzie.

"No, no!" Kenway protested emphatically. "Always wanting to give somebody the works, you are, Mac. We have no evidence to warn him that anything he says may be used in evidence, and we could not question him directly as to his whereabouts and movements without warning him. It was different with Mrs. Andover, because we knew that she had been in the cottage that night. I'll see what the doctor thinks of what we have learned so far. He may have found something at his end which may confirm what we have obtained."

Doctor Manson heard the tale of the investigations, as he sat in the study of his flat. He poured out a drink for the inspector, and listened to the end without speaking.

"Very interesting, Inspector; very interesting, indeed," he commented. "And especially the bit about the other man visited by Mrs. Andover. Any idea who he might be, if it wasn't Appleton?"

"Mackenzie thinks it may have been a Mr. Betterton, who lives about three-quarters of a mile away, has plenty of money and an amorous reputation."

After his guest had left, Manson sat silently reviewing the available evidence gathered during the day's investigations, his brain striving to find the keystone which held all the parts together. The recapitulation did not afford him even a modicum of satisfaction.

"It looks as though the thing is going to turn out into the Eternal Triangle with two men at the meeting sides,' he mused. 'And yet—"

He switched off the lights and went to bed.

"—and yet this kind of triangle does not usually result in this kind of murder," he concluded, as he got between the sheets.

He resumed his investigation, mentally refreshed, in the laboratory next morning.

The laboratory, which was the domain of Superintendent Doctor Manson was a well-lighted room occupying almost the whole of the top floor of New Scotland Yard. Along one side and end of it ran a continuous bench, save where it was broken by sunken porcelain sinks under the windows.

Bunsen burners, test tubes and beakers, evaporating apparatus and other chemistry appliances littered the shelves above the bench. Glass-fronted and indexed cases round the walls contained thousands of specimen microscope slides, including those of the blood corpuscles of almost every animal, fragments of cloth drawn from hundreds of makes of materials, hairs and samples of fur from animals of all countries, together with feathers of birds—enough material to identify by comparison alone nearly everything that could be brought to the laboratory for a verdict.

Along the length of the room opposite the bench, doors opened off into dark rooms, enlarging rooms and X-ray, infra-red and ultra-violet ray rooms.

Within the short space of three years Doctor Manson had built in the shell of the top floor of the Yard this formidable crime-fighting machine—the most complete scientific criminological laboratory in the world.

In the centre of the room stood his own 'bench'—a large square table with a white porcelain top. It was on this that he now placed the exhibits brought back from the cottage at Thames Pagnall—the envelopes containing the fluff from Canley's overcoat, the fibres from the patterned rug in the cottage, the cigar ash from the ash tray. They were followed by the little cake of earth against which his foot had clicked, the thread caught in a rough splinter of the table, the cigar butt which Inspector Mackenzie had found on the railway line, the hairs taken from the hats of Canley which had been hanging on the hallstand, and also the hat which had been found in the garden of the cottage.

Doctor Manson inspected them one by one, debating with himself. Finally, he pulled towards him the envelopes containing the cigar ash from the floor and looked around the laboratory.

"Wilkins," he called. The chief assistant of the laboratory came across. The doctor passed the envelope over. "Cigar ash is your hobby, is it not?" He laughed. "Here is a cigar and some ash. Give them a name, will you? And whether it has been recently smoked, or not? It belonged to a person who has died very suddenly. Any dampness about the cigar you may put down to the fact that it was lying out in the open all night."

Wilkins carried the exhibits to his own bench at the far end of the laboratory; and Doctor Manson, looking round, picked up the hat found in the cottage garden.

When he had first seen the hat he had regarded it with a considerable surprise. This was transformed into astonishment by the more detailed examination.

The hat was well worn, and not too clean. With a distinct air of distaste the doctor commenced foraging in the interior. It appeared to add to his surprise. Merry, entering the laboratory, noted the signs.

"Anything wrong with the hat, Harry?" he asked.

"I'm not sure, Jim. Didn't Mackenzie say that Canley had no occupation?"

"Except racing, Harry. Why?"

Doctor Manson preferred the hat to his deputy, and indicated the inside. "It seems to be permeated with foreign matter of some kind," he pointed out.

Merry investigated. "Dust apparently," he said. "But *inside!*"

Exactly. Dust outside I can understand. But dust inside a hat savours rather of occupational contamination, and that in a man who had no occupation." He turned back the inside leather band. "It's even behind the band," he emphasized. "What on earth is it?"

Merry inspected the discoloration. It appeared to be minute grains of a whitish substance, mixed with grease and dirt. "Can't make it out," he said, "we'd better put it under the microscope."

The examination produced a little more information. "I should say that it is lime, Harry," Merry reputed. "And what looks like—could it be stone?"

"Cement!" Doctor Mason supplied the answer. "It's cement dust."

"Now, what the blazes was Canley doing wallowing in cement?" asked Merry, in surprise.

"I don't suppose he was, Jim. This hat gets curiouser and curiouser. Let me have a look at it."

The doctor searched round the interior with a lens, and picked out two or three short hairs adhering to the grease. Carrying them to the sink, he placed them in a test tube, and washed them with a few drops of ether. Examination through the microscope again revealed the hairs now to be black in colour, from the head of a person, and with the tops square-cut.

"He'd had a haircut within twenty-four hours of his death, anyway," said Merry. "The points of the hair are not even starting to get rounded yet."

"But that doesn't explain the cement dust, anyway."

"I suppose it *is* Canley's hat?"

Doctor Manson looked up in surprise. "The point had not occurred to me, Jim," he admitted. "I had taken it for granted." He made a gesture of annoyance at the oversight. "We've a few specimens of the hair of Canley somewhere, if I remember. Sort them out, and we'll soon see if they agree."

Merry opened one of the seed envelopes and slipped on to a slide a couple of the hairs snipped from Canley's head. They were brown, with the points fully rounded.

"It is *not* his hat!" Doctor Manson exploded.

"Then whose the devil's is it?" said Merry. "And what's it doing in Canley's garden underneath a window where there are confused footprints?"

"That, Jim, is a question which has to be investigated." He rang a bell. "See if Inspector Kenway is in the Yard, Bellows," he said to the constable who answered. "Tell him we want him here."

Kenway listened to the story of the hat. "Black hair and all mixed up with cement," he repeated. "And dirty. It couldn't be flour, I suppose, Doctor, could it, because that would just fit Appleton, who is a grocer."

Manson smiled. "You seem intent on hanging Appleton, Kenway, don't you? No, it could not be flour, not unless Appleton mixes cement with his flour, and I expect the housewives would tell you that."

"Or their husbands," suggested Merry. "That might be better."

Kenway giggled. "I'll go down right away and scout round," he said.

Doctor Manson nodded agreement. He looked up and saw Wilkins hovering round the desk. The laboratory assistant was carrying in one hand a porcelain tray holding the cigar ash from the ashtray confined under a glass covering; in the other hand similarly protected was the cigar butt.

"Settled it, Wilkins?" asked Manson.

"No, Doctor." The assistant paused. "Did you say that this ash came from this cigar?" he asked.

"Presumably it does, Wilkins. I did not say that it did—that is what I wanted you to tell me—" He looked suddenly alert. "Is there something wrong with it?" he demanded.

"Very much so, sir. *There is too much ash.*"

"What!"

"There is too much ash here to have come from the consumed portion of the cigar," repeated Wilkins, patiently.

Merry whistled through his teeth. "I smell a rat, I see him forming in the air, and darkening the sky, but we'll nip him in the bud." He misquoted Sir Boyle Roche.

"I thought that you would like to know before I went further into the analysis," added Wilkins. "Perhaps in the circumstances, you would like to take it over yourself, sir."

Doctor Manson sat down again at his bench. "This, Wilkins," he says, "opens up possibilities."

"More than we have yet realized, Doctor," broke in Merry. He had looked over the covered tiles. "Because," he pointed out, "there is still ash that Wilkins has not included—the clump we gathered from the floor, and presumably, the bit that was thrown away during the journey from the cottage to the railway."[6]

"To be sure." Doctor Manson's voice had a timbre of annoyance at his oversight. He made no physical sign of it, however, but sat down and began peering at the ash through a lens. After a few moments he gave vent to a sharp exclamation, stood up, and motioned the chief assistant to take his place.

"Have a good look at the ash, Wilkins," he said. "Tell me if I am mistaken in thinking that there is something peculiar about it."

Wilkins pried among the carbon, separating a little of it from the remainder. After a pause he glanced up. "Can I use your microscope, Doctor?" Manson nodded, and watched with professional interest Wilkins place a little of the separated ash on a slide, cover it with a mica cup, and slip the slide under the eyepiece.

After a prolonged look, he rose, crossed the room to a cabinet, and from a drawer extracted half a dozen slides, each containing a few grains of some object.

One by one he placed the slides under the microscope. Finally, using the double eyepiece, he compared one simultaneously with the Canley sample.

The result satisfied him, for he sat back. "Yes, Doctor, there *is* a peculiarity about it," he announced. He was dogmatically emphatic in his decision. "There are two kinds of ash here—one from this cigar, which is a Havana blend of leaf. The other came from a Jamaican cigar. The two ashes under the microscope are quite distinct and different." He waited for any comment.

Doctor Manson nodded. "That was my own conclusion, Wilkins," he said. It was characteristic of the scientist that he would not rely on his own unsupported view, though he prided himself on being able to distinguish sixty different kinds of cigar and tobacco ash.

"And what about the ash from the floor?" he asked.

"It did not come from the cigar we have here. It is Jamaican."

"A bit of good thorough analysis, and helps me considerably," commended the scientist.

6. This was, of course, another wrong deduction, this time on the part of Merry. No ash was flicked away outside the cottage.

CHAPTER XXII

INSPECTOR Mackenzie scratched his head and let his slow-moving mind dwell on the story that Kenway had told him about the peculiar hat. A minute or two passed, and then he looked up from his aimless circumambulations. "That's funny," he said. "I never heard of Canley being anything to do with cement."

"I didn't say it was Canley," replied Kenway, patiently. "All I have said is that the hat seems to have belonged to somebody who has something to do with cement." Kenway was beginning to despair of Mackenzie altogether. "In fact, he seems to have lived among cement," he added.

"You mean that the hat doesn't belong to Canley at all?" The truth seemed to be sinking into the inspector's mind. "That's about it," replied Kenway.

"Then who the devil does it belong to?" Exasperation raised his voice to soprano pitch that made Kenway think of eunuchs.

"Who would make a habit of hanging up their hats in Canley's garden?"

"That's what I'm trying to get from you, Mackenzie," Kenway gestured impatiently. "Is there any cement mixing works round here?"

The inspector shook his head. "Nothing like that," he announced. He thought for a moment. "Best we can do is a concrete works," he announced. Kenway jumped. He recalled the stone dust found in the hat.

"Concrete!" he ejaculated. "That's our pigeon. That's even better. Where are these works?"

"Out towards Walton. London firm. Make paving slabs, and wall sections that look like bricks, and—er—all that kind of thing."

"Then we'd better hurry along there and make some inquiries."

The manager of the London Concrete Company sighed mournfully. "You really can't expect me, Inspector, to identify the hats of each of 200 employees, now can you?" he protested. He inspected the head-gear, plaintively. "I can't possibly say if it belongs to one of our men."

"No, I suppose not," Kenway agreed. "Do you happen to know if anyone here had any associations with Canley?"

The manager shook his head, negatively. "I don't even know all the people we employ here," he replied. "The best I can do is to pass you on to our yard foreman. He might be able to help you."

The officers found the foreman ensconced in the yard office. He listened to the recital of their worries and rubbed a hand over a chin which looked blackly dirty, but wasn't; Mr. Bailey was a dark man who had to shave twice a day in order to present a respectable appearance!

"Not exactly an association with Canley," he said, and seemed to be picking his words carefully.

"Something to do with Canley, then, eh?" suggested Kenway.

"No, Not 'im . . . his daughter," replied Mr. Bailey.

"His daughter!" Kenway sat up and took notice. "I think, Mr. Bailey," he said, "that you ought to tell us the story from the beginning. Who is the man you have in mind and what has his daughter to do with Canley?"

The man hesitated. "I don't want to say anything that will do him any harm, sir," he explained. "I don't really know much about it meself, only what I've heard in gossip in the pubs, and so on."

"Bill," interrupted Mackenzie, "you'd be doing him more harm in not telling us anything you know. We've nothing against the man, only we found his hat in a funny place, and we want to know how it got there. Who is he?"

"It's William Harker, Inspector. The gossip is that his daughter, Elsie, has been going round with Canley on the quiet, and he ain't got too good a reputation with women, as perhaps you've found out."

"Did Harker know about this association, Mr. Bailey?" Kenway waited interestedly for the answer.

"That's the point, sir. Although damn near everybody else seems to have known of it, daddy didn't. But he overheard some of the men talking about it here the other day, and there was a bit of a row."

"What kind of a row?"

"I don't know exactly. I wasn't here. But his pal, Harry Johns, was there."

"Can we see Johns?"

"Sure, I'll get him." He went into the yard and returned with a stockily built man, and made the introduction. The line of inquiry was conveyed to him by Mackenzie.

"Well, Mr. Mackenzie, it wasn't exactly a row," Johns explained. "William didn't know anything of Elsie and Canley, but overheard two of the men discussing it in the canteen. They didn't know that he was on the other side of the wooden partition."

"What happened when he overheard?" asked Kenway.

"He came round and went for them as gossip-mongers. They said that he was so bloody sanctimonious about other people that he ought to look after his own folk better. William looked at me and asked me if it was true what the men said. I had to say as 'ow it was, me having seen 'em together on two or three occasions at night."

"And what did Harker say to that?"

"Nothing. He put on his hat and pushed off."

"Ah!" said Kenway. "His hat." He uncovered the head-gear and displayed it. "Do you know if this is his hat?" he asked.

Johns nodded. "I reckon it is," he said. "It's the one he generally wears."

"Was he wearing it when he left after that bit of a row?" Johns nodded.

With that the two officers had to be satisfied.

"Now what do we do?" asked Mackenzie.

"Well, Mac there may be some reason for the hat being in the garden. Perhaps we'd better see Mrs. Skelton. She might know something about it."

The doorbell clamoured vociferously at the little house of Mrs. Skelton, and the Skelton household assembled little by little—Mr. Skelton, his wife and five children. They huddled round the doorway.

Inspector Kenway opened the conversation. "Had Mr. Canley any callers during the evening before his death, Mrs. Skelton?" he asked.

The woman shook her head. "No," she said.

"No tradesmen, for instance, or messengers?"

"Nobody at all. Why? What's the matter now?"

Kenway produced the hat. "Do you know anything about this?" he demanded.

"Oh, aye. That's Mr. Harker's hat."

"Are you quite sure?"

"Sure? O' course I'm sure. I've seen William Harker at choir practice twenty year or more. And always in that same hat. He never wore no other as I knows of 'ceptin' Sunday best."

"And where did you last see him wearing it?" quizzed the inspector.

"Why, the last day as I cooked for Mr. Canley. I remembers as I'd just left his supper all ready and was finishing a nice cup of tea, which same was me perks, when William comes to the front door."

"What!" Kenway was startled into a shout. "But you've just said that nobody visited the house on that evening."

"O' course nobody particular come, but William did. I don't reckon him as visitors. I've known him too long."

Inspector Kenway threw up his hands at the queer reasoning of the feminine mind, which distinguished between visitors and people they knew! He returned to the attack. "So Harker was at the cottage on the night that Canley was killed, eh?" he asked. "Would you be kind enough to tell me as accurately as possible when he came and what happened. This, by the way, is important."

"Well, as I said, I was just finishing a cup of tea when there was a whacking bang on the front door. I opens it, and there stands William. And in a tearing rage he was, too.

"'Where's your master?' he yells at me. 'Master, I says. I got no master. No man masters me. Just let one try.'

"'Where's Canley?' he roars at me. ''Ow would I know,' I says. 'Anyway he ain't in.' 'Then what time will he be in?' he says. 'I don't know' says me, 'and I'll be much obliged if you'll get off the doorstep and let me go home.' 'You tell him I'll be back,' he says. 'Whatever's the matter with you,' I says. 'I've knowed you this twenty year, William Harker, and never see'd you in such a wicked temper. Can't be civil, you can't.'"

"And what did he say to that?" asked Kenway.

"He just glared at me and turned and stamped down the path. Fair 'mazed I was. But it weren't any business o' mine, so I gets me bag and leaves by the front door, 'cos the back door has to be bolted from the inside. So I starts off home as I wanted to get some fish and chips as we hadn't a thing in the 'ouse—"

"Yes, yes," broke in Kenway, hurriedly. "And that was the last time you saw Harker, was it, that night?"

"Yes. O' course I—"

Kenway did not want to hear any more of the Skelton family life. He interrupted the coming discourse. "Was he wearing this hat?" he asked.

"Oh, yes, o' course he was. He always wears his hat."

"And he was in a flaming temper?"

"Not 'arf he wasn't. Funny, 'cos William he don't go letting himself jump off like that. Good husband and father he is, and a regular chapel-goer. But he were proper gone that day, I must say."

"Thank you, Mrs. Skelton." Kenway moved away.

"Welcome, I'm sure. Only too pleased."

"Looks like William went back, as he said he would, and did Canley in," said Mackenzie as the men walked away together.

"Just because Canley was carrying on with his daughter? Doesn't seem feasible to me. Must be something more than that in it, Mac. Has he got any particular friend we could have a talk with?"

"Well, there's Harry Johns. He's a friend of the family for years. I know where to find him."

"Then back to John we go."

It was from Johns that the men a few minutes later heard the full story of William Harker's tragedy. "The daughter is going to have a baby," Johns explained. "William has sent her away, but I don't think he'll be able to keep it quiet."

"You weren't able to find him after Mrs. Harker had told you the story that night?"

"No. Couldn't find a trace of him."

"Do you know what time he got home?"

"Mrs. H. told me it was after midnight."

"Did he say where he'd been?"

"All she could get out of him was that he had been walking all round the place."

Kenway hurried his fellow inspector back to the police station. The doctor, he said, must hear the story.

Dr. Manson, to whom Kenway had telephoned the gist of the story, hurried down to Thames Pagnall. In the police station he heard the more detailed recital. He tapped with his restless fingers on the arm of his chair, the old harbingers of anxiety, the wrinkles appeared in the corners of his eyes.

"Who and what is this man Harker?" he asked.

Inspector Mackenzie looked across at Sergeant Bunny. "He's a decent sort of a chap, sir," the sergeant explained. "Goes to the same chapel as me. He's eddicated is Mr. Harker, and a famous preacher round the country."

"A preacher?"

"Yes, a lay preacher, sir. Goes round all the local chapels and gospel halls telling of the Word. But mind you, he ain't no 'oly Jesus," he added—a description which struck Doctor Manson as rather quaint. He smiled slightly. "Except on Sundays he likes his pint as much as anybody," the sergeant added.

"Well, he seems to have been bent on exacting some sort of satisfaction from Canley," decided Doctor Manson, "and there is no doubt that he was on the premises on that fatal night—"

"And in such a hurry to get away that he left his hat behind"—succinctly from Inspector Mackenzie. "Not, mind you, that I think William Harker is the kind of man to go about murderin' anybody."

"You'd better get hold of him, Mackenzie, and let him speak for himself."

It was a quarter of an hour later that he appeared. A constable knocked at the inspector's door and opened it. "Mr. Harker," he announced. The preacher entered.

Inspector Mackenzie pulled a chair forward and motioned him towards it. Harker waved it away, and stood waiting. He stood tense, his lips tightened across his mouth. So far he had spoken no word.

Doctor Manson held out the discovered hat. "Is this your property, Mr. Harker?" he asked.

Harker spoke for the first time. "It's mine, yes," he admitted. "I lost it. Where did you find it?"

"Where did you last wear it?"

"It would be two or three days ago."

"Do you know where you lost it?"

"No. I can't think where I lost it."

"Where is your daughter, Mr. Harker?"

"Elsie? What has my daughter to do with you?"

"Where is she?"

"She's gone to her aunt's in Worthing."

"To have her child, Mr. Harker?" Doctor Manson raised a hand to stop the flow of words that were about to come from the man. "Understand Mr. Harker, that I have the utmost sympathy for you in this distressing business. I hear you well spoken of by everyone, and I know that your daughter has made a mistake in her friendship with a certain man. This is a case in which the sins of the children will be visited on the parents, which is in direct contradiction to the Biblical edict of which you will be aware.

"But there are serious matters which we have to ask you," he continued. "The man was, of course, Canley. Where were you on the night that Canley died, Harker?"

"I don't know where I was."

The answer reduced Inspector Mackenzie to a state of bewilderment. Doctor Manson eyed the man for a moment. "You don't know where you were?" he asked. "Surely you must have some idea? What were you doing?"

"I was walking under God's skies, wrestling with my soul and my earthly passions," said the man.

Doctor Manson looked at him curiously. There was a certain sincerity about his speech that was impressively innocent. He uttered the statutory warning. "Mr. Harker," he said, "there are certain questions which I as a police officer have to ask you. I have to warn you that you are not bound to reply to them, but that anything you may say in answer will be taken down and may be used in evidence. This hat which you have admitted is yours was picked up in the garden of Canley's cottage the morning after he was found dead on the railway. What were you doing in that garden?"

Harker looked surprised. "So that's where I lost it," he said. "I might 'a known, considering."

"What were you doing there?"

"I went to see Canley, to get justice for my child."

"Justice? Is that all you went to get?" asked Manson. "You did not go for, shall we say, vengeance?"

"'Vengeance is mine. I will repay, saith the Lord'," said Harker. "It is not for the likes of us to interfere with the workings of the Almighty. He was a bad man, one of the worst, a blasphemer, a fornicator and living in adultery. He broke all the Commandments, and God punished him according to His Law."

"God didn't," Doctor Manson said. "Canley was murdered. Did you see him that night?"

"I did not see the man at all."

"Harker." Doctor Manson spoke quietly and seriously. "You went to that house round about seven-thirty o'clock. The woman Skelton was there. You were in what she calls a wicked temper. You left there without seeing Canley, who was not in the house. When you left you were wearing your hat. That hat was found underneath a window at the back of the house, and there were marks on the earth below the window showing that it had been trampled on. What time did you go to that house again, and what were you doing round that window?"

"Did you stand underneath that window?" put in Inspector Mackenzie.

The man nodded. "I went back to the house afore eight o'clock," he admitted. "And I knocked, but there was no answer. I knew he should have been at home for his supper at that time, and I reckoned that he had seen me coming and knew what I wanted. He was lying low. I climbed on to the window of the kitchen to look into the house to see whether he was hiding from me. I saw no sign of him. That was when I fell from the ledge and I must have lost my hat." He paused.

"You never entered the house?" asked Doctor Manson.

"I did not, nor did I see Canley. I went with violence in me heart, that I admit. And then in me distress of mind, I tramped round the countryside, repenting me of me passions, and seeking the help of the Almighty in me trouble."

"And you did not kill Canley?"

"Thou shalt do no murder," quoted Harker.

"What shoes were you wearing at that time?" asked Manson. Harker lifted up one of his feet. "These very shoes I have on, now," he said. "I have no others except those I wear on the Lord's Day."

The doctor looked at the soles of the shoes. They were rubber-heeled, and the rubber was worn thin. His face took on a graver look.

"Very well, Harker," he said. "You can go now. But we may want to see you again later on."

Inspector Mackenzie watched the door close behind him, and then turned inquiringly on the scientist. "Those shoes, with the hat, seem to clinch it, don't they, Doctor?" he ventured, in strange contradiction to his opinion an hour ago that Harker was not the kind of man to commit murder.

The doctor frowned. "Let me think it over carefully, Mackenzie," he said. "I have seldom had a more baffling set of circumstances. Does Harker smoke, does anybody know?"

Sergeant Bunny, who knew him best, denied the weed. "I've never seen him smoking," he explained. "He liked his pint of beer or a drop of spirits, but he didn't smoke, not to my knowledge."

CHAPTER XXIII

THE Assistant Commissioner came panting into the laboratory after a hurried climb up the staircase, the lift stopping one storey short of the penthouse attachment. He walked across to the scientist and sank down in a chair.

"What the deuce are you up to now, Harry?" he asked. "I'm told that the village is full of suspects."

"I'm not so sure that it is as bad as that, Edward." Doctor Manson smiled amiably. "But it is a fact that Kenway's inquiries have led Mackenzie to believe that we have an embarrassment of possibles. And

I think Kenway is that way inclined, also." He looked across at the inspector.

Kenway scratched a puzzled head. "I just don't know what to think," he decided.

"Not after that last bit of reasoning of yours Kenway?" asked the A.C. "By the way, how does that stand up to your expectations?"

"I think it would be better if Kenway told you the story of his inquiries and those of Mackenzie, Edward. It will refresh my memory and when he's finished I'll review them."

"Righto, get on with it, Kenway." The A.C. settled down to listen. The inspector gathered his thoughts into order.

"No, Sir Edward," he said. "I see no grounds for altering the suggestion I made that Appleton and the woman Andover might be involved together with Appleton doing the actual deed and Mrs. Andover the clearing up. Doctor Manson seemed to think that the idea was reasonable." He looked across at the doctor.

"I did say so, Kenway—it *is* a reasonable theory. But that does not mean that I support it."

"But that was based, was it not, Kenway, on the fact that Mrs. Andover was away from her home all night, or until the early hours, and might have been at the cottage. How does it go if she was with another man—this person Betterton?" Merry put the pertinent question.

"It has yet to be proved, Merry, that she was there. She said she was elsewhere when she found we knew that her first story that she had gone to her rooms and stayed there all night was not true. She would not say where she had been, only that she had been with someone not Appleton, and that the someone was not even in the same village. It is Mackenzie who suggested that the man might be Betterton."

"Betterton being the old gentleman who can't leave his house?" asked the A.C.

"Yes."

"And if we clear the lady, Kenway, what about Appleton alone?"

"The one fact in that case, Sir Edward," said Kenway, "is that Appleton was not at home all night, and can give no explanation of where he was."

"Or won't give one for reasons which he thinks sufficient," put in Merry.

"Which is not quite the same thing," said the Assistant Commissioner.

Kenway digested this; but stuck doggedly to his point. "The fact remains, sir," he said, "that Appleton was made to look a fool in front of his friends in the Miller's Arms. He could still have gone round to Canley, and asked what the hell kind of game he was playing at. There had been passages between Mrs. Andover and Appleton, and I am quite sure that Canley knew of it, and deliberately led Mrs. Andover to assume that he was going away for the night, and then doubled back *expecting* to find she and Appleton together.

"Appleton must have been aware of this—it must have been obvious to him when Canley suddenly appeared in the pub. I should say that it is the most likely thing to happen that he would go round and ask what was the game. Then there might have been a row and in a rage Appleton wiped him out. Once that was done Appleton had to safeguard himself, hence the plot to make it appear that Canley had walked out alone, as the doctor has deduced. Appleton has lived in the village all his life, knows the times of the trains, the short cut, and the loneliness of the lane.

"And that is the case so far as Appleton is concerned?" asked the Assistant Commissioner.

"Yes," said Kenway.

"And what about this man Harker?"

"There's a very good case against him," said Kenway.

"What!" ejaculated the A.C. "How many people do you want to hang?"

Kenway smiled sheepishly. "What I am doing, sir," he replied, "is what the doctor does—arguing the case against all the suspects."

"Without fear or favour," chuckled Doctor Manson. "Go on, Kenway, it is interesting and instructive. You've been making the inquiries, not me."

"Well, then, sir, the association of Canley with the girl Elsie is only part of the case against Harker. That is bad enough for the family—the girl is having a child by Canley. But what is more important is that all Harker's life is in ruins by the association. For twenty years or more he has been a preacher. He has inveighed against the sin of adultery and vice, and now here he is held up to public opprobrium by the fact that his own daughter is what he would call 'taken in adultery'. That is a terrible thing for him. He cannot ever preach again—and he lived for his preaching and the social position which it gave him in the chapels. Do you know," said Kenway seriously, "I think he regards that as superior to the fact that his daughter is disgraced.

"The motive is enormous. His world in ruins about his ears. He is a poor man and would want, in any case, the father of his girl's child to support her. What is more likely that he would go and see the betrayer? We know that he did go, while Mrs. Skelton was in the house; that he was in a wicked temper, and said he would come back. He was wearing his hat on that occasion, and he went away with the hat. Then next morning after Canley is dead, we find Harker's hat in the garden. He admits he went there."

"How does he explain the hat?" asked the A.C., who had not, of course, heard the story from Harker himself.

"He says that he went back to the house to see Canley, knocked and could get no answer. Feeling sure that Canley was in and had seen him coming up the path, and knowing for what purpose the visit was being paid was not answering, he climbed up on the kitchen window-ledge to look in expecting to see him. He could see no sign of occupation, and then fell from the window. That would be when his hat fell off. It was dark, and he was scared. Either he could not find the hat, or he was too frightened to look for it, or he did not realize that he had lost it.

"The entire point of the case is that he cannot explain where he was between the time that he first went to see Canley and early next morning—which are the vital hours."

"How does he say that he spent the time?" asked the A.C.

"He says he was walking round the countryside wrestling with his soul."

"And nobody saw him—not even the policeman on beat?"

"Nobody, sir. His friend, Harry Johns overheard the row in the works when Harker found out about his girl. He seems to have been a bit scared of what Harker might do, and so went round to the house to calm him down. Harker was out. Mrs. Harker said she was frightened, and would he go out and find her husband. Well, Johns said he would go after him and bring him home. He didn't. He says he could not find Harker anywhere."

"Did Johns go to Canley's?" asked the Assistant Commissioner.

"Apparently not," replied Kenway. "Although I should have thought that was the one place to go to."

"What about the daughter? She seems to be the one most gravely hurt, Kenway. Could she—"

"No, sir." Kenway was emphatic. "The idea did, in fact, occur to me, but Elsie did not leave her room all night after the row with her father."

Kenway sat back.

"And that's all?" asked the A.C.

"All I can say, I think, sir. These are the only suspects. I can find no evidence of any kind against any other."

"Then what do you say to all that, Doctor?" Sir Edward looked across at the scientist with an appraising interestedness.

Doctor Manson sat forward in his chair, in which during Inspector Kenway's précis of the investigation, he had been lolling back comfortably, the while he listened with what seemed a lukewarm interest, to the recital. "We will take the three people whom Kenway has mentioned in the same order that he did, Edward," he began.

"Mrs. Andover first then, Doctor?" said the A.C.

"Very well. I have viewed Mrs. Andover with great suspicion," began the doctor. "Not quite from the same angle as Kenway here— because Canley had apparently played her for a sucker. But because of the possible effect of the playing—the psychological effect. I put myself in her mind, so to speak."

"In what way?" The A.C. showed livening interest.

"Now, she has been Canley's mistress for some time. She had been going round with him to race meetings, and other functions. And she had been spending nights in the cottage. That means, of course, that he was providing her with money. Suddenly he sends her out of the house on the grounds that he has some business to attend to which will keep him occupied the greater part of the night. She goes off with someone else, and he suddenly turns up and surprises them together, pushes her out of the hotel and has a row with her as they go out. I am quite sure that a woman of Mrs. Andover's mentality would at once see in this a plot not merely to catch her out with Appleton, *but as an excuse to rid himself of her for keeps.* So—"

"Hell hath no fury like a woman scorned, eh?" suggested the Assistant Commissioner.

"Exactly," agreed Doctor Manson. "She was missing from her rooms, and hid the fact by saying that she was in them all night; she is a big hefty woman who could carry Canley; she is a local woman who knows the lane very well indeed, and all about the short cut; and she could have thought of the polishing idea. She was an ideal suspect, *but she doesn't smoke cigars!*"

"What's that?" asked the startled Assistant Commissioner. "Doesn't smoke cigars? What the devil has that to do with it?" Doctor Manson smiled slightly. "We'll come back to that point later," he promised. "Let's take the next on the list."

"Appleton," said Kenway.

The Doctor nodded acceptance. "The case against Appleton is that being made to look a fool in front of his friends, and being robbed of Mrs. Andover by an obvious trick, he went round to Canley afterwards, asked him what the hell he thought he was playing at, and, a row following, Canley was knocked out and went west. Whereupon, Appleton for his own safety staged the accident. He knew, of course, of the short cut, and the lonely lane, and so on. Apart from the fact that there is no sign of a row or rough and tumble—"

"I was counting on all that being removed by the clean-up afterwards," protested Kenway. "He obviously would not leave signs of a row in the place."

"Quite so, Kenway. He would try not to leave any obvious marks of a row. But it would be a clever man who could remove everything of that nature. But we need not quibble over that. Apart from that improbability, I must say that if you had come to me a few hours ago with that theory, I should have been inclined to consider it very carefully. In fact—" he grinned broadly—"I *had* studied the position of Mr. Appleton."

"But not now, Doctor?" queried Kenway. "Why?"

"Because of the cigar that Mrs. Andover did not smoke."

Sir Edward blew his nose so violently as to suggest that he was attempting to emulate the effect of Roland's horn at Roncevaux. "Damn it all, Harry," he blasted, "what's all this about cigars?"

"Canley had been smoking a cigar which was found on the line," explained Kenway.

"What's that to do with the woman and the fact that she didn't smoke it?" roared the Assistant Commissioner.

"Will you let me continue?" Doctor Manson became plaintive. He waited for silence, and then addressed himself to the Assistant Commissioner. "If you were going hot-foot to demand an explanation from a man who had served you a dirty trick, would you begin by offering him a cigar?" he asked.

"Not likely," said the A.C.

"Hardly," agreed Kenway.

"Quite so." Doctor Manson nodded. "Well, you see, that is precisely what the visitor to Canley did. So I say that the person in the cottage who carried out the funeral arrangements of the late Mr. Canley was neither the hot-headed Mr. Appleton, nor Mrs. Andover, who does not smoke cigars and would hardly carry any about with her."

"Where is the evidence of that, Doctor?"

"In the ash left in the ashtray and on the floor of the room, Kenway." The doctor proceeded to explain. "There is not only too much ash for the one cigar that Canley is supposed to have smoked, but the ash is of two different kinds of cigars. It is practically certain I think, that the visitor was the one to hand out the cigars. There were no other cigars in the place, although there were cigarettes. There wasn't a cigar box in the place, nor had Canley a cigar-case. If Canley smoked cigars as a habit, or even occasionally, he would buy not one but several. It is feasible, of course, that Canley *did* have two cigars left and gave one to his visitor; but I should be inclined to doubt that he would have two cigars of different tobacco. So that disposes of Appleton—"

"And leaves only Harker," said the Assistant Commissioner. "Now we're arriving somewhere."

"Kenway," said Doctor Manson, "made out a good case against Harker. His life's work is indeed in ruins, for the chapel folk are not likely to follow a preacher whose daughter has committed adultery. Illogical, if you like, but quite understandable. It is no fault of Harker that his girl has gone wrong. It is merely a case, as I think somebody remarked, of the sins of the children being visited upon the parents. But such an argument would not be tolerated by the chapel folk. And, I suppose, quite rightly. Not only Caesar's wife, but his children must be above suspicion.

"But, A.C., and you, Kenway, overlook one point; while Mr. Harker liked his pint as well as anyone except on Sunday, he did not smoke—"

"Conblast it, Harry, the cigars again!" burst out the Assistant Commissioner. "The one person I know who does smoke cigars is yourself. I suppose—"

"I can account for all my movements last night, Edward," the doctor said.

"Which is in itself a very suspicious thing. I've heard you say yourself that a chap with a ready-made alibi is suspect, because the innocent man rarely has an alibi."

"*Touché*, Edward." The doctor guffawed. "But in this case the alibi is quite accidental. However, even in the case of Harker the cigar is not alone in proving innocence. I can quite believe that in his state of mind the man would wander about the quiet roads in distress and might well not remember where he had been."

"After the murder, do you mean, Doctor?" Kenway looked hopeful.

"No, Kenway. He did no murder. A man of his religious fervour would only kill if in the heat of the moment the overwhelming and sudden impulse came to him. Then, he would pick up the nearest weapon and use it blindly. There was no weapon in that room; and there was no evidence of any sudden impulse; and Harker had only heard of Canley and his girl an hour or two before, you know. He couldn't have planned a cover-up in the time—"

"But, Doctor—" Kenway was checked by a roar from the Assistant Commissioner. "Damn and blast it, Harry, you've eliminated *all* the suspects!" he said. He thought the matter over for a second or two. Then: "Every time we seem to be on a good line you go and cut it from underneath our feet," he moaned, pathetically.

"He'd be no good as Blondin," said Merry. "Not unless he had a strong net underneath him."

"No. But damn it, Merry, he makes a good contortionist act." The A.C. giggled at his ripostes.

"Suppose you stop your jesting and let us get down to serious business." The reproof came from the doctor, but was accompanied by a twinkle in his eyes at the by-play. "I may have dropped the line from beneath your feet, Edward," he continued. "But had I not done so I should have found when I crossed the tightrope that there was no landing rope on the other side, and I'd have had to come back over the rope again. Now, you see, I have been able to return when only half-way over. The facts are simple. Let's look at them.

"You said, Edward, that I have eliminated all the suspects. I have eliminated them all but one."

"That one being?" inquired the A.C.

"The actual murderer."

"Who is he?"

"At the moment I have not the faintest idea." Doctor Manson chuckled anew at the expression that came on the face of the Yard's crime chief. He held up the blistering remark that was about to come, by a wave of his hand. "The best I can tell you is that he was a man who not only offered Canley a cigar and smoked one with him, but also partook of whisky with him."

"What evidence?" demanded the Assistant Commissioner, who sought to recall it from the previous night's conference.

Doctor Manson pointed to the glass tumbler standing on his bench. "The other tumbler which we took from the sideboard, Edward. Polished up and no sign of a fingerprint—not even Mrs. Skelton's fingers. There can only be one reason why it is so stainless—it had been used by the visitor, who had cleaned his prints from it. That means that he was drinking whisky with Canley."

"Of course!"

Sir Edward digested this new mental menu, and a thought occurred to him. "If I remember correctly, Harry, you discounted any suggestion of sudden violence. You said that it was inconceivable that such violence would have been used without leaving some trace for us to find."

"I did."

"Now, you have arrived at the conclusion that the visitor turned up with cigars, sat down amicably and was entertained by Canley with whisky. Does that not assume that it was a friendly chat, or a business visit. And then, suddenly, there came a violent row and a desire by the visitor—a sudden desire—to kill Canley, which would, of course, lead to a struggle for life on the part of Canley?"

Doctor Manson sat back in his chair and stretched his legs under the table. His eyes, deep set in the aesthetic face, eyed the Assistant Commissioner moodily, and with troubled vein.

"It would, indeed, seem to be so, Edward," he agreed. "But—"

There was a questing tone in his voice, and his right hand began a drumming on the arm of his chair. The A.C. waited. Manson was still gazing into his face, but apparently unseeing.

"But what, Harry?" The A.C. reminded his investigator of his presence.

"But it doesn't add up, Edward. It counts two and two as either three or five. And we know, don't we, that the answer should be four. No—" he dismissed the idea finally and completely—"this killing was no sudden impulse. Rows do spring up and people are bumped off in unpremeditated murder. But not Canley."

"Why exactly not Canley?" the A.C. asked. "I'm only trying to argue it out, Harry," he apologized. "I am not doubting the conclusions at which you have arrived."

"Because, Edward, had such a thing happened, the state of mind in which a person would be prisoned after so unpremeditated a murder would leave him mentally incapable of covering his tracks with the thoroughness shown in this case, in the way the cottage was left. The person would be panic-stricken. Here he is with a body on his hands, a body he never expected to have if your theory is to hold, and so crystal clear is his thinking and his construction that we don't know a single thing about him. Why even the last train ran conveniently for him as a cover for his crime. No, it won't hold water."

"Yet, he went there as an apparently welcome guest," hazarded the A.C.

"And he was expected," put in Merry.

"How come?" The A.C. looked his interest.

"Because Canley had turned his light o' love out of the cottage, and had made sure by his subsequent actions that she wouldn't be likely to come back that night," retorted Merry.

"Accepted!" announced Sir Edward.

The drumming of the scientist's fingers suddenly ceased on the chair arm. He came out of his reverie. "There is one circumstance, Edward," he said, "which could account for all the facts, and still allow for the apparent friendly nature of the conference in the cottage."

"What's that?" The Assistant Commissioner sat up suddenly, revived interest in his attitude, which had up to now been desultory from lack of incentive or hope of a solution.

"What circumstance?" he demanded.

"Suppose that the visitor was indeed a friend, or friendly disposed to Canley, so far as Canley knew. Suppose he then went to the cottage at the invitation of Canley for some kind of business discussion, which, seemingly was to benefit Canley. That would explain the whisky and the cigars. *But suppose that this person had gone to the meeting with the intention of getting rid of Canley, and with the plot already completely worked out, including the course of action he was to take to disguise the murder as an accident?*

"In other words, presume the amicable drinking confabulation was a blind. That would cover all the loose ends, and would account for the convenient time of the last train. In fact, in such circumstances the fatal blow could have been struck almost to a timetable because, you remember, death had to be at such a time that the blood would still rim on the railway line after Canley had been conveyed there."

"Now we're getting somewhere," jubilated the Assistant Commissioner. "But it's all theory, you know Harry."

"I would rather call it logical deduction," retorted Manson. "To me it seems the only logical explanation of all the circumstances—including," he added slyly, "the actual friendly visit carrying some sort of lethal weapon."

Sir Edward cheered up a little under this new tonic. But not sufficiently to deter him from a final hangover. "And we haven't a ghost of
an idea who he is, Harry? And you've wiped out Appleton."

"Only so far as a visit by him and the woman and a disturbance
afterwards is concerned, Edward. I made that perfectly clear. There
is nothing against the supposition that Appleton went to Canley with
murderous intent. That remains to be tested."

"Or the new nigger in the woodpile, the hypothetical Mr. Betterton," put in Merry.

"You can count Betterton out," came a voice from behind the group.
Inspector Kenway advanced to the front. "Betterton is nearly seventy-
five," he said. "He can't carry himself, let alone Canley."

"Well, that's one eliminated," chirruped the Assistant Commissioner.

The doctor brought the debate back to those still in the running.
"Was Mrs. Andover with Betterton?" he asked.

"I haven't inquired, Doctor, up to now. I thought that I would scout
round and see what I could learn about Betterton himself. Mackenzie
has little doubt that he is the man referred to. She has been known to
visit him in the past. He is, by the way, housebound. He has not walked
outside except in the garden for months."

The doctor nodded. "It would appear from what you say that Betterton is definitely out," he agreed.

"Then we are back with Appleton," said the Assistant Commissioner. He improvised a nursery rhyme:

> "Two little Indians give the police a bone
> One couldn't toddle up, and then there was one."

"And if you waste any more of my time we never shall. Go away,
both of you and leave Merry and I to sort out a few more of these
riddles." He pointed to the remaining exhibits from the cottage.

They settled down to the task. The doctor cast a comprehensive
look at the collection. *"Cum multis aliis,"* he grieved.

"A regular Tom Tiddler's ground. Which shall we take first?" asked
Merry. "Shall we pick one with a pin?"

The doctor decided on the particles of fluff taken from Canley's overcoat, and Merry extracted them from the security of the seed envelopes.

The objects had now dried out from the wet of the November
night mist. They presented the appearance of springy spirals of tough

thread instead of the soft and sodden tufts of material which they had appeared when removed from the overcoat.

"I should think they had better be washed first," suggested Merry, and produced a bottle of ether and a saucer. He took the first of the exhibits and cleaned it, afterwards mounting it on a glass slide, fixing it with a dab of glycerine.

In the magnified view given by the microscope the particle revealed itself as a coarse twisted strand, of some fibre, and dyed red in colour. Similar examination of the other particles displayed the same characteristics, except that there was an occasional variation of colour, one or two of them being blue and another yellow.

Merry pointed to another of the envelopes, and shot an inquiring glance at his chief.

"I should think it most likely, Jim; in fact that is the reason I collected them," Manson answered the unspoken question. The envelope opened, two strands of its contents which had been taken from the rug in front of the cottage fire, were placed side by side on a slide and inspected. Two of the overcoat exhibits were then mounted beside them, and again a comparison made.

"There is no doubt that the two sets of fibres are the same in origin," said Manson.

"The importance of the comparison is, of course, the position which the particles occupied on the coat of Canley," said the doctor. "It is, to me, a confirmation of my reading of the cottage."

"I don't quite get that, Harry." Merry looked a trifle distraught. "I realize what is in your mind, but—*why on the overcoat?*"

"For the life of me I cannot see why myself," Manson confessed. "But on the other hand I cannot see why not."

"But I can." Merry became flamboyantly assertive. "He would not be wearing the overcoat during the talk—remember there was a fire in the room, and a good one judging by the amount of ash there was left. If he fell down while wearing the overcoat, it would presumably be when he was struck the fatal blow."

"Well?" asked the doctor.

"The blow would not have killed him had he been wearing the overcoat. You can't tell me, that any weapon wielded by the unassisted hand of man could have hit Canley on the top of the spine through that thick overcoat, through his jacket, his collar and shirt and killed him in one blow."

"Checkmate, Jim," the scientist said, a little piqued. He sat back in his chair and called the furrows to his brow and the wrinkles to the corners of his eyes. A period of brooding meditation did nothing to elucidate the riddle, a fact which exasperated the scientist, who was convinced that the answer lay in the cottage and in the very room in which the murder had taken place. There had been, he recalled, no similar extraneous matter on the *jacket* of Canley. Why on the over-coat, not on the jacket. Why?

Step by step he went over the stages of the night's happenings in the cottage, as he had visualized them from his inspection, and subsequent corroborations. But nothing came of the recapitulation.

"It won't work, Henry," said Merry. "Canley was killed with his coat off. There's nothing more certain."

The doctor seemed not to hear the remark. He remained still emulating Rodin's 'Thinker'. But a moment later he got energetically to his feet, seemingly becoming once more aware of his surroundings.

"What did you say just now, Jim?" he asked.

Merry looked up, startled. "Only that Canley was killed with his coat off, Harry. We already know that, anyway."

"We knew it, but we did not realize that we knew it. Confound me for a dim wit. That *is* the explanation."

The doctor seized his telephone, and put a call through to Doctor Gaunt. The gruff voice of the medico answered.

"Doctor, you put the death of Canley, did you not, as having taken place about eleven-thirty."

"I said that if I were pressed to give a definite time I would put it round about that time, Manson."

"Because, I suppose, of the temperature of the body, allied to the temperature of the air, and the state of the blood?"

"Those were the main factors, of course," agreed the medico. "And, of course, because of the decapitation," he added, grimly humorous. "You understand that the blood would not have flowed if death had been much earlier? That's the weakness of your case, Manson."

"Quite so, Doctor. But listen—"

He spoke for a few moments, detailing rapidly three points of vari-ance. "Would that lead you to alter your view, Doctor?" he asked.

Doctor Gaunt swore a very un-Hippocratic oath. "It would make a very big difference to the time," he agreed.

"An hour or more difference?"

"It could well be."

The scientist replaced the receiver.

"Case proved?" asked Merry.

"With full marks to you, Jim. Now let us pester something else."

The deputy scientist lifted the tumbler from the table and regarded it with curiosity. "What is the idea of this?" he asked. "It has no finger-prints."

"But a curious iridescence, Jim. I thought it might give us some-thing. You remember that I asked Mrs. Skelton if there was paraffin in the house, or if she used any on the glasses. She denied both asper-sions. Therefore, the iridescence must have come with the visitor."

Merry held up the glass to the lamp, and remarked the prismatic colours acting to the rays of light. "I don't think it is paraffin," he decided. "And it doesn't smell like paraffin. The aroma would not go so quickly from paraffin as it has done here. I should say it is an oil of some kind."

"Give it to Wilkins, and see what he can make of it. And then, I think, we may as well go over to Thames Pagnall, and tell the story of the murder to the Chief Constable and Mackenzie. And at the same time get a few local inquiries started on a new line. We will complete this little lot when we return."

CHAPTER XXIV

COLONEL Mainforce awaited the conference in the police station at Thames Pagnall. A gloomy and unappreciative Inspector Mackenzie sat with him. To the invitation extended to the inspector to reveal the results of the further inquiries he had pursued, he retorted with fore-boding that he had no results to show. Nobody had seen Canley in the village after the incident in the Miller's Arms, he said.

"Well, that is a good point, Mackenzie," said Manson, cheer-ingly. "For it can mean only one thing—that Canley was not out in the village at all. In other words, he was in his own house from nine-thirty onwards."

The inspector looked a trifle surprised at the unexpected success which had attended his efforts. He strove to extend it. He proclaimed aloud that the same result had been achieved in regard to Mrs. Andover. Nobody had seen her about the place.

This, however, did not work out so well. "That, Inspector, is not so good," chided Doctor Manson. "Because, you see, we know that *she* was *not* in her own house. The only cheering point in it is that she was not obviously out and about in the village at the vital times we have associated with Canley's death."

"Well, that's all," announced Mackenzie.

"How have you come on, Doctor?" the Chief Constable asked. He presented the appearance of 'a man of hope and forward-looking mind'. The reply of the scientist justified the prophecy.

"I can tell you now, Mainforce, the full story of the happenings in Canley's cottage on the night he died," he announced, quietly.

The Colonel patted his stomach complacently. He looked at his inspector. "There you are, Mackenzie. I told you so," he trumpeted. He settled himself comfortably in his chair, lit a cigarette, and waved a hand in the direction of the Yard officers. "Elucidate," he commanded, airily.

"We will have to begin some time before the murder of Canley," began the scientist. "Before Mrs. Andover went to the cottage expecting, as she told us, to stay there for the night. Canley was expecting a visitor. I don't know whether he had expected Mrs. Andover to turn up that night. I should think not, otherwise he would have told her not to do so.

"But she *did* appear. He had to get rid of her. It rather looks as if the visitor might have been someone who knew both of them,[7] and he did not want the visitor and the woman to meet. Or perhaps he didn't desire his acquaintance with the woman to be known. Whatever was the reason, he cleared Mrs. Andover out after a short dalliance and he went with her to the crossroads to make sure she would not be coming back to the cottage to see whether he had, or had not returned. From her story, it seems that she thought he was going to Esher by bus. The mistake Mrs. Andover made was thinking that Canley's business was in Esher, not in the cottage."

Doctor Manson paused to light up one of his Sullivans. He blew a spiral of smoke towards the ceiling, and resumed the story. "Now the visit was to be somewhere around ten o'clock—"

"Just a minute, Manson." The Chief Constable interrupted. "Why ten o'clock?"

"Because Canley made an appearance in the Miller's Arms after he had parted from Mrs. Andover, Colonel. He did not go in there to trap Mrs. Andover with Appleton. He might have felt annoyance at seeing her in there with Appleton, and I have no doubt that he recalled all

7. There was no justification, as the reader knows, for this deduction on the part of the doctor. It was wrong.

about their earlier acquaintance before he had taken Mrs. Andover for his mistress."

"Hence the reason that he picked the row with her and got booted out by Ted North, eh?"

"I don't think so, Colonel. When he saw Mrs. Andover there you realize the position he was in, don't you? He had told her that he had to go out on business, and would not be home until at least midnight. That is her story and I see no reason to doubt it. Now, here he was back in the place again. The likelihood of that would be that Mrs. Andover might very well think that the business had been completed very much earlier, or had fallen through, and she might rid herself of Appleton, who was only a stop-gap anyhow, and pay a visit to Canley at the cottage when she had done so. That, seemingly, was the last thing that Canley wanted—"

"How do you know that?" asked Inspector Mackenzie.

"I don't *know* it," said Manson, testily. "Not having any method of conversing with dead men. But it seems fairly obvious, does it not, that if he had not minded Mrs. Andover meeting the visitor, he would not have minded her coming to the cottage while the visitor was there. The point of the whole thing is that he didn't want the woman at the cottage at all, so led her to suppose that he was going to Esher or some other place for the business."

"Some underhand business, do you suppose, Manson?" asked the Chief Constable. "Or was Canley acting as an agent, or go-between to someone working 'under the counter' cloak? We haven't any operators round these parts—that we know of."

"I haven't the slightest idea, Mainforce. All I can say is that Canley was so keen to keep the woman away from the cottage that night, that he was prepared to go to the length of having a row with her, and getting them turned out of the hotel. In the state of mind in which she was when she told him, as she says, to go to the devil, she was not likely to wander round to his house again that night. There Canley seems to have signed his death warrant—at least on that night. For had she gone round to the cottage, I don't think the visitor would have gone to the lengths of murder."

"I should think you are right," agreed the Chief Constable.

"However," Doctor Manson proceeded, "somewhere about ten o'clock the visitor arrived at the cottage—"

"Who was he?" demanded Mackenzie.

Doctor Manson ignored the question, and continued with his story. "He was a welcome visitor, and, as I have already said, was expected by Canley—"

"How do you arrive at that, Doctor?" asked the Chief Constable.

"Because Canley had put out a bottle of whisky and glasses for the two of them."

*"Two glasses?" the Chief Constable looked surprised. "I thought only one glass was found on the table."

"And one on the sideboard, entirely devoid of fingerprints," pointed out Doctor Manson.

"I see." Colonel Mainforce nodded his head slowly. "He put the other back after wiping his prints off it—the visitor, I mean."

"Quite so. Now, Canley admitted the visitor—since there is no sign of forced entry, and there is every evidence of a host awaiting his guest—and the pair of them sat drinking whisky for some time. What was the object of the business I do not know, and cannot even conjecture, but I can say this—that whatever Canley expected to get from it, the visitor expected to get a great deal more, *for he had, gone there with the express intention of killing Canley.*"

"God bless my soul, Manson. What the devil for? And from what source do you get that?"

"From the preparations he had made, Colonel, and from what he did subsequent to the murder. For instance, he had taken the trouble to bring a couple of cigars—"

"Burn me!" said the Colonel. "What makes you suppose that?"

"I think that he purchased one only, and had the other on him," went on Doctor Manson, ignoring the question, "because had he gone to get two cigars, he would undoubtedly have purchased two from the same box. As it was, he had two of different tobacco, and that proved one of his mistakes."

"How?" demanded Mackenzie.

"Because the visitor was a very clever man. You asked me just now, Colonel, how I supposed that the visitor brought two cigars. The answer is that he wanted one, or part of one, to strengthen his scheme. That was why we found the stub on the railway line. Canley was to have been supposed to have walked to the line smoking the cigar, which the visitor knew would be found when the police searched the track.

"The mistake he made, Mackenzie"—he turned towards the local inspector—"was in attributing to Canley the wrong cigar. You see, when he delivered the fatal blow, a stub of cigar was jerked out of Canley's mouth, and shot with some violence to the floor. You all saw it, and I told you that the stub had impinged on the floor in a way different to that which would have been made had the cigar merely been dropped. *Now, the butt found on the railway line was not the cigar which Canley had been smoking, judged by the ash on the floor.* It was the one that the visitor had smoked. *Ipso facto*, there were two cigars, and the railway episode shared the purpose for which one was wanted."

Doctor Manson paused to light another cigarette. He puffed a few eddies of smoke, and then resumed. "Where was I?" he pondered, "before I diverged from the story?"

"You had given Canley a blow which shot the cigar from his mouth," reminded the Chief Constable.

"Ah, yes. The visitor had in some way distracted Canley's attention, and had got behind him. He delivered the blow at the top of the spine, where the neck is fitted on, and with a weapon with which he was familiar and could use with certainty—another proof, you see, *that he had come with murder in his heart, for he had even brought a lethal weapon with him.* All this, I should say, happened somewhere about ten-thirty o'clock; it may have been a little later, but not much."

"I am not disputing your estimate, Doctor, but did not both the doctors agree on one thing—about the only thing upon which they found common ground—that the probable time of death was eleven-thirty o'clock?" asked the Chief Constable.

"They did, Mainforce. And for a time that fact caused me considerable perturbation. Then, the fluff which we collected from Canley's overcoat on the line solved the riddle for me. However, we will deal with that a little later on in the story. Doctor Gaunt will now agree with me on an earlier time of death.

"We have now, you remember, Canley lying dead in the cottage, with his murderer with him. Now we come to the main evidence on which I base my allegation that this was a planned murder, and done to a time-table. *Because Canley had to be dead by ten-thirty or shortly afterwards*, else the arrangements made by the murderer for staging an accident would have broken down." Inspector Mackenzie had been listening to the building-up of the scientist's story with lively obfuscation, and now goggled at this latest claim to authenticity in deduction. He gave the impression that he would not have been surprised to see Doctor Manson's feet develop into cloven hooves, and a tail appear behind him. A growing conviction that there might, after all, be something in spiritualism and mediums began to stir inside him. He voiced his fears as to the means whereby the doctor had penetrated into the mind of the murderer. "How can you say with any certainty that that is so?" he asked.

Doctor Manson eyed him with reflective interest. "Because, Mackenzie, the man had to be clear of the place before Canley was found dead, therefore the train to kill Canley had to be the last train. Any earlier train might have resulted in the following train, or another approaching train spotting the body, whereupon the murderer would not have been safe away with an alibi. Thus, in order that the accident could be realistically staged with perfect safety—as he thought—for the murderer, Canley had to be out of the way somewhere about ten-thirty."

"An hour before the train, Doctor?" Surprise lifted the Chief Constable's voice a tone higher than its usual pitch.

"An hour before the train, Mainforce, yes—for a very good reason. You remember that there were only one set of footprints—Canley's?"

"Yes, which you say were made by somebody walking in Canley's shoes, and carrying Canley to the railway line. That we accept."

"Right! But, the murderer could make those footsteps only once. The dead man could not walk back again, once he had reached the railway. And there were no other footsteps either approaching or leaving the cottage, you know. In other words, *when the murderer left the cottage, carrying Canley, he was leaving the cottage for good.* That is, I think, elementary logic and deduction."

The Chief Constable considered the point. "Yes, I should think, probably, that there is something in the argument, Manson," he agreed.

"Then, you realize, do you not, that before he left the cottage for good, he had to remove all traces of his presence and arrange the interior of the lounge to justify the idea that Canley had left there on his feet, gone to the line, and in walking across the metals, was knocked down by the train?"

"By gad, yes, of course!" The Chief Constable thought for a moment, and added, slowly, "I am beginning to see the earliest workings of your mind in this case. You had decided this on the very morning of the discovery had you not?"

"Pretty nearly, Mainforce. Not, mark you, that I was actually convinced, but I guessed something of the kind must have happened. There was evidence, I thought, of great preparation and careful inspection afterwards, and it could not, of course, be done while the victim was still alive. Then, again, the murderer had to allow a little time for stray passers-by who might be using the lane. He could hardly go carrying bodies along the place unless it was completely deserted. He might have had to wait for a few moments or even minutes. Thus, he had to allow a margin. I do not think that an hour gave him any too much time for what he had to do."

"What did he do?" The inquiry came from Mackenzie.

"Lest you attribute to me uncanny powers, Mackenzie, I cannot say the order in which he carried out his programme, but I can tell you pretty well everything that he did in that time. Firstly, then, he wiped with a towel, or some cloth of some kind, the glass which he had used. He, in fact, polished it of any marks at all, and he replaced it on the sideboard. That, he thought, removed the evidence of any other drinker. Having achieved that, he wiped and polished the whisky bottle and Canley's glass."

The scientist smiled slightly. "That was his really big mistake," he said. "Had he left Canley's glass alone, it would have been scattered all over with the dead man's fingerprints. I do not think that I should have proceeded so carefully to search the other things and the table for prints, had I found on the first object—Canley's glass—a mingled assortment of fingerprints of the same hand. I might, on examination of the bottle and finding only one set of prints, have put it down as unusual, but possible. But it was when I saw the marks of a glass having been raised and put down four times on the table—as shown by the wet rings on the polished surface—and found that, according to the finger-prints on the glass, it had been lifted only once, that my suspicions were aroused, and I made a very detailed examination of the other articles and of the table."

"I suppose the wet rings were planted by the murderer," suggested the Chief Constable. "For a clever man, as you say he was, Manson, he made a bad slip there."

"Perhaps he couldn't help it, Colonel," Merry made the suggestion. "In the stress of the moment, he might not have been sure that acci-dentally, he had not handled the glass. To have left one of his prints on it would have been fatal."

"Possibly," agreed Doctor Manson. "But whatever the reason, the fact remains that he did wipe off all Canley's naturally placed prints. Then, having thus cleaned it, he bent over the body of his victim, and pressed the fingers of Canley's right hand round the polished surface, thus leaving the one set of prints. Why he didn't do it three or four times I cannot imagine."

"Ghoulish." The Chief Constable shuddered a little.

"Self-preservation, Colonel," corrected Manson. "The man knew more than a little about the methods of police investigation. But his trouble was that he did not know enough; one set of prints, as I have said, was even worse from his point of view, in the circumstances, than no prints at all.

"Having 'cooked' the bottle and the glass, the man next went over the entire surface of the table with his cloth, polishing it carefully, and wiping away any fingermarks which he or Canley had made, or which anybody else might have made—including Mrs. Skelton. He left a little of the cloth behind him—a thread caught on a splinter of the rim of the table. I have not carried out an examination of this yet, so cannot say whether it can help us in any way.

"The table done, he next went thoroughly over the chairs and, I expect, over practically every piece of furniture in the room, in case he had by chance touched either of them during his stay. He had to be extraordinarily careful you see. The fact is, he was too careful. The furniture finished, he arranged the bottle, now also complete with one set of Canley's fingerprints—how did he suppose Canley had drawn the cork from the bottle?—and the glass on the table, placed the ashtray close to them, as a proof that Canley had been smoking the cigar found with him on the line, and—I am not sure about this—arranged the chair by the table as though Canley had pushed it aside when he rose from it. The ashtray, by the way was his third mistake, for he had left the ash of the *two* cigars in it, and also more ash than could have come off the cigar that Canley had half-smoked, or was supposed to have half-smoked.

"We are now very nearly at the end of the recital." The doctor paused to light another cigarette, and to marshal his last flight of deduction.

"Just a minute, Doctor," chipped in the Chief Constable. "Where was Canley while his assailant was cooking up the lounge?"

Merry, who had hitherto taken no part in the story, chuckled grimly. "The late Mr. Canley was cooking the *accident*," he said. "And when I say cooking, I mean cooking," he added.

"What Merry means by that analogical jest, Colonel, is this: Canley was all this time lying in front of a roaring fire, with the idea of keeping the body warm and the blood from congealing so that when it was laid over the rails in front of the advancing train blood would flow."

The Chief Constable threw up his arms in surrender. "So that is the reason for the change in the time of death," he said. "How did you guess?"

"Guess? *Guess?*" Doctor Manson raised his voice more in sorrow than in anger. "I never guess, Mainforce. Merry and I deduced it from a line of logical reasoning which we nearly missed. It was, in fact, Canley's overcoat that put us on the scent."

"If I remember rightly, you mentioned the overcoat in this connection before."

"We did—a little out of its place in the story. Well, we can pursue it now. The point arose when Merry and I came to test out the fluff found on the overcoat. We had carefully removed a few pieces of it, and had stored them away for analysis. At the same time, in the cottage, as you probably saw, I picked a few strands out of the patterned rug in front of the fireplace. Under the microscope all the fluff was shown to be identical. The fluff therefore, had obviously come from the rug. But why? And how?

"Merry quite rightly pointed out that Canley would not be wearing his overcoat when he was killed, since no blow could have been fatal through the thickness of it and the jacket and shirt underneath. Yet he was wearing the overcoat on the railway, and it was dotted here and there with these foreign bodies which had been picked up by the rough surface or nap of the coat. And there were no fluffy pieces on Canley's jacket which he was wearing when he fell under the blow.

"The peculiarity worried me, and I sat down to think out a possible explanation. It was then that I realized what I have already told you—that since there were only the footsteps of Canley showing, the cottage must have been prepared before the murderer walked down the lane carrying Canley to the railway. That gave me the startling knowledge that at least an hour must have elapsed from the time of death to the journey—and yet blood flowed freely from the severed neck.

"Once I had reached that stage in thinking, the rest was easy. If Canley did not die at eleven o'clock or eleven-thirty, then some method had been employed by the murderer to keep the blood from congealing. That meant that the body had to be kept warm. There are other ways, such as beating up the blood, but that was obviously not used in this case.

"*There had been a big fire in the cottage grate. What more natural than this man, who knew a little, but not enough about fingerprints, a little but not enough about cigar ash, should know a little but not enough, also, about the action of blood? He knew that it had to be kept warm in order that it might run when the train passed over the neck, and he did not know that if the man had been alive when the head was taken off, the blood would spurt out.*

"How fluff came to be transferred from the rug to the overcoat is now plain. It was, you will remember, only *on the back of the overcoat*. I do not know when the murderer dressed Canley in the coat—whether it was before he laid him in front of the big fire, or not. Probably he would think that the body would be warmer if it was not in the coat—he was wrong if he did think so. In that case he fitted the overcoat over the dead man. He would, of course, have to pull it underneath the body, and then pull the body along to raise it in order that he could get it across his own shoulders for carrying. That was when the fluff was picked up by the nap of the overcoat.

"We are now nearing the end of the journey—for Canley as well as for us here. The murderer had removed Canley's shoes and put them on his own feet. With Canley across his shoulders he left the house—and there he made another mistake in leaving Canley's hat behind. He walked down the lane and up the path to the railway, leaving the tracks plain for all to see—*and for us to realize from the different tread of the heels that it was another person in the shoes.*

"There he waited until the train was due. He probably listened for it, placed the body in the permanent way with the head over the rail, threw the cigar butt some distance down the line to simulate it as being jerked from the mouth by the shock of the train's blow, and cleared off.

"And that, Mainforce, is the story of the happenings in your Thames Pagnall cottage on the night of the tragedy," concluded the scientist.

CHAPTER XXV

Colonel Mainforce sat silent for a space after the doctor had concluded his narrative. Then, having digested it in its entirety, he turned to his inspector. He beamed.

"What do you think about that, Mackenzie?" he asked. "Eh?" His air would have given a newcomer the impression that he himself had accomplished a triumph.

The local inspector's eyes were still fixed on Doctor Manson, who was now engaged in the intricate task of fitting an oversized cigarette into an under-sized cigarette holder, leaving, nevertheless, sufficient draught to allow smoke to be pulled through it. He was too engrossed in the pursuit to be aware of the gaze of the officer, staring as incredulously as would an unbeliever at a *séance*, seeing suddenly a piece of ectoplasm extrude from the medium and assume the face and form of his long-dead aunt who in life had been his *bête noir*.

"Deaf, Mackenzie?" roared the Chief Constable.

The inspector jerked into realization.

"I asked you what you thought of that?"

"Kenway said that the doctor would probably learn more in an hour in his laboratory in London than we would learn in a day down here," Mackenzie said, half to himself. "Looks like he was right, too," he added, in a sudden burst of relief.

"Nothing to do with me, Mackenzie," responded Manson, laughingly. "I am not the wizard, I am merely the disciple of the army of men who in the past have probed the depth and breadth of science, and have applied its principles to criminology. Without Henry and Faulds and Cherrill we would not have known what we know about fingerprints. Without Gross and Taylor we would have been sadly lacking in knowledge of science as applied to the detection of crime, and without Sutherland our expert treatment of bloodstains would be impossible. And, above all, except for Abbe we would never have had the microscope, possibly the greatest detective of any. The point is where do we go from here?"

"You have no *idea* of the man's identity, Doctor?" asked the Chief Constable.

A soporific atmosphere descended on the scientist and Merry. The keenness evaporated. "Not the slightest, Mainforce. We do not know whether he is tall or short, big or slight, though I incline to the view that he is strong, since he carried Canley fairly easily—at any rate he did not falter sufficiently for his feet in Canley's shoes to show up. What he did—and it is the only successful thing he did do, so far as I can see at the moment—is not to leave a single *personal* clue behind him. It is rather remarkable that he did not leave something—a hair from his head on Canley's coat, for instance."

"I think there is an even more remarkable thing," said Merry, slowly and emphatically.

The company looked inquiringly.

"That he has not left behind any clue as to the *reason* he killed Canley," the deputy scientist added. "It is a first clue in all murders—the motive. There isn't a genesis of a motive here, unless we look upon the favours and the possession of Mrs. Andover as a motive. And that gets us back to Appleton, who is the only man we know without an alibi that can be tested."

Doctor Manson looked across at Mackenzie. The inspector cleared his throat. "I've known Ted Appleton a good few years, Doctor," he said. "And I don't think he's the kind to go murdering people. I should think that if he felt badly against Canley for taking Mrs. Andover he'd have felt it more badly at the time, not twelve months afterwards. Ted has been enjoying himself with quite a number of the village—er—er—"

"Tarts is perhaps the word you want, Mackenzie," suggested the Chief Constable; and the inspector nodded in agreement.

"And I can't find anyone who has quarrelled with Canley, or uttered threats against him," the inspector went on.

"Well, Mackenzie, perhaps the information we now have will help a little," suggested Doctor Manson. "We have a good idea of the time of the murder, and of the disposal of the body. We know now that the man did not return to the cottage. He must, therefore, have been about the village between eleven-thirty and eleven-forty-five.[8] There was no train, so he could not leave that way. He must either have walked, gone on a bicycle, or by car. Now, if you can find someone who saw a car or a cycle, or a stranger wandering around the place at that time, it might help. Are there, by the way, any buses running at that hour?"

Inspector Mackenzie did not reply. He appeared to be lost in thought. A glimmer of anticipation came into his eyes, which stole a glance at the scientist. Doctor Manson, catching it, came to a sudden alertness. It looked to him mischievous.

"What have you behind that forehead of your's, Mackenzie?" he asked.

A little rumble of satisfaction came from the inspector's interior. He had come to the conclusion that what had suddenly occurred to him was one up against the doctor. He tried it out.

"I reckon, sir, as how the man neither went by car, bicycle or bus," he said.

"Why not?" asked the doctor, suspiciously.

"I'll ask you a question instead, sir." He propounded it. "Can you tell me how the man got down to a car or a bicycle or the road? Taking what you say to be true as to how he got Canley on the line, I reckon that he put Canley's shoes on the dead man's feet again, so that he would then have to wear his own shoes. Now, sir, there isn't a footstep in the lane except those made by Canley's shoes. That doesn't matter since you say he did not go back to the cottage."

8. Again Doctor Manson's reasoning (as the reader knows) is incorrect.

"But then," he continued, "there weren't any footsteps *down the other side of the embankment,* and if he wasn't going to leave any cycle tyre marks, he would have had to get down to his cycle which he left there. And he'd have to get down there if he didn't walk through the lane again. So how did he get on the road?"

"God bless my soul," said the Chief Constable; and stared at his inspector as though he were some unbelievable curiosity of the world of nature making its first appearance in a zoo. "God—bless—my—soul," he said again.

Doctor Manson also stared. He stared so long that Inspector Mackenzie shifted uncomfortably under the gaze, and wished that he had kept his mouth shut about the whole thing. He gained the impression that he had in some way thrown a spanner in the workings of the scientist's mind and had, accordingly, veritably committed sabotage.

When the scientist replied, it was with some self-criticism. "It argues a poverty of imagination on my part that I should have missed so vital a relation of observance," he said. "Mackenzie is, of course, right. The man would not, in any case, go into the village again if he could help it. If suspicion was aroused, and he had been seen, he would be in a dangerous position."

"Suppose he had walked down the embankment as he walked to Canley's cottage, in his stockinged feet, Doctor, would not that clear the way?" The suggestion came from Merry.

"It would not clear the way to the peril of leaving a vehicle of any kind in the streets of the village to be noticed, or of boarding a public vehicle in the vicinity of the village, Merry." The doctor gazed fretfully round the company, and then into space, seeking some thread of clue to get him out of this unexpected maze. "We'll have to eliminate the circumstance, Merry," he announced; and proceeded to the intense interest of the inspector to put the operation into practice.

"Firstly, would he come by car?" The pair, after a weighing of pros and cons agreed on a negative answer. A car would be noticed. There was a possibility that it might be stopped by the police, or have a number taken by some fiend of a number-collecting boy. And it would have to be left for a couple of hours or more. The same thing applied to a bicycle—only more so; the cycle left for that time might get stolen, and the murderer would then be in a parlous plight for a getaway.

"What about a bus?" asked Merry.

The scientist looked inquiringly at Inspector Mackenzie "There are buses coming into the place from Kingston, Surbiton, London, and a couple of other places, sir," was the reply. "But there are not any out of the place after eleven o'clock."

"Then that disposes of that," said the doctor. "He would not place himself in a dead hole like that."

"And he didn't walk," said the Chief Constable. "He must have had a helicopter."

"No, sir," denied the inspector, promptly. "We should have heard an aeroplane in the district."

"It was meant as a jest, Mackenzie," the Chief Constable explained, rather unnecessarily.

The inspector subsided quickly. He was feeling no little satisfaction at the disturbance which his suggestion had brought about. During the past twenty-four hours, he had come to a realization that he was not a particularly good detective; it was plain to him that he had missed a great many things in the investigation that he should not have missed. He was beginning to develop an inferiority complex. But now, he was his own blue-eyed baby again, and had put Doctor Manson and his assistant, as well as his own Chief Constable, in a dilemma which might force them to throw back suspicion on one of the people who had appeared on the list of inquiries of himself and Inspector Kenway.

Because he, Mackenzie, knew from his own thorough inquiries and those of his staff that not one single stranger had been seen in the village on the night of Canley's death—at least after the time that Canley had died. He said so now, with considerable enjoyment at the effect on the man from London.

"You *sure* of that, Mackenzie?" demanded the Chief Constable menacingly.

"Absolutely positive, sir. More positive than I have ever been of anything in criminal investigation."

"Huh!" said the Chief Constable, and looked in perplexity at Doctor Manson. Inspector Mackenzie was also looking at the doctor. He was saying mentally, 'now, get out of that one.'

The reaction completely staggered him. Doctor Manson looked at his fellow officers smilingly. "Well," he said, "the explanation should now be comparatively simple, requiring only a little concentration. We are stumbling round the same kind of problem as that presented in a famous case in which a crime was committed inside a room which was locked on the inside. When the door was forced a man was found dead there. He had apparently committed suicide by shooting, only there was no pistol in the room. A quarrel had been heard, and when the shot was fired there were people in the passage outside. They raised the alarm and stayed there until the door was broken in; and the room was found empty except for the corpse. The windows were fastened from the inside with screws. There was no way in which the murderer could possibly have made an exit."

Inspector Mackenzie pondered the problem. "If he wasn't there, Doctor, he must have made an exit," he pronounced.

"The officers on the case were in exactly the same position as are we now, Mackenzie, when we say that the man could not have reached the roadway because there is no trace of him showing the footsteps he would have to show. In the case of the man in the room, the solution was simple: the murderer was behind the forced door, and when the company of people rushed in as the door was forced, he joined them as one of themselves. Simple, wasn't it? There is an equally simple solution here. We have exhausted every avenue of escape except the hypothetical door. Our man, it seems, did not go out of the village by car, cycle, bus, or on his feet, because nobody was seen in the village—no stranger that is—at the time he would be making his getaway. And that means, of course, that he did not come to the village in the first place on either of these means of transport—excepting perhaps the buses—or he would have had to take them away with him. He didn't fly, because nobody, I take it, from Mackenzie's remark—nobody heard an aeroplane take off. Then where, Mackenzie," asked Doctor Manson, "where is the door?" He answered the question himself after a few moments' consideration.

"There is," he said, *"only the railway left. He must have gone out by the railway."*

"He couldn't!" Mackenzie's voice rang out triumphantly again. "There wasn't a train. The eleven thirty-five was the last train of the night, either up or down."

Mackenzie regarded the jubilant inspector with drawn brows. "I did not say, Mackenzie, that he went on the railway. He didn't, obviously. There is nothing I can see to prevent him walking along the line to the junction. I take it"—he developed an anxious lilt in his voice—"that there are late trains from the junction, later that is, than say, midnight?"

"Oh, yes, sir." Mackenzie's jubilation deflated like a pricked balloon. "But—"

"Wouldn't it be a bit risky entering the station from the lines, Manson?" asked Colonel Mainforce.

"I did not say that he need have gone all the way to the junction along the lines, Mainforce." He turned to Mackenzie. "Is there a bridge along the lines, giving easy and direct access to a roadway, Mackenzie?" he asked.

"Yes, sir. About half a mile or so along. It passes over a cross-roads."

"Then that offers an interesting suggestion. He could walk the remaining distance to the junction, and I don't suppose he would have much difficulty in avoiding being seen at that time of night, on the station. Possibly he did not buy a ticket and thus attract attention to himself in the vicinity of this area."

"If I were you, Mackenzie, I should endeavour to find anyone who arrived at a station somewhere along one of the junction lines between twelve-fifteen and one-fifteen in the morning, and paid the fare from the junction, being unable to produce a ticket. At the same time, however, you might see if any of the staff at the junction can recall having seen a man arrive on the platform by unorthodox ways."

He rose to go. "I think that is all Merry and I can do here," he said to the Chief Constable. "If our delvings into Canley's belongings which I still have in the laboratory can give Mackenzie any assistance, Mainforce, I'll give you a ring."

A totally unexpected development was waiting to greet the two scientists however, before they could resume their laboratory search into the belongings of Canley.

Doctor Manson had decided to deal next with the papers taken from Canley's desk. "If anything can give us a line on the man and his murderer, I should say it will be the papers," he had confided to Merry.

At that moment the telephone rang out a shrill call. The doctor lifted the receiver and answered.

"Manson here," he said. The voice of the fingerprint chief, Inspector Baxter, replied.

"Been trying to get you all morning, Doctor," he said. "I've news. Wilkins sent me up a card with the prints of the man Canley on them. That all right?"

"Quite all right, Baxter. What of them?"

"Well, sir, he's known. But not as Canley. His real name is Sprogson. He's been inside several times, the last being three years ago at Exeter. Shall I send you his dossier down?"

"Excellent, Baxter."

Merry and he examined the dossier together. "Theft and burglary, eh?" said Merry. "Last time for a robbery at Paignton." He gave the scientist a precis of the incident. "Seems he made friends with the butler at a big house in Shorton Woods—remember we stayed at a place in the woods for a fortnight once, Harry, when we had a golfing holiday at the Paignton Country Club? He got well in with the butler, and seemingly so well as to obtain the safe combination. The butler apparently was left in the house in charge of the jewellery while the family was away."

"Funny arrangement wasn't it, Jim."

"I should think so—Let's see what it says." He read silently for a minute or so.

"Ah, well, that may explain it, Harry," he explained. "Seems the room in which the safe was fixed was more or less a strong-room protected by steel shutters, and having an electric alarm direct to the police station a quarter of a mile away. Canley, or Sprogson, did not know about the alarm, and when he pulled open the safe door, without switching it off, the cops started out."

"Where was the butler?"

"Dunno. Out on the razzle, perhaps. The family were away. Anyway, it seems that Sprogson shot out of a window, was seen by the police and chased. He knocked one of them out, but was finally caught. And he got three years."

"What did he steal?"

"Nothing. But jewellery was missing from the safe. Sprogson said that he had a confederate, and gave his name as Jack Edwins. Police say they saw no signs of another person. However, as they all seemed to join in a tally-ho after Sprogson, perhaps the other chap laid low. Funnily enough, just over two years later the owner of the jewellery at Paignton received a large sum of money in notes from an anonymous person, with instructions that it was compensation."

"Queer story," commented the scientist. "Hardly compensation, since the owner of the jewellery would have received insurance. More like conscience money. Let's get on with these papers, Jim."

The suitcase of the late Mr. Canley was up-ended and its load of papers deposited in the centre of the table. The two men proceeded each to take a sheet in turn, and examine it with a scrutiny that was not only visual but mental. It was not so much the lines on the documents that the scientist concerned himself with as the reading between the lines. The bills, not in themselves objects of much seeming interest, were examined for any clue that the objects obtained might give.

It is the application of psychology to investigation. An account from a firm of ironmongers for a chisel, for instance, when taken in conjunction with the disappearance from a nailed box of a quantity of valuables might well lead an officer with an active mind to a supposedly blameless person who was, in fact, leading a double life.

But there seemed nothing of any particular interest in the bills which were the liability of the late Mr. Canley. A number of them concerned household purchases, such as groceries, etc., curtains and other necessaries inseparable from the possession of a home. There were a number of bills for spirits and cigarettes, and others for car hire, clothes, etc.

Photographs of women, and letters from women, closely perused, afforded no clue to any rival who might be expected to dispose of Canley for circumstances associated with the Eternal Triangle. There were several sheaves of paper scrawled over with contracted words and phrases, which Merry and the doctor took to be notes on the form of various horses, and the peculiarities of certain race-horses.

"Courses for luck, it looks to me," said Merry, who had at one time flirted with the lucky omens of race-courses, owners and jockeys. "Yes," he added, after a moment or two of further peering. "Here is a note that no horse of Richards has won a classic at Epsom. That's wrong, anyway. It's only the Derby that Richards has never won there."

Pushed into one large envelope were a number of accounts which had the old familiar, to Merry, appearance of betting; they were, in fact, weekly accounts from a number of bookmakers. These were scanned closely. A rapid mental calculation caused the scientist to smile at his companion. "Well, Jim, he seems to have done better with his racing than you did," he remarked cheerfully. "So far as I can see he made quite a good thing out of betting."

"He was living on the bookies, that's plain, if these are all the accounts and not part of them," the deputy scientist agreed.

Doctor Manson picked up a book from the pile and opened it. "His bank pass book! Perhaps this will give us a better idea of how much he made from the gee-gees."

He skimmed through the pages. The man seemed to have started his account in the Thames Pagnall bank with a matter of just over £400. There were a number of cheques drawn for amounts ranging from £5, £10 and larger sums. On the credit side of the book were payments-in of sums ranging in value from £10 to £60, and in one case to considerably over £100. In each of these cases payments were denoted as having been by cheque. The cash payments into the account seldom appeared higher than £10, except in a couple of cases where they had reached the figure of £20 and £30.

It was while digesting these facts that Doctor Manson noticed that the payments-in were distinguished by a marked regularity. It seemed as though the man had some regular source of income which never failed to maintain its periodicity. Since Canley had no employment, so far as could be found, the doctor sought for the reason for the fixed credits to his account. After a short pondering an idea occurred to him. He checked off the dates of the payments with a calendar. The result was to show that the payments were usually made on a Tuesday. "They would be, I should say, his winnings," suggested Merry. "Settling day for bookies is usually on a Saturday, and the money, posted off on Monday would be likely to reach Canley on Tuesday morning. He would naturally, as the payment was by cheque, pass it into the bank the same day, since he obviously wanted to be in credit."

Check-up with some of the slips of the bookmakers' accounts already examined, showed this to be the case; in a number of instances, the amounts on the accounts were the same as those in the credit side of the pass book.

Satisfied that nothing further in the way of assistance was likely to come from the book, Doctor Manson put it aside, and turned his attention to another book. This revealed itself as containing personal accounts. It detailed payments made to Mrs. Skelton for her household work and expenses, purchases of various commodities, of food and clothing and personal requirements. It showed also monies paid out in cash; they appeared to be betting transactions on the course, as distinct from the bookmakers' accounts.

It was when he came to study the receipt side of the book that the doctor suddenly developed a keener interest in the figures. For the first time, he noticed, sums were entered as obviously paid in notes. He drew the attention of Merry to the circumstance.

"Probably, the result of the ready money betting on the course, Harry," suggested Merry. "He would pick it up at the end of each race, you know."

Comparison with the days on which the cash payments were made, however, showed that the dates were separated, and at varied intervals.

Reference to the pass book did not reveal that any cheque paid to 'self' by which the personal account could have been augmented, had been cashed. "Then where was the money coming from?" asked the scientist, ungrammatically.

He proceeded to tabulate the figures. The result showed the receipt of £20 on 8th February, and a further £20 on 22nd February, £50 on

19th April, another £50 on 4th May, and a further £50 on 14th June. The next date was 18th July, when the figure was £42. On 30th August, the amount had been £65. In all just under £500 had been paid in notes at comparatively regular intervals.

Consulting the calendar again, the doctor noted that the dates in each case were at the week-end, instead of at the beginning of the week. "They are not, therefore, bookmakers' payments," he commented, "ready money betting or not."

Reference to the racing calendar revealed that, in any case, on three of the dates there had not been any racing in the vicinity of Thames Pagnall or London.

'Queer,' said Doctor Manson to himself. 'Now, where did he get the money?'

Laying the account book on one side for the moment, he took up a third book. This proved to be a personal notebook. Quick glancing through the pages revealed it to consist chiefly of bets placed, and the result of them. There were, in addition, notes of various purchases, and money paid out to the charwoman, and for rent.

Checking these with the bank pass book, Doctor Manson found that the betting transactions corresponded roughly with the paying-in to the bank. In fact, there seemed not much advantage in pursuing his calculations. He persevered, however, more by force of habit than in expectation of discovering anything that might be hidden: and presently his patience was rewarded.

For the week starting 21st April, he found, on totting up, that the weekly summary was much in excess of money shown in the bank statement as paid in by cheques. There was a similar discrepancy in the summary of the week of 26th May.

Unable to account for these, the doctor decided to take each individual betting transaction during the week. There were, roughly, twenty bets; and the result, and the profit and loss, were indicated. Against each bet were written initials signifying, the scientist hazarded, the firm with whom the bets had been placed. The initials 'D.R.' appeared on several occasions. Reference to the pass book for that week showed that a cheque credit from Douglas Rowe. Rowe, the doctor knew, was a bookmaker of repute. Checking on the other entries he identified all the initials except one: on Saturday, 20th April, was the single item '£50,' and against it were the initials 'J.E.'

What, the doctor asked himself, could have become of the £50 difference between the notebook and the bank pass book of that week?

He decided to follow up the individual items of the remainder of the book. Calling to Merry, he indicated the curious discrepancy, and the two began their task of researching.

Quite soon again, in the week 24th May, appeared the same initials 'J.E.' and the figure shown made the surplus as compared with the bank pass book a matter of £40 on 1st September, and the figure went as high as £65.

The two men pondered over the figures; and then, suddenly Doctor Manson realized how the accounts could be squared. If the amounts credited as 'notes' in the pass book on the preceding Saturday were added to each of the weeks' credit, the amounts tallied.

Following this line of investigation the two men now realized that the surplus figure occurred, roughly, one week in each month, They were congratulating themselves on this discovery when, towards the end of the month of August, there came a complication. The initials 'J.E.' suddenly ceased, and in their place appeared a new set of initials. They were 'J.P.' and they appeared after varying amounts from £20 to £50. Strangely enough, these, added to the cheques shown in the bank pass book, corresponded in the same way that the earlier figures had done. The 'J.P.' amounts remained in operation up to the end of October, and the accounts as shown in the bank pass book were accurate, and had no surplus.

"It gets curiouser and more curious," said Merry. "Who and what are 'J.E.' and 'J.P.'? And for what were the regular payments?"

"It would appear to be a fixed income, judging by the regularity with which the payments were made," said Doctor Manson. "Yet there is nothing in his papers to show that he has any income from investments. There is no person or organization fitting the initials either of J.E. or J.P. And there is not, either, any business in which he seems to have been engaged other than that of racing. I wonder—"

He picked up the receiver of the ringing telephone, and called a reply.

"Prints here, Doctor—Baxter speaking. That glass and whisky bottle which Wilkins sent up to us. The prints are Canley's, as I think you know. But they are not natural prints—"

"What do you mean by that, Baxter?" asked Manson.

"I mean, Doctor, that they have been rolled, in other words the prints have been made by somebody pressing them round the bottle and the glass."

"Well, I guessed that, Baxter. It could not be otherwise if my reading of the cottage interior was correct. I did not send them up to you. But probably Wilkins, who did not know the full circumstances, wanted to check up on the prints for me. Anyway, you say they are definitely Canley's, which supports me very well."

"Yes, Doctor, natural or not they are certainly Sprogson's."

"Sprogson's—Oh, yes, of course," said Manson half to himself, as he replaced the receiver. "Sprogson's—"

He stopped at an exclamation from Merry.

"What is it, Jim?" he asked.

"Why, Sprogson, Harry. I had forgotten that Canley was an alias. Now, where's that dossier of Sprogson?" He scouted among the papers on the scientist's desk, and uncovered it. Turning over the pages he read rapidly through them.

"I think that's it, Harry," he announced. "When Sprogson was on trial for the Paignton affair, he said, you remember, that there was another man with him, and gave his name as Edwins. Edwins got away with the jewels, according to Sprogson—or Canley, as we know him. Sprogson got penal servitude, and the man Edwins went free. Now, Edwin's Christian name was Jack—and Jack Edwins makes the initials J.E."

Doctor Manson stared at his deputy. "That, undoubtedly, is the answer, Jim," he agreed. He paused for a moment and then added. "And that, undoubtedly, also supplies the motive for pushing off Canley, or Sprogson."

He dialled a house number on the telephone. "Records?" he asked. "Manson here. Have we anything of a man named Jack, or John Edwins? I'll hold on."

The reply came in a couple of minutes' time.

"No, Doctor, we've no record of a Jack Edwins ourselves. Only thing we have is a notice from the Devonshire police that a man named Jack Edwins was wanted some years ago for burglary at Paignton. Is that the man you have in mind—? Well, he was never caught, and has never been heard of under that name."

"What about a Jack P—something?" asked the doctor.

Another couple of minutes brought a reply. "We've quite a few Ps, Doctor. There is a Jack Pelman, he's a sneak thief. Then there is Jack Peters, the 'con' man. Jack Porkman, pickpocket, Jack Proffers, but he's been inside this past eighteen months."

"All these pretty well known to us?" asked Doctor Manson.

"Yes, Doctor. All old hands," was the reply.

"Then I'm afraid they won't do, Records. Many thanks." He replaced the receiver.

"There is no doubt, Jim, that the motive was blackmail. And that the sums shown as received by Canley were the results of that blackmail. It seems obvious that Canley had recognized his erstwhile comrade of Paignton, and at once levied recompense for the years he served in gaol, while Edwins had the jewels they had both been after at Paignton. And Edwins paid up."

"But only up to August, Harry," pointed out Merry. "Then we get him fading out, and J.P. coming on the scene. Who is J.P.?"

Doctor Manson considered the question. He sat back with closed eyes, and the fingers of his right hand beating a tattoo on the arm of his chair. That was a habit of his concentration. Suddenly he sat up. "It is pure theory, Jim, but I think we are entitled to assume that the two sets of initials belong to one and the same person. I think it may be purely a psychological matter. I suggest that Canley came face to face with the man he had been in partnership with at Paignton, and at once proceeded to blackmail him under threat of revealing his name and address to the police as being the other man wanted for the burglary. Edwins, of course, had taken some other name when he knew he was wanted; he would know that from the newspaper reports at the trial of Canley. I think it most probable that for some months Canley thought of his partner by the old name of Edwins, and thus marked in his note-book the payments as coming from J.E.

"Then, familiarity of some months with Edwins in his new name led him, unconsciously, to think of him no longer as Edwins, but as the man he now knew under the name beginning with 'P.' And, just as unconsciously, he changed the initials to Jack P—. That would explain the two sets of initials."

CHAPTER XXVI

THE Assistant Commissioner heard of the new development discovery without elation. In fact, something of a soporific atmosphere descended on him, on Doctor Manson, Merry and Inspector Kenway. Sir Edward put the gist of it in a nutshell space.

"Well, Doctor, you've worked out the *modus operandi* of the crime, and dashed clever working out it was. You've followed the johnny who did it in every detail of movement. You've found the motive, or think you have—and I agree that it sounds 100 per cent likely. You've worked down the lines until you've seized on Jack Edwins as the blackmailed who became tired of the demands made on him, and removed the blackmailer.

"All this is well and good. But we still are no nearer to putting our hands on the man. I've a certain sympathy with anybody blackmailed, but the law is the law, and he can't be allowed to get away with murder. We don't know a Jack Edwins, who now seems to have become J.P. Who, Doctor, is J.P. and how do we get our hands on him? That is the question?"

The scientist smiled. "To be perfectly candid, Sir Edward, I have not the faintest idea," he conceded. His voice had an apologetic note.

Sir Edward sighed.

"Certain specific things remain to be investigated," added Manson. "Possibly they may provide a clue that will lead us to the mysterious J.P. I don't know."

The Assistant Commissioner cheered up slightly under the tonic of this assertion.

"What do you mean, Doctor, by certain specific things?" he demanded.

"Well, I mean that though the J.P. did not leave any traces of his identity in the cottage, although he left plenty concerning his actions there, he may possibly have left some in the things that we have taken away from the cottage, and which still require expert examination. You never can tell. I am not going to say that he did, but hope springs eternal in the human breast, you know."

"Fingerprints?"

"No. You can take it definitely that we will never catch J.P. by his fingers. He was the most careful man I have ever come across, in that way. He would undoubtedly have gone through the papers in Canley's desk to make sure that there was nothing likely in his opinion to incriminate him, but so far, we have failed to find a single print.

"Either he wore gloves, or he used some other device for tinning over the sheets of paper. And when he locked the door on leaving the cottage, he was still as careful as ever not to do so with his bare hands."

"He must have taken the shoes of Canley off his own feet and replaced them on the dead man, but still, he did not touch them with his bare hands,[9] though he would have been justified in considering himself quite safe at that final stage of his plan. Nevertheless, Merry and I will continue with our examination of the remains of the evidence."

He rose, and with Merry walked off to the laboratory. Wilkins, the chief assistant was hovering round the middle bench which was the doctor's own domain.

"Any fortune, Wilkins?" asked Manson.

"Not much. Doctor. I sent the bottle and the glass to Prints, and they confirm that the fingerprints came from Canley. They say that they were rolled on."

"Yes, Baxter telephoned me to that effect. It was, however, certain before that."

"I've been trying to identify the iridescence on the outside and inside of the glass that came from the sideboard, Doctor," the assistant continued.

"Paraffin?" asked Doctor Manson.

"I don't think so. There is not enough really to be able to test it—it is only the slightest of film—but I have a feeling that it is something heavier than paraffin, and definitely of a vegetable nature."

"I'll have a go at it, Wilkins."

The doctor settled down to the examination.

"Hubl's test, Harry?" asked Merry.

The scientist shook his head regretfully. "There is not sufficient to give any result, Jim," he replied.

"Tissue paper?"

"We can try it, but I have no great hopes of it."

A piece of tissue paper placed against the surface of the tumbler, and heated, produced a stain. The attempt to identify it by a solvent of ether, however, proved abortive.

Half an hour later Doctor Manson gave up the experiment. "I agree with Wilkins that it is not paraffin," he said, "but I cannot identify it. It is, I think vegetable, and it gives a slight alkali reaction. Beyond that I cannot go."

"Then there seems to remain only the fragments of fibres that came from the boot of Canley and from the splinter in the table," said Merry. "And dashed if I can see how they are going to give us any clue to the fellow's name."

9. This was again a wrong deduction. Porter, the reader will remember, wiped the prints off the shoes with the mutton-cloth. Doctor Manson had, curiously enough, proved this but seemed to have forgotten the fact.

"Neither do I, Jim. But we'll try it."

The deputy scientist extracted from its envelope the strand that had been garnered from Canley's boot. He fixed it on to a slide with a dab of wax, and placed it underneath the eyepiece of the microscope. At twenty magnifications the substance of the thread stood out clearly. Merry, after a prolonged inspection crinkled his brows, and shook his head. "I don't get it, Harry," he announced. "Do you?"

"No. I can't place it at all," was the reply.

He crossed the room and from a glass-covered cabinet took a drawer of slides. Each contained a specimen of thread or fibre of material gathered for the purpose of comparative examination. But an hour later, no decision had been reached as to the identity of the Canley exhibit.

"It does not appear to be cotton, and it certainly is not linen," said Doctor Manson.

"Nor is it fibre," propounded Merry.

"Neither worsted."

Doctor Manson looked worried. He called to Wilkins, and motioned to the comparison instrument.

The laboratory assistant, after a spell at the eyepiece, inspected the array of slides. "None of these, sir?" he queried.

"None." The scientist supplied the answer.

"There is an iridescence about it which suggests oil," decided Wilkins. "And it looks a little stiff which also would seem to spell oil that has dried. I should say it has been a soft material but not wool."

"Oil, and soft," mused Merry. "Could it be engineer's waste?"

"No, Merry. Engineer's waste is hard and cottony. Soft and oily— soft and oily—" Doctor Manson stared blankly into thought. "What soft material could habitually get oil on it in the ordinary way of business?" he asked.

"The only thing I can think of, sir, is mutton-cloth," said Wilkins, who was a car owner and did his own repairs. "That is sufficiently soft to polish cellulose without scratching—it's about the only thing that would do the trick, and a car owner might well wipe his hands on a piece, because most car owners use it."

"That is a most valuable contribution, Wilkins," said the doctor, enthusiastically. "It sounds probable."

"I'll slip down to the garage and get a piece, sir," volunteered Wilkins, and returned five minutes later with a handful of soiled material.

Doctor Manson took it. After a scrutiny he pulled out two of the threads, mounted them on a slide and placed them under the comparison microscope. No more than moments were necessary to identify the elusive thread. It was beyond question from a piece of mutton-cloth.

"And oily, too," said the doctor. "That looks as though the oil on our exhibit might well be motor oil."

"And if that is so, Harry, then we can go a stage farther, can't we."

Doctor Manson looked inquiry.

"I mean that if the oil on the thread is motor oil, then it is a thousand to one that the same piece of mutton-cloth was used by Canley's visitor to wipe and polish the glass and the bottle of whisky. And that makes our film of oil on the glass. It isn't likely he'd have a collection of polishing cloths in his pocket, is it?"

The scientist nodded, gravely. "I think you are probably correct, Jim," he agreed.

"And that means that the visitor is one who habitually carries mutton-cloth around in his pockets, has a car, or works with cars which he attends to himself."

"All of which makes up to what?" came a voice. The Assistant Commissioner had come into the laboratory unheard. "What is all this about, Doctor?" he demanded.

He listened to the results of the examination, and nodded his satisfaction. "We seem to be getting a little nearer to the man we want, Doctor," he said.

"We have, at any rate, established *the class* of man, Edward," retorted Doctor Manson. "And that means eliminating about 25,000,000 of the population."

"So there are only 25,000,000 suspects left, eh, Harry?" He grinned delightedly at the joke, for Doctor Manson always held that the best way of investigating crime was to eliminate the innocent, thus leaving only the guilty.

"Possibly a few less, Edward. For we can cut out everyone outside a ten-mile radius of Thames Pagnall."

"And everyone in that area who doesn't mess about with a motor car," suggested Merry.

"That, if I may say so, reduces the number to a few thousand," said the Assistant Commissioner.

"We can, I think, go a little farther than even that." Doctor Manson spoke quietly, and when he spoke deliberately and quietly the Assistant Commissioner and the Yard officers looked at him with a lively interest, for the quietness of his voice was a sign that the doctor was getting nearer to the heart of the problem upon which he was engaged. Sir Edward now looked at him.

"What do you mean by that, Harry?" he asked.

"That of the few thousand people to which we have now reduced the suspects, Edward, you can take away all those whose Christian name and surname do not make up the initials J.P. For those are the initials of the man who visited Canley on the night that he was killed."

"Eh! What's that?" The Assistant Commissioner looked staggered at the news.

Doctor Manson revealed the results of the investigations into the bank pass book and the account book found in the desk of the dead man.

"God bless me soul," ejaculated Sir Edward. "Well, that ought to reduce the number to hundreds," he opined.

"I should have said about fifty," suggested the scientist. "And that is about as far as we can go, I think. I have now exhausted all the materials out of which I can screw any information."

"There is just one more, Doctor." The interruption came from Wilkins, who had been busy at a bench near one of the sinks.

Doctor Manson looked up inquiringly. The laboratory assistant was kneading a small piece of something between two pieces of damp rag. "What have you there, Wilkins?" Manson inquired.

"The piece of dirt which Mr. Merry said had been picked up from the floor of the cottage, Doctor. I thought we might as well find out what it is."

He came forward with the exhibit. "Look at it," he urged.

Doctor Manson took the piece of soil. Under the influence of the kneading in damp cloth it had become converted into a gluey knob which could be moulded into any shape, and retain that form.

"Looks like a bit of the soil from my confounded garden after a wet day," said Merry. "That means it is clay."

"Clay it certainly *is*," agreed the doctor. He lapsed into thought. "I don't recall any clay in the lane round about Canley's cottage," he said. "Do you, Merry?"

Merry shook his head. "The earth was moist and soft, Doctor, but I should not have thought it clay. It didn't hold water in the footprints, though it left excellent impressions."

"That would mean a fine sand, rather than clay." The doctor lifted his telephone receiver and asked for Inspector Mackenzie at Thames Pagnall.

"What kind of soil is that in the lane, and neighbourhood of Canley's house, Mackenzie?" he asked.

The inspector thought for a few moments. "I reckon it's sand on gravel mostly, Doctor Manson," he replied. "The kind that goes flat after rain and then dries under the sun like concrete. At least that's what it's like in my bit of garden, which is in the same area. But I'll ask Constable Jenkins. He lives not far away from Canley's place."

He went away, to return after a minute or two. "Yes, that's right, sir," he announced. "Sand it is, just like my garden."

"No clay?" demanded Manson.

"No, sir. There's very little clay round these parts. All sand, and fine sand at that."

"It is the little bits of white that interest me, Doctor," interrupted Wilkins. "They look to me like chalk, or something."

Doctor Manson cut off a segment of the soil, and with a knife separated a number of the white particles. These he placed in a shallow porcelain dish and carried them over to the sink. There, with a fine brush he gently brushed all traces of the clay away. The water in the dish which had at first become a pale yellow from the clay gradually assumed a dirty milky colour.

"Looks like lime," said Merry.

"I think it is unquestionably lime, Jim. But the microscope will settle it."

It did. Limestone is composed of microscopic shells— *foraminefera* is the scientific name—and under the microscope these were plainly visible in the sediment of the white particles from the clay segment.

"The piece undoubtedly came from the visitor's boots, Harry, and we know that there is no clay round Thames Pagnall. Therefore, it is likely to have come from—where?"

"Argument on that does not seem difficult," retorted Doctor Manson. "The soil must have been picked up by the boot while it was wet. It would not dry while the person was walking on that damp and foggy night. It must, therefore, have dried while he was in the cottage where, of course, it became detached from the instep. The natural conclusion, therefore, is that it was picked up on the visitor's native heath, so to speak. That interests me, because I can think of only one circumstance under which a person would walk through a mixture of lime."

"And what would that be?" inquired the Assistant Commissioner.

Doctor Manson did not answer the question. Instead, he said, "I think, perhaps, we had better have another chat with the Thames Pagnall people. The remainder of the case seems to me to be merely a matter of local routine."

CHAPTER XXVII

COLONEL Mainforce, the Chief Constable, and Inspector Mackenzie were waiting for the doctor and Sir Edward in the police station at Thames Pagnall. Manson had driven down in his big black car.

He took the long-about route which reached, first of all, the junction down the line. Twice, for no apparent reason, he called at roadside garages and had a supply of petrol put into the tank, while he carefully walked round the garage inspecting the premises, and the men at work there on repairs to vehicles in various stages of age and breakdown. He apparently saw nothing to interest him further, for he made no remarks.

At Thames Pagnall he drove into the police station yard, and the company foregathered in the inspector's office. Inspector Mackenzie eyed his London visitors hopefully; and expressed the hope verbally.

"Yes, I think we may have something to comfort you in your tribulation, Mackenzie," the scientist said, soothingly. "We have, in all probability, narrowed the suspects down to a comparatively small number. Since we started out this morning the number has been further reduced by two," he added, inconsequently.

The Assistant Commissioner, who did not know quite all the views in the mind of his scientific investigator, scratched a puzzled head.

"We, in fact, know the name of the visitor to Canley on that night," added Doctor Manson.

The Chief Constable jumped. "The devil you do?" he said. "Who was, or rather, is he?"

"A man named Jack Edwins."

The Chief Constable looked at his inspector. "Know a Jack Edwins, Mackenzie?" he demanded.

Mackenzie thought through the names of his flock. "Can't recall the name, Colonel," he replied.

Doctor Manson relayed the facts concerning the Paignton robbery, and his conclusions that the uncaptured man, Edwins, was the man who had rid himself of Canley.

"Blackmail, eh?" said the Chief Constable. "Nasty business, I don't like blackmailers."

"Neither do I, Mainforce. But then, neither do I like murderers. And there are ways of getting rid of blackmailers without killing. Since it seemed that Edwins had made retribution for his jewel haul, he would not have had a great deal to fear from the police."

"Anyway, we don't apparently know an Edwins round here, Doctor," said the Colonel.

"No, I supposed not, Mainforce," retorted Manson. "He would hardly be likely to retain that name since the police force of the country were looking for him, and, of course, would still pull him in if they found him. He has some other name, of course. Edwins died on that night at Paignton."

"What would be his other name, Doctor?" asked Mackenzie, ingenuously.

"Don't be a ruddy fool, Mackenzie." The Chief Constable barked a rebuke. "If Doctor Manson knew his man he'd have pinched him by now. You don't suppose the fellow has been round broadcasting his new name, do you?"

Doctor Manson smiled. "Well, Colonel," he said. "We can go a little farther than a blank wall."

"How far can you go?"

"Let us do a little recapitulating on the knowledge we have acquired of the man, and see where it gets us," suggested Manson. "Firstly, then, he is a man of some 5 ft. 8 ins., strong, and used to lifting and carrying weights."

"Why 5 ft. 8 ins., Doctor," asked Mackenzie.

"Length of stride, Mackenzie," retorted the doctor. "Canley, allowing for his longer stride—you remember the worn heels—would have a stride span of about 2 ft. 4 ins. The murderer, if he were 5 ft. 8 ins. would normally span about 3 ft. But we have to allow for a reduction in his stride on this night—"

"Why, Doctor?" The inquiry came from the Chief Constable.

"Because he was carrying a burden—Canley. The fact that the prints he made with Canley's shoes were firm and unlaboured proves that he was not only a man of some strength, but was used to lifting and carrying a weight. The effect of that weight, however, would be to shorten his natural stride. I work it out, therefore, that Canley's weight would reduce the unknown man's stride to about that of Canley himself when alive—and that should be about 2 ft. 4 ins.

"Next, he would certainly have worn an overcoat when he came to the cottage. Nobody would be out on a night like that without some protection. In all probability there will still be a few fragments of the rug fluff on that coat. It is very hard stuff to get rid of, even by brushing, and he must have conveyed some of it from the overcoat of Canley, during the time that he was carrying him from the cottage to the railway line."

"Um! Doubtful, I should think, Doctor. But anyway, we aren't much nearer identifying him so far. There's a lot of 5 ft. 8 in. men in the place; it's more or less a normal height."

"True, Mainforce, but we have not finished the recap, yet. Let's take the third point. I think he will almost certainly have traces of oil in his right-hand jacket pocket."

The doctor detailed the examination of the threads of cloth that had been caught in the welt of Canley's shoe, and on the splinter of the table. "It was impregnated with oil," he said, "and thus caused the film of iridescence on the polished tumbler, for which I almost blamed Mrs. Skelton's use of paraffin.

"Now that cloth must have been in his jacket pocket. He would not be wearing his overcoat in the house during the time he was staying there; and he obviously brought the cloth for a specific purpose. He no doubt had worked out that things would have to be polished to remove the fingerprints that would be left about the place by he and Canley."

"Um!" said the Chief Constable again. "We'll give you that one, Doctor."

"Kind of you, Mainforce. Then we will pass on to a point number four. He possesses a pair of boots which may be rubber-soled or may not be, but at any rate have rubber heels, not of the revolving kind. And the heel of one boot, probably the left one, is badly worn and is showing in the centre two fixing nails through the rubber. They made the parallel scratches on the polished floor of the cottage, you know."

"Why the left boot?" asked Mackenzie.

"Because there were only one set of scratches, which suggests that considerable pressure was exerted by that foot to force the nails through the rubber, Mackenzie. Otherwise there would have been other scratches. Now, the scratches were just behind the chair in which I have assumed that Canley was sitting when he was struck down. Therefore, since in striking a heavy blow, the impetus would be gained by tensing the body on the *left* leg, the nails are probably showing through the rubber of the left boot. That clear?"

Inspector Mackenzie, after striving to get round the logical argument, and failing, grunted his satisfaction with the hypothesis.

Doctor Manson smiled. "Good," he said. "Now we come to the last but one of the points. The man we want is working somewhere where building or repairing operations are in progress, such operations including bricklaying or plastering."

"Eh! That's getting a bit nearer, Doctor," the Chief Constable said. "Where does that bit come from?"

Doctor Manson explained the analysis of the piece of caked dirt picked up in the cottage. "The fact that there is no clay in the neighbourhood of the cottage, or in Thames Pagnall itself, would suggest, would it not, that the soil was brought in by the visitor? Now there is a considerable amount of lime in the clay. Does that suggest to you, as it does to me, that there is a patch of mortar outside the premises on which the man is working? It is, I agree, more or less pure theory, but I think it bears water."

"And the last point, Doctor?" asked Colonel Mainforce.

"Ah, the last point!" Doctor Manson chuckled audibly, and provocatively. "The last point is really important. It is the man's name—"

"Good God, Doctor!" The Chief Constable glared. "Do you mean to say that you've been giving us all this theory stuff, and all the time you've known who the fellow is?" he snorted.

"Not quite that, Colonel. We know only part of the name. The Christian name seems still to be Jack. But the surname, which was Edwins, now begins with the letter 'P'. Jack P— is the man we are after."

The doctor produced from a pocket the account book left behind by Canley, and demonstrated how he had worked out the connection between the amounts from J.E. and J.P. "It is pretty certain that the two are one and the same, and that the change to J.P. came unconsciously," he said.

"So there you are," ended the doctor. "That's the entire story."

The Chief Constable and the inspector digested the doctor's recital, and chewed the cud of his investigations. It was the inspector who first broached any comment on them.

"I reckon there's an awful lot of people whose names begin with the letter P, Doctor," he said. "And we've no idea where to start looking."

"That's true, Mackenzie," Colonel Mainforce pronounced his agreement. "God knows where the fellow is now, Doctor. Might be in Scotland. He'd be a fool if he stayed anywhere round here after doing in Canley. If he followed the path you have trod out for him after he left Canley on the lines, he'd probably take a train for as far away as he could get."

"Would he?" asked Doctor Manson; and looked at the Chief Constable with intriguing interest. "Would he, do you think? Why?"

"Well, dammit, Manson, wouldn't you get going?"

Doctor Manson ignored the personal chunk of the question.

"Then perhaps you will tell me, Colonel, why the silly ass went to all the trouble of devising this most detailed and timed plot to kill Canley. Tell me why," he repeated.

"Why?" Colonel Mainforce stared at the scientist in bewilderment. "Why?" he repeated, parrot-like. "Because he was being blackmailed, of course. Blast it, Doctor, you've spent nearly an hour telling us yourself."

"I have done nothing of the kind, Mainforce. I have told you in the first place, how the murder was committed. I have told you who the man is, and what he is like in appearance, how far apart his legs stride, and what he was wearing. But I have not told you why he plotted this murder. You ought to have been able to realize that for yourself. And so ought Mackenzie."

"You'd better not waste any more time, Doctor," put in Sir Edward Allen, after a glance at the audience, who seemed from their expression to be reaching a point at which the mental aberration of the scientist was in a state of grave doubt. "They think we're potty."

"Let's hear it, Doctor," agreed the Colonel. "I can't make head or tail of you or Sir Edward, but I'll put my shirt on you just the same."

"Very well, then, Colonel," began Manson. "It is really quite simple as you will agree when you've worked it out. Now, the first time that our man got entangled up with Canley was in Devonshire—at the burglary. What did he do? He did just as you are suggesting he has done on this occasion—he scooted right out of the district, and he was never traced. Now, in some way, most unfortunate for him, he ran into Canley, or Canley ran into him, and he was at once recognized. The blackmail then started.

"But why did it start? And, more important still, *why did it go on*? That is the answer to your riddle. And I can see no logical flaw in the reasoning of my rejoinder to it."

"And the rejoinder is—what?" asked Colonel Mainforce.

"That if Edwins was being blackmailed by Canley, why did he not emulate his action of the earlier day? Why did he not say, 'this is not good enough. I am not going to pay this chap my hard-earned money. I'm getting out'. Why, in short, did he not vamoose the ranch?"

"Perhaps he did not want to give up his job," hazarded the Colonel.

"Wasn't much good keeping the job if he was going to pay about ten pounds a week to the blackmailer, was it. Because that seems to work out as the amount he was paying. Surely he could have gone somewhere else where he would again be lost to Canley, and where he could get a job that would allow him to keep his earnings. Instead, he stays and works out a most complicated method of getting rid of Canley by the most hazardous means of wilful murder, in the hope that the crime would be thought an accident, and never traced to him. Again I ask you why?"

Doctor Manson sat back and waited for the answer from his hearers. None was forthcoming. Colonel Mainforce looked the bewilderment he felt at the trend of the conversation.

"Well, why?" he asked, after a pause. "You've something in that head of yours, Manson, but damned if I can see what it is."

The doctor lit a cigarette before replying. He lit it slowly and deliberately, playing with his audience—a little trick of which he was inordinately fond. Then:

"Well, Mainforce, and you, Mackenzie, I will put forward the supposition which has occurred to me, and which I think will prove to be correct in the more essential details. Suppose then, that this Jack Edwins, or Jack P— is *not* in a job at all. Suppose he could not run away from his blackmailer without utterly ruining himself." Manson paused. The Chief Constable looked his mystification. "If he wasn't in a—" he began.

"Supposing that he is in his own business. A prosperous business," the doctor checked his sentence. "Then his only means of getting rid of Canley would be to get rid of him in the physical sense. And knowing that, he plotted the murder to look like an accident. Would not that explain all the answers we want?"

"Jiminy Cricket," said the Colonel. "Of Course!" He eyed the doctor thoughtfully. "And I dare say you have some idea of the business and where it is," he decided.

"Of where it is—no, Colonel. I have not the least idea except that it is somewhere within easy reach of this place. Of the business—yes, I have a pretty shrewd idea. Work it out for yourselves. What manner of man is it that uses mutton-cloth to wipe away oil, and carries a piece of it around with him in his pockets?"

"Are you trying to pinch my chauffeur, Doctor," asked the Chief Constable, jestingly. "I won't have him arrested. Best one I've ever had."

"A motor mechanic," said Inspector Mackenzie, suddenly. He thought again. "And in business for himself," he added, musingly. "You mean that he's got a garage, Doctor?"

"I mean just that, Mackenzie. It's taken a long time to make you see it. But you have it at last. Our J.P. is a garage proprietor in some part of this area where there is clay, and where building extensions or repairs of some kind are being undertaken. Search for that and you'll find him."

"Sounds like Middlesex," said the Chief Constable. "That's the place where we mostly find clay."

"Which reminds me," suddenly thought the scientist. "Did you ever trace anyone who did not pay their fares at the booking office at the junction, Mackenzie?" he asked.

"Don't know about the junction, Doctor," was the reply. "But down the line on trains passing through the junction, four people paid excess at the barriers. There was one at Alton, another at Claygate, a third at London Road, and a fourth at Staines."

"On what trains?"

"Trains which passed through the junction after midnight, Doctor."

"Which of those places is in Middlesex?"

"Only Staines."

"The ticket collector know the person at all?"

"No, Doctor. We asked that, but he said he could not recall the man. He did not, of course, pay any particular attention to him. Just took his money and gave him the official receipt." Doctor Manson considered the position. "Then, I think we will try Staines," he said.

The four men piled themselves into Doctor Manson's car, and set out on the quest. The Doctor drove the car into Hampton Court, and turned left at the bridge, that gem of an erection with the most beautiful lines in the south of England save, perhaps the new Waterloo bridge.

A quick run of a few minutes brought them to the police station at Staines. From the inspector there, the Doctor obtained a list of garages in the neighbourhood.

Through the Borough of Staines the car passed along the route which long years before the Barons of England must have taken on their horses, when they went to the meadows of Runnymede, there to wrest from the King the freedom of a people. Mackenzie, fortunately, knew the district pretty well, and the list of garages were taken in their order of route. In front of each the car was halted, and the scientist passed a critical eye over the set-out and attendants. Once he got out of the car and walked into the building, ostensibly to make some inquiry. But he returned after a minute or so, and taking his place at the wheel again, resumed the search.

It was an hour before the garages of the town had all been eliminated. The Chief Constable looked bored.

"Well, Doctor, that is the last of them," he announced. "Where do we go from here?"

"Not one looked anything like the place I visualize," retorted the doctor. "I think that it must be in a more open country."

"In that case we'd better try the outside," suggested Sir Edward. "If we turn left at the top of the street here, we can get on the second-class main road, get into the country and return via the By-pass road. How far out do you reckon we should go, Harry?"

Doctor Manson thought the problem out. "No farther than makes Staines railway station the nearest station," he suggested.

"Then we'll say a couple of miles," decided Mackenzie.

The secondary main road was negotiated as far as the next village, with occasional stops by Doctor Manson to regard with close attention the wayside garages and service stations along it. At the village the car was swung in a half-circle, and travelling through a narrow lane struck the By-pass road.

They were half-way back to Staines when Doctor Manson, who had been driving with one eye on the road and the other on the buildings and erections at the side of it, suddenly pulled up sharply at a garage which lay some 500 feet back from the metalled road. The garage was a neat and attractively painted green and white structure, and bore the name 'The Green Service Station' across it.

It had obviously been quite recently renovated, for the paint looked new, and a low wall of red bricks had been built between the property and a side road on the left.

Doctor Manson nudged the Chief Constable. "This, I think, is the place, Colonel," he said. He pointed to the space between the wall and the cemented run-in. A dump of mortar stood there, and marks showed how it had been trod into the ground between there and the garage workshop.

As the car drove in, a man came forward, wiping his hands on a piece of mutton-cloth.

"Get the car filled up," whispered Manson to the Chief Constable, and left the driving seat. He walked to the door of the garage, and glanced inside the office. Opposite the door, on the wall, was a framed certificate of a motoring trade organization. Written in the space reserved for the name of the holder were the words 'Jack Porter'.

'J.P.' said the doctor, to himself, quietly, and returned to the car. He paid for the petrol, climbed back into the driving seat and left the garage.

A hundred yards or so down the road he drew into the kerb, and stopped. He turned to his colleagues.

"The name of the man, Colonel," he said, "is Jack Porter. I have no doubt that he is the man we want. He has the right height, the right appearance, and there is the mud and the mortar, and he is in Staines, whence came a man after midnight that night with no ticket from the junction."

"Looks like it, Doctor, I agree. What are we going to do?" asked the Chief Constable.

"You can't do anything, my lad," was the retort. "He is not in your area. And however much I believe my theory, it has still to be proved, you know."

He thought for a moment or two, and then propounded a way out. "I suggest that we go back into Staines, and you, Inspector, see the Staines inspector. Tell him that you suspect the man Porter of a serious crime in your area, but have not yet obtained all the evidence you want. Make him realize that the evidence can be got only if the man's premises are examined, and that you do not want to alarm him by searching while he is there."

"Then tell him that the man is suspected to be Jack Edwins wanted for burglary at Paignton and for whom a warrant is still in existence. The Staines man can then take him into custody on that warrant, and hold him for you on the more serious charge."

"When you have him safe, Colonel Mainforce and I will join you at the garage. Let the Staines man take him to the station."

It was half an hour later that the inspector drew in the garage runway. Porter came forward to service them.

"Are you Jack Porter?" asked the Staines inspector.

"That's my name, yes, sir."

"I am Inspector Tarrant of the Staines police, Porter, and this is Inspector Mackenzie of the Surrey police. You answer the description of a man named Jack Edwins, who is wanted on a charge of burglary with a man named Sprogson at Paignton, but who disappeared at that time. You are not bound to say anything—"

"My God, after all these years," interrupted Porter. "All right, inspector, I don't deny it. But I made restitution years ago. I sent all the money back."

"Where do you live, Porter?" asked the inspector.

"Over the garage, here, sir."

"Very well, you had better come with me."

"Is there anything wrong, Jack?" Mary Porter stood at the foot of the stairs, glancing anxiously from her husband standing between the two officers. They were in plain clothes, but a certain air of officialdom about them, as she had glanced through the flat window upstairs, had sent her hurrying down to the garage.

Porter looked at her, anxiety in his eyes. "They want me for that Paignton business, Mary," he said; and there was a touch of hopelessness in his voice.

"But—they can't, Jack." She turned to the officers. "We made restitution years ago," she pleaded. "We sent all the money back—"

"There was a warrant out, Madam. It has to be served," the Middlesex inspector explained.

"Never mind, Mary. It won't be for long. I shall be back in a day or two, on bail. Take care of the place, won't you."

He kissed her tenderly, and turned and walked away with the officers.

The police car passed that of Doctor Manson on the way back to Staines. The two cars stopped and Inspector Mackenzie joined the doctor and the Chief Constable.

"Well?" asked Manson.

Mackenzie nodded. "He admitted that he was Edwins, Doctor. He said that he made restitution. He lives over the garage, by the way."

As the police car sped towards Staines, Doctor Manson drove into the yard of the garage, and made his way inside. Mary Porter, confronted him, inquiringly. "I am afraid, sir," she said, "that the garage is closed for the moment. My husband has had to go away on urgent business, and we have not a man for the time being."

The doctor's eyes rested on her and there was a trace of regret in his voice as he spoke. "Mrs. Porter," he said, gently, "I am a police officer, and so are these two gentlemen with me. I am very sorry, but I must ask you to allow us to search your home." Mary paled, but made way for them to enter the door at the bottom of the stairs from the garage. "You will not find anything in our home," she said. "My husband sent back the money for the jewellery years ago. He always meant to do that, you know, when he found out that he was unwittingly a thief."

"Unwittingly a thief?" Doctor Manson asked puzzled. "Unwittingly a thief," Mary emphasized. "I think I had better tell you the full story, because I am sure you do not know it, and it will help my husband."

"I should like to hear it," said Doctor Manson, gravely. And in the tiny sitting-room above the deserted garage, Mary Porter told in her quiet voice the years' old story of Yew Tree House, Paignton, of her meeting with Jack Edwins, their courtship, of her warning to her lover and the flight from justice, a fugitive of fate.

As Doctor Manson listened, alertness went from the scholarly face of him, and into it instead came shadows of greyness, and the eyes seemed to sink even more deep-set than usual. Colonel Mainforce looked at him anxiously when, once, he half-turned his chair so that he could not see the face of Mary Porter. He thought he was ill.

From that position the doctor spoke. "You said, Mrs. Porter, that your husband repaid the full value of the jewellery to the people at Paignton. When was that?"

"Just under three years ago from the time of the burglary, sir," was the reply. She hesitated. "I do not want you to think that I am blaming my husband," she begged, "but if I had been able to join him after the burglary and before he had disposed of the jewellery, it would have been sent back immediately. I know that the police would have accepted the explanation of Jack's presence there. But it was not until long after the jewels had been sold that I knew anything about it."

"You did know eventually?"

"Yes, and I agreed to use the money." She looked frankly at the three men. "It bought this garage. I think that life owed something to my husband for the trick it had played on him. It was I who insisted that, from the money we made, restitution in full should be made."

Softly she told of the struggle and the years of building up the business with the drain of the weekly contribution to the restitution fund and of the eventual clearance of the debt and of the conscience of both of them. And a great pity welled up in the heart of the scientist and of the Chief Constable, knowing what they knew of the end of the story so soon to come.

"And now, gentlemen, you are at liberty to search my home," said Mary. She looked proudly at them. "You will not find anything here that is not ours, earned with the sweat of my husband's brow, I know that." She led the way to the bedroom, and left them.

Doctor Manson crossed to the wardrobe. It contained two suits, one of blue and the other of brown material. Behind them was an overcoat of heavy cloth, rough-surfaced and with a check pattern on quiet lines. Listlessly, with all the interest of the hunt seemingly departed from him, the scientist examined it. He picked off the surface one or two short threads of some kind or other. Carrying them to the light from the window he inspected them through his lens.

"I cannot be sure without putting them under a microscope," he announced. "But I do not think there is much doubt that they are the same material as we found on Canley's coat." He returned the overcoat to the wardrobe and rummaged in the bottom of the furniture. Presently his hand emerged carrying a pair of heavy boots.

"Leather soles—no good to us," he said, and returned to the wardrobe.

"These look like it," and he turned up a pair of black shoes, of a lighter weight. The soles were of rubber material, and so were the heels. With the Chief Constable at his side, he looked closely at the heel of the left shoe. The rubber was worn down to the heads of the two sprigs driven through the centre of the heel.

"Just as you said, Doctor," commented Colonel Mainforce. "Any more evidence you want?"

For reply the scientist returned to the wardrobe, and looked over the two suits. He took out the darker of the two. "He would use the darkest suit he possessed, I should think," he said. "Did you notice when we drew into the garage in the first instance, Porter drew a piece of mutton-cloth from his right-hand pocket and wiped his hands?" he asked.

He turned out the right-hand pocket of the jacket and examined it. The examination was more or less a form, for a distinct stain of oil marked the lining.

"Just one more thing, and I think the tale is complete," the scientist commented. He led the way down the stairs, and out into the front of the garage. Taking from a pocket a box of matches, he emptied them out. Then, walking towards the road, filled the matchbox with some of the trodden portion of soil from round the dump of mortar. "That is all," he announced.

"Do we charge him, Doctor?" asked Mackenzie.

"Let me get back to my laboratory, Mackenzie, and test the threads and this portion of soil, first. I would like to make sure."

He drove back to Thames Pagnall, dropped the Chief Constable and Mackenzie, and set the nose of his car in the direction of London.

An hour later the telephone bell rang in Inspector Mackenzie's office. The inspector lifted the receiver.

"Manson here, Mackenzie," came a voice. "You must charge him."

* * * * *

In the police station at Staines, Jack Porter listened to the charge— "that you did wilfully murder James Canley, at Thames Pagnall—"

"Oh, Mary—Mary—my dear, my dear," he whispered quietly, under his breath; and those were the only words he said, then or later.

"I shall take you to the prison at Guildford, Porter," explained Mackenzie, "and there you can send for your legal representative." Porter nodded.

A police car took the couple to Staines railway station, and from there to the junction; the last time that Porter had stood on that platform was the night that he had walked along the line from Thames Pagnall with the burden of Canley freed from his back.

At the junction Inspector Mackenzie waited with his prisoner for the train to Guildford. Round the curve it came from London turning towards number four platform. Alongside it, racing at full speed came a Basingstoke express, which would pass along platform four. Its whistle shrieked as it approached the station.

With a sudden jump Jack Porter leaped back from the escorting Inspector Mackenzie, and hands above his head dived straight in the track of the express. Screams of women mingled with the cries of men and the screeching of the wheels of the train as the driver applied the emergency brakes.

The station-master and porters shepherded the waiting passengers into the exit, and cordoned them there until the line was cleared of all that remained of Jack Porter.

He lay in the permanent way a yard from the end of the platform. He lay flat on his back, but with his body crumbled—and headless. *The engine of the express had decapitated Porter as the engine of the local had decapitated the body of James Canley.*

Three hours later Doctor Manson drove up to the garage on the By-pass. He had imposed upon himself the task of breaking the news of her husband's death to Mary Porter; and of the charge that had been levelled against him.

Mary heard him to the end, dry-eyed, calm with the dreadful calm of hopelessness and despair. Then:

"But, sir," she asked, "why should he want to murder this Canley. I have never heard his name, and my husband at no time has ever known a Canley to my knowledge. Why should he murder the man?"

Doctor Manson placed a hand gently over those she had held out imploringly as she asked her question.

"Mrs. Porter," be said, "James Canley was—Sprogson."

"Sprogson?" The word came in a whisper. "Jack never told me."

"He was trying to save you from anxiety, I think," said Manson. "He paid Sprogson for his silence for months."

"I see. So that is where our money went. And I blamed Jack for—Oh, why didn't he tell me. We said always that we would have no secrets from each other."

Doctor Manson took a card from his wallet. He placed it on the table. "This is my address. Mrs. Porter," he said. "Will you come to me for any help you want, or any advice. It will be at your service at any time." He thought for a moment, hesitatingly, then seemed to make up his mind.

"Mrs. Porter, I would like to tell you that the only words your husband spoke after his arrest were these: 'Oh, Mary—Mary, my dear—my dear'." He turned, pressed her hand in his and left.

Mary Porter stood in the little living-room; she stood as though she was carved in marble itself. She stared through the window into the busy road outside the garage, but saw nothing of the traffic that raced past; her eyes wandered over the mental panorama of the years. She saw the café in Paignton, the entry of Jack Edwins, the smile, the first walk along the sands as the band played in the bandstand to the host of holiday-makers.

She saw her lover on that night she had begged him to end his association with Sprogson; she remembered the pain of the months of waiting, the reunion in London, and the years of happiness and building in the little garage.

Like an automaton she walked down the stairs and into the garage. She wandered round, remembering the planning which had purchased this and that of the fittings for the happy years of the future.

Strewn across a bench lay the overalls that her man had stripped off when he went away with the police officers. Her hands went out to them, and caressed them.

"Oh, Jack—Jack," she said softly; and her voice broke and there came the relief of tears. Mary Porter cried as a woman cries once only in a lifetime, whether her lifetime be twenty or seventy years.

EPILOGUE

SIR Edward Allen and Manson sat together over a tea table in the window of a famous London club overlooking the Mall, and the park beyond it. The Assistant Commissioner had heard the end of the story.

"A fine piece of work, Harry," he said. "It was a thousand to one against the murder ever coming out. I have never known science more devastating in any case you have solved than in this one."

Doctor Manson kept his gaze on the strolling people in the park across the Mall. There seemed a certain resignation in his attitude; and the cigarette was staining with nicotine fumes the whiteness of his long, delicate fingers. It was nearly a minute before he replied.

"I have never concluded a case with less satisfaction, Edward," he said, and there was pain in his voice. "Porter had made good, he had made restitution, and was building up a business by craftsmanship and hard work. And now all that is gone, and his life, too, has gone—for a rogue like Canley. If only he had come to us and told us. After all those years the punishment, if any, would have been nominal only. There are times when I hate this job of mine, Edward."

He stood up.

"Let me go home," he said, and his voice was shaking. "I am no company for anyone today—nor do I want any company."

The Assistant Commissioner, silent, watched him go slowly through the door, and out into the open air.

THE END

Made in the USA
Coppell, TX
31 August 2021

61532830R00144